W9-CHZ-036

HONOR BOUND: BOOK SIX

ANGEL PAYNE

This book is an original publication of Angel Payne.

This is a work of fiction. Names, characters, places, and incidents either are the product of the author's imagination or are used fictitiously, and any resemblance to actual persons, living or dead, business establishments, events, or locales is entirely coincidental. The publisher does not assume any responsibility for third-party websites or their content.

Copyright © 2018 Waterhouse Press, LLC
Cover Design by Waterhouse Press, LLC
Cover Photographs: Shutterstock

All Rights Reserved.
No part of this book may be reproduced, scanned, or distributed in any printed or electronic format without permission. Please do not participate in or encourage piracy of copyrighted materials in violation of the author's rights. Purchase only authorized editions.

Paperback ISBN: 978-1-947222-27-4

HONOR BOUND: BOOK SIX

ANGEL PAYNE

WATERHOUSE PRESS

*As always, for my generous and giving man...
for joining me on this journey so bravely and
steadfastly. I am forever in love with you.*

*And...to all of you who encouraged me to write
"the weird book" and help me rejoice in my
weirdness each and every day.*

*You are the paint in the sky...and the dreams
none of us have imagined yet.*

Stay weird!

*Special thanks to my hand-holders on this
book! It wouldn't be here without you!*

Carly Phillips

Carrie Ann Ryan

Jenna Jacob

Kennedy Layne

Melisande Scott

Riane Holt

Tracy Roelle

Victoria Blue

CHAPTER ONE

"Hi, gorgeous. You wanna play lions? 'Cause I'm ready to chase your meat."

Shay Bommer stared as the little redhead in skintight jeans wobbled on her five-inch heels and finished the line with a playful roar. He expected her friends, a group of ten women at a table in the corner of the LA International Airport bar, to applaud her drunken effort. Clearly, they'd concocted a crazy version of double-dare-you to pass the time, and she'd drawn the wrong straw.

The moment provided more proof for a theory Shay had observed in nauseating detail lately.

People did strange fucking things in airport bars.

A hand snaked around his waist from behind, elegant fingers topped by slick blue-black nails. "I have a better game," murmured a voice just as sultry as the redhead's. "I wanna play war. You lay on the ground, and I'll blow you up, baby."

Hell.

Six months undercover with one of the world's most notorious criminals, and the worst bullets he dodged these days were lines like that.

Remember why you're doing this. Remember who you're doing this for.

He swung a polite smile at the redhead and then swiveled to peer at her friend, an equally petite woman with a deeper tint to her mahogany pixie cut, showing off ears with four piercings apiece. "Ladies, I'm flattered but—"

"Ohhh, noooo," flirt number one protested. "We don't like the sound of that 'but.'"

"Not to be confused with the butt we *do* like." Her friend slid the goth fingernails under his ass, squeezing him through the fabric of his tailored dress trousers. For the fifteenth time tonight, he missed his regular camouflage "work attire" worse than Scout, the Siberian Husky who'd been like another brother to Tait and him through boyhood.

"You're so gorgeous." The first woman pushed his knees apart and stepped in for a feel from the other side, sliding a hand over the fabric covering his cock. "Oooo, and *hard*. You don't just look like Superman, do you? You feel like him—"

"*Everywhere.*" Her friend kept exploring, finally wrapping eager fingers around his balls. "Mmmmm. He's not Superman, Brynn. He's Ironman."

Shay tensed. He threw a subtle but thorough glance around the room, wondering if he'd missed anything on the first five sweeps. *Ironman.* How the hell had the woman blurted his radio call sign? Had Cameron Stock, the evil prick he'd been hanging out with for half a year, directed the woman to act shitfaced in order to drop the name and see how he'd react?

Or are you freaking out like a little girl now, Bommer? For fuck's sake, her fingers are all over the junkyard between your thighs—and the size of your "pipe" isn't a state secret. You may have earned the nickname by setting timed run records in PT, but your cock isn't a bad ally for the cause.

He rolled his eyes at the smartass in his head as the woman nuzzled his neck. When her margarita-heavy breath hit him, he had the answer to his dilemma. Her hit on the name had really just been stupid coincidence, though he rarely believed in that kind of cosmic shit. He couldn't afford to.

Brynn sidled closer, fitting the apex of her thighs against the same part of his anatomy. "Come on, stud. What about it? Ellie likes to share, and so do I. Two redheads, grounded by fog in the same airport as you, with a room waiting for us over at the Hilton..."

"And at least one of us isn't wearing panties." More margarita breath fanned his face.

Brynn giggled. "Make that neither of us. Horny, panty-free dancers from a hot Vegas show. Find a blue moon somewhere in that muck outside, and you've been handed a once-in-a-million memory, honey."

Part of him screamed to simply agree with her. That same part filled his imagination with a fantasy painted in shades of *ohhh, fuck,* and *yeah.* Both women kneeling before him, servicing his cock in all the ways any heterosexual male dreamed. He'd find a way to clamp their nipples as reciprocation for their naughty behavior before they licked every inch of his erection, preparing him to fuck them both...

Thoughts he didn't dare indulge for another second. Not now.

He pushed off the barstool, rubbed the back of his neck, and faked an awkward laugh. "I'm certain you're right, ladies, but I can't. I'm here on business. My colleague should be here any minute."

The reply was a string of lies. Where the fuck was Wyst? The guy was thirty minutes late. *Not* a development Shay wanted to take with the normal calm that had earned him a fast place in Cameron Stock's inner sanctum. But tonight, everything was different. Within the hour, they'd solidify the plans that would make this burglary happen, finally bringing him to the last stretch of this disgusting mission.

Shay had been working closely with the spooks to make this shit go down as seamlessly as possible. His personal investment in taking out Stock was intense. Last year, Stock helped engineer a scheme that nearly drenched the US West Coast beneath a nuclear fallout cloud, a plan thwarted in an operation by his brother Tait's Special Forces team—though the price had been devastating. Tait's ladylove, Luna Lawrence, had eventually died as a result of the standoff's violence. The trauma had turned Tait's heart into a husk and his liver into a distillery. And watching that shit happen? Shay grimaced from the memories. The term "emotional waterboarding" fit the bill nicely.

But exacting revenge on behalf of Tait was only the first half of the picture. Shay never lost sight of the second goal for this escapade, equally driving every step he took and move he made. He was going through this hell to find another victim of Stock's rise to criminal glory—a piece of prey who'd then been forced to become a cog in the monster's machine.

A cog he'd once known as Mom.

His gut turned. It certainly wasn't a new experience, especially if he counted all the years that had been wasted since she "deserted" them, as their father had always alleged. He'd been only nine. Tait was ten, though he was counting the days until his eleventh birthday, when he'd enjoy the six-month period when he could say he was two years older than Shay. Life's concerns were so simple. They were still a halfway-functioning family. Dad's drinking was still just uncomfortable instead of unbearable. He only went after Mom once a week rather than every other day—until the four-day bender that had ended with her leaving in the middle of the night. And never coming back.

Hearkening the start of the shit years.

Tait did his best to make sure they were safe when Dad got bad. There was the "hideout" in the basement next door courtesy of Mrs. Verona, stocked with canned food for emergencies, thanks to Uncle Jonah. Mrs. V always baked fresh cookies, too. Damn, he wanted those cookies again. He wanted the long conversations he and Tait had while savoring them.

Most of all, he wanted all the time he'd missed with his mother.

Whom he and Tait had joined Dad in vilifying for the last eighteen years—when she'd never intended to leave forever.

Who had signed on with Cameron for six months but had been forced by the man to stay for the rest of her life, used for her brilliant scientific mind—and probably a lot of other hideous things.

Who'd been forced to erase Melody Bommer and instead live as Melanie Smythe, never once permitted to contact Tait and him. Not just a stranger to her children. A ghost.

Now, Shay was achingly close to raising that ghost. To finally finding and freeing her.

All he had to do was help Cameron's team steal a commercial airliner.

After an hour, when they'd landed the bird, he'd be standing at the front door of her lab.

It was going to be a night for tricky feats—beginning with peeling off the women who'd redraped themselves against him.

Where the *hell* was Wyst?

His cell vibrated on the bar, dancing across the sticky granite to notify him of an incoming text. *Not a second too soon, dickwad.*

"Sorry, ladies. I really need to get this."

While the message saved him from the paws of his new fan club, it also slammed him with disappointment. Only three people knew the number to this phone, all smarmy sons of bitches. The device belonging to Shay Bommer, not "Shane Burnett," was secured in a locker in Langley, Virginia, its voice mail stating he was on deployment and didn't know when he'd be back.

He yearned for that other phone now. For even five minutes on the line with Tait. The last time he'd seen his brother had been such a bizarre fluke. Shay had just gotten started on this assignment and was working his way into Cameron's good graces, finishing one of the man's "special projects." They'd been on the island of Kaua'i, where Cameron had attempted to sell a beachfront estate to the North Koreans for use as their forward base in an assault on the western United States.

To Shay's shock, Tait and his sniper teammate, Kellan Rush, led the op to crush Cameron's scheme and save the estate's owner, an islander named Lani Kail. The whole episode actually helped seal Stock's buy-in on Shay's cover but had nearly made Lani another casualty of the man's evil. Not a great twist, considering Tait had damn near proposed to the woman after she was safe. Tait's fresh love for Lani made him deaf to any explanation Shay had for his involvement with Stock, officially turning Shay into a traitor in his brother's eyes.

The four months since then had been complete hell. And this text likely represented an extension of the ordeal.

Yo, Shane. You still at the airport?

Called that one right.

Shay clenched his jaw again. In addition to violating the team's rule about refraining from personal names on all mobile communication, Wyst also confirmed he wasn't at the airport, meaning the great airplane heist was again a no-go. *Damn it.*

Am I supposed to be anywhere else?

The sarcasm wouldn't translate, but Wyst wouldn't get it even if he stood here for the verbal version. The guy's DNA strand had taken a leak during the distribution of higher brain function, making him Cameron's ideal lap dog.

Guess you've been waiting for me. Sorry. Was eating dinner.

Shay refrained from gibing about whether the guy would indulge a manicure or a *Friends* rerun after eating. Mainly, he worried about Wyst actually answering.

So Cameron's called off the op again?

Once more, there was a hell of a lot more he burned to type. No, to demand. Like why the hell they weren't moving on the plan when the Pacific Ocean itself was cooperating tonight, dumping fog porridge over half of LA. He watched the departure-gate crews get itchier by the minute, waiting for word from the control tower that every flight would be grounded until morning. Their wait wasn't long.

After a few minutes, the PA system crackled. "We regret to inform passengers"—*blah blah blah*—"due to abnormal fog and dangerously low visibility"—*blah blah blah*—"Los Angeles International Airport will reopen at six o'clock tomorrow morning."

It was such a rarity for LAX, the crews clapped like kids on Christmas. In a way, it was. All the tarmacs had just been turned into Cameron's airliner goody bag, complete with a cloak of subterfuge to better enjoy the "fun."

So why the hell was Stock stalling this time?

New tactic. No joy on taking golden egg tonight.

Not enough yolk to hatch the plan. Extra roosters called to watch the henhouse.

"Fuck."

Now the guy switched to code speak? "Not enough yolk" likely meant none of the jets outside had enough fuel in them, even for a short hop to the desert outside Vegas. But that defense was thin. Why couldn't Stock get a couple of fuel crew IDs falsified, since he'd passed off Shay and Wyst as "airport contractors" for the last month? And "roosters" in the henhouse clearly referred to extra security for the terminals, determined to keep the largest airport in the state a drama-free zone tonight.

That defense didn't wash either. Stock had a shit ton of resources for this kind of thing. He'd called up a small mercenary army to face Tait's Special Forces battalion in Hollywood last year, not to mention the team of pretty-boy cutthroats gathered by his bitch, Gunter Benson, for the Kaua'i adventure.

So what wasn't adding up here?

Shay hoped to God it wasn't his cover story.

His next text exchange with Wyst would supply the answer to that.

When is hatch time rescheduled?

If Wyst's answer was evasive, he'd know the jig was up. It'd be clear Stock had learned about Shay's true purpose and was plotting to cut him out of the mission—and into a bunch of little pieces too.

Shit.

It would be time to risk contacting his CIA point man, Dan Colton. He'd need an exfil fast, if he lived that long. Finding a place to disappear for the night would be a priority. Trusting the LAX security team wasn't an option. He had no way of knowing who Cameron owned around here.

Escaping to the Hilton with his two new dancer friends suddenly seemed the best plan for the night—if they really weren't working for Stock themselves. Which, despite his earlier assumption, was an option on the table again.

How the hell was he going to figure them out? Getting them naked wasn't a fail-proof answer. Wasn't like he'd find wires or trackers. Cocksuckers like Stock had sneakier ways of keeping tabs on a guy these days, especially if they'd researched their prey and learned he belonged to several high-end BDSM clubs in Pensacola and Panama City. Wasn't a secret that he was tapped to teach rope-bondage classes when he wasn't tromping a desert or jungle with his Seventh Special Forces Group operational detachment, as well. All those women had to do was entice him into a little rope play, knowing he'd throw his entire attention into the scene, before distracting him just enough for Stock to put a bullet through his skull or a knife across his throat.

It'd be a viable theory if he still had conscious women on his hands.

He turned back toward the bar in time to hear the *clink* of Ellie's piercings as her head dropped to the marble. A contented smile was plastered on her lips.

"El?" Brynn leaned over and poked Ellie's shoulder. "El? Heeyyy, wake up. We were just starting to have some fun. Ellliieeee...woooo hoooo...anyone home?" She knocked on El's head like it was a neighbor's front door. When she added doorbell sounds, Shay wrote off his suspicions of the girls as Cameron Stock conspirators. Or sadly, as potential playmates for the night.

As he allowed his big head to deliver the depressing news to his small head, another text came in from Wyst.

New hatch time. 8 AM tomorrow. Sunset Airlines #403 to Sin City.

Papa Fox wants hens as insurance now.

Meet at the gate by 7.

So much for the rest of his hard-on. A strange recognition followed. While the update pushed one concern off his shoulders, another replaced it. The blatant details of Wyst's message proved Shay's cover story was still rock solid but also revealed their target wasn't an empty airliner anymore. *Papa Fox wants hens as insurance.*

Hell.

The burglary had turned into a hijack.

Shay glowered at his cola on the bar. He was tempted to shove the drink back and demand something stronger but didn't. Watching Dad pickle his liver into an early death, as well as Tait's temporary surrender to the bottle after losing Luna, guided him to pick and choose his dance cards with Mistress Booze.

Besides, Ellie and Brynn seemed determined to use the cards for everyone in the room.

"Ellliiee! Wake uhhh-hup. Hunk-of-hotness is off his phone and looks like he's gonna punish us for getting so turpsy. I mean tits-bees. I mean *tipsy*."

Shay held back from huffing again. At any other time the girls' antics would've coaxed him into an indulgent chuckle, but he couldn't shake off tonight's tension. The feeling turned into a freak case of Papa Bear syndrome. The hijack wasn't set to go down for another ten hours, but he couldn't stand thinking of the pair, embracing life with such mindless happiness, to be anywhere near this airport when it did.

"No," he told Brynn. "I'm feeling benevolent tonight. No punishments for you two. Let's just get you both on a shuttle back to the hotel, and—"

"Thank you, but they're okay."

The soft dictate didn't come from Brynn. It sure as hell didn't come from Ellie, who giggled in her sleep and then started snoring. *Then who...?*

Shay stared at a third woman who'd broken free of the estrogen pack in the corner. *Damn.* How'd he gotten so distracted that he stopped focusing on his surroundings? Clumsy shit like that landed guys like him at the wrong end of blades or bullets.

Especially if they were wielded by a beauty like her.

Holy fuck.

But so what if she were here to kill him? He almost prayed for it. With her face as his last sight before the other side, Hades wouldn't feel like a penance for the messy turns of his life. Seven years in Special Forces, taking more lives than a man should be comfortable with. Relationships that had ended with even worse carnage. A fucked-up obsession with honor and protectiveness, learned entirely from characters in the movies he'd sneaked into rather than doing homework, likely meaning he had no concept of the shit at all.

But in this moment, he yearned to. Practically craved it as he soaked up her heart-shaped face with its bow of a mouth, along with thick-lashed eyes framing irises that entranced him like skies on the verge of wild storms. Her nose wasn't a petite cliché and was decorated with a sapphire stud that matched her gaze. The same navy blue color adorned the ends of her hair—holy God, what hair—its near-black waves tumbling down her back despite her efforts to contain it in a loose braid.

She was otherworldly. Ethereal. He felt like a knuckle-dragging ape in comparison, especially because words still eluded him.

Finding his tongue didn't get easier when the woman bent to help Ellie, giving a view of her cleavage that banged another wake-up call for his cock. She'd never be a curvy pin-up star, but what she had was tight and firm. Two ideal handfuls.

"El," she murmured to her friend. When the woman only snored louder and pushed her away, she resorted to a full yell. "Ellie. *Ay.* Come on; you can't do this. Let's go back to the hotel, *corazón*, where you can sleep it off."

"Looks like Ellie's one step ahead of you, beautiful."

Her eyes widened when he slipped in the endearment. Through the moment after that, he basked in the searing paradise of her appraisal of him. He lifted his gaze, answering her heat signal with a return beacon of his own. Thank God the messages were comprised of raw sexual attraction, undetectable by the spooks' radio chatter experts. If that were possible, the guys in the control room would interpret the exchange as a plot to blow something up. Not that exploding something here was such a bad idea...

Her scowl threw a soaked blanket on his illicit thoughts. "Look, Mr....uh..."

"Burnett." The cover name rolled out easily. Six months of regular usage came in handy. "Shane Burnett. But please make it Shane." *And please say it in your sweet, spicy accent, too.*

Brynn tittered again. "If you bellow something like 'only my father's called Mr. Burnett,' I'll *die.*" She used an exaggerated baritone for the middle portion.

"Good news." He smirked a little. "Nobody will be writing your obit tonight." He'd called his father many things over the years, but nothing resembling the respectful address. Tait had actually tried it once and had been whacked into the wall for being a cheeky jokester.

"Well," said the newest arrival to their exchange, tugging on a blue-tipped strand of hair. "*Muchas gracias* for that, at least. Now what do we do about El?" She shifted her fingers to the ends of a tie-dyed scarf, seeming lost. Shay took advantage of the chance to scoot closer. The top of her head barely came to his armpit. Once more, he fought the sensation of feeling like an ape next to a butterfly. No. It sounded better in the language her accent hinted at. An exquisite *mariposa.*

"Ladies." He tagged it with another smile, relishing the chance to bury the ugliness of tomorrow beneath tonight's courtly façade. "Perhaps I can be of service."

The two women stared as if he'd really turned into a giant

chimp. Was that a good or bad thing?

"Holy shit," Brynn finally blurted. "Maybe I really will just die—but only if you're waiting on the other side, Mr. Shane Burnett."

Okay, a good thing. He breathed easier. Until the *mariposa* stepped forward again.

"We're grateful for the offer," she stated, "but we'll manage everything fine. Have a good evening."

At least Brynn was still on his side. She glared at her friend, grunting with impressive force. "Zoe Margarita Madonna Chestain," she snapped. "What the hell is wrong with you?"

"Besides that you're loving an excuse to babble my full name?" The woman kicked up one side of her mouth. Part of Shay's gut followed suit, kicking to life at her mirth. The way it made her eyes shimmer no longer aroused his body alone. She really was an exotic anomaly, intriguing him deeper by the minute. He yearned to see her face come alive with a thousand more expressions. How did she look when she laughed? Cried? Or parted those curvy, sweet lips on a long, breathy orgasm...

"You deserve every pissed syllable," Brynn fumed. "What's wrong with you, spewing with the 'tude when the world's last chunk of chivalry is standing here in *that* suit, offering us the aid of *those* arms?"

Zoe Margarita Madonna Chestain had the grace to blush. She lifted her gaze to his. "I'm sorry, Mr. Burnett. It's been a long day. We had performances at all ends of the city today, and we're a little tired."

He swung a glance toward her snoring friend. "Never would've guessed."

"I don't mean to be rude—"

"Then don't be." He made good use of the interruption.

Before she could speak again, he stepped over, slid a gentle grip around Ellie, and then pulled her off the barstool and into his arms.

"Lucky bitch," Brynn muttered. "And she won't even remember it in the morning. Irony is such a douchebag."

The woman's drunken giggle wasn't shared by her friend. Zoe was glaringly sober, verified by the half-drained water glass on the table near the purse she grabbed—and her taut expression while doing so. Shay weathered another twinge to his gut—and a fresh surge of blood to his groin. Deduction dictated she was a dancer. Every move she made flowed into the next, never giving his attention respite from her supple muscles and well-trained grace. *Damn.* She was probably flexible as shit too.

Fine. He was attracted to her. A lot. That still didn't explain the "twinge." He mentally backtracked the feeling. He'd first weathered it when realizing he'd ticked her off with his boldness. *Not* normal shit. Since when did he care about irking anyone other than Tait, his CO, and lately, Cameron Stock? Indulging in "caring" meant a sacrifice of focus.

Nope. Not normal. Not acceptable, either.

Which was why he now smiled at her, trying to be a gentleman and smooth her ruffled feathers?

Forget unacceptable. He'd moved straight on to surreal. The shit wasn't helped by his fascination with her peregrine beauty. She treated him to an unguarded moment of it while gathering her friends' purses, letting him stare his fill of her huge midnight eyes and temptress's lips.

All too quickly, she cast her gaze back down.

Just like a flawlessly trained submissive.

Goodbye, surreal. Hello, torture.

This isn't the time for dungeon fantasies, asshole. Tame your dick and focus your mind.

"The Hilton runs regular shuttles to the outside curb," Zoe told him after she walked back over. "At least I hope they do now."

Brynn answered the quizzical stare he threw to both of them. "Their shittle—err, shuttle—van was all broken when we called for it a couple of hours ago." She turned her hands up, fingers splayed like a little girl. "And we're all in heels. And it was after dark. And the hotel's, like, a bunch of blocks away. A drink sounded good, and they told us the fix time wouldn't be more than an hour."

"Which was two hours ago?" Shay couldn't help a wry laugh after Brynn answered with a sheepish nod. In all seriousness, he wondered if their hot-ass Vegas show company had considered hiring a bodyguard to travel with these girls. If any of them were his woman, he'd be demanding it.

Zoe's heavy sigh broke into his speculation. "Let me call them again. Maybe they took down my number wrong, or—"

"Fed you a line just to get you off their backs," Shay interjected.

She yanked up her chin. Little sparks appeared in her eyes, tantalizing cobalt against the deep blue. "Which means what?"

So much for not irking her again. Fine by him. He was a little rankled himself now, largely from how cavalier she—and her half-wasted friends—were about their own welfare. "It means they're likely not going to pick up even if you do call, Miss Chestain."

Her lips twisted. She'd obviously expected what he said but didn't like it. "Fine. Then we'll just take a cab."

"Bet your ass we will."

"We?"

He repeated the brow-jerking thing before glancing to her friend still totally toasted in his arms. "So you're saying you can handle all of this yourself, tiny dancer?"

The stubborn woman tightened her pout. "Look...Mr. Burnett..."

"Let's go. The taxi queue is this way."

CHAPTER TWO

Damn it.

Zoe almost spat the words aloud, despite risking another heart-halting "look" from Mr. Shane Burnett. She could ignore her animal-level attraction to everything else about the man—his thick chestnut hair, sinful gold eyes, model-perfect jaw, and linebacker-wide shoulders—but when he turned on *the look*, something strange happened to her bloodstream.

Strange. And magical. And terrifying.

It had been a long time since she'd had some scary magic in her life.

Too long to be projecting such feelings onto a stranger in an airport bar.

She'd first seen him use "the look" on his phone, glowering at the thing as if willing the texts on it into submission. He'd likely succeeded too. God knew how *her* knees went weak, surrendering to the heat that flowed between them and the most tender folds of her body, from just watching him. *Caramba*, the man was all her favorite flavors, and none of them were vanilla. She would've bet her favorite shoes he was a lifestyle Dominant—and imagining him in a Dom's skintight leathers, holding a flogger in his hand instead of a phone... approaching her across a dungeon with *that look* on his face...

Ohhhh, yes.

Ohhhh, *no.*

She couldn't foster that fantasy again. Ever. The near-disaster with Bryce had taught her that much. Her submissive dreams were doomed to be just that. Dreams. If she had a drop of truly submissive blood in her body, fate had dried it up well before she could do anything about it.

No, it wasn't even fate's fault. When Mom died, *Papi* had fallen apart. Someone had to take care of Ava, and Zoe was the obvious choice. Maybe the angels had forgotten about her being only eleven years old. She'd been livid with them for a while, of course, but now saw it gave her a stubborn strength she was proud of.

Most of the time.

On other occasions, she opted for full retreat. Seemed the easiest route tonight with Mr. Sexy Scowl. She'd gone for duck and cover, sipping her water and checking her phone, praying El and Brynn would get a clue about the man's polite rebuffs. Before that could happen, Ellie had become Sleeping Beauty on the bar. Then the man himself had gained a name. He was no longer anonymous-fantasy-Dom but Shane Burnett, a businessman with endless patience for her friends, a captivating smile, and a protective streak as huge as the arms in which he now held Ellie.

And one more "little" thing. A presence that pulled on her like the moon did the tides.

Which was why she could muster nothing but a prissy huff before following him out of the terminal and into a cab.

What the hell was she doing? She had to take care of the others, not just El and Brynn, yet she let Burnett load the three of them into the cab. But she was aware, perhaps better than most, that dominant men could also be abusers. Though Burnett directed the driver to the Hilton, what plans did he have for the three of them after he got them to the room?

Images blared to mind of tomorrow's headlines, relaying the news that she, El, and Brynn had been beaten to death by an unknown attacker...

She shook her head free of the melodrama. Resolve time. She simply wouldn't let him get past the lobby elevators.

For the time being, he offered a true favor. El was down for the count, and Brynn was blasted. Handling them by herself really would have been a bitch. The ride was only four blocks, but every inch of it was going to be hell. In all the most tantalizing, torturous ways.

Zoe realized it the second Burnett slid into the car and closed the door. Even after he unloaded El, letting her head slide down into Zoe's lap, he seemed to consume the taxi's back seat. With Brynn opting to grab shotgun in front, Zoe found herself the sole object of the man's concentration—and he drilled it into her without mercy. Or apology.

The car's confines seemed to shrink more. She breathed deep, battling to calm her racing nerves, but wound up drenching her senses with his scent instead. Earthy strength, woodsy spice. An escape to the forest in the middle of Century Boulevard. *Wow.*

Time for Plan B. But returning the man's stare was another failure. Why did he keep studying her like the rest of the world didn't exist? The neon signs of the airport district whizzed by—Girls on Fire, Strip-A-Rama, Boobalicious Beauties—but the temptations could have been dust mites for how weakly they dragged his attention from her.

Ohhh, God.

Wait.

Maybe he was gay.

The possibility was such a relief, she smiled for a second.

That was all the time he gave her to enjoy the feeling. As he extended his arm along the top of the seat and then dropped two fingers to her nape, the inquiry on his face intensified. His gaze was again a wordless query, seeming to question whether she'd welcome him or shirk him.

Before she could help it, a long sigh spilled from her lips.

Burnett's alluring mouth parted a little. His jaw undulated in quiet assessment, flashing with a small tic of muscle.

Her whole body zinged with awareness.

Crap.

Not gay.

She scrambled for a logical argument. This was insane. Unreal. Serendipity that only happened in movies, to people who had perfect lives and all the right lines prewritten for them. Not someone like her, who'd made a *desastre* of her last "relationship" and now must have a tattoo on her forehead, visible to men only. *Hit on me; I haven't had sex in almost a year.* People who could summon a drop of moisture to their mouths instead of letting their tongue turn to cotton from the simple press of a man's fingertips.

"You're tense."

He murmured it between a couple of El's snores. Wait. That wasn't El. It was Brynn, who slumped against the window like she'd pricked her finger on the same enchanted spinning wheel as Ellie.

Great.

She pulled in another breath. And was hit by another arousing wave of his fresh forest smell. *Vaya*, it was nice. Why did a guy in a designer suit smell like he'd just stepped off an alpine hiking trail? Further, why did she sense he'd ditch the suit for the trail in a second? With that jaw, that hair, and those eyes, he was stunning enough to fill one of the Rolex watch ads on the billboards overhead, yet he claimed he was in the airport for business. Now he was stuck in a dingy city cab, in the middle of a freak LA fog bank, with two women who might rouse from their drunken stupors any second just to barf on him—and a third who'd gone dizzy from the effort of resisting his smoke-dark stare.

She finally managed to answer, "And you, Mr. Burnett, are nearly a stranger."

One corner of his mouth lifted. "A nice one"—he trailed his fingers up the back of her neck—"unless you ask me not to be."

There was a rebuff in her brain for that. Somewhere. But as he emphasized his point by sifting his fingers into her hair and pulling by the tiniest degrees, all she could do was gasp. The sound trumpeted what he'd just done to the sensitive nerves between her thighs.

"Damn," the man whispered.

Zoe straightened with a jerk. "What is it?" she demanded. "What'd I do wrong?"

"Wrong? Not a damn thing, beautiful." He chuckled and rubbed the back of his neck. "As a matter of fact, if you do things any more right, I'll be bugging out of the Hilton on *three* legs."

She surrendered to a nervous laugh. At the renewed curiosity in his golden-silk eyes, she explained, "You sure you're just a mild-mannered businessman, Mr. Burnett?"

"Define 'mild-mannered.'" He kneaded his neck harder. "Why'd you ask?"

She settled her back against the cab's door and regarded him for a long moment. "Because you talk just like the army sergeant who's going to be my brother-in-law come New Year's

Eve."

His expression didn't change. But if it was true what the New-Agers said about a person's energy having a color, his just amped from focused purple to alarmed crimson. Before she could discern why, he flashed an extra-smooth smile and countered, "You know, I'm tempted to boomerang that at you."

What was this? A hint at playful? The switch-up gave her hope of gaining back some composure. "Is that so?"

The man leaned forward, matching the angle of his head to hers. "Are you sure you're just a mild-mannered dancer, Miss Chestain?"

She arched a brow. "You're asking that of a Las Vegas backup dancer, mister. They make us check our 'mild-mannered' cards at the door."

"Ahhh, yes. That's right. A dancer for a 'hot' Sin City show."

"Did Brynn and El tell you that?"

"They supplied the 'hot' part. The rest is original material."

She tossed her head the other way, giving the move some spunk. The man was comfortable to talk to when she stopped fantasizing about him with a paddle in his grip or his hand on her ass. "You know 'Sin City' isn't exactly new, right?"

She raised a hand to put the cliché into air quotes but lowered it when he straightened his head, zapping her with the full, delicious effect of his darkening stare. "Sin itself isn't original, little dancer. But what one does with it can redefine a man." He jolted her anew when scooping up her hand, rotating it over, and then dipping his lips to the center of her palm. "Or a woman."

So much for comfortable.

Or any semblance of rational.

Do it again. Oh God, please do it again.

Fortunately, her brain was more cooperative than her libido. One second of clarity later, she successfully yanked her hand back. "You're a naughty man, Mr. Burnett."

She didn't have any strength—or motivation—to add humor. That didn't stop the guy from smirking again, looking like a *Survivor* player who'd found the immunity idol. "Nah," he drawled. "Just a grunt doing my job, ma'am."

She narrowed her gaze. "Who *really* likes doing it with a shitload of those cute military words."

For a second, long enough for her to notice, his smile wavered. "Some of my best friends are ground pounders," he supplied. "That probably explains it."

"Hmmm."

She didn't alter her gaze. He maintained his too.

"You don't believe me," he finally asserted.

Zoe bit the inside of her bottom lip. "Actually, I do. But that's the trouble."

He propped his head on a tripod of the fingers that had just been on her skin. "Why?"

She had an answer. But the best way to phrase it? *Caramba.* Thankfully, her confusion lasted for all of two seconds. "What the hell. It's not like we're going to see each other again." She squared her shoulders. "Because there's something else you're not telling me, Mr. Burnett. Maybe a lot of something elses. And—"

"And?" His soft smile matched his prodding tone.

"And I can't figure out why that bothers me." She frowned and glanced back up. Not unexpectedly, his stare awaited her again, though now his neck was taut, and his strong lips pressed together. He seemed poised and ready.

For what?

"I understand that," he murmured.

"You do?"

"I want to know more about you too." Even as the driver guided the car around a tight turn, requiring him to grab Ellie's calves to stop her from slipping off the seat, his focus didn't waver. "A lot more than we can handle in a five-minute cab ride."

Zoe had done her part to prevent El's fall. But releasing her grip from her friend's elbow played her hand back into Burnett's grip. Her breath snagged as his fingers, massive and warm, closed around hers. *Dios,* he had big hands. So certain and strong. Was there a shred of truth in the adage about the size of a man's hands in correlation to his other...parts?

Get your mind out of the gutter. Now.

Fat chance. She wet her lips before stammering, "Five minutes can be an eternity."

He molded his hand tightly around hers. "Is that so?"

"Mmm-hmm. Just ask a dancer trying to look sexy during a major show finale at a dance rave pace."

He chuckled. The expression spread over his face, igniting it into a captivating sight. She'd have no trouble with taking up a new hobby—counting the flecks of topaz in his eyes. "You have a very good point." Just as quickly, those specks heated. "So maybe we should take full advantage of our eternity."

Once more, everything from her head to her toes felt like electric lines in a hurricane.

Stop. This is crazy. The temptation they flirted with...all the ways she longed to define *advantage* and *eternity*... They were ridiculous, dangerous fantasies. He was a stranger. A man possessing only a name and some vague occupation.

And a stare that dissolved the hinges on some of the deepest doors in her soul.

She turned to the most dependable go-to in her wardrobe of emotional defenses. Dark humor. "With one of my friends snoring in the front seat and the other drooling in my lap?"

He considered that for half a moment before setting her hand free—in order to raise his touch to her face. Alluring officially gained a new ambassador as he grazed his knuckles along her arm during the trip. "I only require the use of these." He caressed the corner of her right eye. "And this." He drifted his touch over her mouth.

Before she could think about containing it, a long sigh escaped. *Dios.* The man didn't look beneath her neck, let alone drift his touch there. So why were her panties already drenched, taunting her with the liquid he'd just coaxed from her most secret tunnel? Why did her heart thunder and her pulse careen?

"Miss Chestain?"

His prompt was a command, ordering her to answer whether she was capable or not. "Huh?"

"Look at me." He curved his thumb beneath her chin and gently tugged up. Her gaze was again filled with his face—only now, his boyish charm was gone. The garish neon of the club lights, joined with the glow from the stoplight ahead, turned him into the granite-hard Dominant she'd previously only guessed at. "And now, I want you to answer me."

She swallowed again. Flames and icicles fought for control of her limbs. *Caramba.* The power of his fingers on her face...it was the beginning of her end. "Yes, Sir."

No, no, no! She clenched her teeth and closed her eyes, fighting to lock him out—even as her senses predicted what he'd say next. What he'd command next...

And how every cell in her body wouldn't give her rest until she answered him.

"How long have you known about your submissiveness, Zoe?"

CHAPTER THREE

Nail on the head.

The catch in Zoe Chestain's breathing, along with the flair of her dark-blue eyes, blared the victory cry through Shay's senses.

He'd taken a calculated risk on the question. While it was ridiculous to think of his life being stable enough to keep a steady subbie, he'd become damn adept at picking one out in a crowd—and Zoe had given herself away from the start. The way she moved. The way she watched *him* move. The way that made her lips part and her breath quicken. And then that defining moment, when she'd ducked her head with such sweet deference, all but daring him to stride across the room and stroke her hair in praise...

Fuck yeah, that moment.

The clincher? Hearing those two perfect words, tumbling so naturally from her lips. *Yes, Sir.*

He longed to hear her say more. Yearned to know more about her, especially the steps she'd taken in the D/s lifestyle. Had they been huge strides or just curious explorations? Had she even experienced Total Power Exchange before? If so, what had happened to make her so shy about this side of herself? Had someone messed with her in the wrong way? Not honored the gift of her trust? He couldn't imagine a Dom with this woman at his feet not wanting to drop to his knees beside her and thank God for the treasure of her.

He practically held his breath, waiting for her answer.

The cab jerked to a stop at the Hilton's lobby doors.

Damn it.

He couldn't help noticing Zoe's big whoosh of breath. As he paid the driver, she actually thanked the man and wished him a good night. Somebody was a little too happy to be off the hook.

Enjoy the freedom now, tiny dancer. I'm not done with you yet.

He didn't want to give his ego full credit for the promise, though his brain blared a reminder. *Careful, buddy. She's already wise to the army-boy vibe. Your call sign may be Ironman, but she's peeling back the armor. You really want this to go that much further? To risk exposing who you really are?*

He turned the voice off to care for the more urgent pair of matters at hand. Brynn needed to be roused and Ellie somehow muscled from the car. As Shay handled things with El, Zoe opened the front passenger door and went to work on waking her friend.

Her *chica* woke with a cute little start, releasing the same drunken tigress she'd been back at the airport—only at a louder volume. "I got the eye of a tiger, a fighter, dancing through the fii-ire—c'mon, Zo, sing with me, baby!—I am a champ-eee-on, and you're gonna hear me rooooar!"

Zoe gave her friend an indulgent smile as Brynn slumped against her. "You don't want me to go there, girlfriend; we both know it. Besides, you've got this handled."

She threw a sardonic glance to Shay as the doorman let them in, and Brynn treated everyone in the lobby bar to a miniature Katy Perry tribute while Zoe picked up the room keys. Though Shay kept his attention fixed on Brynn's antics, he continued his unfaltering study of Zoe, including how she recommitted herself to the all-business air while turning from the desk. Shit, did that mien say things—like her obvious consideration of the options for now giving him a tactful goodbye. The challenge was Ellie. Brynn was still in no position to help, and hauling one's friend to the room on a bell cart was only excusable during New Year's Eve and Mardi Gras.

The woman's dilemma intensified as men waved money at Brynn, shouting requests for other tunes. As the damn fool girl grinned, ready to indulge them, Shay drilled a glare at the bastards. Before they finished backing down, Zoe's ambivalence cracked. She grabbed her friend, nodded at Shay, and then led the way to the elevators.

Once they entered Brynn and Ellie's room, Zoe pulled back the sheets on one bed so Shay could slip El in fully clothed. On the other side of the room, Brynn attempted to strip. The woman shucked her T-shirt without effort, but the painted-on jeans weren't as cooperative. Still humming the Katy Perry anthem, she hopped around until stumbling onto the bed and falling back asleep.

Zoe gaped at her friend, stunned into silence.

Shay snickered. *Hell.* He couldn't help himself. She'd been so I-am-Woman-Hear-Me-Roar all night, making her awkward moment an enticing surprise.

He couldn't help another laugh. Shrugged as if to apologize but let out another. Though Zoe shot him a glare at first, one glance at her friend had her giggling too. They laughed harder as Brynn rolled over, her jeans still locked around her knees, her lips mumbling through the final bars of her song.

"I have ibuprofen in my purse," she murmured. "Maybe I

should get it?"

He mellowed his laugh to a smile. She seemed to always think three steps ahead of everyone, and those thoughts were always full of kindness. "Good idea. Grab some water to go with it, and we'll set it on the nightstand for them." He nodded toward Brynn. "I'll handle the rest of this."

He had to admit, he'd peeled more cooperative wrappers off taffy before. When Zoe came back from the bathroom, he was still battling the denim around one of Brynn's ankles. When she was finally free, he gently tucked her under the covers before following Zoe from the room.

Once they got to the hall, they both leaned against the wall, releasing relieved breaths. He let a long moment pass, though it was total torture. All he wanted to do was pivot around, press her between his body and the wall, and lean in for the kiss he'd been craving since he met her. Now it was *his* turn at the clumsy shuffle.

"Wow." He tried to laugh once more.

"What?" She glanced up, caught him staring, and returned to tracing the pattern on the carpet with her ankle-booted toe.

"I haven't felt this dorky since I was sixteen. For the record, that's a long damn time."

She looked back at him for a pulse-grabbing second, flashing a captivating grin. "Mr. Burnett, I'm pretty sure you and 'dorky' have never crossed paths."

Though she tossed the statement out with plenty of sass, the essence of her submissiveness flowed over him once more, this time with her voice as an added pleasure. The silk of her soft accent was an offering to him, a test run of her trust that danced around the answer she never gave in the cab. Clearly, the progress wasn't easy for her, and he was moved by her bravery. It stabbed to the core of everything he loved about being a Dom. The first tendrils of her surrender...believing in his ability to take her courage and transform it into more...

Holy fuck, did he want to try. They had a lot of hours until dawn.

Or maybe not.

She stopped the process at the gift of her words. Her stance remained rigid, her arms tightly folded. Despite this wild, wonderful energy flowing between them, she scooted away by a nervous step.

Shay didn't let her get far. He leaned toward her with renewed resolve. Damn it, fate didn't simply plop a connection like this into any Dom's lap, during any random airport closure. There weren't a lot of magical things in his life anymore, which probably explained his obsession with *this* gift. He was determined to fight for it, at least a little.

He reached, gently cupping her elbow in his hand. When she didn't resist, he slid his fingers up the back of her arm. "Tell you what. I'll confess about the dorky skeletons in my closet if you spill about the submissive ones in yours."

She squirmed again. Turned her head and gazed back down the hall. "I...really should go back over to the terminal. Someone else may decide to take a snooze on the bar, and—"

"And you're not their mother."

That compelled her head back up. The surprise in her eyes wasn't a shock, but he couldn't stand the idea of her bolting from him either. *Not yet.* There were deeper layers to this woman. Depths he was strangely, intensely curious to explore.

Summoning his biggest *cojones*, he lifted both hands to bracket her shoulders.

"Mr. Burnett—"

"That's not easy for you to hear, is it?"

"Easy or not, it's just not accurate. I'm the dance lead on our show, which means technically, I *am* their mother."

He lowered his head, leveling the trajectory of their gazes as much as he could. "Agreed, though I suspect you're a willing natural for the role, as well."

Her brows jumped. He'd either stunned her or insulted her. Perhaps both. "Willing? Natural? Well, it certainly wasn't what I expected when I accepted the job."

"Why?"

"Because I've been taking care of people, in some way, shape, or form, since I was eleven."

"Then you must be good at it by now."

"So I've been told."

"And tired of it."

"Haven't been told *that*."

"Really?" He was genuinely bewildered and didn't hide it. That shadowed her gaze with curiosity too. Shay took advantage of the chance to scoop a hand beneath her chin, maintaining the silent, potent lock of their eyes.

"Let the kids take care of themselves tonight, Mom."

Conflict took over her face as if he'd asked her to blow up the hotel instead of trusting her friends to behave like adults. It didn't surprise him. They'd met less than an hour ago, but he already saw letting go was a back-burner issue for the woman. She'd been taking care of others for so long, she'd nearly lost herself.

It made him a little furious. A hell of a lot more sad. She had no idea how stunning she was, how she mesmerized him even as she stood there working her lips against each other, turning them the color of crushed berries. For the twentieth time, Shay battled the urge to ram her against the wall and show her exactly what it felt like to be "taken care of."

Focus on something innocuous.

Not happening, either. Even her goddamn earlobes were delectable, begging him to dip his head and taste them...

"Fine," she quipped at last, cocking her head in defiance. "For argument's sake, let's say I leave the kids alone and let them stumble back on their own. You going to stand there and tell me there's nothing in it for you, Burnett? That you don't simply want the chance to poke around for my skeletons a little more, *señor?*"

Her intelligence, showcased with that mix of adorable and incisive, poured even more juice into the elixir of his attraction to her. "Guilty." He raised both hands. "You got me. But your skeletons *are* damn appealing, *señorita.*"

"To a guy like you."

He lowered his hands, letting a weighted moment go by. "Yeah. To a guy like me." Their gazes met once more, conveying a mutual understanding. From the way they both emphasized "guy," it was clear they meant *Dom.* "Who, if I'm not mistaken, might be very interesting to a woman like you."

"That's where you're mistaken." She pushed from the wall, letting him see the sadness that sliced across her face. "I'm not a woman like that." A little snort followed. "Look, I've been... curious...in the past, okay? There was a time when I craved the Dominant/submissive thing. I had a boyfriend who even helped me try it all out, and—"

"And what?"

A deep furrow returned between her brows. She shook her head before answering him in a whisper. "I suck at submissiveness, okay?"

"Zoe." It was all Shay could do not to laugh. "Beautiful, breathtaking Zoe. I find that statement harder to believe than a cheap carny psychic."

"Sure. Because you know me so well."

"Because I know *me* so well. And I know the parts of me that have definitely awakened to corresponding things about you."

Her snort turned scornful. "Keep them in your pants, honey."

He allowed her to break free, only thinking she needed some breathing space—until she stunned him with a parade-perfect pivot and started stomping back down the hall. "You really want that, baby girl?"

He didn't raise his voice on the growl. As he'd hoped, it didn't take long to take effect, halting her cold in those little boots. Her sassy posture accentuated every gorgeous curve of her legs and ass. It all looked even nicer when her spine stiffened. His cock enthusiastically followed suit.

Damn. Their "relationship" wasn't even at triple digits in minutes, but witnessing his voice have that effect on her and getting her gorgeous impudence in return only strengthened his impression about the connection they already shared.

This magic...

So what if she didn't see it yet? He'd already resolved to do the fighting for them both—and recommitted himself to the cause now.

Too bad he was too busy with the mental *hooah* to remember one of the shittiest rules-that-weren't-rules about unconventional warfare.

The outcome of a battle often hinged on the smallest of actions.

Like the one Zoe made in the moment he still struggled to take control of his dick and make his way to her again.

From one of the pockets hugging that cute backside, she withdrew a room key card. Waved it at the door in front of her. The portal beeped, and she didn't waste a second stepping through it. By the time Shay caught up, she'd turned around, one hand on the inside light switch, the other on the door. Her gaze returned to its guarded anger. Her lips were a tight line.

Shay reined back another growl. It was fucking impossible to fight for something with a door slammed in one's face.

Nearly slammed.

"Thank you again," she murmured, "for the help with Brynn and El. You racked up the Good Samaritan points tonight, okay?"

He risked sliding his toes to the threshold of the room. Then tilting up her face with his thumb once more. "I have a lot of those already." He wasn't lying. In his years with the teams, he'd stopped counting how many kids he'd guided from landmine fields, rations he'd distributed to villagers, and even kittens he'd pulled out of trees. "What if I simply want to cash them in?"

Her breath hitched. As she let it back out in shaky spurts, he dared pushing a whole foot forward.

"Burnett..."

She moved her hand from the wall to his shoulder. To push him away? He chose to ignore the possibility and was damn glad he did. The next instant, her fingers curled into his sleeve. A visible tremor claimed her.

Shay moved his other foot into the room. Slid his thumb along her jaw, toward her ear. He framed the other side of her face with his index finger, pulling her mouth steadily closer.

"Please," she whispered.

He lowered a hand to her waist. "I love the way you say that, tiny dancer."

The endearment earned him a high-pitched little cry, vibrating from her throat into his fingers. His bloodstream thundered in response. His cock surged through his pants, now pressed against her stomach.

"Hell," she gasped.

"Feels a lot more like heaven to me."

"Please. We can't."

He drew back a little, making sure her gaze was consumed with the hot intent of his. "I'm going to kiss you, baby girl. If you still believe that when I'm done, then I'll turn around, leave you alone, and never bother you again. Sound fair?"

She blinked hard. With every dip of her dark lashes, her eyes glittered more intensely. Her chest pumped, deep and hard. Technically, none of it told him *yes*.

But none of it was *no*.

He fitted their bodies together. Slammed his mouth atop hers. As he did, his spirit pumped a fist with its revision to his battle wisdom from earlier.

Small actions could definitely determine outcomes.

But bold actions created awesome explosions.

CHAPTER FOUR

She was in trouble.

Hot, wonderful, beautiful gobs of it.

Shane Burnett and his mouth—and his hands, and his arms, and his thighs—were the hard, incredible ringleaders of the mess. Even before he prodded her lips open with his mouth, he brought a waterfall of heat to her blood, a cascade of need to her skin, a profound pleasure to every sense she possessed—and probably a few new ones too. As he deepened their kiss, she matched his rough growl with a whimper that echoed through every corner of her body at once.

He consumed her already—as she knew he would.

Pulled out every dark, sinful craving of her soul again—as she feared he would.

A corner of her mind tried rationalizing the sensations. *Holy shit.* Waterfalls? Cascades? *Cravings?* Would she next start comparing the man's touch to a shower of stars? And could she be blamed? The only male touch she'd known since January had been from the guys in the show, who fantasized about caressing each other when they had to fondle her for the steamier numbers. Dating hadn't been a consideration. After the disastrous night in the dungeon that had officially ended her relationship with Bryce, she'd declared herself an intimacy disaster zone. Ten months later, it was just easier to keep the barriers up.

There was nothing safe about Shane Burnett. And nothing

remotely easy.

He groaned against her lips as he shifted their bodies, making room for the door to thump shut behind them. Zoe sucked in air through her nose, yearning to keep the contact of their mouths intact. Shane groaned his approval, spreading her lips wide before sweeping his tongue into the deepest corners of her mouth. His hands splayed to her shoulders, dropped along her rib cage, and finally gripped her hips in fierce possession, sliding her against the bulge that reigned the apex of his thighs.

He finally pulled back, fanning her face with his lustful breaths. "Please don't tell me the Samaritan points are still my only option tonight."

She smiled. "Please don't tell me that running after the kids is mine."

He answered that by screwing his grip tighter to her hips and hiking her higher on the wall so he could kiss her at a direct angle. *Holy hell.* Maybe the man's touch was made of stars. Her body felt like a damn meteor shower as he controlled her positioning against him...and that meant the blatant slide of her pussy along his huge erection.

"Speaking of the kids," he said against her lips, "how long do you think we have?"

Zoe pried her eyes open. "How long? For what?"

"Until your roommate stumbles in."

She grinned wider. It was refreshing to be with someone who knew so little about her world. Even Bryce, for all his surface charm, got a little tiresome about showing off her lead dancer status, as well as her comp show seats and other perks, to all his friends. "The lead gets her own room, Mr. Burnett."

His groin pulsed against hers. "Fuck."

She giggled again. "Yes, please."

He dipped his gaze to her lips and kissed her soundly there again before returning her to her feet with a reluctant expression. "In that case, grab your phone."

Her smile fell. "*Qué?* Why?"

"Safe call." His brows jumped when Zoe stared like he'd just said *squirrel farts*. "You think I'm going to ask for your nakedness and trust after knowing me a little over an hour, without a safety net of some sort?" His gaze turned dark bronze. "You need to call or text a friend, preferably one who isn't drunk at the terminal, and tell them that if you don't contact them in three hours, they need to call the Los Angeles PD and send them to this room."

"*Mierda.*" Zoe had slipped her cell out but froze, eyeing him as if the squirrel had done more than fart on him. "You're joking, right?"

Shane stepped back, clasping his hands at the small of his back and widening his stance. "Not by any stretch of the word. Your trust is key to me, dancer. As much as you'll give me, as far as you'll let me go. The power here belongs to you as much as me, and having a backup for your safety gives us a clearer path to that."

He looked thoroughly dominant now. Totally breathtaking. Nevertheless, Zoe blurted in confusion, "I'm still not sure I understand."

The man shook his head. Great. Now he had her a little scared as well as a lot muddled. "Why don't you sit?"

Clearly, the polite phrasing was a courtesy. As tempted as she was to go for a cheeky comeback, something in her psyche nixed the move.

She lowered her butt onto the edge of the bed.

Shane positioned himself directly in front of her. She looked down at his shiny black dress shoes, strangely afraid about looking up again—and embracing that sweet thrill.

"Zoe, what do you want from this—from me—tonight?"

A pile of rocks tumbled into the base of her throat. "You... You just want me to say it?"

"That would be the purpose of the question. Yes."

"I...I just can't..."

"Take a deep breath. I'm not asking for fancy words. Just tell me the way you did when you explored the D/s dynamic with others."

She nervously licked her lips. "There weren't *others*. There was only one, okay? And he sure as hell didn't ask me questions like that."

Burnett let out a slow breath. "Let me guess," he stated. "The conversation revolved around how *you'd* serve *him*, all the things he'd do to you, and all the pleasure *he'd* get out of it?"

Zoe pressed her hands together between her thighs, sandwiching her phone with them. The sizzle from their kiss had faded from the room, aided by the palpable tension from Shane—no doubt because he discerned how her silence confirmed his accusation.

In return, she couldn't let go of her shock. How had he known? He'd quoted, nearly word for word, what Bryce had said to her on both their disastrous visits to the dungeon outside Henderson. But Bryce hadn't been the only Dom in the place saying things like that. She'd simply been the only sub who didn't seem to get mushy from it.

"He wasn't a bad guy, okay? Just because *I* couldn't get with the program or be turned-on because—"

"Your Dom didn't learn anything about your needs *before*

you two stepped into the dungeon?"

"Look, we dated for a few months first. We got along great. He knew a lot about my needs alrea—" His angry snort not only stopped her but irritated her. "Forget it. I don't want to hash this out with you tonight."

"Believe me, dancer, your asshole ex-Dom isn't what I want to fixate on, either." His grim laugh turned his features into a portrait of dark sensuality, especially as he snaked a hand around the back of her head. "*You're* my priority tonight." His long fingers curled into the roots of her hair, pulling gently, until Zoe sighed in bliss.

"And...and you're my priority too." She only had these few special hours with him. It was what she had to believe. For all she knew, the guy was actually based in Vegas too, but something about him, lingering in his eyes and voice, said his passion was only ever on loan to a woman. There'd be nothing between them after the hours in this room. That meant every moment counted more. Every touch. Every word. Every kiss.

"Good," he murmured, his grip tightening. "God*damn*, you're beautiful."

"You asked what I wanted?" she whispered. "Well, it's this." She reached to press a hand along the breathtaking line of his jaw. "To see more of this desire on your face. To know whatever I'm doing is okay...is good enough to please you. To see how I make you feel and to feel it with—"

She hesitated, suddenly embarrassed—until realizing the tremble she felt through Shane's body was definitely not his way of stifling a chuckle. Instead, as he cradled the other side of her head, he emitted a low, lush, aroused growl. The sound was so sexy, her skin tingled.

"Don't stop there." The veins in his forearms stood out as

he yanked her face higher, pinning her with his heated stare. "Say it, Zoe. The whole nasty, sexy truth of it. You want to feel my cock inside your body, don't you? You want me to fill your beautiful cunt until you scream from being stretched by me... fucked by me?"

"Yes." She quivered. "That's exactly what I want. Your hands all over me. Commanding me. Showing me how to please you..."

She surrendered to breathlessness when the thunder from his throat took on a savage edge. The world narrowed to a pinpoint. Every heartbeat was a struggle. Even that awareness was impossible to grasp as he rammed his mouth to hers again. With her head bent back, she was an open vessel for his lust, accepting every vicious stab of his tongue and drop of his passion. There was no other choice. And she didn't want one.

She cried out in protest as he pulled away. Shane hovered his lips above hers, letting their breaths continue to tangle as he softly ordered, "Get the fucking safe call handled, Zoe. I have plans for you."

"Yes, Sir."

She finished it off with a giggle, mostly out of nerves. The man didn't copy the humor. He turned back toward her while pulling off his jacket, jaw set and brows arched, turning her into a puddle of equal parts fear and arousal. "Patience, girl. You'll be speaking that 'Sir' for me again very soon and sounding just as beautiful doing it. Get the call handled first."

Puddle? She was a whole lake of sensations now. "Yes, S—" While stopping herself in the nick of time, she hit the button showing a picture of Ryder with a dazzling grin on his face and a margarita in his hand.

There was no way her best friend wouldn't answer. Once,

the guy had even picked up on a frantic call from her while having sex. After her sister Ava, he was her lifetime rock for the worst storms. They'd been through calculus, prom, college applications, dorm life, real life, and moving to Vegas, where they'd both nearly starved for two years before Zoe landed her first show gig while Ry was picked up by the city's biggest modeling agency.

Halfway through the third ring, her friend's smartass baritone filled the line. "How's la-la land, hot stuff? Everyone good and passed out now? Have you tucked everyone in and are calling to squee about meeting David Gandy in the hotel bar, who insisted on showing you what *really* rhymes with 'candy'?"

Zoe had no idea how she kept a straight face. "Actually... it's better than that."

There was a rustle on the line. She'd made Ry sit up. "What the... You're serious, aren't you?"

"Yeah. I sorta am."

"Fuck. Me."

"That's *my* line tonight." She tugged her bottom lip with her teeth and bashfully glanced at Shane. "At least I hope. That's why you're getting the honor of the safe call."

"Thank God. Your ticket is *way* overdue for a punch, Zo-Glow."

She couldn't help a soft giggle at his nickname for her since high school. "Thanks for the vote of support."

"So..." Ry extended the word with anticipation. "*Is* it David Gandy?"

She laughed harder. "Better, sweetie. *Much* better."

After Ry confirmed details with her and then expelled a celebratory whoop even Shane could hear, she disconnected the call with a smile.

Her mirth dipped into perplexity all too fast when she looked up—and found a similar smirk on Shane's face.

"What now?" she blurted. "Did I do it wrong?"

He instantly frowned again. "Why do you keep obsessing about 'doing it wrong'?"

She tugged at the edge of a pillow. "You were smirking."

"I was *smiling*."

"Why?"

"Because it's beautiful when *you* smile." The admission caused a chain reaction across his gorgeous features, as if bigger doors of comprehension opened in his mind. "Baby girl, you're breathtaking."

Zoe dropped her head to hide her flush. This was *loco*. So silly. She was a dancer in one of the sexiest shows in Las Vegas. She was used to *a lot* of people ogling her, cheering for her, and desiring her, all while she was dressed in a lot less than a T-shirt and jeans.

But none of those fans, even the ones who came to the show weekly, ever truly knew her. None saw her as this man did, even though he'd only met her an hour and a half earlier. None had ever studied her as Shane did now, or called her *breathtaking* in a way that had nothing to do with what she wore, how perfect her makeup was, or how alluring her dance steps were.

Even standing six feet away, he could awaken her whole body with the knowing caress of his molten gaze and cause her to blink back tears because of the thousand ways she already felt connected to him.

Dios. They hadn't even taken their shoes off.

Had she ever felt this way with Bryce?

Contemplating the answer made her teeth clench. And the backs of her eyes burn.

"Whoa." *Great.* Their chemistry included him noticing every inch of her struggle, despite how she tucked her chin to hide it. He crossed to her again, tugging beneath her chin with a couple of long, beautiful fingers. "You're not supposed to be crying...yet."

She attempted a dismissive laugh. "And you're not supposed to be so..."

"What?"

"Sweet. And sexy. And *still* smiling."

"Oh?" He dipped his head. "Is that so?"

"Doms don't smile."

"Hmm. Is that what it says in the 'Dungeon Rules for Dummies'? Same place you got the notion you're a sucky subbie? Guess I missed that riveting bestseller."

She looked back down and pressed her lips together. If she didn't, a zinger of a retort was certain to fly from them. She wouldn't be able to sift the snark from the words, either—which meant she'd get hammered with his *look* again. And now, any of the methods he'd choose to enforce it...

Ohhh, yes. Best to *callate*—shut her mouth—than lure out too much of the Dom who lurked so near the man's surface. She wasn't stupid. She only had a few hours of Shane's time. A fleeting taste of his passion would have to be enough, so tempting him to share a whole meal wasn't something her senses, perhaps even her soul, could take...

He interrupted her thoughts by nudging her face up even higher. "Where you going, baby girl?"

She blinked slowly. Clearly, his charge referred to emotional, not physical, distance. "N-Nowhere. Don't gawk.

It's the truth. Honestly, I just—"

"Just answer my question, beautiful. It wasn't rhetorical. How big is that mental research paper of yours now?"

Mierda. Connection or not, he wasn't going to make this easy. With the arrogance in his stare and the expectant angles of his brows, impossible only began to describe his persistence.

"Fine," she snapped. "You want to know? I *do* have a list—and contrary to what you may assume, I didn't just pull it out of my ass." She stepped away from his grip. "Were you *not* listening earlier? I'm not some starry-eyed girl who's only read about D/s in romance novels. I had a man in my life who cared enough to try it with me. I failed him." She shook her head, hating the way his eyes tightened and his jaw clenched. "So stop it with your brooding stare and your continuing mission to dissect me, okay? I don't want or need your damn Dommy pity."

His eyes widened. "'Dommy pity?' Is that where you think I'm going?"

"It's laser-etched in your eyes, Burnett. You think I've been misled, maybe even abused. You want to paint yourself as my he-man hero—and you're so cute about it, I wish I could grant you the wish—but the truth is, I'm not a helpless damsel. I have *never* been anybody's victim. That's a fact you need to deal with. *Sir.*"

The word spewed out as accusation instead of respect, a mistake realized much too late. Tension washed over him like storm clouds on a mountain range. No. Not just tension. She'd hurt him. He took this seriously. It was already clear that he took the role of Dominant as an honor to be accountable for, not an excuse for commanding a woman into sexual favors. That alone earned him more awareness, arousal, and respect from her than Bryce ever had.

And echoed one set of words through her mind as his silence stretched on.

Oh, shit.

Her dread grew as he grabbed her shoulders, drew her to her feet, and then slowly pulled her close, reminding her even more of the growing electrical storm between them. When would his thunder break loose? His lightning? Her breath hitched, her senses sizzling with consciousness. Every inch of his body was equally taut, hard, commanding.

"Zoe. Look at me."

His voice, soft as wind but strong as rain, pulled her head up. His golden gaze waited for her, its ferocity barely leashed. *Damn. Damn. Damn.* She was scared. Really scared.

And had never been more aroused in her whole life.

Her whole body confirmed the conflict. Her shoulders burned where he still held her, though now the heat radiated into the tips of her nipples. The center of her belly, awakened from the edict of his huge erection, curled with anticipation. Her thighs clenched against the muscled ropes of his, sending tingles to the tips of her toes.

"I'm sorry," she finally rasped.

He dipped his stare to the lip she nervously bit. "Why?"

She glanced away. Zoe knew he watched every moment of the action, making it more important to get her answer right— including its contrition. "Because...I suppose I'm being a brat."

"Hmmm." He rubbed circles into her shoulders with his thumbs. *Dios*, even that felt good. "That's probably true. Anything else?"

She pushed out a little huff. "Fine. You're probably right about the dungeon research paper."

"Approaching a mini novel?" He kept his baritone low and controlled. And thoroughly captivating.

She indulged another tiny fume. "Yes. Probably."

"And you *like* all the facts you've learned? Is that it?"

His adamancy stunned her into silence. *Vaya.* Burnett actually thought she might answer him *yes*—and hadn't reacted by ordering her to her knees, yanking at her hair, or ripping off her top. Though the options sounded like paradise, what he'd really done was a huger broadside. Knowingly given her a peek at his vulnerability. Wasn't that a big "Dommy Don't" in a lot of books? Yet now, she was even more fascinated with him. She yearned to reach to him, learning the new lines of his face even as she soothed them...

She surrendered to the craving.

Then rejoiced as he did the same.

He was beautiful. She reveled in stroking the fullness of his eyebrows, the strong slope of his nose, the forceful cliffs of his cheeks. As Shane explored her face the same way, she felt a smile bloom. A silent reverie. A perfect proxy for time.

She'd called her best friend with the knowledge she'd be getting naked with this man but couldn't imagine nudity being more magical than this. Or more intimate. He stole her breath with his intense concentration, tracing the little curves at the bottom of her nose and then drawing a finger into the deep indent of her upper lip...even learning how ticklish she was at the base of her ears.

In return, she discovered a lot of new things about him too. Scars. The man was riddled with them. One at the base of his throat. Another hidden just inside his hairline. A few nicks along the left side of his neck. He'd either moonlighted as a stunt man five miles north in Hollywood or had been through a few war zones. While she burned to complete the riddle, she also sensed the answer wasn't as simple as one sentence—even if he were inclined to give it.

She gave herself over to *this* moment instead.

As Shane's fingers learned more of her physically, he opened more of her spirit. Zoe relinquished the energy because *he'd* gifted it to *her* first. The feeling was surreal. She knew Shane still controlled every moment of what happened, guiding every touch and stare they gave each other, yet she'd never felt more important in her entire life.

Was *this* the beginning of what D/s was all about? Was this why so many referred to it as "Power Exchange" and raved about the purity of its connection?

Her soul echoed with the only answer that made sense.

Yes.

Her heart joined the chorus as Shane formed a frame around her face with his hands, tilting her head up for a long, deep kiss.

He took over her senses in a different way than before. The storm still gathered in him, but the front was more potent. He kissed her deeper, not harder. He didn't leave a corner of her mouth unexplored. His mouth widened hers with carnal intent, demanding even more of her submission. He used her tongue as a plaything, sucking it and then giving it back, twirling it in time with the whimpers she emitted, beseeching him to do more.

Yes...more...

She couldn't be blamed for the urgency. Just his kiss revved her blood better than her favorite vibrator, especially during the moments when he backed away, letting her anticipate his next action. Every nerve ending in her body awakened. A thousand drums began tattoos in her sex. Her lungs started rationing her breath to her throat. And she seriously started to hate her clothes.

Shane's face betrayed his concurrence. No more smirks. No more persistent charm. The storm had taken command. His eyes darkened. His jaw clamped. His arms coiled as he plummeted his hands down her back, grabbing her shirt in fistfuls, the movements timed to his rough breaths.

He held back on kissing her again. Instead, he watched her face while sweeping his hands beneath her shirt. His stare heated as he clawed the length of her spine with his fingernails, eliciting a keen deep in her throat.

"Sh-Shane. That feels so— Ahhh!"

She gave up the scream as he dropped his head to scrape her neck with his teeth. Shivers cascaded as he followed the burn with the silken perfection of his tongue. Zoe jammed her hands into his hair, urging him on. The strands were thick and soft and perfect in her grip.

He groaned deep while suckling his way to her ear, shoving back her hair with his nose in order to bite the flesh there with more force. The surge of pain jacked her heartbeat, making her shriek the same second he snapped her bra free.

"Perfect," he praised, his voice husky. "You're so fucking perfect, baby girl."

His adoration made her head spin. Her blood simmer.

Before her world careened.

Everything in the room spun before her eyes as he twirled her around, making her face the bed. He shoved her shirt over her head, letting her bra tumble free after it, and then re-anchored her by yanking her back against him.

Zoe gasped as her nipples responded to the air-conditioning, though she owed just as many shivers to his big, conquering hands, marking every inch of her exposed flesh as his willing territory. His touch was hot and bold, claiming her in giant swaths from the waist up until he scooped his fingers around both her breasts.

Her head fell back against his shoulder. She moaned, once more breathing in the forest musk of his scent as his thumbs rolled against her skin. He tightened those seductive circles, nearing the center of her breasts with each rotation.

"Ohhhh..." *Vaya*, what his touch did to her. How exquisite he made her feel. God had skipped her on the way to endowing Ava with the great boobs in the family. Though Zoe always made the most of hers by working with costume designers on strategic padding, their nude truth was something her lovers tolerated instead of appreciated. But caught beneath Shane's touch, she was a goddess. Adored. Caressed.

"*Ay!*"

And pinched. And tugged. Hard. Then again. She screamed again, bucking against him.

"Sssshhh." The bastard was calm to the point of infuriating. "Breathe for me, Zoe. That'll help you process it better."

"Process *it*?" she flung. "You mean your torture pinchers?"

He sucked at the curve of her ear once more. "It's only my fingers, beautiful. Not even real nipple clamps. Though fuck, these sweet little cherries would look incredible if I did put real ones on you. I'd buy you a pair with dangling sapphires. They'd match that gorgeous fire in your eyes..."

A growl took over his tone as he closed his fingers again. When he started twisting at her nubs as well, rolling and tugging, she squirmed harder.

"*Burnett!*"

"What?" So serene. So maddening. So sexy.

"It hurts, damn it!"

"And you're not handcuffed to anything, beautiful. Step away anytime you like. We haven't even established a safe word, though you can call a red on me anytime you need. Is that what you're doing?"

"No!" She huffed. "I mean...I don't know." *Damn it.* Giving up on anything in her life hadn't been an option since hitting double-digit birthdays. But was it giving up if Shane placed the safe word in her control, gave her the choice to stop everything? Fully acknowledged her power as well as his?

"It's okay not to know." He gave her a break. While twirling her tips with his thumb and forefinger, he grazed his other fingertips along the undersides of her breasts. The new sensations, mixed with the zings left behind from his pinches, were amazing. "Ssshhh. Breathe."

"I... I'm confused." *Understatement of the century.*

"Let me guess. It wasn't like this with the Dom behind Door Number One?"

She closed her eyes. Like that helped against the memories of that first awful night with Bryce. And the second. *And* the third. Her sexy cop boyfriend had transformed into a different person as a Dom, like Walter White donning the damn Heisenberg Hat. He'd always kept his face shrouded in darkness, concealed by the dungeon's deep shadows—though he sure as hell made sure she could see his cock. Right after he strapped her down to a spanking bench by her ankles, knees, elbows, and wrists, he shoved the swollen thing at her lips. *Take the whole thing down your throat, or I'll flog you until you scream. Service me well, you slutty little subbie.*

"*Sí.*" She finally found her way back to the present, forcing a nod for Shane. "But...it's okay. I'm here now."

"Oh, yeah." He rumbled the word through his whole body, along with hers, while suckling her neck. His fingers drifted toward her nipples again. "You really are."

Zoe released a long breath. "And I'll try to stay."

"Mmmm. That's my good girl."

His praise made her tingle. Even so, she charged, "But I can step free any moment I want?"

"Affirmative," Shane murmured. "But dear God, I hope you don't." He tightened his touch, tugging at her sensitive nodes, again twisting harder at the erect points. "Stunning, amazing Zoe...I could look at you all night. Play with these magnificent tits for hours."

"And I..."

"What?"

"I almost want you to." As far as hiding the astonishment in her voice? Forget about it. "But how is that possible? Even though you're hurting me..."

"Only a little."

"Only a *little*?"

He spread warm breath along her neck as he slowly pulled on her taut areolas. "Only because it feels so good to have this effect on you."

"Ahhh." The breathy syllable was all she could manage. *Mierda*, what an "effect" the man had. Every new pinch brought a jump to her pulse and a jolt to the depths of her tender folds. She pulsed for him now. *Ached*. Because of the pain he'd brought her—and the expertise with which he delivered every moment of it.

"You like it, don't you, baby girl?" He rubbed her with the pads of his thumbs again. Growled low as she let out a long moan. "You like the way I touch you. And yes, you like the pain. You like it because every time you take more of either, part of your spirit becomes mine. And you like that too. You long to know how I'm going to return that gift to you, converted into something new by my passion...my power."

His words sounded like they'd been tossed through a filter of shale. Joined with the pressure of his erection against her ass, Zoe was helpless to fight the demolition of his seduction.

"*Vaya*. Yes." She lilted the words with hope. Maybe she really could do this. Perhaps it would all be different this time. Everything *felt* different, thanks to this man who'd seen her soul from the start...who focused on her like it was their last night on earth.

She mewled as he skidded one of his hands down to her hip. Cried out as he used a belt loop on her jeans to pull her tighter against him. His other hand flattened against her throat, locking her head back. He ravaged her neck in another greedy bite. The whole time, his crotch pulsed against her backside. The ordeal had to be hell for him, but the simple knowledge of how she affected him... It was like taking a drink of the world's best sangria. Sweet. Wild. Delicious. Addicting. Her limbs went limp, washed in the potency of it—but she didn't fall fully into the mush puddle. She hadn't paid for that privilege yet. And submissives always had to pay first. In some way.

Shane broke her reverie with a new growl. "You're going somewhere else again, baby girl. Someplace that's not on my approved destinations list."

"I'm sorry. It's...it's so hard to fight it..."

"Then why are you?" He slid his fingers over her eyelids to close them and then spread his fingers across her forehead. "*Don't* fight it, tiny dancer. This is exactly what I want. Your surrender, from *here* first. Breathe. Then yield it to me."

Beneath his touch, her brow furrowed. "But don't you want me to—"

"Let it go." He pressed the pads of his fingers above her eyebrows. "That's all I want from you right now." The strength of his voice helped his effort, ushering pools of honey through her mind and body. "That's it, beautiful. You've already been here, remember? You were ready to give it all, but then everything switched back on. Shut it all down again. I'll light it back up."

"Promise?"

"Oh, baby girl, I certainly do. You'll be amazed at the places we'll go together."

She still struggled to decipher his words, but the man made it damn hard to connect two coherent thoughts together. He didn't ease up on the sensual cavalcade, either. He stroked a hand through her hair and started pulling with commanding tension. His other hand strayed lower, playing in her navel for a moment before continuing lower.

Zoe sighed as he unhitched the button on her jeans. Once more as he lowered the zipper. And as his hand slipped beneath her panties—

"Ohhhhhh!"

His fingers were nirvana.

"Fuck." His growl was a verbal version of his touch, slow and dark and seductive. "You're perfect, Zoe. So fucking perfect."

A shaky sigh stirred the air. She vaguely recognized it as her own. Didn't matter, anyway, not when she needed to focus on the long, warm digits that parted her flesh, waiting for him in engorged readiness. Though Shane didn't say a word, his harsh breaths conveyed his own pleasure, swirling hers higher as he pushed back the hood of her clit.

Don't stop. Oh, please don't stop!

God heard her prayer. He moved a second finger down, gliding it over her most sensitive nerves in a perfect sweep. A mewl tore up her throat. Shane gave her an approving grunt as he continued his exploration, reaching the edge of her most intimate entrance.

"Ohhhhh!"

Zoe's whole body stiffened. Streaks of silver and gold appeared behind her eyes. Who the hell was she kidding? Her whole body was suddenly formed of the lightning. She was electric and alive, brilliant and dazzled.

And terrified.

She pulled in a quivering breath. And never let it out.

"Whoa, baby girl. Ssshhhh. Easy." Shane rolled his hips, forcing her body into the same lazy ocean motion. "Let it out. Let it go. Trust me, Zoe. We'll get there, I promise."

"Sooner than later," she gasped back, "if you keep all of this up."

"I'm keeping *a lot* of things up, baby girl."

"No shit."

She wasn't sure how he'd react to that. She was guilty as hell when it came to deliberately goading the man tonight, but her new confession was simply the truth. Thank God he discerned that, proving it by turning her around again. At once, he brought her body flush with his and slammed his mouth back down to hers.

Before their lips touched, Zoe caught a glimpse of his face. The glory of him flipped her heart all over again. The passion on his stunning features was defined by the gold hues of the hotel's floodlights, sifting in through the curtains. Her imagination instantly re-outfitted him from the business attire into a gladiator's galerus.

It was her last cognizant thought for a while.

Forget nirvana. The man took her straight to heaven, though she was certain she blushed to her toes as he forced her jeans and panties down her legs. He simply hoisted her a few inches off her feet in order to kick off her boots himself. Her jeans followed within seconds, leaving her completely naked before him. Thank God for her Spanish and Greek heritage. Olive tints were awesome for hiding the pink of uncertainty.

After he set her back down, Shane relocked his stare with hers. The light from outside hit his irises directly now, turning the caramel silk into an amber glow. With his chest pumping on hard breaths, he pressed her hands to the buttons on his shirt, silently ordering her to set them free.

Inch by tantalizing inch, she released the fabric, exposing the naked breadth of his torso. "*Dios mio,*" she whispered.

"What?"

"Maybe you *are* an alien."

"*What?*"

She shoved the shirt farther back and then all the way off his torso. His pecs were like plates of steel, his abs ridges of defined perfection. A tattoo of swirling smoke covered his left shoulder and bicep, with a bold capital *I* wrapped in the middle. "You. You're..." She bit her lip. "I'm a dancer. I've been around some beautiful men in my life. But this..." She stepped back, letting him laugh at her quivering cry. "You're otherworldly." The itch from the back of her mind pushed forward again, begging to be let out. "Either that or you secretly moonlight as a model."

"Do I look like I model?" His gaze narrowed. "Answer that very carefully."

She laughed. He didn't. "Fine. You're leaving me only one other option for a conclusion."

"I'm afraid to ask."

"Conditioning this excellent usually comes courtesy of the United States military, Mr. Burnett. Or is it Sergeant? Or Captain?"

She almost held her breath waiting for his answer. If he confirmed her contention, what would she do? She'd declared a freeze-out on military men once, not a surprise to anyone considering the ordeals her sister had endured by falling for a string of jerks in uniform. That was before Ava found herself a soldier who obliterated those stains and then put a giant ring on it for good measure. After witnessing Ava's happiness with Sergeant Ethan Archer, Zoe had reconsidered her stance, even giving it another go with Bryce. He'd been a proud member of the Las Vegas PD for a year at that point, seeming like he'd gained enough distance from his US Marines days to accept a few imperfections in people—perhaps even his girlfriend.

Right.

She'd been too scared to research the point beyond that whole disaster, opting to keep her remaining D/s fantasies intact—until tonight, when Shane Burnett had stepped out of her dreams and into that airport bar. Now here she was, naked in his arms, perhaps more than physically—and the man's features were an agonizing zero for clarification.

He gave her more of the mystery when grabbing her wrists and redirected her hands over the muscles she'd just been craving. Zoe moaned as he guided her fingers up his taut stomach, over his massive chest, and then atop the shoulders that bunched, beneath her exploring fingers. Encouraged by his aroused hiss, Zoe let her lips follow along the same path.

"Zoe. Sweet baby girl. *Yessss.*"

Perhaps it was good she had no brain left. If she had, the thing would've been blown apart by everything about this experience. He actually let her touch him. And dear God, how he caressed her in return. Connected with her. Called her sweet and beautiful and told her about all the ways she pleased him—yet through it all, never let her forget exactly who called the shots between them tonight.

Him. Only him.

And she didn't want it any other way.

The confession pealed joy through her heart as Shane pulled her off her feet again. This time, he used the motion to lower her to the bed, following her to the mattress. Once more, she wondered if she was living out a movie script, including the most devastating leading man she could ever ask for. Everything was included except the sultry R&B soundtrack.

"Still convinced I'm secretly a little green man from a planet made of cheese?" he finally whispered.

She ran a hand up his muscled neck. "Like you've been labeled 'little' a day in your life."

She expected him to chuckle. Instead, a frown formed across his face. "That'd be a negative," he muttered. *Aha.* More military talk. The words practically beckoned her to call him out again. Burnett wasn't stupid; he knew it, too—but as she pulled in breath for the words, he sucked them from her with another hard kiss.

Dios, this man and his kisses.

He didn't even give her time to regroup. Thunder gathered in his chest, rougher than before, as he pressed his forehead to hers. At the same time, he positioned his knees inside hers and shoved them wide. With a harsh grunt, he swept her arms over her head, capturing both her wrists beneath one of his.

Zoe writhed, whimpered, and shivered. Maybe he'd truly thrown her into a rocket and taken her to another planet. Everything was so surreal. His hands were now forged in iron. His stare was hammered copper. Even the abrasion of his wool pants inside her thighs was a visceral reminder of the delicious contrasts between them. Steel against soft. Command met with compliance. A Dominant preparing to take his submissive.

Yes. Oh, yes.

She didn't realize the word had tumbled out aloud until Shane brushed his lips to her ear and growled, "Like this, do you?" A deeper sound rolled out of him as she managed a jerky nod. "Me too, baby girl. Restraining you like this. Feeling you move under me, knowing I'm going to be inside you soon. Knowing how I'll fuck you until ordering you to come for me..."

"Ohhhh. *Sí. Asi me gusta. Por favor...cojamos.*"

"Soon, baby girl. But that doesn't mean you have to stop begging." He swept his mouth back up, taking passionate nips at the corners of her lips. "Damn. The things you say, Zoe. The way you say them... They make me so goddamn hard."

She lifted a little smile in answer. "And the things you do... they make me..."

"It's okay." It was a demand more than assurance. "Tell me. Don't leave a fucking thing out."

"They make me wet." She blurted it before losing the nerve. "And...hot. Everything tingles. Even my nipples. *Especially* my nipples. Burnett—"

She barely pushed out the name before he tore it from her lips with a hot, hungry assault. When he finally dragged away, he growled, "Call me Sir now. I need to hear it wrapped in your lust."

She nodded. "Y-Yes, Sir." But as soon as the words spilled out, so did heavy tears. She blinked and thrashed her head to the side, bracing for Shane's blowback on her emotion. When men saw tears, it was like having acid spilled on their balls. Maybe she could hide them by keeping her face in the shadows...

He didn't issue a sound.

Instead, he pressed lower—and began wicking the tears off her cheeks with his lips. Sheer shock pulled her face back around. His action was by no means tender, but it wasn't angry, either. He was passionate, even hungry. Feasting on her tears. Treasuring them.

That was it. He didn't just amaze her anymore. He knocked every shred of logic from her brain. Tumbled the apple cart of her composure. Wading through the applesauce aftermath, she cried harder.

"Yes." His exhortation, rough but fervent, stopped the air in her lungs. "Fuck yes, tiny dancer. Don't stop giving it to me."

She couldn't fight him if she tried. And *Dios*, how she was tempted to try. She was bared to him in so many ways now. She was a blubbering mess, half her makeup likely gone, yet Shane kept drenching her in his smile, his burnished beauty growing with every minute. His gaze turned molten as he rained more kisses over her face. His lips glistened from the bath of her tears. His jaw, already hardened by the room's shadows, intensified another degree as he reared back, released her, and withdrew a condom from his wallet.

"Keep your hands there," he instructed quietly, tossing his pants and the wallet toward the couch. "You're so fucking mesmerizing like this. Keep your hands tangled in your hair like that. And your nipples jutted up. Incredible. You humble me, baby girl. Offering yourself like this... Fuck...what a gift."

The sting of her tears worsened. It was too much to handle. He was too damn beautiful. Too many of her fantasies were coming true at once. It was a situation set up for failure, probably hers. She needed to safe word out and make him leave before she messed up and turned this into another grueling memory.

She gained new courage by beholding the heat on Shane's face. And the harsh breaths lifting his chest. And the arousal parting his lips as he set aside the condom in order to free his belt—and then his fly.

"*Mierda.*" Astonishment drenched her voice. "Sh-Shane. *Sir...*"

"It's your fault," he muttered. "I was dust from the second you walked up in the bar."

"There's nothing dusty about that."

She nodded at his erection. Correction—at the most magnificent cock she'd seen in her life. Even the marble statues at Caesar's Palace couldn't compare to the huge, hard length rising from the patch of auburn curls between his thighs, with its flawless crown gleaming at the top. Even the slit in that dark red bulb seemed carved by the angels to perfection.

Dios. Had she really almost safe worded on him—and missed this? How had her pre-estimation of him been so wrong? She'd been a dance lead for over a year now. Sizing up men, as well as costume parts to service every inch of their boy parts, was a job requirement. She hadn't been wrong about those guesses in a very long time. This was a lesson learned in an interesting way. Presumptions could turn into shocking ass biters.

She tore her sights from Shane's crotch to his face. Surely she wasn't the first woman who'd dropped her jaw on his toes in reaction to his "gifts," but nothing close to a gloat defined his features. His lips remained tight. His stare was taut. Every chiseled line of his face conveyed nothing but raw desire, open lust.

Stomach, meet heart.

"Do you get it now?" He closed a fist around his shaft. "Do you understand what you've been doing to me since the second I laid eyes on you?"

A gulp pounded down her throat as he kept caressing his broad length. She longed to raise her arms and touch him too, but her desire to honor his wishes was more important. He enjoyed watching her like this, physically proving her surrender to him—in so many ways, a bondage that meant more than the real thing. And in this position, she was forced to open herself to him more...to show her need thoroughly through her gaze.

"No different than what you've done to me, Sir."

He prowled back over her body with the stealth of a mountain lion, and sank his mouth onto hers with thrusts of growing need. He finally positioned himself on one elbow so he could keep his face level with hers as he ripped open the condom and rolled it over his stunning length.

Longing curled in her core, escalating into a moan up her throat. The sound detonated again when Shane recentered himself, elbows planted on either side of her head. He locked his hands atop her wrists and slid his erection between her labia...spurring her whole body to tremble.

"Ahhhh." Her head fell back into the pillow with the groan.

Shane answered with a low snarl, finishing it with an extra

savage note. "Very nice, but not enough, baby girl." He nipped her chin. "I need more. You're going to give it to me, and you're going to do it now."

A merciless mix of expectation and anxiety made her whole body clench. What did "more" mean? They weren't on a leather-padded bed in the middle of a BDSM dungeon with a hundred rig points. On the other hand, he'd shown her the pointlessness of all that simply with the force of his fingers on her breasts. Was she willing to trust that more from him would be an experience just as surprising...?

She answered that by swallowing deeply and then summoning two words to her lips.

"Yes, Sir."

His snarl turned sensual. He softly kissed her on the mouth. "Good girl."

She gave him a tentative smile. "I want to please you."

He scrutinized her for a long moment. "And that scares you."

"A little. Yes."

"I know. And it's okay." His gaze roamed over her face with heavy-hooded heat. "That's why you're still going to talk to me."

She didn't hide her surprise. "You...want me to..."

"Yes." He kissed her fast but went on. "You want to please me? Then words are what I want. Talk to me in that incredible voice of yours, Zoe." He stroked the tips of his fingers from her palms to her wrists. "Tell me what you want. You know where I stand already."

"And you don't think I stand in the exact same—" She dropped into silence from the power of his sudden glower. Then gasped from the new press of his cock through her folds.

By every saint in heaven, that felt so good. "*Dios.*"

"Mmmmm. I like that look on your face, baby girl."

"I like what you're doing to put it there, Sir."

"Good." He trailed his mouth from one side of her face to the other. "Very good. Now tell me more."

His voice dropped into a warmer register, melting all over her senses, tantalizing every inch of her pussy. "I...I like the feeling of your body against mine," she murmured.

"Yeah," he encouraged. "Very good. More. Naughtier. Dirtier." He rocked their bodies together, his shoulders captivating as they strained, his thighs massaging the insides of hers. "What part of my body?"

"Your...ummm..." What was wrong with her? She was used to slinging biological terms all the time during rehearsals. It was nothing to ask for certain things to be thrust or grabbed or lunged. This sudden embarrassment was baffling. And she could get over it. The man's own words helped her. *This is exactly what I want...your surrender. Let it go.* "Your cock...Sir."

"Yesssss. And where do you want it?"

Her eyes slid shut as his growl made everything throb. Her nipples, her pussy, even the roots of her hair awakened for him. He was a new definition of commanding. Her huge, hard, dominant dream.

"Inside me." She was a little surprised at the gasp in her voice. "Please. Inside my pussy."

"Good. *Good.* Doing what, baby girl?"

"Fucking me." Her mental tethers fell away, useless against the heat of his desire, intensified as he slid his cock along her folds, moistening himself with the cream her body gave. "Fucking me hard and deep."

He pulled away a little, making Zoe cry in protest until she realized his purpose, to position his broad head at the entrance of her deepest core. He didn't stop there. Her walls convulsed as he tested them, inching in a little. Then a little more.

"Your body's pleading for me, baby." His whole frame vibrated as he forced his entry to a halt. "But I need to hear it from your mouth too." He pushed the hair from her forehead. "Beg me for it, Zoe."

"Yes." The acquiescence burst out eagerly now. "*Dios*, yes, Sir. Please. *Please*. I need this."

"Tell me you're sure. I'm not a small man. I'm going to stretch you."

She twisted her wrists beneath his grip. Her blood was on fire. Her core strained and tightened, forcing her to lift her hips. "I'm sure. I'm sure."

"Again." He pressed his lips into her hairline. "Say it again, damn it. I want you to be sure. I'm going to fuck you hard, Zoe— and I'm not going to be gentle about it."

"Do it." The words were pleading rasps. *Dios,* she needed him. His smoldering, sinful smell. His looming, hard weight. His cock, swollen and magnificent, promising to fill her body in ways she'd never imagined. "Fill me, Shane. Fuck me. Take me. Dominate me. Please!"

CHAPTER FIVE

Damn.

Damn.

Damn.

How the hell had he ever thought this woman would be a fun and forgettable fling?

Stupid question. Nonexistent answer.

He didn't just want her. He craved her. And accepted, with grim resignation, that this might be the only time he'd have her. Even if he wasn't eyeballs-deep in this dangerous ruse with Stock, what he'd ask of her was too much. He was already living on borrowed time, considering all the occasions he'd been dropped into parts of the Middle East that people didn't want to know about.

No. That moroseness didn't belong here, in the rare gift of this night and the tight heaven of this woman's body. But his desire for her extended beyond that. Zoe was so unbridled in her passion, so eager with her kisses, so open about her insecurities and what she perceived as her "failures"...and then so willing to let him help set her straight about how wrong she was.

It was official. She was his submissive dream come true. He had the hard-on, more raging than any he'd had in a while, to confirm it. God help the woman.

"Spread wider for me, baby."

Her eyes reopened, likely drawn by the lusty tension

in his voice. Sure enough, as their eyes met, he watched fear tighten her features. She attempted a ready smile, which only drove in another knife of compunction. She was being so brave, refusing to safeword no matter how much his cock strained her tender tissues. At the same time, she drove him insane in all the most awesome ways. Damn, she was tight...and, despite her strain, getting wetter by the minute. Thank fuck for basic human physiology.

But all the lubricant in the world wasn't going to make some aspects of this any easier. He was big. She was small. Period.

Shit.

As a precaution, he wound his hands tighter around her wrists. She noticed, of course. "Shane?" Her query was sweet and tentative and sexy as fuck. "Is everything okay?"

Guilt pushed the repeat key whether he welcomed the shit or not. *Is everything okay? Yeah, just fine and dandy—except for the fact that our minds mesh but our bodies may not.* Didn't mean his dancer wouldn't get satisfaction; he'd just pleasure her in different ways—right before his ice-cold shower.

"Listen to me." He lined his stare up with hers again. The shadows of the room turned her eyes into gold-kissed midnight. "Red still means stop, Zoe. Got it?"

"I don't want you to stop."

"You may take that back in another minute."

"I don't. Want you. To stop."

Hell. She flashed what had to be her sexiest glare of the night, eyes flashing and teeth bared. *Little wildcat.* He rolled his hips, letting her feel the new blood surging there. Zoe hissed and arched her back, pointing her breasts straight up at him. Her nipples were waiting, practically taunting him. He pounced, biting into one and then the other. She let out two high keens, though he chopped the second cry short with a new mash of his lips atop hers.

In the midst of filling her mouth with his tongue, he took over her pussy with his cock.

She screamed into his mouth. Jerked her body against his. And seated his dick deeper inside her.

He'd never felt anything more perfect.

"Shane." She gave it in a wobbly whimper. Twisted her wrists inside his hold.

"It's okay," he murmured. "We're there, tiny dancer. We're there, okay?"

"It...it hurts."

"I know. But in a sec—"

"It's amazing."

He stopped. Just for a moment. Then blinked in bafflement. Hell, he was even indignant for a moment, thinking she might be dangling a kinky lie just to please him, but the glow on her face was real. So were her erect nipples...and the tension of her legs around his thighs, urging him to move again.

And the dreamy wonder in her voice as he renewed his deep thrusts. "I...had no idea."

"About what?"

"That it could feel like this." She sighed as he pushed in harder, driving her body into the mattress. "That it could be this good."

Shay groaned. Good? This was so far above the stratosphere from good, it was outer space. He didn't know if he'd ever felt anything so perfect. So tight. So right. "No arguments from here, baby girl."

"I can feel you...everywhere."

"If it's too much...too painful..."

"It's okay. I've been a dancer since I was eight. Pain and I have an interesting agreement. It's good to me if I let it be boss for a while."

"Hallelujah."

She started to giggle again, but he fucked the sound into a high scream. Shay groaned in return, savoring the feel of her silken sheath around his throbbing shaft. She trembled, arched her neck, and groaned, wordless entreaties for more. As he pumped with more force, conflict assaulted. Ruefulness that he'd possibly found the most perfect submissive in the world for him and only had her for one night. Relief for the exact same reason. If he had any more time with Zoe Chestain than these rare hours, he'd be a man in big trouble.

"Harder, Shane. Deeper. Please!"

Big trouble.

He pressed his forehead to hers. Reveled in the slick tango of their sweat as he drove farther in. Zoe moaned and gasped, her hands curling into fists, her toes pressing at his ass. She panted faster with every lunge, her nipples poking his chest, her pussy quivering against his abdomen.

"Not yet." Shay commanded it, slowing his pace in emphasis. "*Not yet*, baby girl."

She shot up a wild glare. "Are you kidding? Shane—"

"*Sir*."

"Sir...damn it...I... It's so good. I can't just—"

"You can." He captured her lips in a salty kiss. "And you will."

"But—"

"You're a submissive, Zoe, despite how some assmunch of a Dom tried to convince you otherwise." He leaned to show her the conviction in his gaze. "And you're going to prove it to both of us now. You're not only going to hold back your orgasm for me, but you're going to earn it by pleading for it."

She glowered again. "Yes, Sir."

He pinched both her breasts. "You're cute when you're pissed."

For a second, she only gave an aching moan. Could've had something to do with how he rolled into her, doubling the friction to her pussy. "And you're maddening when you're cocky."

"And I like it when you say *cock*. But it'd sound a lot better in the phrase, 'Please, Sir, make me come with your cock.'"

He punctuated with a hard thrust, conveying the tone was a gibe but the intent wasn't. As he'd hoped, Zoe's eyes rolled back in her head.

"Ohhhh. Sir...please make me come with your cock."

"Perfect. You're so fucking perfect, Zoe."

The moisture of her new tears didn't come as a surprise. He hadn't issued the words as empty praise and knew she wouldn't take them as such. *Shit*. If he ever got his hands on the dickhead poser who'd messed up her mind like this, made her feel so far from the stunning submissive she was...

"Thank you, Sir," came her sweet whisper. "Will you give me more? Please? Until my pussy comes around your cock and makes you explode with me?"

"Damn." He'd sure as hell cut the butterfly from her chrysalis, hadn't he? The naughty benefits were wonderful to reap. "That would be a gigantic affirmative, baby girl."

He committed to the promise by releasing her wrists and sliding his hands to her ass cheeks. With his fingers splayed across her flesh, he ground her pussy harder on his cock, setting up a hard, primal rhythm for the demand of his body on hers.

"*Vaya,*" Zoe cried. "*Sí. Ayyy. Mas adentro. Mas duro. Cojame, señor. Cojame.*"

Shay groaned. Here was another reason their passion was best confined to one night. Any more sessions full of that wicked Spanish sex talk and he'd be a deer in the headlights for this woman. He let the gorgeous filth of her words shoot up his cock and flare into his head, now buried so deep in the velvet of her womb.

"Again," he ordered, working his fingers into the crevice of her ass, working her deeper onto his shaft. "Beg me again with that perfect mouth of yours, Zoe. Fill my cock with your dirty, beautiful words."

"Yes, Sir," she rasped. "Ohhhh, yes, Sir. Take me hard. Fill me deep. Fuck me until you let me—"

"Come." Any consideration of drawing this into a hedonistic fantasy were decimated by her untamed submission. Now, he only wanted to grant her every drop of pleasure her wet, tight little body begged him for. He couldn't bear to make her pussy wait any longer. "Come for me, Zoe. Come around me. *Now!*"

Her body quivered and convulsed. Her head sank against the pillows. Her scream consumed the air.

Her orgasm squeezed every inch of his cock. Flash-bombed his self-control into nonexistence.

He detonated too.

And for the first time in his life, finally understood why some poets compared climaxing to death.

Having faced the possibility of his own check-in to hell on several occasions, he'd always tossed off those writers as French fried dumb shits. Those asshats had never been in the middle of a gun battle against jihadist maniacs, with smoke thick as London fog and brass raining the air. No way in hell could death and sex have a damn thing to do with each other.

Until now.

The universe narrowed. His vision was a pinpoint of white heat and sheer ecstasy, tunneling his mind yet blasting his senses. With logic and spirit fused, he floated through one moment and then slammed to earth in the next, aware of every breath that flowed through his lungs, every beat that hammered his heart.

Yeah. He was dying. In all the best, French fried ways possible.

The most incredible part? He wasn't doing it alone.

Zoe. The muscled sculpture of her body. The olive silk of her skin. The soul-snatching beauty of her sighs as tremor after tremor coursed through her, massaging every drop of his climax out of his cock and into her welcoming heat. For one second, he even imagined that the latex barrier between their bodies had dissolved and they were skin-to-skin, connected even more deeply.

Slowly, she slid her legs from his hips. Even more slowly, Shay withdrew his hands from her ass. As she sank back into the sheets, he straightened in order to stay inside her for at least another minute.

One minute more. Please.

Fate actually listened this time. Sort of. While he was given the respite, it didn't relieve the wordless weight from the air between them. He watched Zoe swallow and then close her eyes before dipping his lips to the hollow at the base of her throat. He moved up a hand to continue a soft trail between her breasts, kissing her there too.

Her heart thudded loud enough for him to hear. A solemn knell...without poetry this time.

He pressed his face into the creamy valley of her skin, soaking in the seconds they had before the energy of their explosion faded. Zoe sifted her fingers through his hair, the movements conveying her own awareness that the shadows were soon to come. Wasn't that the fucking rub? They'd likely ignited a radius of five miles with the intensity of what they'd just shared, which made these minutes feel like a trip to the caves of Afghanistan.

Wait. He'd been to those caverns. This was worse.

"Stay here." Even the ten seconds he took to rise and toss the condom were agony, though they imparted an opportunity to dash to the bathroom, dampen a washcloth, and bring it back with him. Zoe sighed as he gently toweled off the front of her body. Before long, he wordlessly directed her to turn over. He couldn't let the opportunity pass to once more appreciate the masterpiece that was her ass.

"Mmmmm." She wiggled the two sweet globes as he stroked the cloth over them. "That feels really good...Sir."

He smiled and smacked her lightly. "Method to my madness. I didn't get a chance to properly appreciate *this* side. Though if you keep up that teasing, I'll do more than appreciate."

"Promise?"

He battled not to take her up on the offer. Fuck, it would be nice to see how the impact of his palm affected her glorious backside. But he let the silence stretch once more, still steadily stroking her. After a few minutes, he set the cloth aside but continued the strokes. During the downward sweeps, he glided his knuckles along her skin. On the upward, he used the tips of his fingers.

"So tell me about the asshat," he finally said.

Her shoulders tightened. He expected the reaction but didn't let up his touch.

"Which one?"

She giggled. Shay didn't.

"You're a smart woman. Why don't you answer that one?" For good measure, he infused it with a growl of command. Didn't do a shred of good. Though Zoe raised her gaze to meet his, she had guardrails up on her eyes. High ones.

"Isn't this the time when you ask me what there is to do in Vegas besides gambling and shows? Then I ask if you're in LA for business a lot and where you originally come from." When he didn't respond, she fumbled on. "Then we talk about the holidays, and I get to tell you how great my tamales are, and—"

"What was his name?"

She snorted. He tried not to let on how much it enchanted him. They didn't have time for enchantment. Or small talk. He craved to get deeper inside her—delving into her spirit this time. And perhaps help to heal it just a little more.

You know, no matter what, it'll still be a task half-finished, right? Her issues on this shit have long roots, man—far beyond what a single fuckwit did to her.

Halfway was better than *no* way. Maybe he'd at least give her some food for thought, a direction to go after this that included some good, solid sense for the next time she ran into a wannabe Dom. He owed her that much.

No. It was about more than that. So much more.

It was about giving her what she needed.

Her submissiveness... He'd never experienced anything like it. He felt like he'd stumbled onto a rare flower in the middle of the jungle, ready to burst open for some lucky man. Instead, she'd damn near been yanked out like a weed. It was time for her to see the sun. To grow again.

"You really don't want to know about my tamales?"

He stretched out beside her, propping his head on his hand. "Unless 'tamale' is the clown Dom's name, then no."

She sighed. In her eyes, he watched her inner debate. The woman was really something, actually considering whether to give him some more sarcastic lip. Shay made sure she watched as he propelled a stare down at her ass. *Go ahead. Give me a reason to spank it, baby girl.*

He admitted a slight twinge of dismay when she huffed in surrender.

"Bryce." She rolled to mirror his position. "His name is Bryce. Happy now?"

His chest tightened. "Is? Or *was*?"

Her lips curled in a knowing female grin. He didn't relent his glower. Fine. He was jealous. A little. At least for another hour, he was well within his rights, anyway. The nation's toughest judge would agree, considering all the places he'd been inside her body—and the rare piece of himself that had been peeled back in return.

"He's not dead," she countered, "if that's what you mean. At least I don't think so."

He scowled deeper. "And that means...what?"

"He's a cop. Well, *was* one. I guess he still is. I haven't heard otherwise. We haven't talked in a while."

"Good."

Her eyes flared. Shay stared back, still unapologetic. She dipped her head and sidled a little closer, likely guided by pure instinct, a kittenish bid to regain his approval. Though she'd never lost it, the action moved him. He had a feeling she didn't get to play kitten very often.

He tunneled a hand into her hair, tugged her face up, and kissed her soundly. Warmth suffused her features—and all of his senses. "So tell me more about Clown Dom Bryce."

She tossed a quick but disparaging glare. "We met after a show one night. There was a big convention in town, and the hotel requested police support to make sure all the dancers had protection getting to our cars."

"And he was your dashing escort."

"Something like that." She pulled a strand of hair from in front of her eyes. "We dated casually at first, and the sex was that way too, but open-mindedness is practically a prerequisite for a Vegas cop...so I had some wine one night and got up the nerve to tell him about my kinkier needs. I confessed that I'd always had some interest in power exchange, and he jumped on board pretty fast."

"No shit," Shay drawled.

She hitched a little shrug. "It was the beginning of the end, as they say."

"Sure," he murmured. "As they say."

She narrowed her eyes again. "*Now* what are you thinking?"

He narrowed his back. "How do you know I'm 'thinking' anything?"

"Seriously?" It was a good thing her little eye rolls were so cute. That, combined with the snarky tone, would earn most subbies in his presence a good swat or two. "Because you hide your thoughts so damn well, is that it?"

Shay gazed intently at her. Actually, that usually *was* it. He wasn't called "Ironman" just because he was hung well, ran like a rocket, and was able to hump it out of hot zones with a couple of injured guys on his shoulders. The name stemmed from his ability to hide the effort beneath it all. He was the guy with the steel poker face.

At least until he'd met her.

Whose uncanny insight into him was rivaled only by his brother's.

Which terrified him worse than a hill full of hostiles with loaded RPGs.

Time to steer this conversation in the right fucking direction.

"I was thinking that most people don't just decide they're kinky one day, even to please a boyfriend." He ran his hand up her back, beneath her hair, to embrace her nape. "You've known about your tastes for a while, haven't you?"

The sarcasm dissolved from her smile. It left behind a softness so captivating, he forgot to blink. "My mom died when I was eleven. Needless to say, life sucked for a while— but in those first few years, I learned I was pretty good at taking care of my dad and sister. I enjoyed it too. When the teenage hormones flooded, I transferred that pleasure into my dating life. It started out with stuff like baking cookies for my boyfriends, helping them with homework, giving them back rubs." A subtle blush flowed over her cheeks. "Once I had my first steady guy, when we were juniors in high school, I'm afraid the libido took over."

Shay drifted his hand to her cheek. "I'm sure he was grateful."

She giggled. "There certainly were no complaints—until the night of our senior prom."

"What happened then?"

She sneaked her bottom lip beneath her teeth. "It was a special night. I told him I wanted to celebrate by giving myself to him in a new way."

He couldn't help smirking. "Let me guess. Ropes or cuffs?"

"Both."

A laugh tumbled out. "That's my girl."

Nix the laugh. Cue the internal barrage of what-the-hell. *That's my girl?*

Had his sanity left his body with the load of that orgasm? Maybe it had, judging by the way those words flowed out like he was simply asking about her tamale recipe.

He coughed in an attempt to make recovery easier for them both. Fat fucking chance. "So I take it the prom night plans didn't go well?"

She winced. "None of my attempts at kink really have."

"Including your time with Bryce," he supplied.

Zoe twisted, gazing at the ceiling while her body still faced him. The position didn't look very comfortable but was sexy as hell, so he zipped it. "It wasn't like we didn't try. We *definitely* tried." She grimaced and then shrugged again. "Perhaps it was the blind leading the blind."

"You think?" Shay snorted.

She batted his shoulder. "Things went from comfortable to weird in a few weeks, so we decided to break up." She'd left her hand where it was and now used a finger to trace a line from his shoulder to his pec. Her finger followed the scar he'd gotten from falling on a couple of swords, damn near literally, during a night mission in Paktika. Had to love those insurgents and their creativity with the booby traps.

"How'd you get this nasty thing?" she murmured.

"How'd you get so good at changing the subject?" He lifted

her finger and nibbled the end. "You and Bryce?" he prompted. "Broken up?"

"We separated for about three months." Her gaze took on a resigned sadness. "I basically gave up on the kink dream at that point. Figured my independent streak was embedded too deep and I'd never get the hang of it, even in Las Vegas."

"You want me to call major bullshit on you now or later for that?"

Her exotic mouth lifted at the corners. "Maybe you should just spank me."

"Maybe you should quit while you're ahead on that." *Because if you don't, I'm going to make sure you* hobble *out of here tomorrow, girl.* "So, three months?" he forced himself to echo. "The two of you reunited after that?" After she nodded, he asked, "Why?"

"The blame for that rests thoroughly on my little sister's shoulders."

He scowled. "You dissin' on your baby sib?"

She clubbed her forehead with the back of her hand. "Oh, no. Are you one of *those*?"

"We're cute, aren't we?" he countered. "And so misunderstood."

The three words were possibly the truest thing he'd ever spoken. Even if there'd been a free chance to contact Tait in the last six months, his older brother would've refused the call. Like the rest of the world, Tait was convinced Shay had gone rogue on his duty and his team, turning to "the good life" as one of Cameron Stock's hired guns. Last he heard, Tait had even requested transfer to JSOC's new group of boy-toys based out of Hawaii, the Special Hostilities Readiness Command, aka the "Sharks." The acronym wasn't the only perfect fit for the nickname. Every man on the team was selected for their tenacious dedication to missions. One of the top targets on their list? Stock's ass, of course.

What the SHRCs didn't know was that thanks to him, the CIA and FBI knew exactly where Stock's slime tracks were. But the spooks' secrecy was because of him too. If word got out that Shane Burnett was actually Shay Bommer, the intel would eventually make its way around to Cameron. Shay's eye sockets would get an instant renovation—with bullet lead.

"While I was figuring out how to solve the issue of the kink itch, my sister got officially engaged to her Dom." She waved a dismissive hand in the air. "He'd proposed already, but when the rock came a few months later and they were official—that was when she told me he was her Dom too." Her stare, still directed at the ceiling, tightened a little more. "Seeing Ava that happy... It gave me hope."

"So you called Bryce again." His tone was tight. It was difficult to watch her relive a hope that had clearly not been satisfied.

"Fine," she confirmed, picking at the pillow's edge, "I called Bryce again."

He resettled his head, confirming his deeper focus to her. "And?"

His chest clenched when new tears sprouted in her eyes. "You know how disaster stories are sometimes bloodier the second time around?"

Before he could stop it, the pain beneath his ribs was intensified by a sharp breath. Shay hitched up onto an elbow, barely refraining from shaking her shoulder with his free hand. "What happened? Did the bastard physically hurt you?"

He wouldn't be romping in Stock's circles forever. Once

he found Mom and rescued her, he'd practically be in Vegas anyhow. How many Bryces could there be in the city's police department—especially ones who could, with a little digging, be traced to dalliances in the lifestyle there?

"No," Zoe spurted. Her answer came almost too fast for Shay's liking, but he detected nervousness more than deceit in her voice. "Perhaps that was the problem," she added, looking down.

"Huh?" Shay retorted.

"Let's just say...I wasn't his flavor of naughty."

"Still in the dark here." He wasn't lying. The woman's willingness to please a Dom was clear as the gorgeous nose on her face. How could she not be a man's most favorite flavor of *anything*?

"I was a little more vocal about things when we went back to the dungeon," she explained. "Listening to Ava talk about what she has with her Sir... It made me bold about asking for what I wanted."

"Which is...?" He sensed he could prewrite her answer already but still wanted to hear it. There were few things more exhilarating than watching a submissive start to articulate her hopes, fantasies, deepest desires. And with *this* submissive, he wouldn't forget the magic for a very long time. Perhaps not ever.

"The connection," she supplied, the ends of her lips turning up. "The *exchange* part of it, you know?"

"Yeah." He rendered his reply with soft understanding. "I do."

"I want that tangle of souls. That awareness of every breath my Dom makes...and knowing he's aware of all mine." She shook her head. "That sounds so stupid."

"The fuck it does," Shay snapped.

"Really?" When her inky lashes turned up and revealed the hope in her eyes, his chest didn't hurt anymore. For a long moment, he wasn't sure he felt anything anymore. His attention narrowed to nothing but her breaths.

"Yeah," Shay murmured. "Really." All too fast, ire bashed at his senses again. "I'm going to regret asking this, but what *is* his favorite 'naughty flavor'?"

She exhaled hard. "Not exactly sure, but it's definitely someone who has a better knowledge of blowjob techniques than me, as well as a deeper working knowledge of using the F-word in colorful sentences."

Shay released a disgusted hiss through his teeth. Her talents in the verbal turn-on department had been exceptional in *his* book, but that wasn't the issue here. Bryce's asshat-in-Dom's-clothing act was. "So he played the *flog her then fuck her* card," he muttered. "Should I even ask if he bothered with aftercare?"

He almost regretted the outburst. Zoe squirmed a little before murmuring, "He took me out afterward. It wasn't bad. We snuggled a little before the game started."

"The *game*?"

"Yeah. The Angels were playing the Yankees, and Trout was on a hot streak that week. The bar had the game on, so—"

"Whoa." He sat all the way up. "Let me get this straight..."

Her "Dom" took her to a dungeon, stripped her and used her, and then took her to a bar afterward—so they could catch the damn ball game?

He barely bit himself back from spewing it. Clearly, the woman had no idea that a trip to "Wings 'n' Wins" was a shitty excuse for aftercare. "Never mind," he said instead before pressing himself over her again.

Without pausing momentum, he sank all the way, taking her mouth under his once more. She tasted so perfect, like spice and cream and sex, and it occurred to him in a daunting rush that their time together was dwindling by the minute.

He only gave her a moment to catch her breath before taking another long, deep sample of her lips. He only drew back when he'd coaxed out a moan that matched his own.

"I take it you're not into the Angels and the Yankees?" she murmured.

Shay ran a thumb across her cheekbone. "I have an angel right here in my arms."

Her face lit up with the smile he'd hoped to inspire. "Hallelujah," she drawled.

Their laughs mingled before their mouths fused. Shay inhaled hard, breathed her in, reveling in her willingness to part her legs when he skimmed his hand down, blatantly seeking the heat at the center of her body.

"Ohhhh," she cried as he found her pouting flesh, pressing his finger to her most sensitive button. "Shane. *Yes.*"

He bit her upper lip with demanding pressure. "No. Use my other name, baby girl."

"S-Sir." Her compliance was immediate and raspy. "Ohhhhh...Sir...that's...mmmm...really nice."

"Yes." He ran the edges of his teeth over her bottom lip too. "Very nice."

After a few seconds of letting him kiss her like that, she whispered, "Do...do you have another condom?"

"Not a relevant question," he countered.

"I don't understand."

"Didn't ask you to. This moment is all about you. Your

surrender. Your pleasure. Give it to me, Zoe. I want it all...one more time."

She pulled in a breath as if preparing to protest, but when Shay shifted his hand, slipping two fingers into her warm little cunt while keeping pressure on her clit with his thumb, he won her over. After a stunning moan ripped up her throat, she lifted her hips off the mattress. A wanton sigh tumbled off her lips. "*Sí...sí...*"

"Good girl," he encouraged. "Arch up for me, beautiful. That's it, Zoe. You're so perfect. So goddamn sexy."

"*Ay Dios mío!* It's so good..."

"Yeah," he growled. "You're right. Your cunt feels so good around my fingers. So sweet for me. So ready to come for me. And that's what you're going to do, Zoe. You're going to let me fuck you with my fingers until you come for me again."

Just a few minutes later, she climaxed with breathtaking passion, rocking her mound against his touch in a shuddering mix of laughter and tears. Shay closed his eyes for a long moment as her body constricted around his fingers, reliving how good it felt when his dick was in the same position.

After her body went limp and she melted back to the mattress, she gazed up at him with bottomless-lagoon eyes. "That was...amazing."

Shay kissed her forehead. "That, sweet lady, was proper aftercare."

He began a sarcastic laugh, expecting hers to ensue, but should've known the woman would take him by surprise without even trying. The press of her fingers on his jaw tugged his stare down to her face, cast in angles of solemn softness. "I think I've become a new fan of aftercare."

"It's not one of my favorite parts for nothing."

That *did* inspire a giggle in her, filling the time it took Shay to pull the blankets over both of them. He pulled her close, tucking her head into the crook of his shoulder and draping her arm over his chest.

"I do have one objection," she murmured into their comfortable silence.

"Oh?"

"I think you've ruined me for sleep."

"Sorry." He brushed her shoulder with the tips of his fingers. "But not really."

She batted his chest. "Evil." After a glance at the clock, she moaned. "*Mierda*. Five thirty is going to hit like a hammer. But we all have to be on that flight. The mayor is bringing a group of bigwigs to the show tomorrow night. If we're not on Sunset flight number four-oh-three, there *will* be hell to pay."

Shay barely refrained from freezing his fingers on her skin. They sure as hell felt like ice now—a horrific contrast with the fire clawing through his gut—and the words of Wyst's text, scorching back into his mind's eye. The messages were still saved on his phone, in his jacket, not more than a dozen feet away.

New hatch time. 8 AM tomorrow. Sunset Airlines #403 to Sin City.

Papa Fox wants hens as insurance now.

Fuck.

Zoe and her friends were going to end up being the "insurance" of Cameron's new plan.

Unless Cameron could be stopped.

But if Shay did that, his cover would be severely

93

compromised. He'd blow the sole chance he had to rescue Mom. If Cameron didn't kill him first, he'd be standing with Dan Colton in an office somewhere, staring at files representing years' worth of investigative work by a dozen different agencies in twice as many countries—all blown to hell. And Stock would likely be a ghost once more, disappeared to God knew where, as invisible as a terrorist general in the caves of Afghanistan. And once again, just as dangerous.

Fuck.

His rule about life was getting a giant shot of justification—fueled by the fact that he'd just violated it in shit-righteous glory.

Caring was a luxury for those who wouldn't jeopardize lives when they indulged it.

That included every speck of feeling he'd basked in for Zoe Margarita Madonna Chestain.

Which meant he had to get out of here. Now.

CHAPTER SIX

Zoe sat up, pulled the sheet against her chest, and peered at Shane. Make that *gawked*.

What the hell had just happened?

She rewound her brain, trying to click on the thing she'd said or done to flip the man's spigot from hot to cold in seconds.

"Shane?" She hastened to correct herself. "Uhhh, Sir?" Was she even supposed to call him that anymore? He'd changed so fast and now bolted from the bed so urgently, she was seriously lost about decorum. "What's wrong? What did I—"

"Everything's fine." But his tone, now forcing the cordiality, blared otherwise. "Everything's just fine."

He tossed an equally feigned smile while yanking on his pants. His hair tumbled into his eyes. He scraped it back with one hand, unwittingly taunting her with the perfect flex of his bicep. Less than an hour ago, he'd been braced on those arms while meshing his body with hers, gazing at her like he never wanted to leave. Now he couldn't get dressed fast enough.

She tucked the sheet closer while battling an idiotic wave of ire. *He doesn't owe you anything. If anything, he gave you something. Two brain-bashing orgasms and one renewed hope of finding your submissive side.*

Either conclusion should've silenced her terse mutter but didn't. "I guess your idea of *fine* is much different than mine."

The man had the grace to grimace. He paused with an arm

95

jabbed into his shirt, leaning down to kiss her on the mouth. "It's late, baby girl. You said that yourself. You're dancing for the mayor tomorrow night. You need your sleep."

At the risk of looking pathetic, she grabbed his collar and tugged. "And you're the Energizer Bunny, so you don't?"

His eyes darkened in a mock glare. "Did you really just compare me to a rabbit?"

"Hmmm. A bunny, actually. A pink one that likes to beat on a big drum."

"Well, I'm tempted to beat *something*." He slipped a hand down to tug on one of her nipples. "Or some*one*."

"Yes, please."

Despite the seductive sigh she gave, Shane slipped out of her reach. His posture retightened as he turned and fastened his shirt. "I have to go. I'm sorry."

She had a feeling he didn't say those words often. They ground out of him as if he were heading to the gas chamber. Zoe leaned against the headboard and studied him carefully. The man moved with such athletic grace, every action fluid but practical. She'd bet the breast he just tweaked that he was a gifted dancer too.

They weren't the moves of a man who sat at a desk all day. Or even traveled the country with his ass on planes, sipping martinis and making "business deals."

What the hell was he really all about?

Nothing about his posture or his face, both newly stiff, gave her a clue. And Zoe *was* watching. More intently than she should. Watching Shane put his clothes back *on* had turned her stomach back into quicksand. He was like some CG creature from a fantasy film, a half god dipped in bronze and then sent to earth for the sole purpose of seducing mortal women into his lair of sin...

Single ticket to the lair of sin, please. One way? Perfect.

She yanked the sheet tighter around herself. *No.* Craving him again would only postpone the inevitable. She had to accept that the dream-come-true of this night had come to an end.

"*Sí*," she finally answered him, forcing strength to the tone and a matching tilt to her jaw. "Perhaps it *is* best that you go."

There. Done. That had to make it easier for him to shove out of here and get to the fire he clearly had to put out.

So why the hell did his face contort as if she'd just jabbed his side with a lighted torch?

"Zoe—"

"*Shane.*" She sliced her gaze up at him with as much severity as her tone. Like that did her composure any good. The second her gaze hit his again, her lungs constricted all over again from the torment in his eyes.

Torment? Seriously, chica?

She stood by the description. Either he really was leaving here to walk into a fire, or the demons in his soul were nastier *cabróns* than she assumed. Since the latter was more likely, she reached for his hand again.

"It was wonderful, okay?" She curled the tips of their fingers together. "Every minute. I mean it."

"Yeah," he replied. "It was. Thank you."

She slipped her hand free. "I really am tired."

"Yeah," he repeated, lowering next to her again. He plumped the pillows and arranged the blanket around her. "I understand."

Zoe glanced away, swallowing against another influx of tears. When was the last time someone had tucked *her* in?

"*Gracias,*" she managed, forcing herself not to focus on his hands, so big and assured and comforting.

And gone. Soon.

He continued for a few more seconds before raising a hand to her face, tracing the arches of both her eyebrows. His own pushed into a tight *V*. "Why don't you sleep in and just take a later flight? Planes leave for Vegas every five minutes out of LAX."

He was right about that. And there was genuine concern beneath his murmur, but she heard something else too. The verbal version of that damn agony from his eyes. It made her long to yank him back down before somehow turning time back by an hour. It was also why she had to squeeze her eyes shut and roll free from his tingle-inducing fingers. "I'll...I'll be fine. I need to call Ry back, and he'll likely keep me up the rest of the night wanting a report card on you anyway."

That should've stressed him out enough to finally leave. If he insisted on getting out of here—and for his own strange, haunted reasons, he did—then dragging this out any longer wasn't benefiting either of them.

There weren't any ropes here—of any kind.

It was best to keep it that way.

But damn it, the man once more shocked the hell out of her. Instead of the tension she anticipated from him, Burnett presented a picture of gorgeous confidence, beaming a subtle smirk while leaning back, and crossed his arms. "Report card? Is that so? Well, then...where do I hit on the bell curve, Miss Chestain?" His tongue swept his lower lip, slow and alluring. "I hope I brought enough apples for extra credit."

Despite everything that screamed *uncomfortable* about this moment, Zoe giggled. "You blew the curve up before the apples made it to the desk, Burnett, and you know it. Now kiss me and go to...wherever you need to be going." She pretended preoccupation with her cell as she finished that but gasped as he pulled the device from her hold. "What the hell? Shane? What're you—?"

She froze when she heard her name being yelled from the device—by Ryder.

"You did *not*," she gasped. "Shane! Give me the—"

He easily held her back with one arm. "Good evening. Is this Ryder? Excellent. Name's Shane Burnett. How are you, man?" He glanced to her, sliding half a smile that threatened to melt her so totally, his physical blockade wouldn't be necessary. "No, no. She's fine. She's right here. I'll hand you over in a second. But she's mentioned you two having a little chitchat and that doing so might keep her up until dawn. As you know, the woman has a high-profile performance tomorrow, and my concern is for her health." He paused, listened, and then nodded. "Glad you agree. I know you'll do the right thing and let her get some rest so I don't have to do anything like use the number I've stored for her in my phone for a three a.m. emergency break-in on the call...or even track down *your* number or anything. Thanks. Know I can count on you, man."

Zoe's jaw dropped. She managed to close it again as he handed the phone back over, though her lips parted as he bent once more to settle a perfect, soft kiss on them. When he pulled up, she shook her head, not even trying to hide her bewilderment.

"I don't know whether to say thank you or fuck you."

Shane gave her a little frown. Didn't seem as if he had the answer, either. He only kept his gaze on her, permeating and unwavering, fading the room—and then the rest of the world—

behind its golden intensity. "If you did either, I'd probably be a lost man again," he whispered. "Or perhaps I'd be found... A scarier idea."

Zoe swallowed. And longed to say so much. And couldn't think of a damn thing to utter. What the hell had he meant? Lost and found? Being afraid? Worst of all, why did he snare the very center of her gut with every syllable, tying her more tightly to him, when...

When he knew what he was going to do in the very next minute.

Without another word, he straightened, grabbed his jacket, and left on steady, silent steps.

In the ensuing silence, the air vent kicked on. Someone slammed a door up the hall. A fire truck siren blared in the street below.

Zoe barely registered any of it.

Only the incessant thrum of her heartbeat made any sense.

The pounding grew louder in her brain and harder in her blood. It pulled her to her feet like some primitive tribal guidance system, drawing her toward the door he'd just closed with such quiet finality. She reached for the knob, a smile of hope brimming. He was there, just on the other side. She could feel him...could almost hear his soft grunt of deliberation as he wondered whether to knock again.

She'd handle the choice for him.

As a precaution, she looked through the peephole, just to be sure she didn't catch him leaning on the door and accidentally topple his balance.

The hall was empty.

Her heart sank to her stomach. She pushed a hand against

the emptiness where it once lay. Curled it into a shaking fist.

"Zo? *Zo?* You still there?"

She blinked. Ryder. How had he gotten here? She glanced down. *Mierda,* he was in the phone. The one still in her hand.

She lifted the receiver to her ear as Ry muttered something about refusing to listen as she and Shane got their kink on again. "I'm here," she snapped. "Don't have a kitten. I'm here."

And Shane's not.

There was a definitive silence from Ry's end. At last, her friend gasped. "Oh. My. God."

"What?"

"He rocked your world, didn't he?" One-person applause filled the line before a loud *clunk.* "Damn. Sorry. Got so excited, I dropped the phone. Maybe I'll drop it again just to prove the point. Hell, Zo. Tell me everything. Don't stop until you get to the part where he ordered me to make sure you sleep tonight. But do it fast before he emergency jams our asses."

Zoe sighed. Words collided, clamoring to get out, along with a part of her that never had the chance to be a fifteen-year-old, giggling over the phone to a friend about an awesome date. She reached deep for that girl now, beseeching her to come out and tell Ry about the most incredible night of her life...

With a man who didn't want to play lost *or* found with her.

She fought to hold back tears, which only turned them into sobs. *Are you really going to do this, Zo? Because it's weak and absurd and really pathetic.*

Ryder's comforting tone worsened the ordeal. He only used it when he knew, through the special sorcery of best friends, that she really needed it.

Shut up, Ry. Please, just shut up.

"I have to go," she finally blubbered. "I can't do this."

"Okay." Damn him for not even hinting at a demand for explanation. "We'll do 'tinis when you get back." When she only filled the line with a slew of snot-filled snorts, he pressed, "Hey, Zo?"

"What?" she finally snapped.

"It's going to be okay, hot stuff."

But after she managed a goodbye, she bowed her head and shook it, knowing otherwise. "Okay" wasn't the word someone used when fate had handed them fireworks so good the explosions could likely be seen in space, only to let the show fizzle away without a fight. "Okay" wasn't what she'd be for a long while to come.

★ ★ ★ ★ ★

The conclusion clung to her like a damn fungus even as she boarded the plane for home the next morning. Thank God her oversized sunglasses and fedora lent her privacy as Brynn settled next to her.

Or not.

"Damn." The woman giggled, even in the midst of her hangover. "When did they change VIP to stand for Very Incredible Pecs?"

Zoe turned her head a little but didn't take off the glasses. Her puffy eyes were really scary. "What are you talking about?"

Brynn frowned. "Are those shades hiding your new blindness, missy? Please tell me you didn't miss the hunk buffet in the front seats."

"I was busy making sure you didn't trip down the aisle."

"Not a valid excuse, Chestain. Their biceps needed seats of their own—and there were at least four of them. One even looked like your type."

The comment was an unintentional stab. She gazed out the window at the last wisps of last night's fog, relating completely to their sad fight against the sun. "I didn't know I had a type."

"Oh yeah, you do. I can't believe you didn't see him. Hulking. Brooding. Dark baseball cap. Darker scowl. Couldn't make out the rest of his face. I wonder if he's on the run or something. Wouldn't that be sexy?"

A laugh escaped, despite the lead weights taking the place of her lungs. "You're incorrigible."

"I think he did look up a little when we passed, but only at you. Hmmm, Zo. You could be the Bonnie to his Clyde."

So much for the humor. "No, I couldn't."

"I'll bet on-the-run sex is way hot."

She pulled out her new romance paperback. Time for distraction by the only Doms who made sense to care about. Fictional ones. "Not interested, Brynn."

Her friend broke out in song. Of course. "I'm a cowboy, on a steel horse I ride—because I'm wannnted, dead or aliiive..."

"*Not interested*, Brynn."

Especially because, no matter how hard she tried, Shane was unshakable from her senses. She practically felt his eyes still riveted to her, smelled his rich forest scent on the air, and trembled from the potency of his presence.

Which was ridiculous. And more pitiful than her sob-fest from last night.

She had to get a grip. Return to reality. Now. Last night was a fantasy come true, but like a sexy stage illusion, it was over. The colored lights were off, the makeup stripped free. She had to be grateful for even receiving a goodbye from Burnett.

The man clearly didn't want *threads* from last night, let alone strings.

In short, her life was no different this morning than it had been twenty-four hours ago.

The logic didn't fortify her battle against weeping all over again.

Which meant this was going to be the flight from hell.

CHAPTER SEVEN

How the hell had he booked himself a first-class seat to Satan's front door?

Best not to dwell on the answer to that for long.

As the plane backed away from the gate, Shay allowed himself just one sliver of relief. Zoe hadn't glanced his way once at the gate or during boarding. Too preoccupied with keeping Brynn upright, the woman had gotten no inkling he was on board. He planned on keeping it that way.

Cameron would give them the go-ahead nearly the moment the aircraft made acceptable altitude. The second they received his green light, they'd all pull on their black ski masks—could Cameron get any more cliché about this shit?—and they'd blow open the cockpit door with one of Ross's nifty cold fusion mini-bombs. Once that happened, Ross, Nori, and Kaziro would move in, putting magic ninja squeezes on the pilots so Nori could change the jet's course as soon as possible. Meanwhile, he and Bash would join Cameron in controlling the crowd.

Including Zoe and her troupe.

His get-out-of-stress-free card expired. He clenched his jaw so hard, his ears burned. He kneaded both armrests with white knuckles.

Bash, seated next to him, didn't miss any of it. "Flying get you nervous, man?" he drawled. "So how'd that work out for you on all those airborne missions?"

"Fuck you."

Damn. He wished he had the freedom to be nicer. In other circumstances, he and Bash would likely be great friends. The guy was smart. *Really* smart. Vigilant. Funny. A keen observer of every person he met. That was the problem. If Shay started even a casual friendship with the guy, Bash's suspicion would instantly click in. There was no bromance in terrorism and piracy.

Bash's chuckle, coming from the middle of a chest that likely accompanied the word "barrel" in Webster's, wasn't a surprise. The guy's freak quotient needled way to the left of normal. "Relax, cupcake. We'll be on the ground before you know it, arrived at target. Then the only thing we have to worry about are a couple of hundred hostages—though I think we may have gotten lucky in that department. Heard there are a dozen Vegas showgirls on board. You know what that means, don't you?"

It took all of Shay's talent at subterfuge to fake a glance that looked lascivious. "Lots of comp buffet tickets?"

The guy humored him with a snort before growling, "Flexibility, man. Bitches who can bend their body any way we command. If we find some rope at Stock's little *desert resort*, we'll have our own personal Barbies to play with. Sweet, yeah?"

Shay forced down deep breaths. It wouldn't do him—or Zoe—any good if he lost composure now. Times like these, the art of fantasy was a damn good thing. Just thinking of landing his fist in Bash's face went a long way toward coaxing out another smile—and abolishing his visions of ever hanging out with the guy as buddies. "What makes you think Cam's going to allow that?"

"Sometimes you don't ask permission, dude. Besides, it's

not like we'll be moving the new *passengers* on board this thing right away. They're experimental science freaks. Some of them are hooked up to machines and shit."

Shay pretended to ogle the flight attendant in order to emphasize the "casual" intent of his next question. Cameron had made no secret about his passion to get a plane landed at the desert complex, which happened to be "conveniently" located somewhere near Area 51, one of the government's most intensely guarded pieces of land. The airspace in and around the base, which hadn't even been publicly acknowledged until last year, was still heavily restricted—as in fly-over-here-and-you're-dead restricted. Cam was just as cagey about his reasons behind needing to get inside with an airliner in tow. His agitation about the mission was even worse today—ever since changing the mission from stealing an empty plane to a craft filled with two hundred hostages.

Because he had other people to exchange for them?

People Bash referred to as "science freaks."

Was Mom one of those freaks now?

"Won't Cameron need help with all that?"

Bash grunted. "Right. Like he's going to let us touch any part of his gold pile. Those mutants are his ticket to world domination, dude."

"And you never asked for a cut of that pie?" He pulled the safety information card from the pocket in front of him and pretended to peruse it. "You've been working for Stock for a long time. You don't think you deserve it?"

Bash answered with a vehement shake of his head. "Even if I did, just don't want it. For a long time, neither did Cam."

"What do you mean?"

"Back in the day, he was a much more fun guy. We pulled

off smaller fraud scams and made a shit ton of money, which he turned around and spent in the Hollywood scene. He had a big-ass mansion, nice pool, stocked bar...the whole nine. Was a decent director too. Actresses liked working with him, so that meant the tail was sweet and plentiful. But then he hooked up with Ephraim Lor, and the fuckery got really weird. That Lor... He was a piece of work. He was about the crazy shit, you know? He'd go on and on about how we'd become the face of history and have a legacy that would go on..." He rolled his eyes. "Christ. What a wing nut."

Shay restrained himself from nodding in sympathy. He was intimately familiar with the chaos Lor had caused. That "wing nut" had almost destroyed every state between Mexico and Canada, as well as his brother's sanity. Thank fuck Tait had survived Luna's death and was moving on—though the definition of that now included his relentless search for Shay under the umbrella of the SHRC black-ops team.

"But Lor's not around anymore, right? Didn't he die in that whole episode at the studio?"

"Sure, but it didn't make any difference," Bash muttered. "I call that the beginning of the end for Cameron."

"You're serious, aren't you?"

"Uh-huh. When we all reconnected in Barbados after that mess, Cam was...different."

"In what way?"

"He snapped, dude." The guy's lips twisted. "If I believed in whacked crap like soul-jumping and reincarnation, I'd say part of Lor leaked out and crawled its way into Cam."

Shay was glad for a reaction he didn't have to feign. "You're right. That's whacked crap."

"I know. I know."

"Cam is all about the money. Always was, always will be."

"No argument there." Bash reclined his seat, ignoring the huff from the guy in the three-piece suit behind him. "It's just *how* he looks at the money now. He used to be about cars, wine, and women. Now it's all about guns, alignments, and entertaining fat foreigners who are into some scary shit. He's started taking insane risks. That whole episode over in Kaua'i... starting a bidding war between Iraq and North Korea for the chance to take over that estate as a forward-operating base..." He blew out harsh breath between his teeth. "These are world powers, Burnett. North Korea has *nukes*. Between you and me, I was glad we got made on that one."

Shay nodded tightly. He didn't have to pour on the acting job much for it. "Bit too heavy on the Johnny Danger angle for me too."

"Right?" His consensus spurred Bash on. "What if both those assholes were playing Cam and planned on eventually uniting for their cause? We wouldn't be sitting here, that's for damn sure. It'd already be World War Three."

"So what's your take on this one?"

"I don't have to think anything. This is my last gig, dude. I'm done with this bozo. As soon as we get paid up, I'm gonna steal a transport of some sort and then get my ass to Vegas. Got a guy there who's going to help me change my identity and fade behind the neon signs." He backhanded Shay's chest. "You're welcome to join me, Burnett. This time next week, we could be balls-deep in a lot of fun, man."

Shay returned a convincing enough chuckle. "Doesn't sound like a half-bad idea."

The shitty thing was, it really didn't. For a while, he'd at least be in the same city as Zoe. He could look after her from afar, make sure no asswipes messed with her...

"But why wait, right?" Bash drawled. "You catch my drift now?"

He frowned. "Uhhh, not exactly."

"The *dancers*, Burnett. You saw them come on board, yeah?"

If he was referring to every step Zoe had taken down the aisle, then yes. "Sort of. I was running down the plan in my head, and—"

"Shit." The guy extended the vowel, turning the word into two syllables. "You're a real moron sometimes. Those bitches are soooo sweet."

Shay held up both hands. "I believe you. I believe you."

"Didn't you say you knew a bit about rope-suspension bondage?"

He tried to hide his wince, betraying the regret he felt for shooting off his mouth during that conversation he'd used to "bond" with Bash. "I don't remember. Honestly, my Dom days were a long time ago." He didn't need to pretend that one, either. It had been almost a year since he'd last had the privilege of tying a willing subbie up.

"You *did*, man," Bash interjected. "So help a guy out. It's my last mission before going off grid, right? Let's string up a couple of these beauties. My dick is dirty, and soap on a rope sounds really damn awesome right now."

Shay managed a smile while grinding his fist into his opposite hand. But turning his hands into a furious mortar-and-pestle was preferable to the alternative—smashing in Bash's jaw before ordering him to stay the fuck away from Zoe and her friends.

Cameron put a decisive end to his dilemma—though, at

the same time, stirred a new one. The man unbuckled and stood, dipping nods to everyone on the team, signaling them to be ready. Shay's gut wrenched as he watched everyone straightening, watching, readying. Wyst eyed the air marshal, whom he'd ID'd by hacking the FAMS rosters a few hours ago, with a wicked glint in his eyes and a fist wrapped in spiked foil—not that the bruiser needed the shit. Ross would go first toward the cockpit, with Nori and Kaziro on his heels, while Shay and Bash pulled wingman duty for Stock.

That was the plan. Easy. Elegant. Evil.

And there was still time to stop it. Still time for *him* to stop it.

But at what cost?

Bash had just confirmed Stock's gelatin of a mental state. The man had become a demon about accomplishing this mission and the lives he'd take to accomplish it. If Shay shattered his own cover and called Cam out, it would just feed the man's hunger for history book glory. All too clearly, he could see Stock ordering Nori to power the plane into a nosedive. And Nori, a kamikaze born eighty years too late, would be his willing bitch. They'd all be dinner for the Mojave Desert coyotes inside an hour.

Shay grimaced as bile seared his throat. He sent a mental broadcast to whatever higher power was in the mood to listen, asking them to expedite the encrypted message he'd sent to Colton from his phone after leaving Zoe's room. The move had been a huge risk, one he hadn't chosen earlier for purely selfish reasons. If joining Cameron in hijacking a flight got him closer to Mom, he reconciled that as the price to be paid for the cause.

But learning Zoe would be on that flight?

It shouldn't have changed a fucking thing. But it did.

It changed everything.

Somehow, in the space of less than three hours, *she'd* changed everything.

Damn it.

The anger ricocheted through his head, along with nausea and dread, as he realized this was really going to happen. He had no choice. Switching out the black hat for white at this point wouldn't just be futile but stupid. Black kept him on Stock's inside track, which meant he still had a fighting chance to rescue Mom and get out of this alive.

Just as importantly, he had a chance to keep Zoe alive.

Holy fuck. If anything happened to her during this damn stunt...

"Gentlemen." The flight attendant's snippy tone zeroed his senses in on the moment. She directed the charge at Ross, Nori, and Kaziro as they moved into the aisle. "You must stay seated. The captain hasn't indicated it's safe to—"

Kaz rendered her unconscious with an expert blow to the side of her neck. As she crumpled, he caught her and then effortlessly dragged her to the galley. When he came back, he pulled his ski mask down in time to confront the air marshal, a guy in bad-fitting khakis who charged forward with a growl. Kaz, who took his ninja calling as seriously as Nori did the kamikaze, dropped the officer with a series of efficient punches and kicks. Wyst cursed, his fun taken away.

Just as a woman screamed. Joined in an instant by Mr. Three-Piece Suit. Then half the other passengers.

Shay muttered the F-word while yanking down his mask and bolting into the aisle behind Bash.

It was showtime.

CHAPTER EIGHT

"Mmmpph." Zoe followed the grunt with an irritated moan. With a soft piano tune layered over the sound of ocean waves in her ear buds, along with the lulling motion of the plane, she was almost asleep. Every mile they flew closer to home meant another mile farther from Shane Burnett. Thank every saint there was.

She wasn't so grateful for Brynn's urgent grabs at her elbow. Or the rapid-fire shoulder whacks that followed.

What the hell?

She yanked her buds out and cracked one eye open in a glare. "*Corazón*, please; can you ogle the guys by yourself? I had a crap night's sleep, and— Brynn?"

Her friend's face wasn't fixed in the rapture of spotting new man candy. It was frozen in what looked like pure fear. "Zo." Her lips trembled. "Oh, my God."

She opened her other eye. Silently followed Brynn's stare toward the front of the plane. From that same direction, a woman shrieked. The sound was a detonation switch on the air, arcing fear through the cabin. Then terror.

Zoe sat up, now awake. Her heartbeat hammered as she gaped at the scene ahead. Seven men in ski masks. Unconscious flight attendants. *Dios*. It seemed surreal. Too far away. This couldn't really be happening. Not to *her* life.

Wasn't that the familiar refrain by now? Last night, she'd wondered if her time with Shane had been a movie happening to someone else, but it had all been so warm and wonderfully real. Now, she clung to that reality instead of this one. Reaching out to Shane and his strength and rewarded by practically feeling his power on the air again. If she breathed deeply enough, she even caught hints of his woodsy scent...

Brynn cried out, along with half the women on board, as one of the men knocked another unconscious. The guy on the floor must've been the air marshal, because his aggressor pulled a gun from the middle of the man's back before turning it over, barrel side up, to a person she assumed was the gang's leader. Her estimation was validated when three of the men followed that guy to the middle of the plane. Two of them moved around him to march deeper into the cabin while he grabbed the intercom handset and clicked it on.

"Good morning, ladies and gentlemen. As you've likely discerned, our flight plan for the day has been altered." The man spread his arms with the gun still in his hand, making the passengers at the barrel's end cringe. "There is no need for alarm. We're not here to hurt anyone, merely to borrow you all as insurance for arrival at our final destination. Please sit back, relax, and enjoy the journey."

As he said that, a small flash erupted at the front of the plane, as if explosives had been set off. A bunch of men joined bellows with the women's screams but Zoe frowned, confused. There had been no sound from the blast; there was still no smell.

"You're cracked wider than a cheap rubber, asshole." The eruption came from a man seated a couple of rows back. Zoe closed her eyes, asking her favorite saints to lend the guy some good sense, but the *idioto* wasn't listening to anything but his own fear, manifesting itself as bravado. "No need for alarm, yeah? Forgive me if we don't buy a line of your bullshit."

The "asshole" narrowed his eyes. Fury flashed so brightly in them, Zoe could see his aggravation even from where she sat. But when the man spoke, his voice was all talk-show congeniality. "We only want the jet, my friend. All of you are simply our insurance of getting it to our desired location. As far as trust? I cannot force you to give me that, buddy—but I guarantee that your day will proceed better if you simply hand it over."

Shouts and exclamations filtered out from the cockpit. The pseudo-explosion had been a tricky device intended to blow the door, and it was successful.

The outlaws now had access to the plane's controls.

Zoe wasn't the only one to reach that horrifying conclusion. More women screamed. Some, like Brynn, broke into sobs.

The dimwit from two rows back erupted with a new string of profanity, all involving their hijackers with goats, dildos, and their mothers. Zoe silently prayed for him again, but the moron was intractable. "What's your name, asshole?"

The man cocked his head. "Does it matter? You're doing such a good job on all those inflections of *asshole*. Maybe we should leave it at that." He followed it up by strolling farther back in the cabin, motioning a pair of minions to follow him—though the term "minions" was up for interpretation. Both men were the size of small houses. Zoe supposed that helped when a guy was tasked with hijacking a plane without any weapons, though their teammate, leaner than both by at least fifty pounds, had just knocked out a flight attendant and the air marshal with his bare hands.

"You coming back to intimidate me, *asshole*?" the idiot

sneered. "Because you don't."

The leader sighed. "Sit down, my friend."

"No."

"*Sit down.*" The goon who'd stopped in front of Zoe and Brynn unfurled it in a low, threatening growl—immediately causing trembles down Zoe's arms and legs. Quivers that unexpectedly turned hot...and sensual.

What the hell?

She scrubbed her palms against the tops of her thighs. She had to be in some kind of crisis shock. Feeling like this was *loco,* plain and simple. The fact that she'd just had the best sex of her life, with a man possessing the same dark panther quality to his voice, didn't help the cause. And yeah, there was that little burr in her brain, too—the continuing memories of him with all his clothes *on.* The recall of what they'd shared when they weren't blowing up the hotel room with their passion. The longing that made her practically feel him in the air, so close and big and powerful, all over again...

Are you actually fighting wet panties at thirty thousand feet, because of a hijacking cabrón *who happens to have a voice with a little resonance to it?*

Crap.

He also happened to have long, strong fingers. And a high, defined chest. And a proud, firm stance that practically bellowed a dominant nature...

"You're a bunch of goddamn bullies." The obstinate ass was at it again. "And I like to eat bullies for breakfast. Come on, everybody. Let's take down these bastards!"

The guard next to them growled lower than before. His leader told the man, "Effective *takedowns* rely on a little something called surprise. And a bigger element called a brain.

Since you clearly have neither, shut the fuck up and sit down."

"Listen to him, gumby," said the goon in front of them. *That voice* again. Zoe dug her knuckles into her thighs and fought back a moan. *You are being ridiculous. And completely pathetic.*

"You want me to sit down? Make me, dickhole."

The next sound out of the man was his tormented wail—a second after the single *pow* of the fired pistol.

Zoe surged to her feet alongside Brynn. The guard with the growl shoved them back down, but not before they saw the man who'd dared the rebellion against their captors. His right knee was nothing but a bloom of blood.

"Shit!" Brynn dissolved into tears. Zoe pulled her friend close, acknowledging her own need for comfort in the gesture. She shook worse than a krump dancer on three energy drinks, though was pretty certain Brynn would never notice.

"Y-You—" the *idioto* stammered. "My knee! I'm— I'm—"

"Damn lucky I'm in a cheerful mood." The man with the gun sounded like he'd just snacked on the remaining bullets in the pistol. If they only got so lucky. Zoe was pretty sure the air marshal wouldn't have boarded with a less-than-prepared weapon. Her suspicion was confirmed when the man lifted the gun, ensuring everyone took note of the barrel. "Anyone else in the mood to play cowboy? Come on up; I'll slide on my spurs."

Other than the soft sobs weighing the air, everyone fell into silence.

"He's bleeding badly." The interjection came from Harmony, the member of their cast who matched her name the most perfectly. The woman was a peace accord on two legs. "Mister, I can see you're devoted to your plan, but do you really want a man to bleed to death for it?"

The minions shifted uncomfortably. The guard toward the back of the plane, with a chest that needed its own zip code, muttered, "Can't hurt to ask if there's a doctor or nurse on board."

Zoe swallowed hard, pulled free of Brynn, and raised her hand. "I can do it."

"No, you *can't*." Brynn yanked her back.

"No, you can't." Mr. Growl's concurrence, with an ample infusion of dungeon-worthy command, rose her hackles. It wasn't just his arrogance. It was the way his presence wouldn't leave her libido the hell alone.

"Yes," she snapped, "I *can*." She swung her sights to his boss. Though the guy was significantly shorter than Growl Man, he emanated vibes that freaked her the hell out. Nevertheless, she jerked up her chin and stated, "I'm the captain for our troupe. I can wrap any part of the body. It'll at least stop the blood until we land...wherever we're landing."

The man rolled his head again, considering her offer. It gave her arrogant guard an opportunity to pin her with a tight, unreadable stare—well, as much as he'd let her see. The guy wore his mask differently than the others, yanking it into slits around his eyes and tucking the fabric around his lips, making his mouth indistinct, as well. He was so strange. And unrelenting. And infuriating.

"The authorities will be kinder about your sentencing if you don't allow him to bleed out," Harmony interjected.

Zoe caught her friend's eye through the gap in the seats. "*Corazón*, he's hijacked a jet with hundreds of people on board. I'm not sure how kind anyone's inclined to be right now. On the other hand, murder in the first never made anyone's life *less* complicated."

The man laughed. "Aren't you two a lovely surprise?" He nodded. "Fine. Tell my boys what you need and then wrap the jerkass up. After that, I'm taking a couple of you lovely ladies to the cockpit to help your new pilot on the radio."

Brynn gasped. Zoe barely heard the sound. She breathed deeply, trying to summon a shred of warmth to the ice in her chest. "Wh-Why? We're dancers, not air-traffic specialists."

The man slid her a patronizing smile. "Thanks, honey. I'm aware of that already. But you're also one thing my boy Kamikaze can't be."

"Oh?" She managed it past gritted teeth. *Damn*. The man and his boys were sharp, using radio call signs instead of proper names with each other. It meant she'd have to work at paying attention to other details about them—a skill that, ironically, Bryce had helped her hone.

"Women," the man supplied to her query.

"Excuse me?" she returned.

"I need a woman's voice," the man explained while helping her into the aisle. But once she stood next to him, he didn't let go of her hand. She shivered as he raised his grip to her nape. His ice-blue eyes glittered from behind his mask. "The boys running the show at military command are going to be more patient with their guns if a woman is pleading for the souls on board."

"Their...guns?" she managed to get out. "Isn't that an extreme assumption to make?"

"Not when one wants to land an airliner at Area 51."

"Area 51?" She plummeted her jaw. While she was no expert on all the urban legends and speculation about the base, she was more than aware of its main fact. Nobody entered without the most high-level security clearance. And no commercial aircraft dared a flight plan into its airspace, let alone a full landing. "Have you lost your damn mind?"

His loose chuckle defied his iron grip as she tried to wrench away. "Oh, you *are* a delight. So much spirit and passion. We're going to have fun together, aren't we, *mi chiquilina*?"

"I'm not your *chiquilina*. I'm not your anything. Let go." She swallowed, glancing to the pistol in his other hand. "Please."

To her dread, he raised the gun's barrel and slid it along her cheek. "I like the way you say that word. Do it again."

Her breath, what she dared to take of it, left her in uneven spurts. The weapon was a cold taunt on her flesh.

Until it was suddenly shoved away.

She gaped as Growl Man's fingers twisted around his boss's wrist. In seconds, the man was forced to drop the weapon. Before she could regain the composure to step back, her savior clamped a steely arm around her middle, swept her behind him, and didn't let go until she fell back into Brynn's lap. He followed her down, low enough to lean over both of them—ensuring she should just write off breathing for the foreseeable future. His proximity gave her a close-up of the brilliant gold shards in the depths of his gaze.

Gold?

His eyes were...gold?

But unlike the gaze of her dream Dom from last night, cutting into her with slices of molten seduction, this bastard's eyes wielded nothing but callous daggers. He jabbed several of those blades into her before uttering one word.

"Stay."

Zoe was stunned to feel herself nodding instead of flinging back her own metaphorical daggers. What the hell was wrong with her? Midair crisis or not, she didn't take orders like a dog, especially from a hijacking mercenary who sounded like he'd morphed with a Doberman himself. She forced her teeth into her tongue, congratulating herself for the wisdom of the move when she watched him square off against his boss.

Vaya. Separately, the men were intimidating. Nose-to-nose, they were terrifying. Two sets of broad shoulders, every bulging muscle defined by skintight black. Two unwavering glares. One loaded gun, now recovered from the floor. One *human* weapon who'd already proved that really didn't matter.

And breathing? Still impossible. Zoe didn't know if she needed to faint or crawl out of her skin.

"You want to tell me what the fuck that was all about?" the leader challenged.

Growl Man grunted. "First off, you want to change the world or chase pussy? Decide now, man. I'm sure we'd all be happy to have 'Kaze turn this bird around for a landing in the middle of Mexico instead of the suicide zone we're about to enter."

His boss huffed. Zoe watched him assess the other man, perhaps questioning the guy's motives. She admitted her own curiosity about what he'd find. Why *had* the guy whisked her away from him like that? Something wasn't adding up.

"Is that it?" the leader finally charged. "Or is there a 'second off'?"

Her savior nodded at the gun. "Yeah. How about locking down the safety on that heat?"

Boss Man rolled his eyes. "Jesus. When did you become Safe Side Superchick?"

"When I boarded a flying can full of pressurized air with you. But hey, if you want to blow an accidental hole in the hull and render this bucket un-flyable—"

"Fine, fine." The leader thumbed the lever into place. "Christ. I let you get away with so much cheek."

"Yeah, yeah. Flattery still won't get me to suck face with you."

"Bite me."

"No, thank you. Not into mini sausage."

Zoe couldn't decide which ordeal was worse, their bro-flirt banter or the sudden explosion that interrupted it. The blast, visible through the windows on the plane's left side, rocked the whole aircraft. When another followed, closer and to the right, the airliner listed to the left.

Zoe burrowed into Brynn. They didn't let go of each other even after "Kamikaze" realigned the plane. Shrieks, profanities, and horrified bellows punched the air.

Mierda. Her friend was right last night. Irony was a douche. She and Brynn had originally bonded because they were adrenaline junkies, joining Jacy and Holli for a four-girl ride on Insanity at The Stratosphere on their first girls' night out. There was a big damn difference between roller coaster terror and real terror. She'd endure the *pretend* Insanity every day over this ordeal.

Everyone's attention swung toward the front of the plane again. Zoe could only discern that someone from the airline's crew had attempted to tangle with one of the hijackers. Stripes on the man's uniform confirmed that the brave soul was one of the pilots, obviously not as disabled as the hijackers preferred. Zoe was joined by many others in wincing as the man was subdued by the bad guy, who fought like Bruce Lee incarnate.

As the ninja tore out a coffee maker cord and hogtied the pilot with it, another hijacker burst from the cockpit and raced down the aisle toward the leader. "We're through the magic mirror, boss. Officially in A-51 airspace."

"Really?" Growl Man's rejoinder dripped with sarcasm. "Thanks for the update. And here we were, thinking we'd simply crossed paths with a psychotic skeet shooter."

"Hey." His leader glared. "Play nice, assface." He cocked his head. "That's normally not a problem for you. What the fuck has crawled up your backside?"

"Other than knowing that those two shots were purposeful misses? And that the next one won't be?"

For some strange reason, the guy finished by sweeping another glance down at her and Brynn. For an even stranger reason, Zoe wished he'd do it again. Despite his gentle-as-a-porcupine manner, there was a protectiveness in him, a ferocity that made her feel he'd leap in front of bullets for her, if this nightmare came to that.

Caramba. This was crazy. A textbook case of captive falling for predator to lessen the terror of the trauma. She needed to get real again. The leader of these lunatics had just shot a man's kneecap off for tossing a little lip. The ninja up front had taken out both pilots, the air marshal, and a flight attendant in about two dozen punches. All these men were one mental snap away from actually exacting lives for their cause.

It was clear. She couldn't afford the luxury of trusting in silly romance anymore. Fate had given her some incredible hours with Shane, but that kind of lightning didn't strike twice. If she wanted the memories of him to live on, *she* had to live—and stop imprinting his qualities onto this coldhearted criminal.

The engines changed speed again, coinciding with a shift in altitude. They were already descending. The comprehension hit her with hope and dread in the same heartbeat. Boss Man didn't aid her conflict by hauling her back to her feet and then pulling Brynn up after her. "They're not going to fire again," he said to his skeptical minion, "and our sweet dancerina dolls are going to help seal that deal."

Zoe kept her fingers twisted into Brynn's. She nodded back to the man who held the bloody mess that had once been his knee. "What about wrapping him?"

"Changed my mind," the man drawled. "You can fix him up when we're safely on the ground—which now makes him a good incentive for helping us out. Right, honey?"

Her nerves screeched like a fork on glass. It was the second time the man used the endearment on her. Two times too many. Growl Man seemed to agree. His tall frame tensed and he stepped closer, once more giving off an aura of protectiveness she couldn't ignore—but had to resist. Those two factors, as well as the situation they came wrapped in, contributed to her own snarl of a response.

"Fine. Let's get this the hell over with."

★ ★ ★ ★ ★

If this experience was nerve-wracking from the cabin, it was a composure killer from the copilot's seat in the cockpit.

Zoe bit her lip as she looked out the windows, across the desert and its palette of tan, sage, and copper. The Sheep Mountains glowed in the morning sun up ahead, flanked by the Spring Mountains to the west and the Muddy Mountains in the east. The valley they formed was filled with the sprawling checkerboard of the Las Vegas metropolis.

Weirdly, she remembered the first time she'd seen this

landscape, from the passenger's window of Ry's Acura as they'd approached down Highway 15. To a born-and-raised Tacoma girl, the vistas around Vegas had been an alien world, stark and unforgiving, but the last three and a half years had taught her differently. The desert was now full of many textures, moods, and colors—and it was home.

No. It was only the start of what she knew as home.

Home was also the couch back in Tacoma, where she'd cried so many times on *Papi's* strong shoulders over blown auditions or asshole boyfriends. Home was happy hour at Commonwealth with Ry, clinking dirty martinis and making up naughty labels for every hunk who walked in the door. Home was going to be the altar at the winery in Sonoma, when she watched her little sister walk down the aisle to begin her new life as Mrs. Ethan Archer.

She had to get home.

She couldn't die today. She *wouldn't* die today.

The affirmation gave her the strength to raise her head. And push words out of her lips.

"Okay. I'm ready."

Boss Man's lips lifted the inner edges of his ski mask. "Good girl."

Zoe glared. "Let's not go there again, *pendejo*. Just tell me what the hell to say so we're not blown out of the sky."

His mouth sobered, but his eyes retained the gleam, still going for the tease. Zoe barely refrained from shuddering, but was glad she did when another hijacker leaned in, punching a button on the console that made her dizzy from its levers, switches, and lights. Two fingers of his other hand tapped his thigh, confirming he was the status messenger they'd seen before.

"Hello? Hello? Sunset flight four-oh-three, do you copy?" came a frantic baritone from the cockpit speakers. "Sunset four-oh-three, be advised that this will be our final attempt to communicate with your aircraft. We've intercepted passenger cell transmissions from your plane, and we know what's going on. We're willing to discuss demands, but if you don't alter course out of this airspace *now*, you'll be blasted out of the—"

"No!" Zoe screamed it. "Don't shoot! You'll be killing hundreds of innocent civilians!" They'd never coached her what to say, but it felt logical. And terrifyingly truthful.

"Errr, to whom am I speaking?" Now the baritone almost sounded like a different person. Zoe was grateful for the guy's gentler side. Adrenaline and stress still techno-stomped her nerve endings. "Hello?" the man prompted again. "Identify yourself at once, ma'am. To make this perfectly clear, we're not fucking around anymore."

"Neither are these guys," Zoe snapped. "The air marshal's unconscious. They used some kind of Jedi-ninja chokehold on him. His gun's been used to shoot another man. The guy's not dead but bleeding a lot, and they won't allow him medical attention until we land. There are more bullets in the gun, and I'm certain this man will use them if provoked."

Boss Man let out a satisfied whoosh. "Couldn't have said it better myself. Thank you, honey."

"Fuck off," she retorted.

A harrumph rustled the connection. "Sounds like you're doing your best to keep those scumsuckers in line, young lady."

Zoe tried to smile, appreciating the man's attempt at comfort. "I'm not sure that's what I'd call it, sir. Sometimes you just have to put one foot in front of the other."

"Spoken like some of my best soldiers."

"Or some of my best dancers."

"What's your name, firecracker?"

"Zoe Chestain. I live in Vegas."

"Zoe, I'm General Kirk Newport. I'm going to do my best to get you get home safely."

Any thread of ease she'd allowed herself was canceled by the pistol's barrel, pressed to her temple with ruthless force. "Social hour's over," the leader barked. "Stay on task, dancerina."

Zoe dipped a tense nod. "General, this man is serious." Panic started to win over composure. Her chin trembled. Her words wobbled. "Please, *please* let him land the damn plane."

Boss Man ground the pistol tighter against her head. "Beautifully spoken, Miss Chestain, but I believe General Newport already knows how serious I am. Don't you, Kirk baby?"

Curiosity snuck in around her fear. *Kirk baby?*

"Cameron. It's been too long. Wish I could say it's a pleasure to have found the rock you crawled back out from, but you know the adage. Honesty's the cornerstone of a great relationship."

Okay, there was history between these two. Would that bode well or worse for a safe landing once they got done with their pissing match?

"Honesty." The man behind her sounded like he'd just chomped a cyanide pill. "Have you ever known a day of the shit in your life, Kirk?"

"And do you really want to dredge up the past now?"

"'The past.' *That's* what you're calling it now?"

The general let a low snarl reverberate through the line. "I'm two minutes away from giving those F-18s permission to fly back in and blow your ass out of the sky."

"But you won't."

"That so, dickwad? Then you're crazier than I thought, Cam."

"I prefer calculated risk taker, but you call it like you see it. We'll see what the *world* says, after those jets blow a packed commercial airliner to shreds."

Brynn, pinned against the cockpit's entry threshold by the ninja who'd taken down the flight crew, let out a sharp whimper. Zoe twisted her hands together in her lap until they burned.

"Was that really your plan, Cam? You think the upper muck gives a shit about the PR fallout of this? You remember everything that's at stake here, don't you?"

Slowly, the pistol barrel slid away from her face. Zoe still didn't let herself breathe, unsure whether to exhale in relief or start confessing her sins before death. *Forgive me, Father, for I have sinned. I used a lot of bad words yesterday. Then there's the issue of the man who gave me two orgasms that I'll confess, but only if you let me remember...*

Her captor spoke again. His determined tone revealed nothing about whether to finish her supplication.

"I remember everything, my friend," he stated. "And that's why I've left a memory stick of very interesting information with...let's say a dear friend. If I don't leave the base within twenty-four hours with this plane full of our valuable new guests, my friend will know to take that information to the nearest news outlet."

A long pause preceded the general's response. Zoe glanced at Brynn, whose thin lips confirmed her suspicions. The man was taking a moment to seethe.

"You wouldn't fucking *dare*."

"Kirk." The word was a tease in its condescension. "You know, for better or worse, I'm a man of my word."

The general was noisier about his fury now. There was a loud *thump*, several seconds of static, and then a harsh grate. "And if I do give you clearance, you jizz-slurping shit?"

"My friend feeds the stick to his pet crocodile." The guy actually laughed. "It'll go well with the clock, right?"

Newport's reaction, once more sucking up an interminable pause, gave her lots of time to stare at her hands, still torture-twisting in her lap. She listened to Brynn make an attempt for normal breathing. In the meantime, the pilot took the aircraft lower, aiming for a set of domed buildings that appeared like a collection of buttons on the desert floor.

Newport finally clicked back on. "Sunset four-oh-three, you have clearance to land at KXTA," he bit out. "Groom Lake Tower will guide you in, but you must patch to them on secured radio frequency. Dial in your radio accordingly."

"Thank God." Brynn's whisper was thick and tearful. Zoe longed to echo her friend's outlook but was stopped by a volition from deep inside, an instinct she couldn't explain. The tension in Newport's voice was only her first trigger. The weird energy flowing off Cam the Boss Man was the second. His anticipation bordered on violence, creeping her out even more.

"General Newport," he drawled with scary serenity. "Thank you for your time. A pleasure, as always."

"Fuck you, Stock."

The hijacker next to her cut off the line with a low laugh. His boss joined him. Brynn fell silent again. Zoe just gulped, battling the chaos of her mind, now revving toward a dreadful conclusion.

"*Ay Dios mio,*" she stammered.

One trigger. Two triggers. And now the third, slamming into her with the force of a Mack truck.

Fuck you, Stock.

The lead hijacker's name was Stock. *Cameron Stock.*

She knew that name. With horrific clarity.

As the director of *Dress Blues,* the TV show Ava had worked on as a stylist, the man had once been her sister's well-liked boss—until he'd colluded with the terrorist who'd almost killed Ava and Ethan. That radical, Ephraim Lor, had been shot and killed in their failed plot to launch nuclear warheads at all the western states, but Stock had escaped and been a ghost ever since.

Not anymore.

Not here, where he shared a fist bump with his minion as his pilot guided the plane lower. Not now, a moment in which he indulged in a victory that had come from the fear and pain of others.

No. He wasn't invisible anymore.

Which meant Zoe no longer had to guess where to aim her fury, frustration, and hatred.

She whirled and sprang to her feet. As she'd hoped, the move landed her in front of Stock. Fear almost slammed her back down, but desperation and exhaustion—likely mixed with stupidity—rejuiced her bravery, firing up her arm. In one whisk, she ripped Stock's cap off his head. The stunned expression on his square quarterback face was practically worth the risk by itself—but she wanted more out of the bastard than his shock.

Preferably his blood.

"*Percanta,*" she spat. "You're dirty and disgusting, and so are all your trained monkeys."

The weasel lunged at her, but Stock shoved the guy back, not wavering his insolent grin. "But I like monkeys. Don't you... Miss Chestain? Hmmm. I knew another Chestain once. Well, I didn't *know* her, if you follow me. Not that I didn't want to. Seemed like she'd be a good fuck, but just never—"

Zoe punched the man as hard as she could.

It felt great.

She wanted more.

Growl Man's entrance into the cockpit only spiked her rage higher, especially at herself. She'd practically had gooey panties over the *cabrón*. Had let herself tremble from the timbre of his voice and practically *thanked* him for yanking her away from Stock's flirtation. But he wasn't some noble antihero. Putting Stock's face to this crime had crystallized the realization. Whatever had motivated each of these men to this act, which remained a mystery, they were still criminals, crawling in the sludge just shy of terrorism.

As Ryder would say, *damn straight*. Not a drop more of her misplaced hormones would be wasted on the creep. Unmasking him would help her accomplish that better than anything else.

"What the hell's going on?" His growl was back in place, just as daunting and riveting as ever, but Zoe only smiled at it now. She was immune to it now. Empowered. In control.

She stomped toward the guy. Growl Man countered by shuffling backward.

Which wasn't supposed to happen. Nor was it supposed to make the hairs on the back of her neck turn to spikes. *What the hell?*

"Boss," he leveled, "why the fuck are you letting her—"

"Everyone calm down," Stock ordered. "Just calm the hell down and—"

"Have you flipped?" Growl Man snapped. "Put your lid back on."

"Okay, listen. Your cheek isn't cute anymore. You want to help? Restrain your little gal-pal, dickwad. We're landing this bird in twenty minutes, damn it, and—"

Zoe cut Stock off. By shrieking.

It was the closest description of the sound her throat made after she reached, uncapping Growl Man—who shocked her by not letting out a single growl.

And stunned her even more by looking just like—

"No."

He didn't just look like Shane. He *was* Shane.

"*No.*"

It all made such sense now. Horrible, hideous sense. His strange behavior last night after she'd told him her flight information. The way her body reacted to the vibrations beneath his careful growls just minutes ago. But she'd refused to believe it. Had denied the horror of it.

The most magical lover of her life was a criminal. Had helped to take hundreds of people hostage at thirty thousand feet. Had assisted in nearly getting them all shot out of the sky.

This isn't happening. This is your sleep-deprived mind manifesting a disgusting nightmare. Just keep standing. Reality will kick back in soon.

She continued to blink, certain it would happen. Positive he'd become someone different. An outlaw with bad breath and a broken nose. Someone without that pleasure-giving mouth. That alluring, dominant jaw. Those thick, dark waves that felt so good between her fingers...and her thighs.

"Zoe." He turned her name into a ragged prayer. "Zoe—"

"Don't," she gritted. "He's a monster, and so are you!"

He grabbed her by both elbows. She wrenched and shoved. *Run! Run!* But where? She didn't care. Anywhere, even a few feet away, would be better than what she did now, curling trembling fingers into his black shirt. What the hell *was* she doing? Even her damn hands betrayed her, reaching for the flawless muscles beneath his clothes, seeking the sweet pleasure they'd given her last night, instead of this awful nightmare.

Her whole body convulsed, combating a sob. The sound burst from her anyway.

She had to hate him now. No. She had to *forget* him. Discard everything she knew about him. *Thought* she knew.

"I can't," she rasped. "I...I...can't."

Dizziness assaulted. She held Shane tighter, watching her name cross his lips again, but couldn't hear. Her ears buzzed like a thousand cicadas had flown in. Blackness pushed at her vision, intensified by exhaustion, disbelief, fury, and heartache. She batted a hand, fighting it.

Fighting...it...

The darkness descended deeper.

Her mind surrendered. Her body followed, losing all strength. She was limp, helpless, truly part of the nightmare now. But before she tumbled completely, she felt herself smiling. Just one inhalation brought back the smell of the forest after a rainstorm...and the perfect musk of Shane's skin.

CHAPTER NINE

If life in Special Ops taught a guy anything, it was about the gap between expectations and reality. The way you practiced the mission and the way you ran it? Usually universes apart. Guns jammed. Eggbeaters crashed. The 4-1-1 was wrong. And sometimes, guys died.

Yeah. "Dead" sounded like a great choice right now.

He screwed his fist against his chest while glaring around the sparse, chilly room deep inside the complex they'd landed at, condemning himself for the morosity. When Death was a groupie in a guy's life, clinging for a chance to get in the tour bus and fuck everyone it could, it wasn't a cool idea to swing open the door and issue the bastard an invitation.

Really, idiot? Probably wasn't a hot idea to indulge a one-night stand knowing you were less than twelve hours away from hijacking an airplane, either—as part of the mission you were so invested in, you agreed to six months of deep undercover work. But you told Colton you could stay sane about this. You took the mind-fuck tests, proved you could keep all the emotions in tidy compartments. So stop wishing to buy the goddamn farm and get your shit back together.

Who was he kidding? This was about more than compartments falling apart. More than just his mind staying off the mind-fuck hamster wheel anymore.

It was about Zoe. And the way he'd messed her up in bigger ways than he'd imagined.

He set aside the smart pad that had helped confirm that conclusion, hating what he'd read in the mission files he'd pulled. The intel was a brimming bucket of corroboration for his suspicions after her words on the plane.

He's a monster, and so are you.

She'd soaked it in enough venom to poison ten men. The accusation was her Biblical truth, rooted in something deeper. Shay realized it even before she'd passed out cold in his arms.

And now, she'd been out for so long.

He didn't count the minutes she'd roused just before they landed, though he probably should have. He didn't know many women who'd stir from a dead faint, sobbing while trying to belt him, before falling under again. That had been almost an hour ago. The nurse had come and gone three times to assure Zoe was simply wiped and dehydrated, but he remained skeptical—and stressed as fuck—about that.

The combo was a perfect stage-setter for Act Two of this ordeal.

The part where scared shitless was added to the mix.

Damn it, Zoe. I can't let you slide under my skin anymore.

But that was exactly where she'd burrowed.

He let out another heavy breath. She stayed motionless against the pillows. An eerie stand-in for the vibrant *mariposa* he was used to.

Wake up, baby girl, and I'll even let you punch me.

Unable to restrain himself any longer, he slid his hand beneath hers, and found her pulse with a couple of fingers. The steady but soft beat wasn't reassuring. Could have had something to do with the IV in her arm, along with the hydration bag that still dripped fluid into her depleted body.

You need to get her out of this nightmare, asshole. Alive.

And then you need to leave her the fuck alone and let her live the rest of her life without your filthy hands all over it.

He glided his hand up to her cheek. Goddamn, she was beautiful. Even now, so much paler than usual, bronze light seemed woven into her skin. Her lips were still a collection of exotic curves. Her eyelashes were thick feathers against her cheeks.

He prayed like hell for the moment she woke up.

In the same moment, he dreaded it.

She moaned softly. Her nose scrunched, making the sapphire stud glimmer. Her brow knitted. She'd been doing that a lot. Until now, he'd successfully battled the urge to reach and stroke her discomfort away. With his fingers so close now, he didn't resist anymore.

"Mmmm." She sighed as he traced his thumb over the arches of both her brows. When he got to the end, he reversed the caress, making her repeat the sound. *Fuck.* Even the triumph of taking a little of her pain away shot new blood into his cock. Who the hell was he kidding? The arousal began the moment he'd first touched her.

Not here. Not now.

Zoe blinked slowly. Winced at the bright lights. Closed her eyes again.

"It's okay, tiny dancer." He turned his hand over, soothing her brow with his knuckles. "Take your time."

God knew, they had all the time in the world. Turned out that Cameron's "science-experiment freaks" had been moved to extra-security holding areas, probably as soon as the feds had charted the new coordinates of the hijacked plane. The twist was a blessing. It was taking Wyst a while to crack the codes into the locked-down division, where Shay was pretty sure they'd hidden Mom's lab too. During the wait on the break-in, Shay had time to ensure Zoe was okay before he rejoined Stock and the gang—and to try to clarify himself to her, as well.

That meant giving her the truth. All of it.

Now that she was here and in *this* deep on the plot, he abhorred the idea of keeping any more secrets from her. He couldn't control what she did with all the facts after he pulled back the veil, but the woman had already proven one thing to him with breathtaking certainty. Her belief in their connection. The gift of her trust and passion last night, even with just minutes of validation...he'd been humbled. He still was.

He just hoped to fuck she'd feel half the same after hearing him out.

Christ. When would this all be over?

Theoretically, it could be soon. Rejoining Stock meant he'd also be minutes from finally finding Mom. He *hoped.* The few pages of intel Colton had procured—and it was literally a few—weren't verified. Not even the spooks were allowed to know what specifically happened inside Area 51, which brought more confusion as to how the fuck Cameron had finagled *his* access beyond the base's airstrip—but sometimes curiosity and the cat really were a shitty combination.

It was best to focus on what he *could* figure out, like the request he'd put in to fate for that bowl of good-karma kitty chow. Hopefully, there'd be some vittles left over for a viable exit trail out of this place capable of handling Mom, Zoe, and everyone in her dance troupe.

Zoe pressed her head against his hand...ironically, like a kitten seeking a caress. Shay swallowed back a groan. So much for trying to run the trouser tanker on empty. As his dick threw the hammer down and rammed his pants, he threaded his fingers into her hair.

"Sssshhh, baby girl. Easy does it."

The edges of her lips tilted up. He committed the look to the most special box in his memory. "Shane..."

"Right here. I'm right here."

"Mmmm. That feels good."

"That's the idea."

The lines formed in her forehead again. She licked her lips and emitted a soft grunt before opening her eyes again. Her smile widened as she tilted her face toward his hand.

Forget the agony in his crotch. Her stare carved a canyon into his chest. He was able to return her smile only by stretching it over clenched teeth. When he'd prayed for her awakening, this was the moment he'd dreamed of. And the dread on the flip side of that? Any moment now, its justification would come too.

"Wh-Where am I?" She gazed past him, over the gray brick walls, across the sterile white floor, and down to the hospital-grade bed. When her scrutiny fell to the tube in her arm, her eyes popped wide. "*Ay Dios mio.* What happened?"

Shay took her hand again. And held on with reassuring strength. "Don't struggle for it. Trauma can be like that sometimes. Just breathe deep."

"Easy for *you* to say." Her pointed glance, referencing the fact that he was free from the tubes and monitors, almost made him chuckle. His little sarcasm factory was back. "And what do you mean, trauma?"

He stroked her knuckles with his thumb. "What do you remember last?"

"Well, I remember *you*. And us. And being together at the hotel—but then you had to leave. And I was sad." Her grip tightened in his, making his heart pick up speed. It snapped a missing piece of him into place to be needed by her—but how much longer would he get to enjoy it? "Didn't sleep much after I talked to Ryder." She bit her lip. "We only talked for ten minutes, I swear."

The canyon in his chest turned into a fucking gorge. "I believe you."

"The next morning, I got Brynn and El, and we got on the plane to come home. And then—"

He felt his lips dip.

Here came the nightmare.

Her fingers twisted harder. Her face contorted. "Oh, *Dios*. And then...oh, God...those men..."

She wrenched her hand away. Scrambled backward in the bed. Once she slammed against the wall, she lifted a leg and kicked at him.

"Zoe. Calm down."

"*You!* Oh my God, Shane. You—"

"Can explain," he fired back. "If you'll just—"

"You can *explain*? *Caramba*. Are you serious?" Her voice cracked as she hugged herself. The machines berated the air with beeps. The IV stand rocked, tugging at the tube in her wrist.

It was time to throw down another hammer. The one with the *D* on it. For *Dom*.

"Calm. The. Hell. Down."

On the first syllable, he stood. On the second, he steadied the IV stand. On the third, he wrapped an unyielding hand around her left ankle. With the last, he secured her right.

She didn't like it. Not one fucking bit. Her chest pumped on furious breaths. Her eyes brimmed with tears, their oceans turned to pain-filled seas. As Shay forced her to lie back, the muscles in her legs bunched, still fighting him.

Because there wasn't *enough* tension in the room, the door popped open and a gentle-faced woman in a nurse's smock appeared. In the two seconds he had to do so, Shay pressed Zoe's eyes closed, commanding her to feign sleep again. Though every inch of her body was still taut, she picked up on the hint. Thank fuck.

"Hey-dee ho," the nurse greeted.

"Justine." Shay kept his reply cordial but brief. In the hour he'd known her, it was glaringly clear Justine had a schoolgirl thing for Stock and was texting him updates every ten minutes. "What's up?"

"Is everything okey dokey?" She flashed a smile more fake than a toothpaste ad. "Miss Chestain's monitor board just lit up like Christmas morning."

"Just a bad dream," Shay supplied. "She was all over the place. I managed to calm her down."

The answer seemed to mollify the woman. For now. "Well, let's hope she *dreams* about waking up soon. Cameron's made his good faith move with those government goons by freeing all the passengers except those dancers. Last bus left about fifteen minutes ago. That means every one of those dancers is an important hostage now. He'll want her back with the others as soon as possible." With a nod, she added, "Besides, it shows them he's organized. Has his logistics straight."

Shay was damn certain Justine wouldn't know a mission logistics chart from the Periodic Table of Elements, but he shot her a grin and a thumbs-up, which satisfied her enough to leave.

As soon as the door shut, he braced himself for Zoe's reaction to the information she'd just overhead. Sure enough, she bolted up like a wildcat pushed by a hurricane. "Hostages?"

He framed her shoulders in his hands and impaled her gaze with his. Goddamn, this wasn't easy. He yearned to get lost in those midnight irises of hers. For her own good and his, he twined his response into a command. "You need to calm the hell down, baby girl, or Justine will come back in and fiddle with all this shit herself."

She sagged in his hold. Pained lines crossed her face. After she took several deep breaths, she rasped, "Tell me. And spare the damn sugar."

Once more, she blew his mind in a brand-new way. What the woman had been through today would have turned most women into a quivering puddle under the table. Not Zoe. She sat like the hospital bed was a boulder in the Kunar Province, demanding the truth without the whipped cream and cherries. And damn it, that was what she'd earned.

"You're a smart woman, Zoe. You know by now that the second Newport knows there aren't any innocent lives at stake, he's going after Stock with the intention of annihilation."

As she nodded, the stark room lighting picked up the prisms in her new tears. "Sure. And the most heart-wrenching *innocents* are pretty young dancers, right? We make for damn good *Breaking News*. So he released everyone else and kept us." Her shoulders stiffened, and she lifted a glittering glower. "And you helped him."

Shay tensed too. Battling her glare with his. Fighting himself with the rest of his body. Fuck, how he wanted to just lean over and kiss her, win her over with the power of his passion as a John Williams symphony swelled and the credits rolled over their happy ever after.

But this wasn't the goddamn movies. Things couldn't be fixed by a lip-lock, some fireworks, and a Hollywood wrap. He had to try to make her understand—before he got her out of this mess and safely back to her life.

That meant he had to start with the truth.

"You helped him," she repeated. "With all of it. Didn't you?" In spite of her tears, every word she spoke was a harsh bite.

"I did." His response came out with firm calm. Some CO in his past had once yelled, during the last mile of a long PT run, that the end of an ordeal was often when one gained the most clarity. Since he'd always kind of enjoyed those runs, he'd never understood the truth of it—until now.

"And you knew what flight it was the night before, didn't you? That was what your text messages in the bar were about."

"As stated, you're a very smart woman."

She returned his attempt at a smile with a disgusted glower. "So our time together, was that some kind of a perverted fun time for you? An extra twist to the Dom game, sexing up a woman before terrorizing her at thirty thousand feet?"

With a clamp of his jaw, he harnessed his frustration. Her conclusion was understandable. And now, if he had anything to say about it, erasable. "I had no idea you'd be on that flight until you mentioned it in the hotel room, after our fireworks finally faded." *And I could barely feel my toes after the magnificence of it.*

She snorted softly. "About the time you decided to bolt."

"And tried to talk you into catching a later flight."

Pain flared anew in her gaze. "You didn't try that hard.

You going to blame the fading fireworks for that too?"

He took the risk of releasing one of her feet in order to guide her hand across to his chest. "To be honest, baby girl, you left behind a lot of live embers."

She huffed so hard, it almost became a laugh. "For a guy who's so good between the sheets, your timing really sucks elsewhere."

"No shit."

Her expression softened. She really was an insightful woman. "You're conflicted about being involved with him, aren't you?"

Shay took a deep breath. Here went nothing. Or perhaps everything. But knowing the nursing station had only a video surveillance monitor, which Justine had been using for the latest episode of *Dance Moms* the last time he checked, this could be his only chance for full disclosure with Zoe.

"He's a monster, a murderer, and a world-class cocksucker on several other levels," he professed. "And as long as I'm dropping your jaw, I know exactly how *you* know that. I know about how Stock played the boys in the First Special Forces Group as a double agent, setting the trap for them that included Ethan Archer and Ava Chestain—your sister. And I know how the bastard and his buddies bribed Archer to dance to their tune by almost unleashing a thousand bees on your sister, making certain her epi pen for her allergy to them was nowhere nearby."

"*Mierda.*" The word quivered as much as her fingers, still pressed between his hand and his chest.

"I understand now why you clocked him," he went on. "Though I've been wanting to do the same thing for months, so now I'm jealous as fuck."

She drew her hand back. He let her. He'd just thrown some wild revelations at her, and the biggest was yet to come.

"Why?" she blurted at last. "Why do you know all this? *How* do you know all this?"

Shay paused to make sure he regulated every note of his reply. "Read it while you were sleeping. In the final mission report."

She arched sarcastic brows. "'Final mission report,' huh? Which you...what...conveniently pulled off the internet between checking your Facebook and watching videos of masturbating cats?"

He couldn't help quirking his lips. "As intriguing as the cats sound, I used a simpler firewall."

Her brows descended. "Firewall? How? Why?"

"Well, everyone needs a good cover story, especially reading detailed shit off a classified mission report."

She nodded with mock understanding. "Sure. The one you obtained with your magical, ultra-high security clearance, right?"

He took another long breath. Her suspicion pegged right at the center of his expectations, justifying his decision to come clean. He desperately hoped she saw enough of his honesty—as well as the connection, compassion, and care he still had for her—to know he was being totally real. "I know it sounds crazy. But I don't have to worry about clearance, Zoe."

She straightened a little. Cocked her head to regard him carefully again, her eyes glinting as if she'd already crayoned the outlines for this picture and now waited for help on coloring in the shapes. "How?"

"Because I'm Special Forces too."

Fuck, it felt good to say it again. *Yeah. I am one of the good guys.* Part of him even wondered if she'd been clever enough to piece it all together, though that possibility worried him. Zoe was one of the most perceptive people he'd met, but if she could sniff out his cover, there was a chance one of Cameron's guys would too.

Needless to say, her shocked blinks came as reassuring signs. And sexy triggers. "What? Are you joking?"

He leaned more closely over her. At the same time, he lowered his voice a couple of decibels. "My name isn't Shane Burnett. I'm not really a random businessman who uses LAX as my second home, and I usually don't get to sit around the bar there—or the bar anywhere—waiting for my dream woman to appear." He warmed his tone and stared deeper into her eyes, ensuring she didn't harbor a single doubt about the subject of his assertion. "My real name is Sergeant Shay Bommer. I proudly serve with the US Army's Seventh Special Forces Group—except for the last six months, in which I've been deep undercover with Stock and his shitheads, on voluntary 'loan' to the CIA."

"The CIA!"

He flattened a finger over her lips. Nevertheless, she repeated it in a harsh whisper.

"The spooks actually have exclusive SFG battalions assigned for their use on missions that require our soldiers' training in things like unconventional warfare and negotiation tactics," he explained. "But this inroad to Stock happened as a result of intel *I* brought to *them*, based on digging I'd been doing on my own."

Her features pursed with skepticism again. He really wished it didn't make her so damn beguiling. "Digging?" she quipped. "What, in your *secret spare time* on a few missions?"

He laughed on top of a grunt. "There's more of it than you think. And this particular search...was important to me."

It shouldn't have surprised him that she picked up on the subtle emotion that snuck into his voice, causing her to press her hand over his. Shouldn't have, but it did. Pleasantly so. "Why?" she followed up.

Shay lifted her hand and twined his fingers through hers. She'd insisted on the truth from him. He'd vowed she'd always get it now, no matter how difficult the information. But in this instance, he was damn glad he'd made that promise—and finally had someone he no longer had to hide the words from.

"Because, after eighteen years, I think I've finally found where Cameron Stock has been hiding my mother."

CHAPTER TEN

Zoe didn't say anything for a long moment. She couldn't.

Every word he spoke was true. She saw it in every tormented facet of his gaze. Felt it in every inch of pressure from his touch.

Which opened the floodgates on a new skirmish in her own soul. *Mierda.* She'd barely learned the man's name—which she'd learned *wasn't* his name—before stripping and sleeping with him last night! No. That was no ordinary we're-stuck-here-so-let's-fuck-here little appointment. She'd opened herself to him, exposed something she'd sworn never to show anyone again. Her submissive soul and all the vulnerability that went with it.

But who the hell had she entrusted herself to? Shane or Shay? Who the hell had shown up in that hotel room last night to rule her body with such knowing dominance, to capture her soul with such perfect care? Had she given herself to a man who didn't exist? And what did her confidence in him last night reflect about her now? Had she become the blind-trust idiot she'd always cautioned Ava from turning into?

Unbelievably, the chaos of her heart yielded an answer.

Perhaps the man's name hadn't been real last night. Perhaps the clothes on his muscled back weren't his own and the ID in his pocket was forged. But none of those things could cancel out what *was* the truth—the connection of her senses to his. The bridge of energy between their gazes. The electricity, sweet yet sizzling, in every touch they shared. The flawless fulfillment of welcoming his body into hers. The exquisite knowledge of surrendering everything to him.

Bridges. Sparks. Fulfillment. Surrender.

Everything she'd sought for months with Bryce—and found in an hour with Shay.

So yeah, she believed him.

And right away, she knew it was one of the best decisions she'd made in a very long while.

But believing him and comprehending him were two different things, actions much further apart than she thought.

He hadn't seen his mom for *eighteen* years. That was only two more than her, but knowing one's mother was really dead, as opposed to knowing she still lived yet never getting to be with her...

To her confusion, tears sprang again. Because of him. *For* him.

Damn him.

Connection or not, he'd deceived her on a bunch of levels. And while she recognized his reasoning, that didn't justify letting him back into her soul now. The man's life was a mess. He'd helped turn hers into one too. But she had to believe this ordeal would be over soon—and once life was back to a semblance of normal, she didn't need any extra illusions about him hanging out, mucking her judgment. It was best to just let him clear the air, since he was so willing. It would be good for them both.

"Tell me." She repeated her command of five minutes ago, gazing directly at him to emphasize the follow-up hadn't changed. *And spare the damn sugar.*

Shane—*Shay*—curled his other hand around hers. In the

fervency of his hold, she comprehended so much. She felt the miles and months of sacrifice he'd endured before this moment, instantly reconnecting to him.

"It's probably best to start at the beginning." He uttered it like an apology.

She smiled back. "I don't scare that easily, Sergeant Shay Bommer." She lifted her arm, dragging her IV and monitor lines with it. "And I'm not going anywhere."

"Okay, then. Ready or not..." He drew in a deep, hard breath. "It begins with my mom and dad. They met when she was conducting some cutting-edge projects at the Naval Research Lab in DC. He was a base guard, assigned to walk her home every night. They both liked classic movies, going to the zoo, and wishing for a simpler life. Over the course of her year assignment there, they fell in love. I always knew that, always felt that soul connection they had, but as the years went by, it was clear that Mom's *brain* needed a lot more feeding than what my dad, my brother, and I could provide, in the middle of a tiny town in Idaho. She started going into Boise on Saturdays, taking long trips to the library, attending scientific lectures at the university..." He pressed his fingers a little tighter around hers. "It made Dad tense. Maybe a little more than tense. Saturdays started to be his drinking days."

Zoe sighed and pulled his hands closer to her heart. "That doesn't sound like a fun weekend."

He attempted a shrug. "He always sobered up before she got back home, but after a while, Tait and I started making excuses to be gone on Saturdays."

Damn. She got weepy again. After quickly palming her cheeks, she rasped, "*Dios.* Sorry."

"Don't be." He quirked up one side of his mouth while

thumbing away the tears at the corner of hers.

"Go on before I decide to really like the way you said that and end up mauling you instead of listening to you."

He let the other side curl up. "Don't you mean letting *me* maul *you*?"

"I stand corrected." She tried to filter out her creamy undertone, but the feat was impossible when his eyes warmed like buttered rum. "Move on, Sergeant, before Justine comes tearing back in here because my monitors are going Gangnam on her."

He groaned. "Right. On to the relevant shit, as my brother would say."

She brushed away a bunch of hair that had fallen into his eyes. "How long did the awkward Saturdays go on for?"

"Little over a year." Painful shadows appeared in his gaze, but he blinked them away. "By that time, I was just past eight years old and Tait was waiting to turn ten. That was when things got interesting."

She frowned. "They weren't already?"

"I'm just getting started, remember? One day, Mom received a call—a summons, really—to go to Washington. The Pentagon, to be exact."

"Whoa."

"Right?" He grinned wider. "Tait and I thought it was hot shit, at least."

She couldn't help tossing in half a giggle. "How long was she there?"

"A long time. Well, at least to us. About two weeks. But man, when she got home, we wondered if she hadn't gone to some miracle spa, instead. Our mother was a different woman."

She liked the little tug at one side of his mouth and felt

herself emulating it. "How so?"

"She had this new...light. I know it sounds corny, but it's true. She was excited all the time. Really happy." His grin softened into a wistful half smile. "Things changed fast after that. *Really* fast."

"How so?"

"By the following week, there were workmen all over our backyard. They converted the old tool barn into a bio-lab for Mom's use."

"You're right." Zoe blinked a couple of times. "That's fast."

"No shit." A soft laugh touched his lips now. She didn't complain about having to watch it. She'd never get tired of gazing at his mouth, just as she'd never forget what it felt like when taking over hers... "Of course, Tait and I thought it was the hugest adventure ever, and—what?"

His question came as she gave in to a careful frown. "Tait," she repeated. "Tait...Bommer." Amazement zinged through her. "*Caramba*. Your brother's in the same battalion with Ethan Archer, my sister's fiancé."

"Bingo," he replied, "at least until last July. Tait's taken an assignment with a new team."

"You don't look like a proud little brother about that." Even a blind person would've noticed the about-face of his demeanor.

"Oh, I'm proud as hell. He's damn good at his job. Just wish that detail didn't include hunting *me*."

"So he doesn't know you're undercover."

"Nobody does outside the CIA assets I've been working with—and now you."

Zoe forced down a long breath to calm her careening pulse. Even without the purposeful regard he gave her, the meaning of his statement wouldn't have been lost. And the honor. He was entrusting her with his most valuable secrets. The keys to his kingdom.

To his life.

"So I take it he believes what a lot of the world does now? That you've pulled a Judas and taken up with the enemy?"

"Worse," he returned. "The enemy who helped kill the woman he loved. But T's always had a weak spot for drama. The week the G-boys took over our tool shed, Tait was convinced they were enlisting Mom to design a new bomb inside."

"Was she?" After the insane twists her life had taken in the last twenty-four hours, Zoe would believe just about anything short of aliens from cheese planets. And perhaps even that, given the setting for this stolen moment.

"Wrong field. Mom was a bio-scientist, not a chemical or explosive engineer. Didn't matter to Tait, no matter how many times she told him. Even after she punished him for trying to float the story at Sunday School, he kept it alive on the regular school playground, turning us both into mini celebrities for a while." He attempted another laugh but didn't get very far. "It helped a little, I guess. Distracted us from the tension that was really going down at home."

Zoe sighed in empathy. "Sounds like things weren't going great."

"They weren't," he replied. "The lab was the beginning of the end. To get even more cliché, it was the best of times and the worst of times. On one hand, we'd never had it so good financially. Whatever Mom was doing, the feds considered it worthy. We had two new cars, repairs to the house, an in-ground pool, all the video-game shit we could ever ask for...not that we went home to enjoy it much, after Dad decided *every* day was Saturday."

"Shit," Zoe mumbled. "Really?"

His affirming nod was tight. "At least he could buy the good stuff, right? Pickling one's liver on a daily basis is so much easier with high-end hooch."

"But it wasn't like your mom could tell the feds to take a flying leap, either. They clearly needed her help, and it was important."

Shay stunned her by suddenly pulling his focus. His gaze lost its reminiscent haze, beaming into her like a golden laser. "You really *are* all about being a good girl, aren't you?"

She straightened against the pillows, arching her brows. "There's nothing wrong with that."

"Not a goddamn thing, beautiful."

So much for indignation. It was difficult not to enjoy the heat of his stare. Except for *Papi*, nobody had ever acknowledged her "responsibility fetish" as a good thing. It felt nice. Better than nice.

"So what happened then?" she prompted. "Things were good but not so good. Your mom was building a bomb in the garage—"

"Yeah." He laughed it out, though his mouth was the only thing carrying the ball on the sentiment. "Damn. She was a lot like you, Zoe, at least what I can remember of her. She was smart, funny... She always smelled good too, like Juicy Fruit and sunshine...and she was so, so beautiful." The misty overlay returned to his eyes. "Dad never stopped telling her that, either. Even when things got weird, he told her how beautiful she was."

The middle of her chest burst into butterflies as his smile finally climbed to his eyes. "*Amor mágico*," she murmured.

"*Sí?*"

Shay gave the stud in her nose a gentle tap. "*Sí.*"

"What did she call him?"

"Her handsome stud." He shrugged as she giggled. "Yeah, it was the corniest of the corn fests. T and I gave them shit for it once we understood the mush, but they didn't stop. He loved her despite the work demands, and she loved him despite the booze." His lips contorted for a second. "That was why so much didn't make sense to me, when I looked back and tried to put it all together. I mean, after Homer started hanging out with us, and—"

"Whoa. Pause button. Ummm...Homer?"

"Sorry," he muttered. "Sprinting ahead of the pack, huh?"

"A little." She squeezed his hand in reassurance. "Who was Homer? A *friend* from DC?"

"You could say that." A discomfited air rolled off him. "The suits were always sending specialists, a new round every week. It was a revolving door of government geeks. But one of them stayed longer than just a week."

"Homer."

"Right."

"So he was a 'special' specialist?"

"Hell, no. He was another government tool, like the rest. Standard-issue haircut, standard-issue personality. His name was Homer, for fuck's sake. He ate Bacon Bits on everything, including his cereal. But when he and Mom hit the lab together, I guess something pretty cool happened."

"I assume it wasn't Tait's beloved bomb."

"To our minds, it was way better. The entrenchment of Homer also meant we got a new fringe bennie."

"Which was...?"

"A menagerie."

Zoe blinked. "As in, animals?"

"Yeah, for real. They came and went, of course—and at first, T and I were a pair of kid-power protesters, thinking the creatures were being used for *nefarious* purposes—but Mom ensured us they were making the animals better with their research, not worse." He gave a lopsided grin. "We were relieved when she was right."

"So Homer and the menagerie became fixtures."

"Bingo," he confirmed. "One week turned into two, then three, then a few months. Mom and Homez—that's what T and I finally started calling him—literally invented a geek-speak language of their own around the project."

She leaned toward him, more fascinated by his story with each minute. "Do you remember any of it?"

He grimaced. "I've tried, but we were kids. If it didn't mention Transformers, Nintendo, or the Husky we hoped Homez would let us keep as a pet one day, we weren't into the grown-up chatter. But I remember their excitement. They were onto something big." Though his tone was steeped in pride, his tight frown lingered. "Dad saw it too—so much that he actually invited the guy over for dinner twice a week."

Zoe didn't hide her surprise. "Generous."

"He wanted to make Mom happy, even if that meant gutting his sanity to make it happen." He deepened her bewilderment by ticking up one side of his mouth. "And she kept loving him, though the drinking got worse."

"So things were a teeny bit dysfunctional."

"We're all a little dysfunctional, Zoe. The goal is to simply find someone who balances yours out."

For a long second, she couldn't decide whether to smirk in

cynicism or frown in disbelief. "Okay, so they were...balanced. Right up until the day Homer left, right?"

"Right."

"And she left with him."

"No."

"What?"

"No." There wasn't a note of hesitation in his voice. "Gotcha, didn't I?"

She surrendered to a baffled smile. "It's not a very typical story." She paused for a moment as another thought struck. "Though nothing's been very *typical* since the moment I met you, Shay Bommer."

She knew better than to get used to the name—both their lives might depend on her keeping up with the ruse that he was Shane Burnett—but the sampling felt nice on her lips. Probably too nice. The man himself was no help for her resolve, moving a hand to her cheek and then caressing the trail of her hairline. Beautiful shivers came, racing all over her scalp, but why'd they have to find their way to the expanding bud between her thighs too? She swallowed hard, forcing herself from moaning at him in abject need...and then bucking her hips up in open invitation...

"You've been so damn brave, Zoe," he murmured. "So strong. Just like Mom was...especially after Homer left."

"What happened?" *You can now return to the innocuous part of our programming, everyone. Thank God.* "Did they finish the project? Or did Washington just summon him back?"

"Neither." He spoke it with certainty. "My research doesn't bear it out, and neither do my memories."

"Okay," she returned. "What *do* you remember?"

"Fights. Bad ones."

She pressed her hand over his when shadows took over his face. "Ugh," she whispered. "So your dad and Homer finally had enough of the gentleman's agreement?"

"Oh, no. It wasn't my *dad* and Homez. It was Mom."

"And Homer?" She didn't hide her bafflement. "But why? Weren't they going to be the new Fonteyn and Nureyev of science?"

"Who and who?"

She couldn't help a beguiled smile. He really was such a big, burly military hunk. Her imagination went off like a sparkler, thinking about all the classic dance videos she wanted to make him sit through. "Maybe one day, I'll have the chance to enlighten you."

"Maybe one day." His gaze turned a soft butterscotch, threatening her focus yet again.

"What happened?" she forced out. "Between your mom and Homer?"

The softness dissolved from his gaze. Then his whole face. "I don't know," he admitted. "Their fights were loud enough to wake Tait and me, but the dialogue itself...either it was too muffled by the lab walls or I just don't remember." He shook his head. "But after the dustups, Mom would bawl and Homez would leave."

"Back to DC?" she ventured.

"That's what we assumed." He pulled his hand away to rub the back of his neck. "It got to be that his time there outweighed his days in the lab with Mom. She was miserable."

A huge fist lodged beneath her ribs. "And your dad definitely noticed."

"Every second," he confirmed. "Finally, after one really bad blowup, Homez bugged out for good. Took everything except Scout, the dog. By that point, we were all kind of relieved. Even Mom." His shoulders clenched. "But Dad didn't see it that way."

The fist punched hard, banishing her breath. "Oh, no..."

His shoulders clenched. "He was drunk," he muttered. "And she was distraught. Conclusions were reached. His temper blew."

"Shay," she rasped. "*Lo siento.* I'm so sorry."

"It wasn't the last time." He flattened his lips, as if berating himself simply for the defensive tone, before going on. "But for some reason, *every* time, she just took it. Fuck, Tait and I were so angry—at her as much as him."

She gulped. At least there were no tears to worry about this time. The grief in her heart tore past the realm of tears. She ached for the little boys he and Tait had been, forced to become men far too fast. "And I'll bet you both tried to stand up to him."

"Fuck, yeah. Of course. But one time, she actually screamed at us to stop. She said..."

"What?" she rasped into his lead-heavy pause.

"She said we were only making it worse."

"*Ay.*" She shoved back her bitterness to ask, "What did you do then?"

He squeezed his neck harder. "What *could* we do? We moved the hell on and tried to stay out of Dad's way as much as possible, especially after she disappeared in the middle of the night, about three months later."

For a second, she let her jaw plummet in freefall. "She just left? No note? No goodbye? No explanation?"

"Oh, there was an explanation. It came from Drake Bommer, who was happy to tell us about the 'stone-hearted bitch' who'd left us and him for Homer, the hunk of scientific hotness. Thanks to his new bestie, Mr. Jim Beam, we had the treat of hearing that one over and over—and *over*."

"*Higueputa*," she spat. *Son of a bitch.*

"It wasn't an easy time for him."

"Are you making *excuses* for the *cabrón*?"

"You think that's what this is?" He nailed his stare back into her. "He was a shit, okay? No pardons for that. But he was also a Bommer—and if I've come to understand anything about that while growing up, it's that his pain ran through deep fucking canyons." He pulled in air through his nose, bitterness still gleaming from his gaze. "Thanks to Cameron Stock, I almost lost my brother to those same canyons last year."

"Don't forget the fine example your father set," she grumbled.

"Well, Tait pulled through. He let his heart, his character, his stubbornness—and yeah, the love of a great woman—take him to a better place. I'm damn proud of him."

Her heart clenched once more. He and Tait were as tight as she and her sister. Like Ava and her, they'd had to be. Would she be as strong if she'd lost Ava's devotion, even temporarily? Would she be strong enough to keep such a huge secret from her sibling? The conflict had to be tearing at Shay.

"So what did you two do then?" she queried, hoping to refocus him. "You had someone to go to, right? Someone to talk to?"

He actually laughed. "We were *boys*, Zoe. The sons of an alcoholic abuser, at that. We sucked it up and moved on because we had to. We were old enough to know that *talking to someone* would likely mean being placed into separate foster homes faster than you can say *ay caramba*."

159

His words forged new hardness in his face. Zoe watched the transformation in wonder. She and Shay had to be near each other in chronological age, but he suddenly seemed eons older. "So you clung to each other for strength," she whispered.

He reeled back a little. "Don't get carried away, Miss Tiptoe Tulips. I don't *cling* to that dork-ass for anything. He smells like a goat and he snores."

Just like that, the man again melted her like a brick of chocolate in the sun. She gazed up at him, hoping her face conveyed the depth of her gratitude for his honesty in revealing his past and his bravery in confronting it for himself.

"Thank you for clearing that up, Sir."

He grinned and bestowed a deep kiss to her mouth. "You're most welcome, baby girl."

She yanked on his shirt, keeping him near for one more moment. "I mean *all* of it."

He kissed her again. A little longer. A lot deeper. "I know."

"So, what happened then?" she asked. "How did you two little men do your *not*-clinging-to-each-other thing?"

"We carried on. Went to school. Kept our noses clean. Worked hard. We had *one* angel on our side, our Uncle Jonah, who took care of crap like signing the school papers and making sure we even got to school—*every* day. No such thing as ditching when Uncle Jonah was around. We made that mistake only once. Shit wasn't pretty."

She brushed her knuckles down the side of his face. "Did you get to have *any* fun?"

"Hell, yeah. Mrs. Verona, our neighbor, sometimes let us help her bake cookies. And once a week, we treated ourselves to the half-price movies. They didn't show the latest shit, but they showed the best. Every Saturday, we survived on a cultural diet of Stallone, Willis, and Schwarzenegger. Take a wild guess what we both wanted to be when we grew up."

She added her grin to his. "Special Forces?"

When Shay nodded, somberness stomped back across his face. "It was good timing for both of us. In Tait's senior year of high school, Dad's liver finally gave out. By the middle of that summer, I took the equivalency exam and became a grad, too. Uncle Jonah put us up for six months while we sucked raw eggs for breakfast and trained like goddamn Olympians, preparing for the physical requirements of the job.

"By the time we signed up for the big green machine, we were ready. We didn't make it a secret to anyone that Special Forces was our ultimate goal. They all told us we were crazy to think we'd both make it past the cuts, but we did." His gaze sobered by another degree. "It was harder for Tait than me—I saw it in every step he trudged and test he took—but damn, I was proud of him. He hung in there, sometimes literally by the skin of his teeth. He's a stubborn fucker.

"For the next few years, life became a blur of working hard and playing harder. When I wasn't training for or actually out on an op, I was increasingly fascinated by the connection that BDSM offered."

Zoe slipped her hand to his neck and squeezed. "Connection. I like that description too."

He scraped his fingers across the back of her hand. "I know."

Before she succumbed to the longing to pull him down and mash their mouths again, she probed, "So what led you to start looking for your mom?" The question was hard to get out. There was a good chance he'd explain that he'd been involved with someone else and the importance of that relationship led to the desire of completing his psychological circle with his mother. She didn't enjoy even the concept of Shay with somebody else, period.

Stop it. Crazy circumstances aside, you've known the man less than twenty-four hours. It was nice with him. It is nice with him. But he's a Special Forces soldier with a thousand other priorities higher than you, including the mission he's on right now. Get over it. Get over him. *Now.*

"It was an act of fate, I think," he started, in answer to her question. Oh, great. *An act of fate.* Here it came. "My CO pulled some strings and secured me ten days of leave in order to be with Tait after the conclusion of that insane op they accomplished in LA. T was a train wreck. Just needed to talk about a lot of shit. Needless to say, Stock's name came up a lot in the conversation. It nagged at me. I knew I'd seen Stock's name well before that.

"Well, one morning, the dots connected. A few months prior, I'd screwed up the nuts to go through the last of Dad's shit. One of the boxes actually turned out to be Mom's. It looked like a lot of old notes from the lab, pages of scribbled shit and scientific formulas that all could've been written in Chinese for all the sense they made to me—but there were lots of names in the notes too."

"And Stock's was one of them," she supplied.

He touched a finger to his nose, indicating she was right. "I didn't think anything of it when I went through the box—just wrote him off as one of the Pentagon's financial guys. But one morning in the shower at T's, everything slammed together, and—" He stopped when he noticed her expanding grin. "What is it?"

"Sorry." She couldn't help the provocative bite to her

bottom lip. "I'm stuck on the part where things slammed together in the shower."

His lips curled up too. He trailed a hand down to her hip. "Are you telling me you're not such a good girl after all, Miss Chestain?"

"I have no idea what you mean, Sergeant Bommer."

He brushed his lips across hers. "Any other time or place, I'd call your bullshit on that, baby girl."

The sandpaper he'd scrubbed over his voice rubbed her in so many new places, in so many right ways. Against her better instincts, Zoe sighed, arched, and pushed her hip higher into his touch. Shay didn't miss the opportunity to grasp more of her flesh, kneading her with spread fingers before heating every drop of her blood with his rough moan.

"This is crazy, right?" she rasped.

When he responded with a silent nod, she knew he understood. Not just the word she used but everything she encompassed with it.

Crazy.

Two syllables that stood for so much more. Like every electron that ignited the air between them. Every perfect minute of the power they'd exchanged with each other last night. And in a strange, sweet way, every day of every year that had guided their life paths to collide in that one airport bar, on that fogged-in night, in a city known more for fabricating connections than really having any. And a final twist, carrying them to the most secret section of desert in the world. Throwing them together once more.

Throwing them?

Or *placing* them?

Yes. Crazy.

And extraordinary. And incredible. And so damn good.

Okay, so things with him weren't going to end with a marriage proposal. But things with him were also...unlike they'd been with anyone else. He saw every part of her. The good girl and the bad girl. The lioness who guarded her inner kitten. The She-Ra who so desperately craved the chance to be a submissive one more time.

Who yearned to be *his* submissive one more time.

"Shay?" Half of it was drowned in her breath instead of her voice.

He lowered his forehead to hers. "Yeah?"

"I'm technically still your hostage, right?"

Every tendon in his perfect muscles stiffened. He released the tension by measured increments, reminding her once more of a mountain lion. Carefully coiled. Hypnotically lethal. "Yeah, baby girl. You definitely are."

His breath heated her lips as he slid his beautiful fingers along her inner thigh. He brought his thumb up, rubbing into the valley there, pushing her open a little more for him. *Caramba.* She almost lost her nerve to press on. Almost.

"So, technically...you can do whatever you want with me... right?"

Nothing changed about him except the aroused tic in his jaw. *Mierda*, she adored that tic. "Is that what you want, baby girl?"

"I'm the hostage. What I want doesn't matter....*Sir.*"

The other side of his jaw gained a tic. She didn't have time to revel in it, though; Shay swept his hips between hers with such stunning speed, even her gasp of astonishment was submerged beneath the harsh grunt of his command. Maybe three seconds had passed, but she treasured each one, knowing he'd understood her emphasis on his title with the crystal insight he had into her needs, her desires, her soul.

She'd given him one word but meant so many more. With her raised eyes and soft smile, she added an underline to all of them.

Take me.

Fill me.

Dominate me.

Please.

CHAPTER ELEVEN

With his heartbeat filling his throat and his blood swelling his cock, Shay slammed a finger to the comm piece at his ear, sending an exclusive hail to Justine's nurse station. As he'd hoped, the woman picked up instantly. As he also hoped, her game show hostess voice seemed a little forced. Things must have been getting intense on *Dance Moms.*

"Good day, Shane. What can I do for you?"

"Lock the door and turn off Miss Chestain's monitors. I'll take responsibility for her condition now."

"Oh! Is she awake?"

"Those were orders, Justine, not requests. Do it."

"Of course." He allowed himself a beat of relief. While Justine's devotion to Stock tiptoed down the path of fanaticism, the woman couldn't be totally blind to the kind of pigs he hired. One of them wanting a quick "sample" of a hot little hostage should have barely lifted her brows. In the end, it didn't. The nurse clicked off the comm with businesslike speed.

Shay jerked the line free from his ear and then tossed it to the mattress behind him. With his other hand, he snatched the monitors off Zoe's fingers but stopped her from pulling the line free from her IV tube.

"Leave it in," he commanded. "I need you good and hydrated, baby girl."

Warmth suffused him at the upturn of her exotic lips—and yeah, about a hundred pounds more pressure to his dick—but in that moment, she gave him more. So much more. For the first time in six months, he was free of every mask he'd had to wear, pretense he'd had to erect, and lie he'd had to tell. The step was surreal, a moment he'd often lost hope of ever experiencing. It washed him in pure euphoria. And terror.

Zoe, noticing every moment of that conflict on his face, pulled him down again. "And I need you to keep being honest with me," she murmured. "So out with it." Hastily she amended, "*Please*, Sir...out with it."

He pressed a long kiss to the sumptuous flower of her lips before pushing her legs apart with his knees. "You're still the hostage, baby girl—but I'm not still your abductor."

She bit her bottom lip, adorably somber. "I'm not sure I—"

"I'm not Shane Burnett." The bark was harsher than he intended. He nipped at her nose as a softening measure. "With you, I can't ever be him again. Do you understand that?"

Her head tilted. "The only differences I see between you and *Shane* are a nice suit, a designer wallet, and a cell phone that wouldn't leave you alone last night. Gucci and Prada are just window dressing to me, and your cell is probably Stock's, which sure as hell doesn't make it important to me. So what's your problem, Bommer?"

He almost laughed. Her clarity astounded him. Humbled him. And he wished he could take it as the complete truth. "My beautiful little dancer," he murmured, "there's a significant difference...you didn't quite catch."

He filled the pause in his assertion by fitting the ridge of his body against the perfect triangle of hers. Zoe gasped, her gaze widening and her torso arching, giving him a perfect eyeful of her sweet breasts. "Ohhh," she moaned. "*That.*"

"Uh-uh." The denial was hell to get out. Every corner of

his mouth was poised to give her a groaning *uh-huh* instead. "That's not the difference I'm talking about."

"*Ay Dios mios*," she mewled. "It's...it's not?"

Damn it. The woman continued her undulations like she was a cloud and his chest her sky, inciting him to react with equal ferocity. Driven by a gust of heated lust, he shoved at the hem of her T-shirt until her bra was exposed. The contrast of the cream lace against her copper skin incinerated his control. He shoved back both cups, revealing the perfect mahogany discs that gave rise to erect dark brown tips.

"Difference number one." He paused long enough to open his mouth against one firm swell, soaking her nipple with the flat of his tongue. "Shay isn't a goddamn gentleman like Shane. Not when it comes to your beautiful tits."

"Ohhhh." It was the only sound she gave as he shifted to her other breast, this time dragging the tip out with the force of his teeth. Her moan lifted into a scream. Her hands, roaming under his shirt, turned into claws against his spine.

"Difference number two," he snarled, scratching his own fingernails up to both sides of her jaw, where he dug his fingers in deep. "I love hearing these lips scream, and I don't care who hears you. I love being the one who's made you sound that way."

Her eyes, wide and wild and stormy, dilated beneath his scrutiny. Frantic air sliced from her lungs as she surged her hips for him, locking her thighs on his. Her body was a full tempest, begging for more of his control. Her spirit was a hurricane, blasting him with merciless gusts and ruthless rain. He accepted it all with open gratitude. She was his storm and he was her god, about to give her energy back with a thousand times more passion and life than where she'd started. He couldn't wait to watch.

"Yes," she rasped as he pressed her harder into the bed, shifting his mouth to her neck, suckling with his teeth and tongue.

"You like this?" He bit into the delicious curve of her ear.

"Ohhh," she moaned. "Yesssss."

"And this?" He shoved a hand against her scalp and yanked hard on her thick, silky strands.

"*Damn.*" The column of her neck undulated as she swallowed. "Yes, Sir."

"And you liked the way Shane did all of this last night too? And the way he fucked you afterward?"

"Yes, yes!"

He rammed his mouth over hers. Claimed her brutally. Filled her ferociously. When he broke off the kiss, he pulled her head back down with just as much force, still restricting her gaze solely to him.

"Difference number three," he uttered into the thick air between them. "Shane fucked you like a pussy."

Her eyes flared like crushed cobalt infused with diamonds. "Oh, God. Holy shit."

He twisted out a feral grin. "Save the prayers, baby girl. You're going to need them more in a few minutes."

A long whimper slid out of her, along with a frantic nod, as he released the fastenings on her jeans. Her expression crunched into confusion as he rolled off the bed. It expanded to a full gape as he flipped her over, and then it was lost to him as he worked on removing the pants with vicious yanks. He could guess, though. Her aroused little grunts conveyed novels to him—and they all hinted at very happy endings.

Her desire was his new vortex, flipping back more latches on the storm doors of his composure. Fuck, it felt great. There was so much inside him that hadn't been out to play in a long time. His chest pumped. His muscles surged. His focus funneled in tighter on his precious subbie. Tighter...

Goodbye, humanity. Hello, Sir Shay. The animal inside clawed at his blood, pounded into his cock, vibrated in every breath. It also growled up his throat as he watched his near-naked hostage, her hands kneading the mattress, her sighs punching the air, and her thighs starting to part, giving him glimpses of her dark-pink pussy lips. Her wet, glistening readiness...

He was well aware they didn't have a lot of time, but took an extra second to let her shiver through his scrutinizing silence. After she'd endured a few more seconds of that tension, he paced to the area near her head. Checked the security of her IV line. Then pushed the hair away from her face.

"Open your eyes, tiny dancer." Damn. Even in that simple act, she performed with exotic elegance. "Beautiful," he praised. "Now look up at me." When she obeyed—lashes so thick, irises so bright, and bow lips parted—he exhaled hard. She was five thousand kinds of breathtaking, a perfect wet dream. He almost wondered if he *was* asleep. His dick provided the answer to that. If this was a dream, he would've lost it and orgasmed already. "Red still means red," he ordered in a dark rumble.

She tossed him that perplexed pout again. "You don't get it, do you? Hostages don't get—"

"Hell." He snatched up a roll of gauze bandaging off the nursing tray and unfurled a length before fitting it between her teeth and yanking hard. After wrapping the white shit a few times around her head, he tore it off and knotted it over one of her ears. She winced when some of her hair got tangled in the tie, but the thickened lust in her gaze was also unmistakable. "Your safe word is now crossed fingers, *hostage*. But you'd better fucking mean it, baby, because now you've gotten me extra torqued. Now nod and tell me you understand."

She complied in less than a second. Shay grunted, proud of himself for his handiwork. The gag was sexy as fuck, adding fire into his certainty to possess her again. At the same time, she wasn't just giving in to the meek captive thing. Her backtalk had been a massive turn-on. Now, her eyes glinted with alternating messages of *fuck you* and *ohhhh, shit*. So damn gorgeous. Dark blue was rapidly becoming his favorite color.

"Good girl," he murmured. Christ how he wanted to keep pacing around this table, playing with her mind and her body and anything else he could get his fingers on and his cock inside, but time was a goddamn monkey on his back. Soon, Wyst would have that extra wing open, and he'd have to jump back to being Shane again—to what he really came here for— though with every passing minute in this room, Zoe felt more a part of that reason too.

She squirmed a little, increasing the awareness that he'd let another silence slip by. "Be still," he ordered quietly. "You're *my* toy now, and that includes the call on every move you make."

She nodded and then lowered her head back to the mattress. The move placed her gaze at the same level as his cock, a fact she certainly didn't miss, judging from her rapid-fire breathing. It sure as fuck wasn't lost on him. She was the portrait of dreams he'd long ago written off as fantasy, the plaything he'd stopped putting on the Christmas list. He'd resigned himself to getting socks and lame sweaters for the rest of his days.

No more sweaters now. Unless he could dress her in them. Then unwrap her *out* of them...

He groaned as his cock threatened to cut its own way from his pants.

Zoe's fingers curled into the mattress while he pulled at his fly, slicing the air with the grate of his zipper. She writhed as he produced a condom from his front pocket and then placed it in front of her face. He decided the move could be her free pass. Inside, he thanked her for it. Her near-nude beauty distracted him from thinking about the moment Bash had forced the rubber into his hand as they'd loaded Zoe onto the stretcher after landing, joking that Shay should make the most of using his "private dancer." Shay had almost given the thing back to Bash by ramming it down the guy's throat. He was damn glad he hadn't.

As he parted his fly, Zoe bit into the gauze. When he pulled out his erection, she released a full moan. Shay was tempted to respond in kind but only grunted.

He repeated the sound as a crystal drop formed in the valley atop his cock. He let it stay there, shimmering inches from her eyes, as he stroked himself from balls to crown with a tight fist. He didn't say a word, knowing her eyes took in every piece of information she needed to know by staring at the force in his hand and the growth of his stalk.

He was going to fill her without liberation. Fuck her without relief. Claim her in every hard, ruthless way he could.

After she watched him like that for a minute, her buttocks constricted. She trembled, clearly trying to stop herself, but sobbed when Shay stopped her with a sharp spank across both her cheeks. "Naughty girl. Trying to get yourself off by rubbing the mattress like a kitty in heat?"

"I...I...shaw-wee." Her voice was filled with lusty desperation.

Shay dipped his hand between her ass cheeks, his fingers slicking into tight, wet warmth. "You *are* a wicked pussy," he purred. "A sweet, sopping little hostage who's ready to be fucked."

"Yesh," she mumbled as he spread her sex wide and stroked her erect clit. "Ohhhh...yessshhh!"

"Hush." He pulled his hand out, joining it with his other to lift her hips high. When her ass was thrust high, he wound his hand back in and caressed her pussy. He stroked her twice and then smacked her once. A stunned keen tumbled off Zoe's lips. When he repeated the treatment, she cried louder. "Much better," Shay praised. "Forget the words, sweet girl. Your only purpose is to scream."

"Mmmmm." Though her tone was threaded with pain, her beautiful cunt sent a stream of arousal over his fingers. She turned even wetter after he swatted her again. And she shrieked even louder. "Oh. Ohhhhh. Owwww!"

Shay leaned close, pressing his body over her and dragging the hair away from her eyes. She stared back up him, looking as untamed and exhilarated and turned-on as he felt.

Then for an instant, just an instant, she kicked up one side of her mouth at him.

The look was so sublime, Shay couldn't help but grin back before sinking his teeth into the back of her neck. He licked away the burn before crooning, "You want more, don't you?"

He held his breath in anticipation of her response. His breathtaking she-cat didn't disappoint him.

No little nod of sweet acquiescence. Or another awkward mumble. The woman let a stunning snarl prowl through her body, joining to the shove she gave with her shoulders and the buck she attempted with her hips. *Attempted.* Shay was ready for her struggle now. He easily braced her thighs, stilling them with steely grips. If that weren't enough, he rolled a hand back over her sex and once more massaged her tender tissues.

Zoe froze. It made him smile. The woman was amazing, already conditioning her reaction based on what she thought he'd do. He hadn't been planning a pattern, but just thinking of swatting her pussy again was now a psychological temptation on top of the physical.

Beneath his swirling touch, her clit trembled. Her lips erupted in an agonized moan.

"Don't you want what's coming next, my hot hostage?"

She swung her head from side to side. "Uh-uh."

"You *don't* want me to spank your pussy?"

"Yesh. *No*," she gasped. "Pwease donnnn't!"

"But it makes your cunt so wet, Zoe. It makes you shake so hard for me."

"Pwease. No. Owwww!" Her cry coincided with the audible smack he made to her mound this time. She dug her toes into the mattress, struggling to push free. Like that was going to work. With one hip still captive in his ruthless hold, he shoved two fingers between the dark honey perfection of her ass cheeks. Without stopping, he plunged them into her deepest tunnel.

"You're dripping again, Zoe. Soaking me with your hot cream. And I can see your tits, hanging over the mattress like darts. They're sharp, erect and aroused." He pulled out his fingers to loom forward again, kissing the valley between her shoulder blades "Your shoulders are trembling. Your skin is gleaming. My sweet little hostage, your lips can try stories with me, but your body says different things."

"Unnnhhh. Mmmmm!" She forced the sounds past the gauze as he reached between her legs from the front. Her intimate flower trembled beneath his touch, and her delicious moan erupted into a needy scream. Her gaze, though shielded beneath heavy lids, followed his hand through every inch of the sweep he made to retrieve the condom. Once he tore into the wrapper and sheathed up, her eyes slammed shut and her breathing doubled.

"Wider." He repositioned his legs between hers and then spread her according to his dictate. Pressed beneath him, she was a heaven of liquid compliance and lusty sighs. She softened as he forced her torso flat to the mattress, angling her entrance perfectly for his invasion.

"Good," he grated into her ear. The roses in her shampoo, the salt in her skin, and the tang of her sex were an ambrosia in his nostrils, filtering straight to his cock. "Very, very good. You're so ready for it, aren't you, little prisoner?"

She gave him the answer already. From the second he guided his rigid length between her legs and was welcomed by her pussy's greedy lips, he was certain the rough foreplay had flipped every switch of her desire. She quivered and pulsed and sweated and writhed, all but begging him aloud for his ruthless discipline.

And damn, how he loved pleasing a sweet little subbie.

And dominating a gorgeous little hostage.

His hostage.

The affirmation cranked his blood to boiling. His savage urges became caveman needs, driving him to mark her shoulders with deep bites before he reared back, digging his hands into her hips and imprinting her flesh with his grip.

After one nudge to retest her readiness, he lunged forward while pulling her back—and didn't stop until he felt his balls smack the trimmed hairs of her pussy.

"Ahhhh!"

Her desperate scream swelled him more. He gritted the F-word at the confines of the condom. Christ, he hoped the barrier held. He'd strained a few in his time, but no woman he'd ever screwed had this effect on him. Made him feel as if he wasn't deep enough, didn't stretch her enough, didn't stamp enough of himself on her, inside her. The frustration made him withdraw nearly to her entrance before thrusting hard into her once more.

It still wasn't enough.

"More." The command razed his throat as he pounded into her sheath once more. "Take more of it, Zoe. More of me. Breathe, baby. You can do it." As her shoulders dropped, her pussy slackened a little. He moved in fast, using the opportunity to conquer more of her body. "That's it. Fuck, that's good. Again. Let me in deeper."

She nodded but then rolled her head, thrashing it. "So muh," she blurted. "So fuh."

Shay dropped his hands to her thighs and began running them inward, forming a *V* around her pussy. With his thumbs, he pushed at the top of her prettily cropped mound. "But *so much* can be so good, little hostage. So can *so full*."

As he offered the seduction, his gaze was mysteriously guided to the side—and drawn at once to the items on the small medical cart there. *Hell.* Maybe fate really was a benevolent mistress sometimes. And maybe he'd just gotten lucky with the inspiration.

Either way, the tube of petroleum jelly wouldn't go wasted.

In ideal circumstances, the shit wouldn't have been his first choice for this—but since his plan was only to have fun with her anus and not get his cock anywhere near it, he felt safe in popping the lid, working the jelly onto a finger, and then dipping that digit to the naughty ring surrounding her back hole. He braced his other hand to the small of her back while slowly pushing his finger inside, expecting his little hostage to become a bucking pony any second.

She met half his expectation. While the keen from her throat was high and frantic, she didn't lurch. Her only resistance came in the form of clenching every muscle she could. That wasn't such a crappy thing. Shay bit back a groan as her channel nearly crushed his dick in all the right ways.

"Ssshhh. Breathe, baby girl. This is *so full* in all the best ways."

"*Mmpphh.*"

"Pretty, but not a safe word. Crossed fingers, remember?"

Damn it.

He paused as she used the cue to raise her right hand.

But her fingers weren't crossed. She really shifted only one of them—to flip him a definitive "bird" of tribute.

He let out a gloating chuckle. "My adorable little hostage... how fortunate you are that it feels too good to fuck you right now. But since you've asked so nicely..." He slicked on more of the lubricant and then fit a second finger into her ass, twisting his hand to work both digits deeper. As Zoe grunted, he began a gentle rhythm in her ass, timing it to how he rocked his dick in her pussy.

Her protests faded into whimpers. Her shoulders sagged. But within a few more strokes, Shay felt her start to push back on his fingers with the inner muscles of her ass. The depths of her sex kept kneading his dick. Her body quivered, easily absorbing his thrusts. When he stretched a hand to her clit, it was a rock-hard nub of readiness.

Holy God. He'd never seen a submissive so completely embrace everything she was. Taking pain for her Dom's desire. Trusting his will with the surrender of her own. Accepting his force and letting it transform with her passion...and heat.

Her obeisance flared his lust. The pressure percolated in his balls, pushing the limits of his control. His thighs clenched and his ass constricted. She heightened the torment by mewling at him in protest with every new inch he gained in her ass, only to massage him harder the next second, coaxing him deeper in. His cock was a separate issue of torment. It was no longer possible to simply rock into her. With every passing minute, the blood beat more urgently up his shaft. He was powerless to ignore it and helpless to control it, letting it drive him into a thundering rhythm on her pussy. Every time he bore down, he gritted filthy commands, binding him tighter to her in nasty collusion.

"Take it, Zoe."

She shivered and sighed.

"All of it, Zoe."

She quaked and moaned.

"You're filled up, Zoe."

Finally, he pinched her labia lips together, pushing her clit into the pad of his forefinger.

"Make your cunt come for me, Zoe."

She froze. Shivered.

Screamed.

Shay detonated too. Bolts of electricity shot up his shaft. He burst in the depths of her body like a neutron bomb fused of ecstasy and agony. Her body continued to squeeze him, milking every last drop of his come. The world centered and expanded at once, spinning his senses, blowing his goddamn mind.

He couldn't let it end there.

He couldn't let her walk away without having her mind imploded too.

After lowering the gag from her mouth, he leaned over and kissed her, savoring the taste of her lingering pleasure. As he trailed his mouth back along her jaw and to her neck, Zoe let out another blissful sigh.

"Sir. Thank—"

"Sssshhh." He'd already cupped her mound with his hand again. The fingers in her ass had stayed right where they were, and his cock was still blissfully buried in her womb. With defined purpose, he pressed the heel of his hand against her mons, matching his beat to the thrusts of his other hand.

"*M-M-Mierda*," she gasped. "Wh-What the hell are you—"

"Rules still apply, baby girl." He rolled his hips, letting his cock and its filled rubber add to all the sensations inside her. "Only screams."

"But...I can't..."

"You can. You *will*. Feel it build...from the inside. All those sweet, sensitive spots deep inside... You'll give them to me now too."

"But I'm not built like that. I—"

"Screams, Zoe." His growl was rewarded by the clench of her tunnel around his cock's crown, confirming she might actually understand. When her stare sprang wide and a stunned cry burst from her lips, he rumbled in triumph. The next minutes were defined by the most beguiling moans a submissive had ever given him, threaded together by sighs of amazement, arousal, need, and even a few tears.

Suddenly, she writhed more violently. She tried to ram her buttocks against his fingers while grinding her pelvis on his other hand. "S-Sir," she panted. "Please. *Please.*"

Shay kissed her slick forehead. "Aching, little hostage?"

She jerked her head in a strange semblance of a nod. "Aaahhhh," she moaned. "More. *More!*"

He broke away to slide a third finger into the petroleum jelly. When he twisted it into her ass with the other two, she let out a high-pitched cry and pushed a fist against the mattress. Her pussy was taut and slick around him, her legs trembling and wobbly beneath him.

"Better, baby girl? With another finger in here?"

"Yes, Sir. Thank you, Sir."

"But you still need it, don't you?"

"*Dios.* Yes. Yes!"

"Then take it, Zoe. It's yours." He pressed into her mons harder. Jammed his fingers deeper into her asshole. "I'm right here with you. You can feel me, can't you? Everywhere inside you."

"I can." Tears trickled out of her with the confession. "I...I *can.*"

"Then clamp down on me and claim that orgasm."

He deliberately made the order into a verbal battle tank. And like a deer caught in front of the Sherman, she exploded into a thousand pieces of sexual mush. Her pussy flooded, her anus constricted, and her legs gave out. As the aftershocks continued, she rolled and cried and swore in Spanish, mixing in a promise that he'd killed her with pleasure, and now she'd pass to the afterlife without forgiveness for her tawdry sins.

Shay, unable to help himself, chortled softly in her ear.

"*Higueputa,*" she huffed. "Are you...*laughing* about this?"

He should've punished her, at least a little, for the snip. Instead, he closed his eyes, reveling in how she summoned such sass with his cock and three fingers still inside her. It was no surprise that she had him almost hard enough to fuck her again. She gave him such incredible pleasure—bested only by the hunger to give *her* more.

With a decisive grunt, he stilled her hips with a shove of his. Then, letting his breath fill her ear and his cock grow in her tunnel, he lowered his hand from her mons to her pussy. And gave just one swipe of his middle finger to the most sensitive hub of her need.

Zoe, being his perfect little submissive, screamed for him. Over and over and over again.

Many minutes later, as her breathing calmed and the shivers of her climax faded, he finally pulled free and turned her over, accepting the conclusion that fucking her again wouldn't be a wise move. Even a pushover like Justine would have limits for a guy's time on some recreational pump-and-dump with a hostage. Still, he took a long moment to brush the damp hair from her dark eyes, lower a soft kiss on her delectable lips, and tell her through a smirk, "Baby girl, *now* I'm laughing."

CHAPTER TWELVE

Zoe didn't hesitate to punch the sexy *chingado* in the muscled meat of his shoulder. The move was more to save face, though she wasn't sure what "face" she had left, considering he'd just turned her into the sexual version of a triple-fried egg. After he pretended deep pain, making her hit him again, he dissolved into more laughter. She gave up and joined him, recognizing he probably hadn't had a lot of chances to indulge even a snicker in the last six months. Her heart filled with warm gratitude, honored to be the one to bring him a little respite in his life.

And then his radio squawked.

"Burnett!" The voice was a little garbled, but she recognized it as the hijacker with the gritty voice and creepy gaze. "Pull your dick out of that bitch and join us in quadrant six. We've cracked the code, and we're back on program with the good shit."

So much for respites.

Shay's gaze gained some new shadows too. She chastised herself for feeling giddy about that. Was it possible that he comprehended it all too? The primal power in the air whenever they stepped near each other... Did he feel it as well? And the pull of their bodies to each other, like they were magnets only able to fuse to one another...and the coils of their souls, only activated by their entwined hands and their crushed mouths...

No. You've gone crazy. You said it yourself, right here, and Shay nodded. He agreed. *Remember where the hell you are and what's happening right outside that door. You think he's pondering tangled souls with you, when the scary side of "crazy" is waiting for his return?*

Thunder boomed overhead. A flash desert storm. Appropriate, considering the flood of perception that crashed through her at the same time.

Danger. It wasn't just a dramatic word in his life. It was reality, waiting to bite him in the ass or worse. Stock and his men weren't just playing around at the soldier-boy thing. Whatever the hell they were here to retrieve, they were serious as hell about it, enough to steal a jetliner, shoot a man's knee out, and keep fifteen dancers behind as hostages too.

Which brought her inevitable reaction.

As she watched Shay rise and reach for a towel to clean himself up, she couldn't fight a tremor of fear. An *intense* one. Even as he smirked at her again, muttering how it was *her* fault he had to stuff a nearly erect cock back into his cargo pants, she couldn't force herself to return a smile.

Shay's grin faded too. His thick hair fell against his frowning brow, turning his gorgeous humor into rugged beauty that wrenched at her heart—and tugged at her tears. He was so stunning. So strong. So unspeakably brave. She dropped her head, unable to stomach the idea of him returning to those evil *cabróns.*

"Dancer? You okay?" His concern only made her torment worse. As the mattress dipped from his weight, the tears came harder. Zoe tried to sniff them back, but they fell anyway, plopping onto the hand he curled over hers.

"Shit," she whispered.

Shay pulled her up and cradled her tightly against him. "Damn it," he muttered. "I'm sorry, baby girl."

"Huh?" She pushed back to fire a glower at him. "Why?"

"You need hours of aftercare, and I can only give you minutes."

His tender tone drew her to bury her face into his chest again. *Mierda*, it was such a nice chest. She pressed closer, treasuring the thumps of his heartbeat. As she absorbed the strength of the sound, she smiled in deep peace—

Just before inspiration zapped it to hell.

She kept her face down, certain Shay would translate her thoughts. She wasn't even sure about acting on them. It was one thing to be inspired but another thing to sell him on the concept.

She had to think fast. Playing on his guilt was a direct route. But could she deal that dirty?

"Meh," she murmured, taking advantage of the chance to sniffle into his shoulder. "Just get me to the nearest sports bar and we'll call it aftercare, all right?"

An angry rumble vibrated out of him. "No goddamn bars for aftercare."

Well, that answered her question. She had no trouble at all with the dirty work. But right now, as desperate as it sounded, she'd do anything to stay at his side. Giving herself so deeply to him... It had felt like finding refuge in a mountain cavern after walking through a storm. But now a bulldozer named Cameron Stock wanted to tear her mountain away—or worse. If the man learned the truth beneath Shay's cover, he'd think nothing of pulling out his handy pistol, jamming it to Shay's skull, and firing away.

She shuddered—and just as fast, castigated herself for it. Damn. She was officially torn between the Zoe who'd sworn off weakness during puberty and the Zoe who'd newly discovered

Shay's remorse-is-ruin button.

But the thought of him lying on the ground, his brains blown into the dirt, swayed her battle in seconds. She gripped his neck and burrowed harder into him.

"Then take me with you."

Shay stilled his hand against her head. His neck stiffened beneath her fingers. "Christ. I really did fuck your brains out."

She huffed. "Listen, I'm not going to sit helplessly in some back room while you—"

"No."

"Shay!"

"*No.*"

"Do you even want to hear my idea? How I can actually help you out here?"

He pulled away enough for her to catch the skeptical jump of his brows. "This should be good."

"You could pretend I gave you a shitload of trouble, so you decided to tie me up and take me to hostage holding yourself. Go all *One Twue Dom* on Justine again. She'll buy every second of it. Once we're past her, you can put me down. I'll smuggle out some of those medical scrubs under my shirt and then can change into them." When his glower hardened to the texture of pounded gold, she twisted her hand in the front of his shirt. "You're here because you think this is where Stock is keeping your mom, right? Seems like a big place, *mi amigo.* You could probably use help. Another set of eyes?"

Shay expelled a weighted breath. "How long have you been concocting this?"

She bit her lip. "Long enough."

He dropped his head, studying her more closely. "You're an experienced dancer, right, Zoe? Then you of all people should know that half-assed planning makes for shitty execution."

She slid a hand to the sharp line of his jaw. "Or a surprise of brilliance."

"Cameron Stock doesn't like surprises. Just ask the guy from the plane who's missing a kneecap now." He wrapped his fingers around hers, closed his eyes for a long second, and then bent his head deeper into her hold. "Cam was telling the truth this morning. He was feeling benevolent, which was why the dumb shit didn't get that bullet between his eyes instead." He slowly shook his head. "The man's not feeling benevolent anymore, baby girl."

"But he doesn't even have to see me," Zoe protested.

"I said no." His voice was grim. "This isn't a movie, Zoe. We're in a top-secret facility that I barely know the exit routes from, and even on that point, my intel is chicken feed at best. I hate doing this to you—"

"Then don't." *Mierda.* The man had her pouting. She never pouted.

"I have no choice, damn it. I'd rather endure your anger than your death, okay? And, by the way, any other time or place, my palm would be branding your backside for that lip."

"Sounds like fun."

"It would *not* be fun. That's a guarantee." Shay barely let her process the strange combination of shivers and tingles from that before scooping a finger beneath her chin. "Listen to me, damn it. *Obey me*, Zoe. The safest plan for you right now is to let Justine take you back to your friends."

"Then just wait for him to kill us?"

"He won't let *any* of you be killed." His jaw turned the texture of his hard gold stare. "To be blunt, you're his leverage."

"So he'll just let us be raped."

"*I* won't let that happen." He kissed her fiercely. "I promise. But I can hide my feelings easier if they're tucked behind my guard dog face. I'll be shit for concentrating on searching for Mom *and* maintaining my cover with Stock if I haven't ensured your safety."

"But how can you promise yours?"

He brushed both thumbs across her cheek—through the tears that had rolled out with her rasp. "I can't." His own voice cracked again. "But I'm going to try, okay?"

As he swept his mouth lower, taking her in what she knew would be their final kiss, Zoe's throat constricted like he'd tossed boulders down it along with his kiss, but she prevented her needy, stupid follow-up from spewing out.

I just found you. I can't just...lose you. Damn it, I have to keep you alive! Somehow. But how? How?

His lungs toiled on breaths as he pushed to his feet again. He stood next to the bed like that for a long moment, keeping their fingers twined until he slanted over her, pressing his lips to her forehead and echoing a command he'd given her hours ago...a lifetime ago. This time, the charge came with a distinct variance.

"Stay." He yanked her face against his chest, clasping her against his stone-hard exterior—and the impassioned heartbeat that filled his interior. "Please."

★ ★ ★ ★ ★

Stay.

Twenty minutes later, she still fumed about his damn decree. She wouldn't have let *any* man get away with such an edict even once, yet she lay here obeying the damn thing for the *second* time.

She had a valid excuse for the first slip, when he'd issued it to her on the plane. Terror had a great way of stealing a person's brain.

A heavy sigh rushed out. She had an equally good excuse for her second lapse. No, a better one.

Shay's fear.

She'd seen it in every shard of his gaze, heard it in all the pounds of his heart when he'd held her close one last time. In every beat of that moment, he confirmed what she'd already sensed, that he recognized the rarity of their bond as profoundly as she did. That in just hours, they'd already built a world together. A place she'd only dreamed she'd ever find. *Hermoso fuego.* The beautiful fire of their power exchange.

It was a world worth fighting for. Yet here she lay, still tethered to the damn IV tube, all but whining like a puppy in worry for her master.

She needed to be helping him. Supporting him. Fighting for him, for *them,* in any way she could.

Having selective brain again, hmmm, Zo? Have you conveniently forgotten that the man is trained to fight and you're not?

She snorted. "*Ay.* I'm not going to just pick up an M14 and go to town. But he needs help, and—"

Help? Really? You going to yell at him to duck bullets and hand him a cold towel for comfort?

How the hell had her own conscience turned into her worst enemy? "You're supposed to be on my side."

And you're supposed to be heeding your Sir.

"He's not my Sir." Hearing her vicious bite on the air imparted new confidence. "He's my damn captor, is what he is, and he's still keeping me hostage!"

He's keeping you safe.

"He needs—"

For you to be alive at the end of all this. But you can't handle not *helping. You can't let it go, can you?*

"I'm sitting here, okay? Being good, keeping my place... waiting to be hauled off to the holding pen."

You have to let it go, Zoe.

You have to let it go.

She winced as her head repeated the phrase. The words were worse than "tech run-through," "pap smear," and "sold out of Ding Dongs" combined. With hard breaths, she fought them back again, shoving them back from the tunnel of memory, knowing—and dreading—what they'd morph into if they achieved that goal.

Too late. The echo chamber of the past grabbed the words and ran. At first, the phrase reprised in her own voice, but all too fast, she heard it in Aunt Lena's voice instead. The woman's usual strict accent marked each syllable, amplified by the stark white walls of the King of Peace Mortuary.

Zoe. You have to let go now. Your mamá *is with the angels. Let her go now, child. They have to take her away.*

She squeezed her eyes. Forced down a breath. Fought to thrust the memory away. Though she managed to clear her mind, the grief clung to her heart, reduced to its eleven-year-old tenderness.

And desperation.

And damn, disgusting helplessness.

She should have done something. There had to have been *something*. She should've known *Mamá's* cough wasn't a normal thing that grownups got on airplanes. She should've made her go to the doctor sooner. Hell, she should've begged her not to go to Greece in the first place. Why did *Mamá* always have to go see *Giagia* and not the other way around?

"You should have known," she whispered. "You should have done something."

Something other than letting go.

She jabbed the tears off her cheeks as the door opened with a *whoosh*. Justine beamed a creepy doll smile while bustling over, a roll of gauze in her hand. Just glancing at the spool made Zoe feel like more of it was crammed down her throat, especially as the memory of Shay's special use for the stuff blared across her mind. She managed—barely—to choke the anguish back as the nurse approached.

"Well, well, well," Justine chirped. "Aren't we looking muuuuch better? You actually have a little color in your cheeks."

Zoe attempted to lift her lips. She couldn't discern whether Justine was friend or foe, and the woman's *Bride of Chucky* stare didn't help in figuring it out. "Sure," she managed.

"Bet you're more than ready for this bad boy to be pulled out." The woman giggled as she turned off the IV drip, peeled the tape off her arm, and then gently removed the catheter before covering the site with a square bandage. "Though we certainly can't say the same thing about *all* the bad boys and their *pulling out* habits today, right?"

It took a much more monumental effort to react "normally" to the woman this time. Whatever normal was around here. The smartass in her brain gave a wry smirk. *What did you expect? You're in the real-life* Twilight Zone, *remember? There's a good chance Stock simply found her here and decided to let her stay.*

A frown creased Justine's forehead. "Damn it," she muttered. "I forgot your juice. We can't have you getting released without juice now, can we? I'll find a little something to help you freshen up."

Zoe blushed furiously as the woman glanced over, clearly eyeing the bite marks at the base of her neck along with the top buttons on her jeans, pulled back on her legs but still unfastened. She colored more deeply with the memory of Shay stripping the pants off her in the fire of his passion. "Th- Thanks."

As soon as the woman disappeared again, discomfort set right back in. Zoe grimaced and squirmed, despite telling herself this was just her psyche being influenced by Justine's weirdness. But everything about just sitting here felt wrong.

Make that *wrong*.

"Damn it." Now that she could actually rise off the bed, she did. It felt a little better to work off some tension by pacing, but the movement also confirmed that she really did feel better. Damn near perfect, as a matter of fact.

Perfect enough to be helping Shay.

Let it—

"Screw yourself."

She barked it at her conscience before turning the whole thing off. Later, she'd search it for the insane monkey now cavorting its neurons, but there was no time right now. Listening to her instinct over her conscience wasn't a natural skill, so she had to focus harder on that innermost voice—even if it *was* lifted to a bellow now.

Correction. A bunch of bellows. All phrased into questions. Disturbing questions. Angles she wasn't sure Shay himself had considered in the ardency of his quest.

So what if Stock had influenced his mom's disappearance? That didn't mean it had been involuntary. What if his mom was here because she'd chosen to be? What if Shay *did* find her—and she instantly turned him over to Stock?

And what if the man had his mother thrust on such a high pedestal, he never entertained a single one of those thoughts?

He needs me.

It didn't just resound in her brain. It throbbed through her entire being, claiming her bones and blood, more deafening than a wall of speakers during the final act at a hard-rock festival.

She kept pacing—and stopped only when Justine came back in. "Oh, lookie," the nurse chimed. "You're up. That's a good sign." She scrunched her shoulders up to her ears while extending a tray of filled cups. "Orange, apple, or cranberry? I brought all three flavors so you could pick. I also brought a fresh T-shirt for you. Thought you'd want to change, and we seem about the same size, girlfriend."

Zoe gritted out a smile as her inner creepazoid alert went off. Justine giggled in return, clearly giddy as a bestie about to plop down on the bed, braid her hair, trade boy secrets, and maybe even make out. In her book, her and Zoe's similar builds and hair color magically turned them into something close to sisters. Next, she'd probably be insisting on a blood oath so they could *become*—

Sisters.

Mierda.

Who would've known? The Demon Pazuzu was actually her ticket out of here.

Zoe smiled again, actually meaning it this time. "Ummm, which one do you like best?"

Justine smiled. "Apple, for sure."

"Then apple it is." She waited for Justine to come closer and set the juices on the bedside tray, astounded how the nurse didn't hear the frantic thrum of her heartbeat. After forcing down a deep breath, she commented, "*Vaya*. Your smock is super cute."

The nurse smiled like a girl who'd just been noticed by the captain of the football team. "Really? Errr—I mean, I know, right? Garfield's the best, huh?"

"Cutest cat ever." Despite her nerves, summoning her inner fourteen-year-old wasn't that tough. "Looks like it holds a lot in the pockets too."

"Oh, yeah. Totally necessary for the job, you know? I mean, if one of Dr. Smythe's animal boys gets riled and starts rampaging, I have to have the tranq gun nearby." She patted the pocket with the larger lump in it, answering at least five prayers for Zoe at the same time.

"Animal boys?" Once again, she didn't have to fake her demeanor. Boys generally *were* animals at different points in their development, but she was fairly certain Justine's context was different—and was a huge reason why Shay's mom had been abducted to here.

Or chosen to come here.

Regrettably, Justine's face clouded over. "I've... I've said too much." Just as hurriedly, she laughed off her disclaimer. "It's best that we carry on."

"Couldn't agree more."

Before she lost her nerve, she stepped forward...and slammed a kiss on Justine's mouth. As she'd hoped, the woman froze, suspended in shock. It bought her the three seconds she needed to pull out the tranquilizer gun, hoping like hell the contraption worked similarly to other pistols. Luck was with her. A fast flip of the safety, a jerk on the trigger, and the dart discharged into the woman's thigh. Justine stiffened again, eyes bulging wide—before she slumped onto the bed right where Zoe had just lain.

"I'm sorry, *amiga*." Zoe wasn't sure her whisper had been heard. Justine was as slack as a tranqed-up antelope.

She took a deep breath, peeled off her top, and then went to work on wrenching Justine out of her smock and hair scrunchie. Thankfully, it didn't take very long. Panged by guilt, she took an extra minute to redress the woman in the T-shirt she'd brought, which really was a nice shade of pink, despite the smirking Garfield on it and with the words *Don't start with me. You won't win.* Well, hell. With her hair loose and her face peaceful, the woman was actually pretty. If the goon who discovered Justine was horny enough, she might even get her own "soldier sack time" today. In the end, the woman might even thank her for this.

And pigs might fly.

And she'd walk outside into a dewy woodland, with birds wanting to fit her for a princess gown and little crystal slippers.

And Shay wouldn't be itching to beat her ass to a pulp once he found out she'd pulled this stunt.

That would be just fine by her. She'd willingly, gratefully, accept any punishment the man saw fit to wield—as long as he was alive to do it.

Using the thought as a cheerleader, she straightened her new outfit, scooped up a clipboard and radio from Justine's station, and turned her path toward the hall spilling out with the most noise.

★ ★ ★ ★ ★

Only fifteen minutes later, she felt like she'd lived through fifteen hours. Maybe fifteen years.

This subterfuge shit wasn't as easy as Emma Peel made it look. Every step she took coincided with another terrified throb of her heart, certain somebody would call her out as an imposter, forcing Shay into a choice between two situations that were hell. He'd have to jump to her rescue and risk exposing his true identity or watch her be "disciplined" by Stock for her stunt, likely by letting his horndog henchmen have some turns with her. She had no illusions that decking Stock on the airplane had sliced her "special favor" with him, a status not helped by tranquilizing her nurse and then roaming freely through the facility's hallways.

Maybe Shay had been right.

Maybe she really hadn't known what the hell she was asking for.

Or the strangeness of the party she'd just invited herself to.

As she sucked up her fear and kept moving down the halls, the scene reminded her more and more of a hospital emergency room. Everything was controlled chaos, with Stock's goons acting as armed directors of medical personnel in full scrubs and sterile gloves. Using the clipboard as a shield for her face, Zoe soon learned that if she stuck to the walls, kept her head down, and pretended to talk on her radio every few minutes, everybody assumed she was just another gear in the machine.

A machine that grew busier and busier as she moved along.

And stranger and stranger.

Despite her clipboard obsession, she managed to snag some long looks at the patients being rushed down the hallways, presumably to be loaded onto the now-empty jetliner. At first, she could only frown in confusion. All the men on the gurneys looked like they belonged in the next *Magic Mike* movie, not a supersecret medical facility in the middle of the desert. Some of the hulks were so huge, they threatened to spill off the tables. It was a sea of rippling biceps, ripped chests, massive thighs... and many sets of boxer briefs that were stretched to the limit.

But then she looked closer. Peered beyond the "scenery," to the patients' faces.

While the men's bodies looked like strip-club fantasies, their eyes were as haunted as D Street crack heads. Their features, while traditionally handsome, were just the skeletons that supported lines of disillusion, despair, loneliness...and pain. The kind of pain she'd often seen while growing up down the street from one of the country's busiest military bases, on the faces of vets who'd returned fresh from Iraq, Kuwait, Liberia, Sierra Leone. The pain of endurance but not obliteration. Of memories that were monsters.

Caramba. Who were they, and what had happened to them here?

She forced herself to look for more clues.

A few seconds later, she barely quelled a gasp of horror. That was a good thing, since it subdued the bile in her throat too.

A blond hunk, beautiful enough to play Adonis in a movie, scraped the hair from his eyes with hawk talons in place of his fingers. The guy behind him was positioned stomach-down on his gurney, the thin sheet on his back covering a shark's fin where his spine should be. Farther in the parade, a guy opened his mouth on what looked like a moan, but a soft lion's roar came out instead. His nose was flat and wide like a wildcat's too.

Zoe slammed against the wall, holding the clipboard across her face to shield her horror. "*Ay Dios Mio.*"

The Island of Dr. Moreau had been transplanted into the Nevada desert. Only Moreau was now Cameron Stock, and these poor men were his wretched mutant experiments.

Or were they?

Who the hell was really behind this? This building was situated on the US government's version of hallowed ground, the most secret installation in the country. Books had been written, TV shows developed, even movies made on the speculation about the activities that occurred here, everything from top-secret spy plane tests to deep-freezing aliens. According to the feds, the very facility in which she stood didn't even exist.

Still hiding behind the clipboard, she tried to connect puzzle pieces. The "chat" between Stock and General Newport, in which Stock had threatened going public with a computer stick. Then Justine's earlier reference... *Dr. Smythe's animal boys...*

What did it all mean? Who were all these beautiful, tortured men? Where had they come from? More crucially, where the hell was Stock taking them? How and why was the government involved?

The questions continued. And who was Dr. Smythe? Stock's partner? His enemy? Did Shay's mother know him? Work for him? Was *he* the reason she'd left so abruptly, eighteen years ago? Was he still here now?

As she wrestled with all the facets of the mystery, Zoe

made sure to continue walking. An object in motion was harder to catch, especially when it was a hostage disguised as a nurse...

Unless that object noticed a distinct change in the hall's air pressure.

She looked up to observe that she'd passed under a significant juncture in the hallway. The connection looked like the entrance to a Rockefeller bank vault. Both walls and the ceiling were reinforced by layers of steel. The double doors, also made of steel and at least eighteen inches thick, were held open by a dozen cement blocks each.

Another glance around, taking in the marked section numbers overhead, confirmed what she'd already suspected. She'd made her way into quadrant six. This was where "the good shit" was happening, as Shay's "buddy" had put it. Now to find Shay, without *him* finding *her*—but what then?

She could be like his guardian angel. *That was it.* Helping without his ever knowing it. There was no way he'd find his mom in this labyrinth, plus keep up appearances with the other men, before Stock ordered the plane to take off again. In the meantime, she'd also check out every escape route possible while listening in on these *cabróns'* conversations. Somebody was sure to mention where Brynn, El, Harmony, and the others were being held. Once she found out, she'd free them too.

Vaya. This was one of the best nonplans she'd ever planned.

From behind the clipboard, she allowed herself a small smile of victory.

The next second, it was choked from her. Literally.

The beast that belonged to the arm across her throat knew exactly what he was doing. Zoe's scream, a logical reaction given the spectacle she'd just witnessed, was plugged into a weak gurgle by a hand that constricted her windpipe at precisely the right spot. Zoe fought the guy—the creature?— for about two seconds before realizing the effort was useless. Instead, she concentrated on staying conscious as he hauled her backward, barely stopping to kick back the door through which he dragged her.

Darkness swallowed her.

No. Not complete blackness. It was simply much dimmer than the glaring light of the hallway. And quiet. Too quiet. She glimpsed a leather couch, but when she inhaled, an antiseptic smell hit her. The room seemed to be another medical setting with a small living room attached.

Terror assaulted all over again. Zoe tried to scream but still couldn't catch her breath. A hidden reserve of strength rose when she thought of that couch again and how this asshole could pin her there. She twisted, managing to get her elbow into his ribs, but it was a tiny win in a big-ass battle. The bear growled before spinning her around, flattening her to the wall, and clamping one of his massive hands over her mouth.

Her dread became euphoria.

Shay wasn't jumping so fast on that joy-joy ju-ju train. At all.

"What the hell do you think you're doing?" His voice was a combination of a hiss and a snarl. He wore his black wool ski mask again, only the thing was rolled back on his head like a cap, somehow making him look more like a criminal. A really pissed off one.

"What the hell do you think *you're* doing?"

Zoe exchanged stunned blinks with him. Even if she had the breath to speak, the prickly words wouldn't have been her first choice.

They peered around together. From the shadows of the room, a woman emerged, shocking Zoe by looking more miffed than Shay. She was older, perhaps in her fifties, but clearly possessed an inner strength that enhanced her natural beauty. Her auburn hair was pulled into a ponytail. Little wisps fell free from it, around the classic angles of her face—

With dark-gold eyes that looked exactly like Shay's.

"*Ay Dios mio.*" Zoe gasped. "You... You're..."

"Dr. Smythe," the woman retorted. "Who the hell are you? And why are you wearing Justine's smock?"

Her jaw fell. "*You're* the animal-boy doctor?"

"I beg your pardon?" The woman pulled up her shoulders, which were encased in a cream button-front shirt that showed off a delicate gold locket around her neck. "Look, I don't know who you are, and I don't even care if you're with Cameron. All I'm going to tell you is that my name is Dr. Melanie Smythe, and—"

"No." As Shay turned fully to her, he whipped the mask away from his head. His hair tumbled free, instantly making him more recognizable—especially if his mother's stunned outcry was any barometer. "Your name is Dr. Melody Bommer, and I'm here to rescue you."

CHAPTER THIRTEEN

Shay was damn glad he had such a good hold on Zoe. No mistake about it, he was still steamed as hell with her, but as a thousand emotions slammed him, it occurred that the woman was possibly the only thing keeping him upright.

Especially as his mother's face crumbled in front of his eyes.

Though he'd dreamed of this moment for at least six months, it was sheer hell to keep holding her gaze—but he did it, digging into fortitude he hadn't accessed since the end of an eight-day mission last year in Somalia. He smelled better now. He felt worse. Much more uncertain. And a thousand times more scared.

"Oh, my God."

If it weren't for the infusion of tears, his mother's words would've been bare whispers. He opened his mouth, intending to be strong for her, but wound up gulping back his own damn sob.

"Oh, my God."

Zoe stepped back as Mom lifted a hand to his face. As her fingers trembled against his jaw, he attempted the first tugs of a smile. "Hi, Mom."

Her brilliant gaze scoured every corner of his face. The rest of her features didn't reveal anything else. What did she see? He'd been through hell in the last few days and probably looked like the floor of a teenager's bedroom. Was she happy?

Proud? Disappointed? Maybe he fell short of what she expected. Or maybe she really *had* left that night of her own choice, never wanting to know him and Tait ever again.

The seconds strained on as he waited for an answer.

Finally, without a word of preamble, she locked her other hand at the back of his head and yanked him down against her. She still didn't say a word. Maybe that was because she was sobbing too hard.

Shay tasted salt on his face too. He didn't care. His tears came harder when he attempted to suck in a full breath.

She still smelled like Juicy Fruit and sunshine.

"Shay," she finally rasped. "My sweet, beautiful Shay."

He closed his eyes and pulled her closer. And, for one moment, didn't let himself think of anything but the joy in his heart...and the fulfillment in his soul.

It ended by Mom's choice. On another little cry, this one full of agony, she pushed him back. Then smacked his chest. "You shouldn't be here! And when the hell did you get so damn big?"

He stepped back, arching brows to match her indignation. "I'm not leaving without you. And Mrs. Verona's cookies have magic growth potion in them. Or so she always told me."

She lifted her hands again, bracing both sides of his face. "I want you to stay forever, but as you probably know, that's not possible." Her fingers quivered again. "I have no idea why you're here—"

"Why the fuck do you think I'm here?"

"Language, young man."

"Ow." He rubbed his cheek where she'd pinched it. How had he forgotten how accurate her aim was on those things? "I'm here because of you."

While his explanation didn't make her freak out, she shot a defined huff that instantly reminded him of Tait. She averted her gaze and jammed her hands into her back pockets, also exactly like Tait. "Me? I don't understand."

He advanced back toward her. "I think you do, Mom."

"Shay." Zoe gently grabbed his elbow. "This would be shocking under normal circumstances. Give her a minute."

"We don't have a minute."

She answered his retort with a blazing glare, muttering something in Spanish. *Shit.* At once, he felt like an asshole. It was a necessary job requirement in typical mission situations, though this situation wasn't anything close to typical. Neither of these women were the "norm" for him, in ways that sliced to the depths of his damn soul. And if he didn't make it out of this pressure cooker with both of them alive...

Fuck.

That possibility wasn't acceptable. At all.

The recognition weakened him. And *that* perception froze him in place. He had Mom to thank for snapping him out of the shit. Her accusing glare, flung at Zoe, realigned his attention.

"Who the hell are you?" She was clearly still hung up on Zoe's stolen identity, though he had to admit, his tiny dancer made even Garfield look fucking sexy.

"Mom, this is Zoe." He wrapped a possessive hand around Zoe's waist. "And she's pretty incredible."

His mother worked her jaw back and forth. "You picked an awfully elaborate way to introduce me to your girlfriend, Little B."

"Shit."

A blush fired up his face as Zoe reined back a giggle. "*Little B?*"

"Yeah. And you can guess which asshat was *Big B.*" Despite his mortification, it was tough to slide irritation over the words. He liked the "girlfriend" part of that. A lot.

Mom's glare returned. "Young man, when did your language hit the deep end of the gutter?"

"First day of boot camp." He puffed out his chest a little when her anger burst into a smile. "I'm Army Special Forces now, Mom. That's why I'm here. Stock and his goons know me as Shane Burnett. I've been undercover with them for six months, working with intel from the CIA to get here...to you."

"Wh-What?" she finally murmured.

"I've come to finally take you away from here, and..."

He trailed into silence once the sunshine of her smile started to fade. Something wasn't right. This was supposed to be the part where she wept harder, threw herself into his arms, and told him how happy she was that her little boy had endured stomping across the globe with a madman in order to finally find her.

Instead, Mom uncurled her arms as if they'd turned to lengths of chain, took two leaden steps, and then hugged him with heavy solemnity. "I can't go with you, Shay."

He grimaced from the scythe of grief hitting his chest. He tried imagining the blade as a reality, cutting him away from her so he could step back. No fucking go. "Can't," he finally grated, "or won't?"

Hell. Could he have been *that* wrong about this? Had Dad been right all those years ago? Had Mom really left them in the middle of the night...willingly?

Her soft sob told him nothing. "Oh, my brave boy. My sweet Shay."

He steeled his posture against her embrace. "Yeah. Right.

Who's *not* feeling so sweet right now." At least he got that out with some force. He couldn't show her the quicksand of his heart right now.

"I know." Her empathetic croon didn't help one fucking bit. How many times had he longed for that voice in his ear? How many knee scrapes, nightmares, and heartaches had he lived through without her? How many Christmas mornings had he and Tait lit their little plastic tree and handed each other presents in aluminum foil, singing the enhanced version of the Rudolph song because it had always made her laugh? And now she had the nerve to talk to him like that, like she *understood* the loss that ripped at his very core?

"No, Mom. I don't think you do."

She bent her head back to gaze up at him. "I love you so much, Little B. And Tait too." Her hand traveled to the locket at her throat. He was close enough to see that the front of it was engraved with two ornate letters: T and S. "But this is more complicated than you can comprehend. There are lives at stake. Lives I saved by coming here."

"Valuable enough to leave your sons?"

Her gaze glittered with fresh tears. With a shaky hand, she reached to him. "Your lives were at the top of the list, Shay."

Zoe gasped something in Spanish. For a long moment, he was grateful to let that sound consume the air. God knew, whatever erupted from his throat wouldn't be so eloquent. Not that there'd be anything there, considering the scythe now had a companion: a battle-ax of shock.

"What?" The word was as raw and wounded as his spirit. And it served as a shitty stand-in for all the questions he actually needed to ask. He'd detained enough people on missions to know when he was dealing with someone concealing a much bigger story—even his own mother. Her eyes, darkened to the shade of pennies, told him everything...and nothing.

She definitely, positively, wasn't here by choice.

She definitely, positively, wasn't leaving here of free will, either.

But why? What the hell was going on?

Before he had the chance to ask her either question, a *boom* shook the building. Glass jars rattled in the laboratory part of the room. Shay knew the sound all too well, though that didn't stop it from frying his nerves.

Instinctively, he yanked both women close and muttered, "Mortar blast."

Zoe, with eyes showing more white than color, tucked herself against him. After his statement, her skin followed suit. *"Caramba,"* she gasped as another explosion hit. "What the hell is happening?"

Before Shay could start on an answer, the door to the hall slammed open. In the portal was a Badlands cliff hacked into the shape of a man. The guy shut the door without looking back, stalking closer with his hard-hewn face set in a determined scowl. Though the fucker was dressed in sand-colored fatigues and a matching T-shirt, which outlined every vein in his muscles, his gait reminded Shay of a forty-something, nasty-ass Komodo dragon. The suspicion wasn't helped when Mom ran into the man's arms.

"What is it?" she queried the guy. Her tone didn't mirror Tait now. It was all Zoe in its no-nonsense strength. *Spare the damn sugar.*

"Company's arrived." The walking cliff sounded like one too. "And it seems they don't care for the cheese in the fondue pot."

Mom's shoulders tensed. "You were good to warn everyone that this might happen."

He nodded tightly. "We knew what to expect." His gaze lifted and pinned to Shay. "You're one of Cam's guys, right? What the fuck're you doing, bothering Dr. S?"

"Gabriel." Mom soothed a hand down his arm. "I want to introduce you to someone very important to me."

Cliff Man took that in with a short grunt. At the same time, he swung his bright-green eyes in the fastest head-to-toe assessment Shay had ever endured, taking only a second to note his resemblance to Mom.

"Huh," Gabriel muttered. "Well, weren't you clever, making the Cameron Stock connection and using it." He narrowed his gaze. "So're you Tait or Shay?"

At least ten smartass comebacks came to mind, but Shay nixed them all. Mom didn't make it a secret that she held the guy in high esteem. As in the pedestal-worshipping kind. "Shay," he replied. "And this is my...uhhh...friend, Zoe. It's nice to meet you...Gabriel, right?"

The guy didn't return his offered handclasp. "Ghid."

"What?"

"It's Ghid," he countered. "Pronounced *geed*." He didn't waver his stare through a meaningful pause.

"Sure." Shay shrugged. "So that's as in...what? Not your real name. Stand-in for your gamer name or something?"

The guy grunted again. "As in Ghidorah, the only dragon who made Godzilla shit his pants. I don't have time to play games."

"Yeah." Shay finally let a subtle snarl of his own unfurl. "I know Ghidorah." Classic monster weekends at the movies had made sure of that. "He was a nasty motherfucker with three heads." And thinking of this grouchy dickwad with *any* of his "heads" near Mom...

Shit.

"Can you two save the pissing contest for another occasion?" Mom yelled over the thunder from another detonating mortar. "I think we've got bigger concerns."

"Damn straight," Ghid growled. "Like getting your ass out of here."

Shay gave a grim smirk. "*There's* something to agree on."

Ghid took Mom by the elbow. "The sooner we get you to the roof and the helipad, the better. Trinity's got the chopper juiced and ready. Sounds like those Special Forces suckwits only have a few more taps of the battering ram left until they're fully in."

So much for seeing eye-to-eye with the bastard. "What the fuck?" Shay snapped. "That's Special Forces out there?"

"Damn it." Mom grimaced. "I thought Cameron had things under control."

"Yeah, well." Ghid's face barely changed, despite the dry overtone. "Guess his fondue wasn't a tasty treat, either."

"Crap," Mom mumbled.

"No shit," Zoe concurred.

Shay glared harder at Ghid. "In case you don't know, lizard breath, they're the good guys."

If it were possible, Ghid's face turned stonier as he pulled out a gorgeous SIG pistol, checked the chamber, and then glanced back at Mom. "You didn't get a chance to fill him in on much, did you?"

"What the hell is that supposed to mean?" But Shay had part of his answer deduced already. It meant that his conclusion from before, that his mother was here because of *both* force and choice, was true. It also meant that all the questions surrounding that theory were back—this time with a load of friends just to heighten the confusing fun.

Because this whole situation wasn't enough of a clusterfuck already.

When Ghid yanked open the door again, that assessment was proven in detail. The other side of the hallway wasn't visible anymore through the smoke, and paint chips dusted everything like snow. A couple of abandoned gurneys now lay on their sides, no attendants or patients in sight, causing Mom to clamp a hand over her gasping mouth.

"Breathe, Mel. You know Simon and Nick would've carried those guys out on their backs if they had to." Ghid's order was the perfect combination of patience and power. Shay admitted it grudgingly. Patience and strength aside, why the hell was Mom trusting a granite slab who spoke of Cameron and his gang almost like comrades and referred to a Special Forces team as *suckwits*?

He forgot the anger as he turned back to Mom. Her lips trembled as she lowered her hand. "But... But what if they couldn't make it? What if they've been st-stopped? What if they got t-taken back and—"

"Taken back where?" Shay asked. Ghid impaled him with a silent version of *don't ask, dude.* But it was too late. Mom's tears thickened, ripping at his chest. And galvanizing his actions. "I'll make sure they made it." Though he couldn't believe what he was promising, the words sprang from the depths of his heart, connected to the desperate little boy who tried to soothe her bruises with ice packs. The man he'd become could do something real for his mother's hurt. "I'll make sure every one of your boys gets on the plane. I promise." When Zoe added her own anguished sob, he leaned and gave her a quick, hard kiss. "Ssshhh. I'll be okay. My cover's still solid. I'm the logical one for this, dancer."

Ghid fired off an approving snort. "He's right."

Hell. The man was making it damn hard for Shay to decide which column to put him in, asshole or ally, which was likely how Ghid wanted it. "What's your destination for the chopper?"

The fucker quirked up one side of his mouth. "I could tell you, but then I'd have to kill you. Not that your corpse wouldn't feel right at home at our rustic little backup camp."

Shay sighed heavily. "Fine. Keep the twenty on your magic treehouse a state secret. Just tell me you can get Zoe safely back to Vegas from there."

"We have plenty of resources. She'll be safe."

Who the hell is "we"? He didn't bother pushing for the answer again. Ghid's enigma act was firm on the shutdown right now.

There was another matter to deal with too. One ticked-off little dancer, now launching herself at him with new terror in her eyes. "*Pendejo testarudo. No. No.*"

Ghid clearly recognized a good moment to pull away when he saw one. "You ready to roll, Doc?" he asked Mom in a tone too intimate for Shay's comfort. Despite every asshole move Dad had pulled, including death due to an exhausted liver, it had never occurred to Shay to think of Mom with someone else. Shit. The notion was reasonable, even justifiable. Just didn't stop it from being weird.

Mom raised a brave smile. "I have to grab my backup drives and the source serums."

"Shit," Ghid returned. "Yeah. Good call."

No more mortars hit the building, which was good and bad rolled together. Instead of the big blasts, gunfire *rat-a-tatted* nearby like Chinese fireworks, indicating whatever team had been sent for the party now had boots on the ground. Though the battle still raged at the other end of the building, adrenaline jacked Shay's blood as he took advantage of the few seconds he had left with his tiny dancer.

His tiny dancer.

He'd have to let go of that concept as soon as this moment was over.

On that dismal note, he hauled her tightly against him. They simply stood for a long moment, absorbing each other's energy, until he sifted fingers into her hair and tugged, lifting her face for one more selfish gaze.

"Damn," he murmured, blown away as if beholding her beauty for the first time...forcing his mind around the miserable truth that it was the last. She finally lifted both arms, tangling her hands against his scalp too, forcing his mouth down to hers. She didn't wait for him to do the invading this time. Her lips and tongue pulled and sucked on him with hot hunger. Her tearful mewl echoed through the deepest reaches of his being. Whatever part of his soul that hadn't been branded by her yet was officially lost to the resistance now.

When he pulled away, her protesting whimper filled the air between them. She kept her hand in his hair, soaking him all over again with the midnight-blue magic of her eyes, as she repeated her sweet little rasp from just an hour ago.

"This is crazy, right?"

Like that perfect moment from the medical room, he pushed their foreheads together and nodded.

"Shay?"

"Hmmm?"

"I'm scared."

"Don't be scared."

"What if—"

"Ssshhh."

He kissed her into silence not only for the words but all the shitty things his mind filled in to the blank after them. Life in Special Forces was all about *what ifs*. Some sucked harder than others. He'd had to confront them every day he went out with the team, including the real possibility of his own death. But that knowledge had always existed in the game room of his mind, like an irreverent neon beer sign. Other than Tait, who fully understood the hazards of his job, he'd never had to worry about anyone missing him much.

In the space of twenty-four hours, the perfect woman in his arms had changed all that. *Damn it.*

Mom reappeared, bearing a small satchel filled with notebooks and rattling with computer flash drive sticks. In her other hand was a clear Lucite box loaded with a dozen tubes, all filled with dark-gold liquid. Shay stared at them. He blinked, struck by a strange memory from those days when Mom and Homez were intense at work on their project in the garage. He had seen Homez with one of the vials in his hand, holding it up so the afternoon light made the liquid glow like—

"Magic honey."

The words fell out of him with the amazement from the memory. Mom stopped and blinked now too. She didn't look amazed. She looked stressed. To the power of ten. "Shay? Why did you say that?"

"Because I was the one who thought of it."

"Why?" Her questions were demands now. "How?"

"During the summer, when you and Homez were working so hard, he used to let me watch him during the breaks you took to go get lemonade and shit." He wondered if she would pinch his cheek again, but she was clearly too upset about something, still beyond his comprehension, to wield the discipline. Hoping to yank free the sword he'd apparently jabbed into her, he went on. "It was only for a few minutes at a time, Mom. He never let me stay for very long. I was just a curious kid, and—"

"He never let you near it, did he?" She jerked free of Ghid's hold, though Shay couldn't tell if the guy had attempted to comfort or restrain her. "The magic honey..." She ran her gaze over him with eyes that were different than a mother adoring her son. This time, her attention was filled with...fear. And horror. "Tell me, Shay Raziel Bommer," she insisted. "I know Homer adored you, and I know you knew it. Did you ever talk him into letting you touch the serum...or taste it?"

As soon as she ignited the question, more years burned away between then and now. His recollections crashed on each other like the gunfire that grew closer and clawed at him like Ghid's impatient growl.

He grimaced as an image rose from that fuzzy fire.

"I... I didn't know," he murmured. "The note... It was from you, Mom...right?"

He should've cussed. Even one of her treacherous pinches would've been better than her motionless silence.

"Wh-What note?" she finally asked. "Didn't know about what?"

He took her hands. Needed to feel her reassurance. The consequences for this one felt much worse than getting grounded for two weeks. "It was the night after you disappeared," he began. "Dad had hit the sauce all day and was already passed out. Tait was watching TV. I went to my room. One of the vials was just there, in a gold holder on my nightstand, with a note."

"Oh, my God," she rasped before squaring her shoulders in a you're-a-mother-don't-you-dare-fall-apart jerk. "Okay, tell me. Wh-What did the note say?"

He looked up at her anguished face. Her lips shook harder than before. Desperate breaths worked in and out of her nose. Without a doubt, if he spoke again, he'd drive the damn sword in deeper. But had he come all this way, worked this hard to find her, to hide them both from the truth—even if that reality wasn't a perfect movie plotline?

He hauled in a huge breath. "The note said...*Magic honey for my Little B.*"

"Oh." There was barely volume in it. "Oh..."

"Shit, Mom, I thought it was from you. I saw it as a sign that everything would work out okay. There was a part of me that probably believed it *was* magic...that by drinking it, I'd instantly teleport to be with you or something."

Their hands were still twined. Mom gripped him back so hard, she trembled from the effort. "He knew," she whispered. "Somehow, he knew I'd signed with Cameron, so he went back to the house and put it there...for *you* to find." Her head dropped forward between her shoulders. "Bastard!"

"Mom. *Mom.* Who're you talking..."

His words drifted out beneath the weight of his shock— because of the agony in her tears. Mom peered at him like he'd been gunned down in front of her. "Homer. I had no idea he could be so cruel."

"What?" Shay uttered. "Why?"

"You drank it." Her voice was flat and grim. "The honey.

Didn't you, Shay?"

Hell.

This wasn't like line-driving the baseball through the kitchen window. He couldn't stick the flower vase in front of the hole and be assured it wouldn't be discovered for another week. They were already out of time. He heard men bellowing orders over the gunfire, meaning it might already be too late to scoot his ass safely back down the hallway. But that didn't mean he could shirk the responsibility of his reply, either.

"Yeah, Mom. I drank it."

He felt nine years old all over again, confessing it. But even his nine-year-old self, who could peg the woman's reaction to a healthy list of shit, wouldn't have predicted the impact of his admission on his mom.

Who fell against him in a dead faint.

"Fuck!"

He and Ghid spat it in unison as the walls quaked again around them.

The military was here. The building had been breached.

Ghid snatched Mom's satchel and the case of vials and thrust them into Zoe's hands. As if Mom weighed the same as those containers, he scooped her into his arms. "This way," he ordered Zoe with a jerk of his head toward the stairwell. "Now!"

Shay didn't stop to ensure if Zoe followed. He prayed she was smart and simply did. He bolted the other direction, sticking close to the wall and praying that CENTCOMM had sent some guys with decent brains in their buckets—and reason in their trigger fingers. If he was lucky, he wouldn't see them at all.

He didn't get lucky.

"*Freeze*, dickwad! And get your ass on the floor right now, before I blast another hole in it!"

He complied without question. He knew better. Though it was torment to rein back his temper, especially when his face was "accidentally" grinded into the floor as they cuffed him, he accomplished the miracle by gritting his jaw and thinking of Zoe. He slid his eyes shut as they rolled him over and a boot pushed into the cavity between his ribs, crushing his hands beneath his body and all the air in his lungs.

But when the boot released, he still couldn't breathe. The voice belonging to that foot, just as angry as the stomp it had delivered, ensured that fact with crushing precision.

"Hello, little brother." Tait flung down a glare full of revulsion and hate. "Fancy meeting you here, asshole."

CHAPTER FOURTEEN

Zoe shivered, curled her legs under her in the patio chair, and wrapped her purple pashmina tighter against her shoulders. It was early November in the high desert, meaning the temperature descended with the sun. Though a few violet streaks lingered in the sky beyond the peaks of Red Rock Canyon, nighttime was definitely on the prowl.

She took another sip of the Cabernet Brynn had brought to go with their lasagna and salad. As the wine slackened her limbs, she leaned back, trying to let it ease her mind and heart as well. A bite of wind rustled through the juniper and willow trees and then across the in-ground reflecting pool, a nice reminder of why she'd decided to rent a place in Canyon Gate and commute a little farther to work on the Strip. When a girl's post-shift happy hour was at two in the morning, it was skies like this, blanketed with a thousand stars, that bested any cocktail for "taking the edge off the work day."

But she'd never had edges this harsh.

The stars began to glitter more brightly, but tonight, she didn't see any friends in them. Instead, they were heart-stabbing reminders of the gorgeous glints in Shay's eyes. The mighty silhouettes of Turtleback Peak and Mount Wilson only made her think of every perfect ridge in his muscles, of how safe she'd felt in his massive embrace. And the wind, stronger now, sucked her breath away just like he had on so many occasions. The first moment their gazes had met. Every single time he'd kissed her. Every second he'd filled her body with his.

The wind died.

It was eerily quiet.

Just like his four days of silence.

All the better to hear the desperate questions on their ridiculous repeat loop in her head.

Where the hell is he?

Is he safe?

Is he alive?

If so—and she wouldn't allow herself to believe anything else—then was he still playing his dangerous ruse with Stock? Or had he returned to his Spec Ops team, gone from the country on a completely new mission?

You knew it would probably go down like this. Even after you learned his truth, you knew the possibility of seeing him again was never as sure as splitting aces.

"Shut up," she muttered, gulping more wine.

Four days. Why did it feel like four thousand? Yet in so many ways, it could've been yesterday...even a few hours ago. She could almost hear the deafening roar of the helicopter again, carrying her, Ghid, and Melody Bommer away from the raid. She could smell the wildflowers in the meadow where they'd landed, near the ghost town in the middle of nowhere. She'd guessed they were at one of the long-forgotten mining camps that were scattered across northern Nevada. Though a tour wasn't offered, it was clear Ghid and his gang had taken over the place as a remote outpost, probably in preparation for exactly what had happened at the base.

The setting had been remote and chilly, a perfect match for the instant plummet of her spirit. Logic dictated that the despair was due to her sudden adrenaline drop, but that concept was paltry satisfaction for a mind still coping with the surreal somersault her life had taken. In a little over a day, she'd gone from watching her friends chug margaritas at LAX to sitting in an old gold panning trough as Ghid and his team refueled a helicopter in a meadow...

Okay, maybe "surreal" wasn't the right word.

Or maybe it was perfect.

Zoe glanced to the lavender bushes lining the yard, waiting for Morpheus or Glinda the Witch to emerge and confirm she'd really jumped into an alternate reality. She probably wouldn't mind things so much then. Glinda rocked great shoes, but bending spoons in a kick-ass leather trench definitely appealed too. *Hell.* What a dilemma.

No.

She knew what a dilemma really looked like. She was just fighting the memory—which, as her mind's eye so lovingly helped demonstrate, only pulled the whole thing closer.

Much too close.

She twisted her scarf harder as the recollection hit with brutal clarity.

She saw every tormented crease of Melody Bommer's face while Ghid relayed that Stock had been stopped from getting the airliner back off the ground. When Melody asked about the "guys," who Zoe assumed to be the strange patients on the gurneys she'd seen in the hallway, Ghid's features had succumbed to rare emotion. He had no answer for her and was clearly ripped apart by it. By the time Melody's tears surfaced, he'd become a human wall again, holding her while she sobbed out phrases about being helpless and pissed and confused, and then pissed again.

Zoe had been unable to sit by and watch anymore. She

couldn't very well blurt that she'd fallen like a lead brick for the woman's son after knowing him for a day, but she could help by taking over the tear-wiping duties. The action was a balm for her. Being closer to Melody helped her notice many wonderful traits the woman shared with her son—the brilliant amber eyes, the caramel highlights in the thick chocolate hair, the strongly angled face—and best of all, the similarities in their personalities. Even in her grief, Melody let out one-liners full of wicked sarcasm. Her protective side showed when she voiced concern about Zoe's growling stomach. But best of all—and oddly, worst of all—her smile was exactly like Shay's, easily formed and persistent in its strength.

When it had come time to say goodbye to Melody, she'd clung longer than she planned...and cried more than she wanted to.

And Shay's silence had stretched on.

At least the troupe had finally been reunited yesterday. Stock and his goons had taken away everyone's phones once they'd all become hostages, only now that everyone in the troupe was the media's hot flavor of the month, a cell company sponsored a big "get reconnected" celebration for them on a yacht at The Lakes. The last thing Zoe had felt like was a party. She dialed in from her own new phone, kindly messengered over to her, and video-chatted with everyone until she couldn't stop thinking about the moment she'd turned the device on, finding fifty texts and phone calls from Ava, about that many from Ryder, twice that many from *Papi*—and a grand total of zero from Shay. The ruse of cheer became too much. She excused herself, hanging up to indulge a self-pity bawl over the stupidity of falling so hard and fast for a man in one damn day.

It almost matched the dumbass move of picking up the

phone when it rang with a new video call, even when she recognized the number as Brynn's. She should have known that no matter how many margaritas Brynn had swigged, her friend would be instantly wise to her swollen eyes and cherry nose—explaining why she, Ellie, and Ryder were here for dinner tonight.

"Somebody's glass is almost empty."

Ry's sing-song, a usual natural for making her giggle, cracked only a small smile tonight. With a resigned sigh, she lifted her glass for the cheeky boy to refill. Ryder sloshed more Cabernet in as he settled into the chair to her right. "Thanks," she said, arching a brow at the large puddle of vino he'd managed to spill to her deck. "Good thing this is used brick."

"And good thing I wore my lined jacket," Ry quipped back. "Holy shit, girlfriend. It's cold enough for Otter Pops out here."

"Then I'd like a Sir Isaac Lime, please." She sipped from her refilled glass. "And the cold is...good. At least tonight."

"Needing a little distraction?" He waited for a decently long moment, like any good friend, but jumped back in as soon as he possibly could. "From thinking of a certain Dom-alicious individual who rocked your world a few nights ago?"

"It's...a little more complicated than that." Though she managed to keep the tears from completely ruining the last of her statement, Ryder's sympathetic *tsk* pushed her over the edge.

"Ohhhh, honey." He fell to his knees next to her chair and pulled her into his warm hug. "Crap. I'm so sorry. Me and the nasty cesspool of my mind. Like you'd be thinking of shag-worthy Shane after all the shit those cockbags put you through, and—Zo?"

She buried her face against his shoulder, letting the sobs

come again. "Oh, Ry..."

"Jesus." He slammed down his wine in order to hug her more tightly. "Zo. Shit, girl. What is it?"

She shocked herself by actually growling. The sound blatantly dazed Ry, who'd never heard her pull a blubber-fest like this since they'd known each other. "Screw it," she finally blurted. "I'm a mess, and I don't care who knows."

That caused the guy to squirm. Ryder might have been a walking, talking expert about everything Sondheim, Prada, and penis, but he also hated rom-coms, Gaga, and people who whined in the gym—which meant a bawling woman in his arms likely didn't rank high on his list. "You want to talk to Ava? I could get her on the phone, sweetie."

"No!" she snapped. "She'll call *Papi*. His cardiac check-ups have finally been better, and I'm not going to ruin that energy two months before her wedding."

He huffed. "So much for not caring who knows you're a mess, hmmm?"

Mierda. The only one who did hot angry better than him was Shay. "*Ay. Callate, pendejo.*" She forced a tease into it, throwing a hand through the trendy new crop cut of his dark-blond hair.

"Hey. Not the hair!"

Just before they debated trying to fling each other into the reflecting pool, there was a forceful knock at her front door.

"Odin's fucking beard." Brynn emerged from the kitchen, intercepting Zoe on her rush to the door. "Did you invite Thor *and* his hammer and not tell us?"

Zoe swung open the portal as the pounding started again. She barely avoided a fist in the face from the man who stood on her porch—correction, consumed her front doorway—like a full-scale Malibu Ken doll.

"Are you Zoe Chestain?" His guttural demand cut the Ken doll impression by half. The accent immediately gave him away as a Texas boy, only it was the Chuck Norris side of Texas, used to confronting a lot of danger.

Which wasn't a great comprehension for her gut. "Uh..."

"Who the hell wants to know?" Ryder stepped forward, producing an inner alpha dog that Zoe didn't know he had. It was stunning. A little scary.

The guy tossed a furtive look over his shoulder as he stomped in and slammed the door. "My name's Dan Colton." He flashed a gold badge. "I'm with the CIA. And you were the dancer with Shay at A-51, weren't you?"

"Don't tell him a thing, Zo."

Ryder had gone to full-on protective hound mode. Now the whole thing was a little irritating. Zoe gave him a bop on the shoulder and a soft she-growl.

"Yes," she told the agent, "that was me. Is he okay? Are you his contact from the agency?"

"I am." His face tightened. "Or at least I was."

"*Was?*" Zoe clutched at Ry. Her body went cold. Oh, God. Didn't they bring priests along when they informed loved ones that a soldier had died?

But she wasn't Shay's "loved one," was she? What *had* she been? A nice diversion, if that? Maybe she should be grateful for Colton's house call, instead of a phone message or email.

"Yeah." Colton's green eyes turned stormy. "I'm pretty damn certain my involvement with the guy is past tense."

From clenched teeth, Zoe demanded, "Which means what?"

The agent pierced her with a harder stare. Whatever he

saw in her face clearly disturbed him. "I was hoping you could tell me."

The urge to drill her fist into the man's jaw intensified by the second. "Tell you *what*?"

"Okay, back up the trolley. I'm not on board." Ryder frowned. "Who the hell is Shay?"

"Ditto," Ellie and Brynn added in unison.

Zoe glanced up, biting her lip. "Remember when I told you it was complicated?"

"Complicated enough to involve the CIA?" Her friend dropped onto an ottoman when she only bit her lip. "Holy shit, Zo."

"Pop a chiller, sparky. Let the man explain." After the sarcasm of her gibe at Ry, Brynn pulled a one-eighty in her cordiality to Colton. "Come in, Agent Colton. Are you hungry? I just pulled some lasagna out of the oven."

"Sure. Whatever." The agent was oblivious to the fact that Brynn clearly thought he was better than Thor and the hammer. His palpable stress crunched Zoe's gut even harder. "So Shay hasn't contacted you at all in the last four days?" he turned and asked her.

Zoe joined Ryder on her worn leather couch. "No. I'm sorry, Agent Colton. I can see how stressed you are about this. If I could tell you anything else, I would."

"How about telling your friends who the hell this guy is?" Ry snapped. "Or was?"

"*Is*." Zoe bit it out before falling against the cushion, cradling her head in her hands. "His name is Shay Bommer, but you know him as Shane Burnett. Agent Colton was his main line at the CIA because he was working with them on an undercover basis, and—"

224

"Whoa," Ry cut in. "Now the trolley's jumped all the tracks."

Brynn stomped back in, oven mitts on the hands she braced to her hips. "Damn straight it has. *Shane Burnett?* The world's last chunk of chivalry from the airport?"

"Shit." Ellie gasped. "The one with the supersized fries in his crotch?"

Ryder straightened. "You didn't tell me about the big fries."

Brynn stomped closer. "You didn't tell *me* that you spent any more time with him after we got back to the hotel."

"And there was time to do that...when?" Zoe shot back. "Remember the hangover you boarded the plane with?"

"The plane." Ryder repeated it like the words brought new revelation. "Oh, *hell*. Shane is Shay. And he was with you during the shit at A-51. So does that mean that Dom-alicious was also one of the dickwads who hijacked your plane?"

"Dom-alicious?" Brynn and El were once more an echoing chorus, complete with their own accusing gapes.

Colton came to her rescue in the nick of time. Rising with a sweep of his impressive height, the man silenced the three of them with a single glower.

"As much as I'd love to hear that story and have a sweet piece of blackmail material to hold over my friend's head, there's a larger cow pile to shovel here." He paced to the patio door so forcefully, Brynn flattened to the wall to let him by. "I officially don't know where they've taken Shay. And I'm freaked as a virgin in a whorehouse about it. Now none of my calls are being returned, my secure email address is no longer accessible, and my key card doesn't work at the office."

So much for the rescue. Zoe surged to her feet. "What

does that all mean? *They* who?"

Before she could interpret anything from his cryptic glare of a reply, her cell vibrated on the dining room table. The window didn't identify a caller. She showed it to Colton, who nodded at her to answer but to keep the device tilted so he could listen. She wiped her clammy palms on her thighs before clicking open the line with a wobbly finger.

"H-Hello?"

Several sickening beats of silence went by.

"It's Ghid."

"Uh, hi." *Hi? Really? Think you can handle things a little better than reverting to the age of fifteen, Zo?* "How'd you get my number?" she charged. "Why are you calling?"

"It's a good thing the I-Man has an excellent memory chip. Remarkably, he was able to dig your digits out of his ass, even in this condition."

Zoe scowled, baffled. "What?"

"Hey...dancer."

In the same instant, his voice lit up her soul and broke her heart. He sounded parched, exhausted, weak...and alive.

"Shay?" It was a combination of sigh and sob. "*Ay Dios mio*. Where are you?"

Another unnerving silence. Ghid's burlap tone filled the line again. "Has Colton found you yet?"

She looked over to the agent, unsure how to answer in light of the way his eyes had gone Hulk-green with rage. "Yeah," he seethed, "I'm right here, assmunch."

"Thank fuck." Shay mumbled it that time, sounding more pained. Zoe winced before exchanging a confused glance with Colton, who spoke up on behalf of them both.

"What the hell is going on?" Colton charged. "Who are

you and what do you want with Bommer?"

Shay came on again, replacing his strain with wrath. "Goddamnit, Colton. Stop being Cowboy Bob. He's not the bad guy."

"And I'm supposed to believe that?" Colton flung. "You've been MIA for four days, Bommer."

"I'm well aware of that, you ass." He sifted the anger from it to add, "And pretty sure today would've been my last one alive, if it weren't for Ghid."

"Nah." A horn sounded in the background to help punctuate it, clarifying the two of them were in a car somewhere together. "They wouldn't have killed you, kid. Not before dicing you up a bit more."

"*Dios.*" Zoe couldn't help emitting another sob. "Then thank heaven for you, Ghid."

Colton didn't look anywhere near ready to join in her gratitude. "*They* who?" he challenged.

Ghid paused before answering—long enough to let a strange, foreboding lump form at the base of Zoe's throat. "The same *they* I'm not going to talk about over the phone, even if we're using a burner." The traffic noises behind him grew a little louder, as if they'd gotten onto the freeway. "And the same *they* who are likely on their way to scoop you both up now."

"Both of us?" Zoe questioned. "You mean Agent Colton and me?"

"What the hell?" Colton charged. "Why?"

Zoe couldn't interpret the snorts Ghid and Shay emitted, roughening the line. Wait. Maybe she could.

Were they *chuckling* about this?

"Let's just say your big brothers don't like it when someone comes and takes their toys, Colton."

The agent frowned. "I don't have any brothers."

"Yeah, you do. The big, happy, Langley, Virginia, family, remember?"

Zoe found herself the lone witness to Colton's stunned glare. She was pretty certain she shared the expression.

Had the *CIA* been holding Shay for the last four days?

"Ghid...that's a big gap of belief to jump," she finally said. "And if it were the case, why wouldn't the feds just call Colton in instead of *scooping him up*?"

"Don't bother answering that, man." The astonishing interjection belonged to Colton, who had his cell pulled out—with an expression that blew from fury to alarm in two seconds. "I'm already looking at the explanation. You're not shitting about this."

"Wish I was," Ghid muttered.

Brynn, pressed up behind Colton's other shoulder, also frowned. "What are all those red dots on the screen?" she asked. "And why are they all bunching up in the parking lot at the grocery store up the street?"

"It's not for a fucking sale on Bugles and beer," Colton muttered.

Ghid grunted. "You're able to track the other agents in the city?"

"For safety and security purposes," Colton supplied. "In this case, mine."

"Yeah, we'll see how long they let that last."

As Ghid declared it, all the dots vanished from the screen.

"Oh, no!" Brynn grabbed Colton's wrist and shook it, along with the phone. To Zoe's surprise, the agent reacted with what looked like enchantment instead of anger.

"It's not an Etch A Sketch, red."

Brynn was too stressed to latch on to the humor. With panic in her eyes, she looked across the room. "Ellie!"

The hail was redundant. El was already halfway across the room, one hand extended. "Give," she commanded Colton. The agent, too nonplussed to argue, complied. By the time El had tapped the device a dozen times and completed her technical magic, the trace dots were so globbed together at the grocery store, it appeared like a blood splotch on the screen.

"Shit," Brynn rasped. "I liked it better when it was an Etch A Sketch."

"Zoe." Shay's voice, though still craggy, now reverberated with his Dominant's baritone. "You're in danger too, dancer. A shit ton of it."

"M-Me?" She hated herself for getting tremulous. The last thing Shay needed right now was a woman going soggy on him. Still, her confusion was legit. "Wh-Why?"

"You know about me now."

"Know *what* about you?" *That you have the strongest arms that have ever held me, know the fastest paths into my soul, give kisses I'd sacrifice a kidney for?*

"I'll explain soon, I promise. You just both need to get out of there. Now."

"We can go to my place." Ryder pulled out his keys. "As long as you all promise to take off your shoes. I had the carpets done last week."

"El and I are closer," Brynn countered.

"None of that works," Ghid ordered. "I guarantee these guys will be pounding on all *your* doors next."

"I've got something that'll work."

Colton's assertion was quiet but strong, enough to still everyone in the room. Still, Ghid countered, "Fine and dandy, spook man, but you can't spill it on this party line."

Colton smirked. "Sure I can." After a second, he called out, "Yo, I-Man?"

"Yeah?" Shay's reply had weakened again, turning Zoe's gut into a pretzel.

"Listen up."

There was a rustling on the other end, as if the phone were being picked up. Sure enough, Shay's next words were louder, right into the phone but just as tired. "Go ahead."

"I want you to subtract eleven from thirteen, then go south but shoot north."

"Huh?" Zoe stammered.

"What the hell?" El and Brynn chorused.

"Got it," Shay confirmed.

"*Huh?*" Zoe bugged her eyes, but Colton maintained his focus.

"I won't repeat for obvious reasons, but it's in the decoder," Shay stated.

"The decoder?" That one came from Ghid. "*What* decoder?"

"The one between my ears. What's after that, Dan?"

"Double your age," the agent replied. "When you've gotten to the target, ask for Oz."

"As in the Wizard of?" Ry sneered. "Oh, this should be fun."

Ellie drummed a finger at Colton's phone. "No time for fun. The red dots are on the move."

"Which means we are too," Colton ordered. "Leave your phones, grab your purses, and let's bug. I'm driving."

"Ry always carries the purses." Brynn stated it as they hung their bags along one of Ryder's long, lean arms. "In the mall, that leaves us free to shop. In a situation like this, I suggest replacing shoes with booze."

Despite the stress lining every inch of his face, one side of Colton's mouth yanked up. "Zoe, I must commend you on your taste in friends." He didn't veer his gaze from Brynn. "They're beautiful *and* smart."

"Awww. Thank you, cutie." Ryder beat Brynn to the punch on a response, though he had an unfair advantage. It was tough for Brynn to speak around the giggle she shared with Ellie as Ry gave an appreciative squeeze to Colton's ass on his way out the door.

★ ★ ★ ★ ★

An hour later, Zoe tried to remember the metaphor she'd conceived while gazing at the stars back home. Something about life and somersaults...

Well, the comparison needed a serious upgrade now. Something along the lines of a couple of *loco* backflips.

She could only see a few stars now, though the light pollution from the Strip was a full fifty-four floors down. That didn't matter when one was competing with a nighttime playground so iconic, some say it could be seen from space. From this picture window in the Vdara's penthouse, all the icons looked like sleek postcards—the gold bastions of the Wynn and Encore, the Bellagio fountains, the Paris's Eiffel Tower and hot air balloon—increasing the sensation that this was somehow all the craziest dream she'd ever had. In a second, she'd surely wake up in her room at the Hilton back in LA, rocking the hangover from hell along with the realization she *had* joined the gang on those margaritas—and that Shay

231

Bommer had been nothing but a perfect man in a magical dream.

"Miss? The food has arrived."

The statement, though soft, was issued in a voice so deep that she felt it to her toes. Just like Dorothy Gale, her dream had its own wizard, though hers wore tailored black leathers instead of a carpetbagger look, rocked two full sleeves of exotic tattoos, and had a face so beautiful, one barely noticed the severe skull cut of his jet-black hair.

"Thanks, Oz," she replied, just as subdued, "but I'm not very hungry."

Furrows appeared in the man's silk-smooth forehead. "Are you unhappy with the accommodations?"

She almost burst out laughing. How could anyone be dissatisfied with this place? The two-bedroom suite, with its modern lines, gray and purple furnishings, and state-of-the-art *everything* for amenities, was fit for rock stars and moguls, not a bunch of backup dancers from a show up the street. When Colton told them he "knew a guy here" who'd promised he'd always have a place to stay, she wondered if that man was the damn owner and exactly what kind of favor he owed Colton.

"No, Oz," she protested. "Everything's wonderful. Really."

I'm just agonizing every minute Shay still isn't here. Wondering if that pained quaver in his voice has gotten worse. Beyond stressed about the completely cryptic directions that Colton gave them and trying not to think about them ending up in the middle of the Mojave instead.

With the telepathy only possible from a best friend, Ryder translated her stress into the most perfect words possible. "Colton, sweetie? While it goes without saying that we all couldn't be happier with your secret hideout, can you enlighten us to how the hell Shay and his friend will find us too?"

Colton finished his bite from the flatbread pizza Oz had brought and then flashed what had to be his eighth complimentary smile at Brynn for the wine choice. "I-Man and I are a couple of action movie geeks. I banked on him remembering the films that were shot in Vegas."

Zoe continued with a perplexed frown, along with Ry and Brynn—but Ellie's eyes suddenly ignited. "Oh, snap on the downbeat! Yeah, it makes sense now."

"It does?" Brynn muttered.

"Damn." Ellie pointed a congratulatory finger at Colton. "That's brilliant, spook man."

Ry's brows pushed together. "Hello, United Nations? Anyone there have an interpreter for 'El Browning Speak'?"

Ellie rolled her eyes. "Sheez, you guys. 'Eleven from thirteen.' That refers to *Ocean's Eleven* and its sequel, *Ocean's Thirteen*. There was only one place used for filming in both the movies—the Bellagio. But he also said 'subtract,' which told Shay to do the actual math. Eleven from thirteen is two. Going south from the Bellagio by two, you end up here, at the Vdara. As far as doubling his age?" She spread her hands. "Since we're on the fifty-fourth floor, I'm guessing Shay is twenty-seven."

A long silence stretched.

Ryder slowly cocked his head at El. "You officially scare me."

El gave a delicate snort. "I have piercings in my ears, sweet thing, not my brain."

"You still scare me."

Zoe, succumbing again to nervous energy, paced back toward the suite's foyer. "I'm still scared, period."

No. She was past scared and now at terrified. What if Shay

and Ghid didn't get here? But what was she in for if they did? Everything still felt in limbo. She still kept expecting to wake up from the dream—

Until reality bashed its way in.

There was a key swipe at the suite's door. Zoe froze, her stomach lurching into her throat. She rushed farther up the entry but was hauled back by Oz, his dark eyes issuing a silent dictate for her retreat. Colton, with pistol now drawn, yanked her even farther back. He pushed her against Brynn, who grabbed the agent's elbow before he pivoted to join Oz. Brynn mouthed two words at him. *Be careful.*

That was certainly the slogan of the damn night.

Wrong.

As soon as the door opened and Ghid staggered in, supporting a man who vaguely resembled Shay beneath his cuts, bruises, and wounds, the night was stamped by a brand-new refrain. It was ripped from Zoe's throat on a scream that began deep in her soul.

"*Ay Dios mio*, no!"

CHAPTER FIFTEEN

"*Zoe.*" Shay hated having to bellow it, but the woman was practically tripping over herself with panic and worry. It made his head pound—worse than it already did—to think of the woman keeping her shit together through the hijacking and the mortar drop at the base, only to tizzy herself straight out one of these windows. "For the twelfth time, I don't need a doctor."

He finished the order by pulling her down on the couch next to him, despite the rocket of pain it sent up his arm. *There. Better.* Fuck, it felt good to have his *mariposa* against him once more. A haven of softness, smelling like cocoa, cream, and roses...

He tucked her tighter, regretting that in comparison, he probably stank like a hobo. Ghid had brought him a fresh T-shirt, work boots, some underwear, and jeans, which he'd changed into when they stopped at a gas station to redress his wounds, but a cowboy shower in a roadside john wasn't nearly what he needed to scrub away the stench from the last four days.

He'd let her go in a few minutes. For now, he needed the assurance that she was real, the verification that he was truly free of the ugly cocoon of the last four days.

Ghid, who crouched next to him, grunted approval of his move. Not a surprise. Ghid had his own version of a Zoe. Her name was Melody Bommer. Anyone with half a brain cell in their head would figure it out after spending thirty minutes

235

with the man. Shay had now logged in a little shy of three hours with him. While the idea of the guy shacking up with his mom had been jarring to accept at first, Ghid had gradually won him over. The guy adored Mom so much, he'd sneaked *back into* Area 51 just to bust Shay's ass out. The lunatic had used the pretext of being some chemical-waste-disposal dude, curling Shay up in one of his steel drums.

In doing so, the man had saved his life. There wasn't a goddamn doubt in Shay's mind about it. If the "experiments" hadn't eventually killed him, then the despair would have.

Zoe snuggled a little closer, earning a soft kiss atop her head from him and a slightly bigger smirk from Ghid. The man had already examined "the nicks," as he called them, from the side Zoe was pressed against, anyway—though when Ghid first used the term, he'd glanced at Shay to communicate how he comprehended the word's irony. "Nicks" could be relative, couldn't they? Shay had been bumped, bruised, and cut up a hundred different ways just jumping out of a plane to a mission target. The sight of his own blood was nothing new. But there was something different about the experience when watching a "scientist" with high-level government security clearance slice a strip out of his chest, then slide it under a microscope slide and make notes about it...

He washed away the horror by gratefully grabbing the beer offered by a lanky dude wearing a T-shirt emblazoned with the expression *PUH-LEEEZ.* The blonde seemed weirdly familiar, though Shay was certain he'd never seen him before.

Christ. What *was* he "certain" of anymore? The reunion with Mom had been two hundred kinds of weird. And the little chitchat with Tait after his brother brought him down? *Fucking disaster* was a better term. Bash, Wyst, and a couple of the other guys had been caught along with him, meaning he couldn't simply blurt the whole truth to T without compromising the entire operation he had in place—and Dan Colton along with it. By the time Tait relented and dragged him into a room for a one-on-one, Cameron hailed him on the radio with disgusting timing. That had deep-sixed any scrap of trust Tait might've thought about throwing his way. Tait had hurled the handset against the wall and then marched him back out to the hall, happily handing him over to the scientists with the clearance badges.

By then, the bad that had become worse took a nosedive into hell.

So no, he wasn't sure of a goddamn thing anymore—except the woman still pressed so perfectly against him.

"Hey, hey, heyyyy, Mr. Shay." The blonde with the weird shirt tried crossing hipster with talk-show host. Neither worked, which the guy validated by muttering, "Shit. I can be lame when I'm nervous."

By then, the connection clicked to the voice. "Ryder." He smiled and meant it. "It's good to meet you." *Hell.* It was good to be alive, period.

Ghid leaned back, nodding his head with what looked like satisfaction despite eyes that glittered with strange green glints. "I have good and bad news, kid. You're going to live."

Zoe tensed a little. "So what's the bad news?"

"That's the bad news too."

Shay really wanted someone to laugh, to confirm he wasn't as batshit as he felt, since he couldn't. Laughing at the nightmare felt too much like tempting it to return. Zoe seemed fond of her perplexed frown, and Ryder was a loyal friend in backing her up.

Ghid to the rescue again.

"Hell's fucking bells." The man pinched the bridge of his nose, but there was a chuckle in his tone. "Mel warned me about the smartass streaks in you and your brother."

Okay, better again. He could smirk and feel safe about it. "Well, half the show is better than nothing, right?" He let his stare drift out the windows, taking in the glittering city lights. "Probably a damn good thing, too. If that goat testicle who calls himself my brother were here right now, I'd be wanting to—"

"Tear open all the stitches that the spooks' finest sewed into you?" Ghid parried. "Is that it?"

"Thanks." He spat it while swigging the beer. The bubbles felt good at the back of his throat, biting at the places still raw from his screams. He forced himself to focus on how good every drop tasted, anything except the craving to tear out the thick black threads holding at least eight gouges in his body together.

"That's what I'm here for," Ghid drawled. "Anytime you need a warm fuzzy, kid."

Shit. The man had sarcasm down to an art. Shay tossed back an equally dry glare and muttered, "Sure. Warm. Fuzzy. Got it."

Only the images bombarding his mind were the polar opposite—literally. Like the morning he woke up from a drugged sleep in a subzero freezer, stark naked, and was timed on how long his body held out until he went severely hypothermic...

Fortunately, rage wasn't so debilitating. "Cheers, mate," he snarled, downing the last of the beer and then heaving the bottle at the wall.

"*Mierda!*"

Zoe's exclamation was a stab of light in his darkness, jerking him back to sanity. "I'm sorry," he murmured, but when she pressed a hand over his chest, he pushed away, jabbing hands into his hair. Of course, his fingers landed on the long set of stiches there too. What had those fuckers said? Something about the importance of gathering a "complete sample"? Oh, *that* was what they called it. Felt like a four-inch scalping to him.

It's over, man. All over. Open your eyes. Focus on what matters.

He forced his gaze open, lifting it to Ghid, who'd moved to the ottoman in front of the couch. "Shit. I'm sorry."

If Ghid had a reaction, and that was a big *if*, it was replaced by another voice, from behind Shay.

"I'm sorry too."

Colton.

Shay didn't want to stiffen but did. His head reconfirmed all the pertinent shit—that they wouldn't be safe at the top of this glass tower if not for the guy and that Colton had kept his mission a very secure secret for six months—but then there were the facts his gut wouldn't let go.

Spec Ops had given him over to the scientists without a second blink, which meant somebody way higher than them had approved the plans for him. Probably *much* higher. But that also meant that at some point, his file had to be run through the system. Which meant that the CIA had to have a chance for throwing a flag on the play—

A flag that had never come.

Leading to his four days in lab rat hell.

Who the hell had the pull to yank him that far off the grid? And why?

239

Then there was the shittiest question of them all—the one that demanded to be voiced aloud, despite how it gouged at his lips with more painful incisions than anything the science monsters had done to him.

"Where'd you go?"

He watched all three words drive into Dan like daggers yet felt no satisfaction about it. The emptiness of that was the worst of all. Their stares twisted into each other. The months of their partnership, their *friendship*, had tied them like forest vines through the last six months, seeded by a mission but grown through humor, honesty, and trust. Seeing the agony on his friend's face confirmed the disgusting truth—the shit that had gone down in Area 51 was as much a shock to Dan as anyone. Maybe more.

"Christ, Shay." His voice was ragged. "Where'd *you* go?"

He grimaced while eagerly accepting another beer from Ryder. "That isn't a peachy answer for me to give right now."

"I've barely slept the last four days."

"That makes two of us."

"Three." Zoe's murmur, thick with emotion, tore at him in bad ways...and good. He was surely going to a deeper part of hell for being a little touched that she'd lost sleep over him.

"They pulled everything from the system." Dan's assertion tugged Shay's head back up. His friend waited for him with a nod of emphasis. "Yeah, man. I mean everything."

"Don't stop there, ball sack." The opportunity to use his favorite pet name for the guy couldn't be better timed. Not if the gravity of what Dan inferred was true.

"As soon as I heard the big brass had sent in that SHRC team to bust things up at the base, I knew it was time to step in and make sure CENTCOMM knew about your cover so that you weren't pegged as a hostile in the mess. But when I went to pull up the file on our op, it was gone."

"Gone?" *Fuck*. The line sounded like an outtake from every lame confrontation scene from every bad action movie made. But unlike fiction, this worse-than-the-worst possibility couldn't be fixed by blowing something up in the next forty-five minutes. "Gone...how?""

"Is there more than one way to do 'gone'?" Dan returned. "They took it out, Shay. It's not in system backups or archives, either. Somebody deliberately extracted every word, note, field intel, and status report we filed on your mom, her connection to Stock, and our progress on the mission."

Dan finished by lowering to the other ottoman. Shay didn't blame him for wanting to sit. He was surprised the guy didn't use the floor itself as a landing strip. As the shock set in deeper, the idea of splaying there himself gained appeal. "What about the guys higher than you in the food chain? Did you take this bullshit to them?"

"None of them are returning my calls, texts, or emails. And as of three days ago, when I went to the office to take my personal backup to them, my key card didn't even work for their floors in the elevator."

Shay braced his elbows on his knees and dropped his head. He gazed down the neck of the beer bottle dangling from his fingers. It was damn murky in there. He couldn't see to the bottom. Pretty ideal fit for this new piece of grand fuckery, its web apparently stuck to the CIA's upper ranks, too. "So the last six months of my life are gone."

Dan exhaled with careful slowness. The sound was painfully familiar to Shay. It was the sound Colton saved for moments he had crappy news to deal and was determined to respect their relationship by dealing it straight. "The last piece of available information I can see is your transfer request off the Seventh SFG, and onto the CIA Spec Ops detail with me."

"Six months ago," Shay said.

"Six months ago," his friend confirmed.

"And after that, I disappeared."

Once more, he had a crapload of information. And absolutely nothing at the same time.

"So what does it all mean?" The query came from Zoe's friend Brynn, who settled next to Dan. She was more sober than the first time Shay had met her and less terrified than the second. And looking a little attached to Dan now too. That was good. The guy looked like he might need it.

Ghid pushed into the silence by unfurling off his seat with fluid grace, again reminding Shay of a prowling Komodo. "This feels like a damn good place to step in," the man stated.

"What the fuck?" Dan challenged. He chilled once Shay extended both hands, backing him off. Ghid had earned the respect, at least for a few minutes. The moves he'd pulled when helping Shay escape from the science monsters were just short of poetry, Special Ops style. Shay had no idea if that was where the guy had learned his swagger, and at this point, didn't care. He was free. If that was accomplished by training from fucking *Sesame Street*, then all hail to Big Bird for the moves.

"Go ahead, Ghid," he assured. "It's okay."

Ghid's nod was far from effusive, though the appreciation was apparent. "Glad to hear you feel that way, kid." He dropped his head again, this time toward Oz. "Okay, big O, bring him in."

So much for camping out on the chill button. Shay couldn't put his finger on what made him hop right back into trepidation mode—perhaps the furtive speed of Ghid's glances or the urgency in Oz's steps toward the foyer—but he knew the instinct to slam his guard back up when he felt it. That proclivity was rarely wrong.

And it sure as fuck didn't let him down now.

God only knew what Tait's arrival would've done to his gut otherwise.

Didn't stop him from giving in to the fury it unleashed on his senses anyway. Without a single regretful thought, he lunged across the room. With every step, the wrath kindled higher. Thicker. Hotter.

"Fancy meeting you here, asshole."

Hurling T's sneer back at him felt every damn bit as good as he thought it would—right before he took the shitwad down in a clean tackle. T's answering roar was just the incentive he needed to drive his knee up into his brother's ribs, making the guy roll to his back. *Perfect.* He straddled T and pulled back his arm, already savoring how good it was going to feel to ram his fist into the guy's jaw.

Somebody grabbed him by the elbow. The grip wasn't very viable, though. It'd be easy to shake them off—

Until the scream pierced his ear. Her scream.

"Are you *loco*? *Madre de Dios*, you're going to break open everything and bleed again!"

He resisted her hold. "Zoe." Then glared down at his brother, who fired back the eyes and snarl of a pissed-off tiger. "Back off. Now."

"Not a chance, *pendejo*." Her spite would've been kind of cute under other circumstances. But her tears? *Fuck.* They were his downfall, and the smart little thing probably knew it. "Shay." Her voice rippled with a sob. "Please. *Please.*"

"Damn it." If Ghid *had* been trained on *Sesame Street*,

his growl was pure Oscar the Grouch, complete with the steel lid for emphasis. "She's right. Stop acting like a couple of five-year-olds."

Shay let go of the hold he had on the classic image of Clint Eastwood plastered on Tait's T-shirt. Dirty Harry really was lucky tonight. "Zoe, let me introduce the goat shit known as my brother. And assmunch, while you're down here, grovel a little at the feet of the woman who saved you tonight. If not for her, your face would be removed from your skull about now."

Tait scrambled to his feet and jutted a hand at Zoe. "Tait Bommer."

"Zoe Chestain. Really good to meet you."

"Likewise, Z—" T stuttered to a stop. "Wait. *Chestain?*"

"Yes, Ava's my sister. And no, Shay and I didn't have a clue until well after we met each other."

"Which was..."

"About five days ago."

"What?"

"Write the movie script later, Mel Brooks." The bark belonged to Ghid. "You're here for a purpose, so focus."

"That's right." Tait rolled his shoulders and winced a little, bringing a little satisfaction. He'd have some new bruises tomorrow. Good. "A *purpose*—" he hurled his growl to Ghid now "—that isn't as clear to me now as it was when you called using details about my mother as bait, Mr. Preston." His face gave in to obvious surprise when looking at Shay again. "What the hell happened to *you*?"

Shay spewed a bitter laugh. "Like you don't know?"

He almost regretted the vicious tone. Tait's face fell into authentic shock. "No." His voice faltered too. "I really don't, Shay. Holy crap. Do you really think—?"

"Come on." Colton motioned toward the suite's living room area. "You two need to sit down and chill."

"Fuck me." Tait's face expanded with more surprise. "Dan Colton. *You're* in on this gaggle too?"

Dan folded his arms. "Cool the fuse, T-Bomb. Preston hasn't been able to get in a word yet."

"Because somebody let my brother off his leash?" He prowled toward Ghid with a new grimace. "This is fucked up. I should be calling and reporting your ass right now."

Though Ghid looked like T had simply told him it would rain tomorrow, Shay stomped forward again. "Christ, T. Back off on the pompous-ass throttle and give the guy a break."

"Like you gave me a break when I walked in?"

"Like you gave me a break after you stomped on me, cuffed me, and turned me over to those monsters at A-51?"

"Monsters? Damn it, what the *fuck* are you talking about?"

Shay grabbed the back of the couch to avoid digging his hands into Clint Eastwood again. "You really going to look me in the face and tell me you don't know?"

"I was doing my job!"

"So was I!"

"You're a fucking traitor, Shay. And now you're a fugitive on top of it. Shit! My own goddamn brother!" His mouth bunched like he was about to hurl. "You know what? I have every damn right to pull the asshole card right now."

Shay openly borrowed from Zoe for his reaction. Sometimes silly girl behavior deserved silly girl eye rolls. "You know what? Forget the goat-shit thing. You're just a goat, T, plain and simple. You'll swallow anything anyone feeds you."

Tait got in a sarcastic laugh of his own. "Doesn't change the truth of the matter. Every soldier and special agent in a fifty-mile radius is looking for your ass." He visibly stiffened when Zoe gasped out something desperate in Spanish. "Sorry, Zoe, but they are."

That sliver of kindness toward Zoe made Shay actually contemplate his brother for a long moment, instead of getting creative with the goat jargon again. "My ass, huh?" When he tacked on a long exhalation, he hated the quaver in it. "Figures. It's the only part of me they haven't fileted yet."

Finally, *finally*, Tait looked at him too—with eyes that saw him once more through a filter other than Cameron Stock. "Christ, Shay. What's going on here? What the fuck are you doing? What are you hiding?"

Ghid stepped over and positioned himself in the center of the seating area, adopting a full drill instructor stance. "Come and sit down, you two."

Shay looked his brother in the eye. "You should probably listen to him."

"It was meant for you too, kid."

"Thanks, Ghid. But I feel fine now."

"*Sit. Down.*"

Tait snickered during his grudging obedience. "You're a tetchy fucker, you know that?"

"Tetchy." Ghid gave another weather report reaction. "That's a new one. Fits, though."

"Mom never used it on you?" Shay asked.

Tait sobered the laughter. "Mom? *Whose* mom? What the...fuck?"

Shay used his brother's astonishment as a chance to regroup his own composure. Missions and their expectations... The dichotomy was a bigger dildo up his ass than before. This sure as hell wasn't the way he imagined the end game of this op fleshing out. Mom was in hiding. T still gawked at him like a criminal. And now, a guy who'd nicknamed himself after a dragon looked like he had some not-so-comfortable fire to barf on both of them.

Forget the Badlands mountains comparison. Ghid had turned into Mount Rainier instead, his icy outer layers concealing a volcano lent an ominous green tint by his intense eyes.

Hell.

Shay took another long swig of beer. Despite how he'd pay to see the sight, Ghid was obviously not preparing himself to sing the *Sesame Street* theme song. He braced himself for the possibility it would be no less easy to hear.

CHAPTER SIXTEEN

Though Zoe's pulse hadn't returned to normal and the air still crackled with unsatisfied male aggression, she was finally able to take a breath. She needed to think about sitting down too. She didn't want to. Every muscle in her body longed to go to Shay, if only to hold his hand through a crappy patch between him and Tait, but these guys needed this moment just for each other—especially when it appeared Ghid was about to lay down some heavy *caca*.

She scooted onto a stool at the bar where Colton had camped out. Oz had disappeared along with the food and her friends, leading to the conclusion that Colton felt it safer they didn't hear the upcoming conversation. Zoe smiled in appreciation to the agent for that.

Her expression quickly changed to a wince of commiseration with Shay. He'd given up six months of his life, perhaps literally, for this moment. Needless to say, the reality wasn't matching the fantasy. She hurt for him while continuing to rein back supreme frustration with Tait. *Deep breaths.* Maybe Ghid's news would help heal their rift a little. She could only watch...and pray.

After another long look at Shay, Ghid pierced his stare into Tait. "Tell me if I've pieced this together right. You were part of the SHRC team that busted up Stock's party at A-51 beginning of the week?"

"Affirmative," Tait said.

"And it sounds like you gunned for that duty because you were hell-bent for leather on locating your brother...because you had some notion he'd gone rogue with Cameron Stock?"

Tait pushed a fist into the couch's arm. "I work with hard intel and verified facts, Mr. Preston, not 'notions.' I'm not the fucking bad guy here."

Shay's jaw went rigid. Even from across the room, Zoe could see the strong tic that vibrated in it too. It was a sin, plain and simple, to remember how she'd seen that tic at work in completely different circumstances...and to feel her pussy throb from the thought of being with him that way again. She atoned for the wickedness by sending up another prayer for understanding between the brothers.

The Creator was a gracious listener tonight. *Gracias. Gracias.*

"T," he murmured, "you've been textbook perfect on everything, man. Nobody's calling you out." He reached to clap Tait's shoulder. "I'm even proud of you for your conviction—despite how that meant throwing me to the wolves."

Tait glanced as if Shay's hand was an alien laser ray. "Am I supposed to say thanks? Because that didn't do jack shit for clearing me from these weeds of what-the-fuck."

Ghid dipped a shrewd nod. "Maybe you'd better start at the beginning, kid."

Shay's inhalation was long and heavy. "'Beginning' is a relative term here."

"Well aware of that." Ghid's expression barely changed, though his wry inflection couldn't be missed. "Let me see if I'm right on the episode recap. You finally went through your dad's old things, and they pointed toward your mother's affiliation with Stock. You followed up on the lead, bringing in your CIA friend here for the fun, knowing he was already hot on Stock's trail. That was when you realized the only way to figure out the guy's game *and* find your mom was going at it from the inside out."

Both Shay's brows arched. "That's damn impressive."

"And right on the money," Ghid returned.

"And right on the money."

Like everyone else in the room, Zoe turned her attention to Tait. The shock on his face had deepened with every word exchanged between Ghid and his brother. Now, with forehead fully furrowed and eyes hardened like gold spears, he attempted to work his mouth around words. "You were with Stock and his gang...because you were *undercover*?"

Zoe whooshed out a breath of relief. She was stunned when Shay didn't do the same, until she realized the source of the pain still carved across his face. His brother finally had the truth but had trouble biting into the elephant of it.

"Yeah, T." His voice was soft, almost apologetic.

"Why?"

"That's the part of the story best told from the beginning." Shay straightened. "About six months ago, I approached Dan about transferring me from the Seventh SFG to the CIA special detail. We kept it far under the radar. My cover story—"

"I know your cover story," Tait grated. "I've memorized every goddamn word of it." He leaned forward and let his head fall between his shoulders. "And drove myself crazy trying to convince myself it wasn't the truth, even when all the evidence—and all the suits clear to DC—told me otherwise."

Tears pricked the back of Zoe's eyes as she watched Shay close his. A strange beauty took over his face, reminding her of the saints she and Ava had studied in Sunday School, newly delivered from earthly torture on their way to celestial deliverance. "Well, your gut was right," he murmured.

Tait's hands balled into fists. "Why didn't you call me? Why didn't you tell me? You had the damn chance, on the beach that night in Kaua'i—"

"I couldn't, T. And you know the hundreds of reasons why."

"I'm your goddamn *brother*."

"And you think if Stock or any of his guys came up the sand and found us cavorting like Frank and Joe Hardy, I wouldn't have been made in two seconds? After that fun plot turn, they'd carve my balls out with dull fishing knives and then feed them to you and Kell while Lani watched." His posture coiled tighter with every word, but he released the tension for a quick smile. "Congratulations, by the way. Lani's a damn good woman. I at least had the time to see how happy she makes you."

"Thanks. You're still a fucker."

"Right. The fucker who found our mother."

"Another fact that parks my ass in the weeds again." Tait twisted, staring like Shay had revealed he'd applied for a mission on the moon. "So you wanted to search for the woman who left us...why?"

Shay's answering smile flowed with unmistakable joy. "Because she didn't leave us."

"Pardon the crap out of me?"

"You remember when I came out to LA during the week after your adventure there? And how I asked all those questions when you mentioned Stock?"

Tait threw his wincing gaze toward the window. "I don't remember a lot from those days, dude."

Zoe smiled with pride as Shay rubbed a reassuring hand

to his big brother's back. "That's all right. I remember for both of us."

Tait nodded. "I know you do. And thanks."

One long moment extended into the next. To an outside viewer, the room seemed to fall into stillness. Zoe knew better. A glance at Dan told her he did too. Together, they watched a pair of brothers begin to cut back a forest of misunderstanding and anger, rediscovering each other on a path of healing.

On a quiet murmur, Shay went on. "After leaving LA, I went back to Florida by way of the storage unit we put Dad's things in. By that time, Stock's name was burned in my brain. I didn't have to look long to find it in a big stack of correspondence to Mom."

That made Tait surge off the couch. As he paced between the couch and window, his eyes conveyed the violence of mental links slammed together. "What kind of correspondence?"

"Well, they weren't love letters. But it wasn't hate mail, either. It seemed like some kind of amicable business deal."

"So what the hell does that mean?" Tait fired. "Mom left Dad...for Cameron Stock?"

Shay took another deep breath. "Hopped on that same ox cart too. At first."

"Until he came to me." Colton offered the declaration as he slid off his barstool. "Obviously Shay's inquiry roped me by both horns out of the gate," he continued while approaching them. "By that point, your brother was a little obsessive about the subject."

Zoe was glad Tait let out a laugh, making her giggle less conspicuous.

"Him?" Tait drawled. "Obsessive? Nah."

Shay rolled his eyes before persisting, "Something really

didn't feel right about the story to that point. We were missing chunks of the picture. When Colton's search results proved that out, I seesawed between elation and nausea."

Tait cocked his head and narrowed his gaze. "Nausea?"

"Oh, yeah."

"Why?"

"Do the math. If we learned that Mom didn't necessarily go to Stock on a willing basis..."

"Shit."

"Bingo."

Tait swung his scrutiny to Colton. "You unlocked intel to back this up? That she was under duress? Even taken?"

Colton's response wasn't what Zoe expected. His Texas swagger had turned into a weird falter. While kicking a cowboy boot at the carpet, he offered, "Wish it were as cut and dry as that, T. Would've made things a lot easier to approach, especially from your brother's point of view. Simple human-abduction charges? We could've just found her, rustled up a team, and extracted her."

Tait sagged against the armoire, indicating he understood Shay's nausea tag now. "And it wasn't that easy...why?"

"The facts we had were *pointers* to abduction, not hard evidence. Your mom didn't leave the house kicking and screaming. She sneaked out on her own, in the middle of the night. The trail fell cold for about six months after that, especially because your dad never filed anything formal about it."

"What happened after six months?"

"She resurfaced to apply for a legal ID in Reno using false docs to indicate her name was Melanie Smythe. That name also shows up on tax records for Cameron's old film development company out of Hollywood, as well as Benstock, the corporation he formed with Gunter Benson."

"Yeah," Tait cut in. "I know all about Benstock, remember?"

When he slouched over and literally looked green, Ghid stepped to him. "You all right?"

"Hmmm." Tait braced his hands on his thighs. "That's a damn good question. Just had my brother inform me that the mom who deserted us didn't really mean to do it but paid for her Louboutins with paychecks from the shell corporation owned by the terrorist who killed someone I deeply loved. So *am* I all right? Why don't *you* answer that question?"

Ghid stiffened—to the point of looking like his spine was fused together by molten fury. "Damn good idea," he uttered, "since you're pretty much wrong."

"Excuse me?"

"You're excused," Ghid returned. "But you're still wrong."

Colton, centered again on both feet, angled hands into his back pockets. "Paychecks were cut to Melanie Smythe from both those companies," he supplied, "but they never showed up in any bank accounts for the woman."

Tait scowled. "What do you mean?"

"Not sure I can be any plainer. We crosschecked the issue every damn way we could. Used your mom's real name, middle names, and variations of each. Played with both social security numbers. All the paperwork on the front and back end was legal; there were just no transactions in the middle." He pointedly cleared his throat. "No wild shoe-buying sprees."

"Back end?" Tait queried. "What back end?"

"Taxes were filed every year on the money," Colton explained. "Everything was legal; no red flags."

"Filed by who? Were you able to trace something there?"

"There's a tax preparer's name on the documents, but the physical address is a vacant lot out in Henderson." Colton grimaced as if he knew how lame the action looked. "It's been like looking for a ghost before the funeral."

Ghid made a clicking sound with his teeth, jerking the agent's attention back up. "Maybe this is where I step in again." When Dan didn't argue—Zoe doubted Attila the Hun himself would cross the man—Ghid nodded to the couch, directing the brothers to sit once more. As soon as they did, he reestablished his wide stance minus the hands locked behind his back. It occurred to Zoe that he might be trying to appear more relaxed. Thank the saints she was getting proficient at holding back giggles.

Shay, noticing the guy's massive fail at trying to be more roadster and less tanker, wasn't so amused. "Sure *you* don't need a drink, dude?"

Ghid gave two gruff jerks of his head. "I'm an ugly fucker but even uglier when I drink. Just get me some more water, would you?" By the time he finished, Zoe was halfway across the room with the ice water pitcher from the table. After he nodded in thanks, he gulped deeply and then exhaled with equal purpose. "What I'm about to say is the truth. It won't feel like it when I'm done, but you need to promise me you'll stay open."

Tait lifted a wry brow. "I think I've had the crash course in 'staying open' today."

Shay squared his shoulders and positioned his hands atop his knees, a sitting version of a full-attention stance. Zoe studied him with a twinge of concern. He looked like a guy about to receive his dishonorable-discharge papers. Given everything he'd been put through in the last week, she didn't blame him. And yearned to be next to him even more.

Ghid gave them both another extended look before going on. "What you said, Shay? About missing pieces of the big pie? Good call. Thing is, you're still missing a few chunks of the thing. I've got them, but they taste a bit bizarre."

The man's brilliant green eyes darkened to the shade of a troubled ocean. Zoe wasn't the only one who picked up on the strange change.

"A bit?" Shay rebounded. "Why does that sound like the world's biggest understatement?"

Ghid exhaled through his nose. "Because you're damn good at discerning that kind of shit."

"He always was." Tait's tone was full of the years he'd been on the receiving end of Shay's perceptive abilities. Zoe could sympathize. She'd only been exposed to hours of the stuff and had come out of the experiences in a tangle of awe and annoyance.

After ticking a brow at his brother, Shay turned again to Ghid. "So where does *this* story start?"

Ghid's awkward posture still prevailed, so he finally decided to sit. "Where most of the good ones do," he told them. "At the beginning. So...you guys remember your buddy Homer?"

"Nuclear bomb Homer?"

Tait's quip had Shay throwing a glance to Zoe. A new giggle sprang to her lips at his I-told-you-so smirk, suppressed by pressing a hand over her mouth.

"Yeah." Ghid leveled another stunner by sliding in half a smile over the end of it. "Mel told me about your little fun with that theme."

Tait's eyes narrowed. "'Mel'?"

Shay shifted a little. "It's what he calls Mom."

"Why?"

Shay backhanded his shoulder. "Why do you think?"

Tait stabbed a new glare at Ghid. Then viciously twisted his lips. "Are you fucking kidding—?"

"Lock it down." Shay turned his move into a steeled grip. "Dad's been dead for a long time. Ghid just risked his ass in a big way to save mine. And he's got pie, even if it's bizarre."

None of them gave the comment even half a laugh. As Ghid pushed his fingers together in a taut steeple, Zoe bit her lip hard. *Mierda*. The man actually appeared like a self-conscious CO himself, about to hand walking papers to a couple of his guys. Her gut twisted in sympathy for him too. "You two never really knew what they were working on, did you?"

Shay looked at the man with extended contemplation, perhaps trying to tell what the angle was on the question. "I know she was a bio-scientist and so was he, so that dictated the focus of their work. We had a damn zoo of research animals at the house for a while."

Tait broke into a dazzling grin. "Shit. The zoo. Now that part was fun. Mom let us keep the iguana in our room at night, didn't she? We called him Messy."

"Original," Ghid muttered.

"What? He *was*." Tait openly moped. "But Homez took Scout back to his place most days, and I wasn't a happy camper about that."

Shay shrugged. "But when Homez left, Scout stayed."

"Barbecue bonus," Tait concurred. "Of sorts."

"Sure."

"I fucking loved that dog. Nearly as much as you loved the

horse."

"Yeah." Shay's return to boyhood joy brought dimples she'd never seen to the corners of his mouth. "Hercules. He deserved that name too. Fucking awesome animal. An Arabian of some sort. Homez would let me sneak in to feed him carrots. I definitely had a guy crush."

Ghid's stare at Shay grew more intense. "Hmmm. That's probably a good thing."

Shay's response was equally as forceful—with discomfort. "Why?"

Zoe was glad to see she wasn't the only one unnerved by the man's vibe of cryptic and creepy. The impression gained strength as Ghid pushed back to his feet, arms angled back as if he aimed to go find a street brawl. But surprisingly, his comeback was built on solid composure. "The animals in your zoo...weren't test subjects. They were Melanie and Homer's inspiration. And...DNA sources."

"Huh?"

"What?"

Ghid stopped in front of the window. "You two might be proud to know that in her way, your mom was a member of a unique Special Forces team of her own."

Shay scowled. "At the risk of sounding redundant, *huh*?"

Ghid squared his stance, leveled his jaw, and fixed them with the fresh laser focus of his gaze. "The research she performed in your garage was part of a very special project, jointly embarked on a top-secret basis by twelve of the world's leading nations. The initiative was given ten years of funding and was simply called *Big Idea*. The sole goal was to combine the knowledge of the planet's greatest scientific minds to craft innovative solutions to the world's biggest challenges."

Tait let out a low whistle. "By 'challenges,' I'm assuming you don't mean shit like the soccer-football discrepancy and asshats who won't pick up their dog's crap."

"Both valid points," Ghid returned, "but no. Big Idea was about addressing shit like the ozone layer...world weather patterns...poverty..."

"Oh." Shay snorted. "Just *that* kind of stuff."

Ghid didn't mirror the sarcasm. Still serious, he stated, "Some pretty amazing shit came out of the project. Though it was all streamlined to the public via different avenues, you can thank Big Idea for biologically enhanced vegetables that resist pesticides, most materials that recycle besides tin cans, and lifesaving improvements in how tsunamis and hurricanes are tracked."

Tait spread his hands. "So how does this circle back to the work Mom and Homez were doing?"

During his question, Zoe's heartbeat leaped by at least twenty beats per minute. Then thirty. Two words from Ghid's explanation slammed like a lightning bolt and then fused with another blow—memories as vivid and disturbing as the minutes that formed them, in the hallway back at the base.

Biologically enhanced.

Biologically enhanced.

She'd still held the water pitcher. It slipped from her numb hand now, crashing to the hardwood floor near the table. "*Por Dios,*" she rasped.

"Zoe." Shay rushed over. "You okay, dancer? Did you—"

"I saw them." She gripped Shay's arm but blurted it straight at Ghid. "In...in the hallway. At the base. That's what you're talking about, isn't it? *They're* what you're talking about."

Her mind raced, shoveling Ghid's pie pieces into all the logical slots. But it still made no sense. It didn't come close.

Ruthless shivers roared up and down her spine. She'd dismissed all those poor creatures as an illusion of her exhaustion, stress, and fear, or at the worst, an evolution of humans forced to mate with the aliens that so many assumed were housed in Area 51.

Not government-sanctioned science experiments.

Not products of some idealistic "project" for mankind.

Not the brainchild of Melody Bommer—the mother of the man who'd wrapped himself around her heart. The man she pressed more tightly to now, who swore softly in his distress for her.

"Zoe, what the hell are you talking about?" Shay finally murmured. She felt him turn his head, probably to look at Ghid. "What the *hell* is she talking about?"

Ghid's labored sigh turned every air molecule in the room into a cactus ball. "Come sit down again, Shay. Bring her with you."

Zoe's knees felt like rubber. Just how correctly had she pieced the pie together? And how thoroughly would she want to throw up after being forced to eat it?

"Forget the weeds," Tait professed as Shay eased her to the couch. "I'm wandering the goddamn forest now."

"Make room because I'm right there with you." Shay dropped next to her with stiff movements. "DNA sources? Ghid, what the fuck?"

Zoe joined them in scrutinizing the man. As she expected, Ghid didn't even try for a fashion-model pose anymore. His posture was firm and his face the same tough mask—though his eyes, searching all three of them now, were a thousand sharp green shards apiece. What he had to tell them wasn't easy. Not by a long stretch.

Zoe twined her fingers into Shay's and squeezed. Hard.

"Their concept started out simply," Ghid began. "The concept of transplanting animal *organs* into humans was decades old when Big Idea began. Melanie and Homer began with a version of that idea. They wondered if they could target human diseases by successfully extracting the blood cells from animals who had the corresponding strengths, then adding them to a serum formulated to activate them in the human bloodstream..."

"Wow," Tait murmured.

"There's an idea for a winning cocktail," Colton added.

Shay was totally silent. The ominous stillness he joined with it was unnoticeable to everyone except Zoe. She knew exactly what he remembered from the base now. And exactly why it led him to clutch her hand with brutal force.

"Shit, Mom, I thought it was from you. I saw it as a sign that everything would work out okay..."

"He went back to the house and put it there...for you... Bastard..."

"What? Why?"

"You drank it. The honey. Didn't you, Shay?"

"Yeah...I drank it."

Without second thought, she offered him her other hand. He didn't hesitate to accept, twisting her fingers just as tight.

"So...did it work?" His words were so taut, they snapped up Tait's concerned stare. "At all?"

With the last two words, Colton's attention was snagged too. While Zoe longed to return their looks with even a small smile of assurance, she couldn't. No use in perpetuating a lie. She couldn't fix this any more than they could. And that dragged her into a grieving silence too.

Ghid regarded Shay with eyes that stunned Zoe with their new intensity—and empathy. "There's a damn interesting answer for that," he stated.

"Interesting," Tait echoed. "Crap. There he goes again with *interesting*."

Ghid headed for the window again, his steps slow yet steady. "At first, the results blew them away. Mel and Homer started with a simple serum blending raven and elephant cells, both animals known for their memory retention. They gave it to a small group of targeted subjects in an Alzheimer's study and had awesome results. While waiting for the numbers to come in on that one, they developed another serum. More complicated. The end game was endurance and running speed."

"Let me guess," Tait offered. "They gathered a bunch of teen guys and told them they could have an advance copy of the new Halo game if they ran a mile in less than ten?"

That actually garnered a tic at one side of Ghid's mouth before he replied, "They used antelope, Iditarod sled dogs, and cheetahs."

Colton took his turn to snort. "In a magical serum? That you fed to—who?"

"Targeted subjects," Ghid replied without faltering. "Again with astounding results." He threw his gaze to Tait and Shay again. "Your mother and Homer Adler were delivering the scientific world's equivalent of shock and awe."

"Shit," Tait responded.

"*Shit*." Shay grinded Zoe's fingers into putty. She didn't care. If he kept holding on, they could weather this together.

Please keep holding on.

"That justifies the menagerie." Tait tapped two fingers on the couch's arm while drilling his gaze into the modern photo art on the wall. "But it doesn't clarify anything else."

"No." Shay's agreement was rough and low. "It doesn't."

"If things were so awesome, then why did Mom leave? And then Homez?"

Ghid's reply was prefaced by an odd change to his face. A toughening in his jaw but a thick storm in his eyes. Zoe sensed it was the man's version of sadness but couldn't be sure. "They'd harnessed lightning in a bottle," he offered, "but had very different ideas about what to do with it."

"And that's why they fought," Tait murmured.

Shay shook his head. "And we thought it was because Homer let us feed the table scraps to Scout."

"Well, *I* did. You were always better about obeying the rules than me."

"No. You were just always there to take the blame instead."

"You made up for it by keeping me sane, brother."

Zoe bit into her bottom lip, dealing with the emotions flooding in. *Dios*, how she could empathize with Tait's words. Though younger sibs were often sheltered from the tough crap, that didn't make them any less important in the grand scheme of things. In many ways, it made them more valuable than ever. She watched Shay take that comprehension in and make it his own. Despite the battered landscape of his face, he'd never been more stunning to her.

They were having to take a painful road back to brotherhood...but they were getting there.

"So what happened, Ghid?" Shay asked then. "Mom and Homer hit an impasse. The results were shitty. We have that part figured out."

Ghid reset his stance before going on. "In a nutshell, Adler got impatient. And greedy."

Tait leaned forward. "Didn't you say Big Idea was subsidized by a government cooperative? Where does greed play into that?"

"Money isn't the only wealth that corrupts," Ghid replied. "Homer felt marginalized and impatient. He wanted to present the Big Idea honchos with some *wow* results, but your mom thought a public ra-ra was still premature. They hadn't had a chance to study the serum's long-term effects. They had no idea about side effects." While grating through his next sentence, he locked eyes with Zoe. "Or deformities."

Colton shifted forward, voicing what they were all thinking. "So Homer took things into his own hands?"

Ghid's face hardened into the hardest scowl Zoe had seen from him. "That's the nice way of putting it."

Tait dropped his fingers to the couch's arm again. "Tell us the not-so-nice way."

"When the holidays came, Homer told your mother he was going back to his country for a family visit. He went to Washington instead."

"And swapped spit with Big Idea on his own," Tait spat.

"Who probably threw their hats over the windmill with glee at the information," Colton added.

Ghid dropped a confirming nod. "They instantly authorized more funds for bigger tests, expanded labs, and new serums—all in the name of scientific advancement, of course."

"Never mind the blatant military applications." Tait tacked on a growl of disgust.

Before all the conclusions were reached, Zoe braced

herself for Shay's tighter hold.

It didn't come.

Instead, he fed her worst fear.

He let go.

Tait grunted. "No wonder Mom popped a thousand gaskets when he got back from that trip."

"So what happened then?" Colton queried.

Shay's interjection was a jagged knife on the air. "Cameron Stock happened then."

Tait's face exploded on a disbelieving glare—quashed by another nod from Ghid. "At that time, Stock had started to make his name in Hollywood. He was working with some pharmaceutical companies who'd backed some film projects and kept his eyes open for new investment opportunities for them. Believe it or not, he met your mom at the grocery store in Des Moines one weekend. He was there scouting locations for a movie, and she was there—"

"Buying us Ding Dongs." Shay's voice was a rough blade edged in deep emotion.

"She always bought us Ding Dongs in Des Moines." Tait's explanation was just as serrated. "Our local grocery didn't carry them."

"Stock saw a biomedical thriller poking out of Mel's purse. He was interested in what she thought of the story. Her review gave away enough about her profession that his interest turned to fascination."

"That doesn't explain Mom's gullibility," Tait snapped. "She's a smarter woman than that. Or at least she was."

"Unbelievably, Stock wasn't always such a huge prick," Ghid stated. "There was a time when the only thing he wanted was to make big money and have a little creative fun in

Hollywood. And he was damn good at both."

Tait's forehead creased. "That tidbit and six bucks will get you a latte and a barista who cares," he growled. "And I'm not him." His lips compressed. "So Mom was standing there with Ding Dongs in the cart and a chest full of pissed off at Homez. I take it she spilled all to Stock?"

"Pretty much." While Ghid's face remained, as always, an inscrutable wall, his eyes gave him away again. Shadows of deep memories turned them into dark moss forests. "And in return, he offered her everything, too."

Tait's shoulders tensed against his T-shirt. "You'd better tell me my mind just jumped to the wrong conclusion about that, man."

"It did," Ghid replied. "Because believe it or not, here's where the story gets uglier."

"Fuck." Shay's reaction came from deep in his gut. Zoe ran a hand up to his shoulder, happy that he didn't shirk her off again.

"Your mom didn't know it, but Homer was already working with others to make all of it happen. Though the funding came from Big Idea, they kept it all *off the books,* with knowledge about the project limited to a select group—and the sad-shit volunteers they scraped up for the program, of course."

Watching the man's eyes was proving to be a wise move. They revealed his soul with heartbreaking clarity. "*Mierda,*" Zoe uttered. "You were one of those volunteers, weren't you?"

Ghid let out a heavy breath. "A man will sign on to do a lot of dumb things when he's desperate," he uttered. "Spend thirty years in prison or sign up for a couple of weeks in a simple science study? That's a no-brainer, right?"

"But it wasn't."

The second Shay slammed out the words, he surged to his feet. The burst wasn't a surprise. Zoe had been the one to feel the tension climb higher through his body. She longed to rise with him, to help him through this, but how could she soothe away the confusion from a situation *she* hardly understood? There wasn't a user's guide for this picture. No handy online video to help ease the soul of a man who'd just learned that his mother's "magic honey" might really have been a tainted elixir.

"Tell me." Shay's voice thickened to a growl, harsh in its demand—but not just from Ghid. He needed the revelation for himself and clearly waged an inner war of self-pride and loathing about it. Elite soldiers insisted on knowing every detail of what they faced, no matter how horrifying the intel.

Tight emotion jammed the bottom of Zoe's throat. Part of her gave in to a girlish swoon at observing the proud warrior side of him. The other part succumbed to her growing dread for him.

Both conditions were distant memories within the next minute.

Ghid replied to Shay's command with a respectful nod. "You deserve to know," he stated, "but sometimes, the telling is best done in the showing."

Without any more preamble, the man stripped off his shirt.

As anyone with a brain would expect, Ghid was as ruthless and chiseled below the neck as above. Every inch of his tan skin was stretched taut over huge mounds of tendon and muscle. It was all a bit too daunting for Zoe, though she gave Melody Bommer a silent high-five for being the lucky female who shared his bed.

And then he turned around.

Proving, in graphic reality, that she'd remembered everything from the hallway with perfect detail. And bringing an insane new meaning to the words *side effects*.

CHAPTER SEVENTEEN

"Holy sssshhhh..."

Dan never completed the exclamation. Shay didn't blame him. The expression was beyond what his mind could produce, fumbling past shock and bewilderment, scrambling for the fortitude just to keep him on his feet instead of crumpling to his ass in a ridiculous ball of horror.

Get your shit together. You're a member of the finest fighting force on the planet. You've been through clusterfucks and firestorms that would spin the heads of most men. You need to look. And see. And try to understand.

Ghid's back...wasn't a back. Instead of muscle and skin, his spine was bracketed by swaths of thick green scales. Shay would've even guessed that the plates were simply painted on, but they jutted from his back at least an inch and shifted with every move he made...which so far, the man subdued to a few uncomfortable shifts of balance. The sight was like a damn car wreck. Shay couldn't help gaping but was sickened with himself for doing so.

When their shock ticked past the one-minute mark, Ghid turned back around. "As you can see, Mel's concern about long-term effects pretty much smacked the target."

"No shit," Dan muttered.

"Fuck," Tait spat.

"Wow." They all threw stares at Zoe in the wake of her awe-filled murmur. The smile she gave Ghid conveyed even more admiration. "So that explains your eyes."

Ghid snorted. "My eyes?"

"Of course. They're beautiful. And fascinating."

Ghid blushed to the base of his neck. Shay joined Tait and Dan in a burst of laughter. The moment was a needed, if temporary, reprieve from this insane revelation.

Insanity. Right. If only that was where Shay's senses stopped. Inside the next ten seconds, he blew past insanity and straight down the highway to terror.

"Fine," Ghid finally huffed. "That's what drinking lizard blood will do to a guy."

"Lizard?" Dan drawled. "You mean those cute little guys who run around on my backyard wall until my dog eats 'em?"

"Hmmm." Ghid pulled his shirt back on. "Nice image, but no. More like a mix of monitors, Komodos, and Gilas—the kind that like human limbs for breakfast."

Dan stepped back. "Oh."

"But if you count rhinos as *cute*, then I guess I qualify."

Shay joined Tait in a smirk as Dan paled. "No. Rhinos aren't cute."

Ghid clicked his tongue against his teeth. "Didn't think so."

All the humor aside, Shay's gut left terror behind and dove into a vortex of raw dread. There was an elephant in the room—and damn it, it might even be him. He saw now that all of Ghid's intense glances had actually been attempts at commiseration. He was officially a member of the Big Idea freaks club now, and the guy had been attempting a series of awkward welcome mats since hauling his ass out of hell. While he was grateful, this was one goddamn card he longed to rip out of his wallet.

Have you learned anything about life yet, asshole? Don't

you know the choices aren't always yours?

Great fucking tip. Because years of choking down MREs, humping his ruck through miles of hell, and getting shot at by crazy jihadists hadn't taught him the lesson already.

He didn't know whether to laugh or cry.

Or break something. Maybe all those fucking picture windows.

Who the hell was he?

What the fuck was he?

If he wanted to find out, he had to hump the goddamn ruck again. And listen to the rest of Ghid's story.

"So what happened then?" he forced out. "When all of you started to...to..."

"Morph out of control?" Ghid narrowed his eyes a little after filling it in. "What do *you* think happened, kid?"

The man's reasoning for the response was clear. By assisting with the answer, Shay could reclaim a couple of things he hadn't had a lot of lately: his identity and his control. He was a trained member of a Special Forces Alpha team, not only capable of connecting this kind of information but processing it at least five different ways and then serving it up an enemy's ass if that was the ordered plan.

Ghid wasn't just a genius; he was a friend.

Shay communicated his gratitude with the nod he prefaced to his answer. "Operating outside the radar allows the government to deny culpability if they have to. In this case, I'm sure the Big Idea folks did everything they could to squeeze you all back down to a damn small idea."

Ghid's gaze turned the color of a moss-lined torture chamber. *Shit.* Zoe was right. The guy's eyes told profound truths. "It was a shit-rough time," Ghid uttered. "They talked about secured camps, maybe shipping us off to an island..."

"*Dios mio*," Zoe whispered. "You're human beings!"

"*Creatures*," Ghid corrected. "At least in their eyes. Walking, talking reminders of their big-time shit on the fan, but not sentient beings with lives or futures to be considered." The guy sent a benign stare to Zoe—well, his stilted attempt at one. "Zoe, before the study, we were all convicts, remember?"

"Who became something else in the name of their science."

"Not everyone's." Tait rose as he professed it. "Just that pudwhack Homer. He didn't present the full facts to the brass. He had a big ego and a pencil dick, and he should have listened to Mom."

"And nobody knew that better than him," Ghid stated. "The guy was the first one out the door—figuratively speaking, since there really wasn't any door. It was a warehouse roll-up with fifteen kinds of security, which they bumped to seventeen even after they started keeping us strapped down all day."

Shay dropped to the couch again, backed by a stream of Spanish obscenities from Zoe. "Christ," he muttered. His blood chilled, a horror martini tossed over ice cubes of incredulity.

"What happened then?" Dan queried.

"I think I know." Tait's gaze followed the dreamlike lines of the print on the wall again. His eyes hazed over with memories. "Somehow, somebody got word to Mom about Homer playing off the Big Idea pier and then falling into the royal drink of fuck-up. I happened to be home sick from school. A woman came to the house, flashing papers and ID, saying she was from some lab in DC."

Shay scooted his head out from the cocoon of his hands. "That's one hell of a vivid recall."

"I'm sure of this one," his brother asserted. "I won't forget that goddess as long as I live. She looked like a living version of Pocohontas. Hell, she was—" He had the grace to squirm a little. "Sorry, Zoe. But she *was* fucking hot."

"Awww, sheez." Shay let his head fall again.

"Pocohontas?" Dan nailed his stare to Tait. "You mean the cartoon I was always embarrassed about pitching a tent over?"

"Hair in the wind, big doe eyes," Tait concurred. "Those legs you couldn't help imagining around your waist and—"

"The subject?" Shay cut in. "We had one, dorks. Can we stick to it?"

Tait shrugged. "Yeah, though my part of the story wraps up there. Two days after Pocohontas came to visit was the last time Homez dared show his face at the house again. That was also the night he and Mom threw down like Rocky and Apollo. We all know the fallout from there, though I'm surprised Homez didn't come back and curse the house just for good measure."

Shay left his head where it was. Low. Really low. *If a curse on the house was all he came back to accomplish, brother...*

"I take it this is where Stock entered the picture for good," he finally said.

"Excellent word selection," Ghid replied. He let several moments weigh in for emphasis. "And though you all may throw tizzies at me for it, I'll say it again... At first, the man really did do some good."

Tait opened another beer and then dragged hard on the brew. "He can take that up with the good-karma angels *after* I drive a Bowie into his throat."

Wisely, Ghid didn't push that issue harder. "The thing

was, Stock had already approached your mom about accepting a research deal with Verge Pharmaceuticals. She'd flat-out turned him down, but he kept in touch *just in case*."

Tait narrowed his eyes. "Because he was such a great guy and wanted to do it for humanity, right?"

"Never said the guy was bucking for sainthood," Ghid qualified. "Cameron was always business first. Brokering the deal would've earned him a pile of flow like he'd never known. But by then, he also had a general idea of the shit that was going down at home with your dad. He started feeling more protective toward your mom...and probably a few other things too."

"Shit," Tait spat.

"You may want to go for the fast recap on this part, G," Shay muttered.

"Acknowledged."

Dan tipped the neck of his beer forward. "I think I can help braid this rope a little tighter. Verge Pharma, right? They invested in a lot of space in Austin in the late nineties. I remember their complex being built. Lots of big glass buildings with spacey-looking security shields. We called it the star fleet." He tossed a quizzical glance to Ghid. "Was that because Melanie inked the deal through Stock?"

Though the answer was obvious, the observation did nothing for Tait's tension level. Shay glanced at him and murmured, "She did what she had to, T."

"Fuck off."

"Shay's right." Ghid braced both legs wide again. "She didn't know where to turn." His gaze sharpened to laser green. "Unlike that chicken fart Adler, she felt responsible for what had happened to us, which was why she left home so abruptly."

Tait's glower darkened. "With the intention of never coming back?"

"That what your turdtastic father tell you?" Ghid waved a dismissive hand. "Never mind. I already know the answer." As he lowered that hand, he curled it into a fist. "Let me be real clear about something. There wasn't a day that passed without your mom having deep conflict about the decisions she made and the consequences you all paid for them. You really think she just walked away, never thinking she'd come back? What kind of a snow globe did your dad dunk you two in? He had a front-row seat for the knock-downs she had with Homer. He knew *everything* that was at stake when she left for DC and that she had every intention of returning after she handled the crisis. And yeah, kids, it was a *crisis*."

A soft sob shredded into the middle of his explanation. The source didn't surprise Shay. Zoe had seen others like Ghid, the men Bash had originally described as mutants. Her face reflected that horror—and encompassed his deepest fears—but he couldn't hang on to that fear when gazing at her. The woman's heart was so huge, every drop of its compassion showed across her incredible face. She took his breath away.

"How many of you were there?" she softly asked Ghid.

"Fifty, maybe sixty," Ghid estimated. "And we all would have been left to die in that warehouse, if not for Dr. Melody Bommer." As he took a breath, a shocking change overcame his whole body. The man's posture actually softened. "When she walked in, with her cheeks rosy from the cold and her hair in all those gorgeous curls..." His shoulders dropped in unspoken surrender. "I had no idea who she was, so I assumed I'd just died and was getting a lucky break from a living angel."

Tait peeked at Shay. "I should be disturbed by that, right?

Why aren't I?"

Shay gave his brother a meaningful smile. "Because he sees her how we do."

"She promised we'd be moving out of the warehouse within a few months," Ghid went on. "Kept her word, too. Five months later, we moved into preliminary buildings at the complex outside Austin. Melody was with us the whole time... and always talked about how she was excited things would be settling down so she could finally get back home to her three men."

He made the last assertion with a defined stare over his shoulder. Shay could see that he meant it, but Tait insisted on the snide asshat angle. "So did you still think she was an angel?" he alleged.

Ghid's riposte was immediate yet composed. "Of course I did. But it stayed capped there until well after your mother took her wedding ring off, after she received word about your dad's death."

Tait snorted before voicing the obvious retort to that. "At which point, she *still* didn't come home."

"At which point, she wasn't able to."

"What the fuck does that mean?"

Ghid picked up his water glass and took a huge drink. "You remember I said that Stock *started* as the nice guy." Another gulp went in. "Well, stories are often filled with twists."

Tait took another long, angry pull on his beer. "*Here's* where we get to the part justifying my blade through the bastard's neck."

"Pretty much," Ghid muttered.

Shay didn't feel like drinking anything. Could've had something to do with the ball of apprehension in his gut, snowballing by the minute. "I take it Stock finally rolled in his gold pile and liked the dirt."

"And the corruption," Ghid added. "He had things and people, especially your mom, right where he wanted them. The Austin location was nice and remote, just where he wanted to keep your mom for good...now that he'd developed full feelings for her." He finished the water—and slammed down the glass. Several fissures ran up the length of the thing before it collapsed into several fragments atop the table. "That was when he made up the blackmail sandwich for Mel."

Forget the snowball. Shay's stomach turned into a full-on warhead of dismay. "Blackmail?" he fired. "In what way?"

"Easiest way there is." Ghid's gaze turned the color of a tormented tornado sky. "He used the two of you."

"What?" He and Tait sputtered it together.

Ghid picked up a bigger piece of the broken water glass, examining the distortions of light through its curved surface. "You both remember your sweet little neighbor, right? What was her name? Something with a V?"

Shay rammed his bottle to the table. "Mrs. Verona." In every syllable, he inserted his unspoken threat. A word against Mrs. V, and the guy would have to stress about keeping his balls whole.

"Watch where you're treading, man," Tait snarled. "Mrs. Verona was the closest thing we had to a saint in our neighborhood."

"Didn't change the fact that she worked for the devil."

"Fuck," Shay rasped.

"You're lying," Tait accused.

Ghid lifted his gaze to Colton. "Double-check my facts, spook-boy. Pull up the woman's financial records and her status as a *location consultant* for his production company."

Shay traded a significant look with his brother. "She never went anywhere," he confessed.

"Because she had to be near the phone. If your mom ever dared to scoot out from under Stock's thumb, Mrs. Verona would be called." The depths of the guy's eyes turned from tornado clouds into furious smoke. "Melody would've come home to find her two little boys with bullets through their brains."

Along with Tait, Shay tumbled into a fog of shock and betrayal. They sat together in silence for a long minute, identically posed with elbows on their knees.

"Why mess with bullets?" Tait finally grated. "She'd probably have just poisoned the cookies."

For once, Shay didn't whack his brother for being a drama queen. "Why bother to bake at all? Tossing us in the garage and turning on the car... There's quick and painless."

Colton, thank fuck, was still able to form a clear head around the subject. "That's a fine excuse through the eighteenth birthdays for these bozos," he queried, "but what about after that?"

Ghid turned to Dan with a steady regard. "You're able to braid this one tighter too, Tex. Rewind your mind by about ten years."

After processing that for a few seconds, Dan's face ignited. "Cork my goddamn pistol. That was when Verge downsized the star fleet." His gaze, strangely matching Ghid's in green intensity, narrowed. "What happened?"

"What do you think?" Ghid flung. "The gang at Big Idea finally figured out we *weren't* all dead and tracked us to the hideout."

"So you had to break camp again?"

"Not until after your mom struck a pure genius deal with them, giving us the green light to move into the facility at A-51."

Shay couldn't figure out how to react to that. He processed the genius reference, but the rest was lost beneath his haze of raging memories—four half-conscious, torture-filled days' worth. The shit churned through him as a physical force, driving him to his feet again. "She...was the one...responsible for transplanting your asses into that hell?"

Ghid stunned them all by turning like a cornered animal. More accurately, a peeved rhino. Fury flashed in his eyes. Shay wondered if a horn really would bust loose in place of his nose. "She didn't have a lot of options by that point, all right? The feds promised us there'd be no more restraints or dissection-style tests. Mel was still tormented about inking the contract with them, knowing she didn't trust them enough to leave us alone in a base that wasn't even publicly acknowledged by the government at the time. But by that point, Stock was out of control on letting the lies and corruption take over his life." He paused, breathing hard, looking ready to wrestle a fucking bear. "*I* was the one who finally begged her to sign again with the feds—after I found Stock just a few inches away from raping her."

"Christ," Shay repeated.

"Goddamn fuckstick," Tait seethed.

"Let my kneecap do a mambo on his ball sack while making sure his left eye socket was a lovely blue to match" Ghid rejoined. "But I told Mel that if I ever caught his naked dick near her again, they'd be adding murder to my rap sheet."

Shay took the two steps needed to lock his stance in front of Ghid. For a long moment, their gazes dueled. It was a hell of a lot harder than he anticipated not to yank the guy into a fierce hug for saving Mom from Stock's perverted attack, but he managed to restrain the PDA. Ghid gave a little nod, conveying he understood anyway.

"So everyone packed up again," Dan filled in. "Melody was able to sever shit with Stock, and the feds promised you all protection inside Area 51."

"We were sure it was for the best," Ghid confirmed. "A lot of the buildings at the base had been abandoned since the top-secret work they did there in the fifties and sixties." A cynical gleam appeared in his gaze. "Despite what the world thinks, we were the most exciting thing to arrive there in years. It's remote and quiet and secure." His jaw tensed. "Which seemed like our idea of heaven."

"But it wasn't." Shay lifted his head. As Ghid met his stare, he knew he'd issued the truth. The grimness of it was stamped across Ghid's formidable face. "So," he followed up, "how long was it until the torture sessions started again?"

Ghid responded with his version of a grimace. "They kept it to what they could get away with when Mel wasn't looking—which wasn't very often. She practically lived in the lab, working like a demon to find viable solutions for all of us to get on with our lives."

"She felt responsible." Zoe inserted it. Her words, along with her eyes, communicated how she related to every choice Mom had made, no matter how wrenching they'd been.

"You could say that." Ghid's reply was a verbal version of the dry air blowing at the windows. "At first she thought surgery might help correct the guys with larger deformities, but all the shit simply regenerated. So she did her best with choices for occupational therapy and specialized career training, with the understanding that integrating most of us back into society wasn't going to be a choice. With the military's help, she also kept tabs on Stock, knowing he'd dipped further over to the dark side after the botched job with Lor in Los Angeles and might one day decide to butt heads with the feds over property he perceived as rightfully his." The guy's tone gained some somber grit. "Funny, what can happen to a regular asshole once he perceives himself as a real martyr."

"Feel you there," Tait murmured. Shay added a commiserating grunt. They'd both seen that insane light in more than one man's eyes during missions in deserts far from this one, watching the sky ignite with rocket fire instead of neon.

Zoe's face crunched with confusion. "I don't understand. If you were all prepared for what Stock did with the plane, why did all the lab's staff simply cooperate with Stock's men?"

"Because those were General Newport's instructions to us," Ghid revealed. "He assured Mel there was a plan in place for everyone's safety, that he had an ultra-elite team on their way to make sure all the Big Idea boys made it to safe ground again." He shrugged, seeming genuinely puzzled himself. "Mel was actually excited. She and I have been making lots of day trips up to the backup camp, preparing it to be a B compound of sorts for the guys. With the feds' blessing, full security's been in place for a month. Newport told us that the op would involve the SHRCs secretly boarding the plane and then taking down Stock's guys in midair in order to pilot the jet to Reno. After that, the guys would be transferred out to the compound." He arrowed his gaze straight into Tait with that. "Instead, we received a little surprise party, complete with special lighting and entertainment."

Tait hauled out his inner John McClane, unrepentant and unyielding, for the comeback. "I could say it wasn't intentional, but I'd be lying. At the time, the mission mantra was a capture-or-kill on Stock and all his men *before* the plane fired engines again. The choice was a need-to-know thing only, shared outside the team by the general, the upper brass at JSOC, and of course, the Big Nick." His use of the military's nickname for President Nichols didn't go lost on Ghid or Dan, though it took Zoe a second to catch on. That was a good thing, since T didn't wait to continue. "We had to assume that Shay was possibly dealing off both sides of the intel deck, but we had no idea who else might be involved, including everyone on the facility's staff."

"And there was no way you could've known that Dr. Melanie Smythe was actually Dr. Melody Bommer," Shay put in.

"None at all." T's reply was rough and low. "Damn it."

Shay swapped a glance with Ghid. Their silent agreement was clear. It wouldn't benefit anyone, least of all Tait, to tell him he'd missed seeing Mom in the hallway by a few short minutes.

"She was gone by the time you got there anyway, T." Shay elbowed his brother in encouragement. "And from what I heard, she got her wish, at least for a while. Most of the Big Idea boys were transported by ground to B camp after the raid, since a lot of the A-51 lab isn't livable right now."

He traded another look at Ghid with the statement. *Most of the boys.* It was accurate, since the poor guys who hadn't made it out the door in the evacuation were certainly the sources of the screams that chorused with his own in those halls of horror. He almost laughed at the second half of his assertion. *Isn't livable right now*. That was even more precise. Living wasn't what a guy did when the lunatics took over the asylum. Surviving was the only goal.

"Well." Tait cleared his throat and flashed a smile. "Glad to know everything gelled out for the best, I guess."

"Yeah," Ghid grunted. "Eventually."

Tait frowned. "Eventually?"

The man's eyes actually twinkled. "Guess you don't remember how your mom likes to plan shit down to the molecule. She wasn't a happy camper when your band of merry men changed things up." Another sound erupted from him. Not a full grunt—probably the Ghid version of a chuckle. "That woman can be quite a feisty little Fifi when she wants to be."

Shay's brows shot up. Tait's did too. "Fifi, huh? You ever called her that to her face?"

"Just came up with it. But hell, now I can't wait to try it out."

"Good luck with that," Tait drawled.

"Won't need luck."

"Right. Just full body armor."

"That's sort of the point."

"It is? Why?"

Ghid's eyes were a damn fireworks show now. "Because she'll get all...feisty."

"Ohhhh, yeah." T grinned with understanding. "I get it. Feisty. Have one of those back home, only she does it most of the time in bikinis that drive me insane. Hell, the first night we met, she made me strip down to my skivs and march my ass through her garden until I—" He stopped and shuddered. "Wait. Jesus on a Ritz, dude—you're talking about my *mom*."

"Oh, yeah."

"Shut. Up."

Shay, while pleased about their fun little bonding session, couldn't sand the edges of anxiety off his blood and bones. The feeling was rendered by the same blade that sharpened him for things like HALO jumps from planes and impending shit storms with hostiles. He was used to dealing with it for a few hours and then buffing it out with some deep breaths and renewed focus on the horizon.

But the horizon was a blur. And every breath just brought another swipe of the knife, cutting a deeper chasm inside, opening the way for his mind to plunge deeper. He gripped his bottle and paced to the window, forcing himself to concentrate on the present, to take in every shape and swirl of the electronic tapestry forming the boulevard below.

It wasn't working.

He still drowned in dread and couldn't figure out why.

Until his brother spoke again.

"Wait another damn minute. If Mom was working with our side the whole time, and we cleared all the residents out of A-51, then who were those G-suits I signed Shay over to? And why did they beat and torture the crap out of *him*?"

CHAPTER EIGHTEEN

Zoe didn't know her heart could break just by looking at someone. This moment proved her wrong.

Her chest clutched from the agony of watching Shay as *he* watched Tait, knowing his brother was finally stringing every piece of evidence together—and arriving at the truth at the end of that line. Tait peered at Shay with layers of new intensity, though beyond that, Zoe couldn't tell if the man was shocked, horrified, confused, or all three. Clearly Shay couldn't discern that answer either, and his torment over that was hewn in every taut line of his body...every haunted, bruised line of his face.

She yearned to go to him. To ease his anguish. But she could only sit there and hope it was enough, her own version of a disgusting hell.

Tait finally jabbed the throbbing blister of a silence. "Shay. *Shit*. Shay." He took a step.

Shay rushed backward by two. "Don't," he growled. "Just don't, T."

"Okay. Fine." Tait tilted his head forward before shaking it again. "Wait. Hold on. Why do they even suspect that *you*—"

"Little parting gift from Homez," Shay growled. "A whole vial of the serum. I drank it the night Mom left, thinking it was some special thing from her."

"Big deal." Tait spread his arms. "You were a kid. Maybe it simply...passed through you..."

Shay made a rolling motion with one of his hands. "Keep

going. You're doing good, broheim. It's the same script I ran when they had me strapped down to that gurney. I don't look like the others, right? I'm completely normal. No scales or horns or fins. Figured they'd test me and then throw me back." A growl, sudden and anguished and angry, ripped out of him. "Well, they didn't throw me back, damn it."

"Okay." Tait stared harder at his brother. "It's going to be fine, okay? You'll handle this. *We'll* handle this. We'll—"

"I don't want to fucking *handle* this!" Shay's sprint across the room made Zoe's heart feel like a caged animal— appropriate for the vicious desperation in every inch of his movements, too. "You know what I want, Tait? I want someone to cut me open from my throat to my balls so I bleed. And I want this monster inside me to be drowning in every drop of that shit. And I want to lie there, watching that fucker drown and die." He gripped the wall, his fingernails scoring the stucco, digging out chunks of it with the force of his fury. "I don't want this poison *handled*, Tait. I want it *gone*."

He disappeared down the hall.

Two seconds later, one of the bedroom doors thundered shut.

Before any of the men could stop her, Zoe rushed to her feet and ran across the room too. She bolted past the bedroom where her friends were piled on the bed watching a *Step Up* movie, to the door still trembling from the force of Shay's slam.

She was glad he hadn't thought to lock it—though as soon as she entered, the tic went off in his jaw, likely damning himself for the oversight.

"Get out, Zoe," he snarled. "Now."

She trembled. *Caramba*. His rage was a force in the room, short-circuiting her in ways she'd never felt before. Part of her understood his frustration and shared his anger. Another part ached deeply for him. And another part, unattached to any logical thought, gave way to her inner cavegirl, responding in its purest form to his caveman...turning the crux of her thighs into a pulsing puddle.

Shit, shit, shit.

She sucked in a breath and dropped her hands to her sides. Through the next breath, she told herself she wasn't an idiot for locking herself in a room with a beast with hunched, heaving shoulders, arms spread, hands flattened against the window.

How she longed to rush to him, molding her body against his back, whispering a reprise of Tait's pledge. It *would* be okay. They'd help him through this, no matter what "this" ended up being like.

That was where curiosity rammed itself into the picture.

Shay had taken his "magic honey" shooter when he was nine years old. According to what Ghid had relayed to them, the incubation period for the other test subjects hadn't been eighteen months, let alone eighteen years.

What had happened differently with Shay? Did the serum affect children differently than adults? Was that the reason Homer slipped the vial to him?

The questions were as daunting as the power of her need to be here for him. And with him...in any way he needed.

She scooted forward by one shaky step. Another. "That's—That's not a good idea," she stammered.

An ominous rumble crawled out of him. "Right. Because the way things have been going has been such a string of *good ideas* lately."

Crazily, that replaced her nervous chill with a hot gust of

anger. "Five days ago, you thought three hours in a hotel room with me was a pretty good idea."

His fingers went white against the dark glass. "Damn it."

"And another one on a hospital bed in the middle of the desert."

"*Zoe*."

"What?" It tore out of her at full volume, and she didn't care who heard. "*Dios mio!* Don't you get it? Every minute, every *second* of those hours was like gold turned into time for me. Before them, I felt like an alien on my own planet, seeking a connection that didn't exist here." So much for breathing deeply. Or holding back the tears that had been pummeling at the base of her throat. "I'm *thankful* for every turn your life took that brought you to that airport bar...that led you to me. And yes, that even conspired to put us on that crazy flight here. And if you answer me one more time with that damn growl, I'll make sure everyone in this suite knows it. Maybe the whole Vegas Strip."

He swung his head around, glowering at her with bloodshot eyes. "Try it, and you won't be able to sit tomorrow."

He meant it. Every word. And every cell in her body, sparking with terror and need at once, adored him for it. This man...turned her inside out. Made her insane.

And infuriated.

"Is this the part where my dutiful 'Yes, Sir' is supposed to make an appearance? Don't hold your breath, Sergeant."

His glare narrowed. "Goddamnit, Zoe."

"Fuck you, Shay."

"You're not making any sense!"

"Bullshit I'm not." Her voice cracked. Appropriate, considering what was going on inside her heart.

A dark huff fell from Shay. He wearily shook his head. "You're the craziest woman I've ever met."

"In case you haven't noticed, crazy's a good thing when it comes to us." She jabbed her chin up, wishing for heels over her flats to help with the defiant posture. At least the flats had a little sparkle. "So if you think you're getting rid of me, just because you think you're some changed creature"—she took another step, reaching out for him—"when it's *you* who have changed *me*..." Tentatively, she lowered her hand to his back. "You need to think again, damn it."

"Zoe—"

"You opened me again. Filled me in so many incredible ways. I don't know how I'll ever communicate—"

"*Stop.*" He left her with only the stark imprints of his hands on the window after he wrenched away. "Stop it, Zoe. Now. Please."

She couldn't listen to him. She *wouldn't*. "Shay—"

"*Damn it,* Zoe!" He wheeled back toward her, his gaze at full dagger force. "What are you going to say? That you *understand* me now? That you once felt like a mutant, so you *get* everything that's going on here? It doesn't fucking work that way! We're not suddenly soul mates because of this!"

Twisting herself back from the temptation to slap his gorgeous face, she retorted, "You're right. We're not soul mates—because of this." She jutted her chin again, refusing to let him go from the direct demand of her stare. "We were already connected, five nights ago, because of things far more amazing than this." A new sting pressed behind her eyes. "Go ahead," she rasped, blinking hard against the tears. "Tell me I'm full of shit for that now too. It won't change the fact that it *is* a fact."

A roar curled out of him as he turned on her again, clawing a hand at the back of his neck. "I can't do this."

Zoe snorted. "Can't or won't?"

As his head dipped, his hand curled tighter. "I don't...know how. Damn it, Zoe, I just don't know how."

"Because you think you have to do it alone." She reached and pressed the button to extinguish the bedside lamp. The movement brought her next to him, a good thing since the sole light in the room now came from the city stretching for miles below. She lifted her hand to his downturned jaw, her fingers sizzling from the burn of his thick stubble. "The mission's over, remember? You don't have to do this by yourself anymore."

He pushed her away, gently this time. "I'm lost, dancer. Nothing's in control."

A rough sigh escaped him. The wind *shoosh*ed past the window. Something with a siren wailed through the streets below.

Chaos and uncertainty outside. Darkness and shadows across the room.

Yet Zoe was suddenly clearer than she'd been in days. Saner. More completely sure of being exactly where she was meant to be.

No. Not exactly.

She slid down until her knees met the carpet. Once there, she leaned forward, tucking her head against his thigh.

"Then control me."

Now everything was right.

Or so she hoped.

Shay's silence extended through an interminable minute. Another. In the middle of the first, he lowered a hand to her head, sifting his fingertips through her hair, inch by slow inch.

He still made no other movement or sound.

Zoe waited.

She battled not to feel as if she searched for constellations in a starless sky. If the midnight of this moment extended for an hour, she'd wait. She let the promise fill her mind as she desperately, stupidly, pressed tighter to his leg. If anyone kicked in the door and burst into the room right now, they'd get quite a laugh from proud, self-sufficient Zoe Chestain, fawning at the feet of a man. She didn't care. She belonged here. Simply being here for him. Offering him...

Everything.

The sudden tension of his hand was stunning but thrilling. When he wrapped his fingers into more of her hair and pulled, Zoe whimpered in a fusion of abrupt pain...and mounting arousal. In an instant, her mind spiraled into an ether she couldn't explain, let alone control. It sucked the breath from her lungs, stopping her heart until it pounded in her chest, begging wildly for air.

She finally pulled in a gasp as Shay rolled his hand to the back of her head, dragging the hair he already had in his fist. He grunted hard as she cried out in full, and then again when he pulled her face up against the ridge beneath his jeans zipper.

"*Dios.*" It was all she had time to gasp before he guided her mouth up and down the flap, the denim stretched taut from the flesh that pounded beneath. Zoe moaned, widening her jaw, letting her mind succumb to her soul's needs for service and submission.

"Sweet baby girl." Shay barely added volume to the gruff yet adoring utterance. "You do want this, don't you?"

"Mmmm." She sighed in place of a nod since his hold was still deliciously restrictive. "Yes, Sir. Oh...yessss..."

He growled in harsh approval before using his free hand to twist the button of his pants free. Zoe sighed again, inhaling the musk of his arousal and the tang of his skin while he directed her face to the top of his magnificent bulge.

"Unzip it," he ordered. "Use only your mouth."

She peered up, rejoicing in the molten light that shined down on her from his gaze. His eyes were the color of new chains, a perfect comparison to the bonds she yearned to form with him. Shay Bommer, in his passion and fire and domination, was rapidly ruining her for any other man. Perhaps ever.

After locking her lips around the zipper pull, she dipped her head, opening every lock of the metal teeth until nothing barred her from his cock except his BVDs. She couldn't help licking her lips while beholding the strained fabric, already dark with an oval wet spot as evidence of his hot desire. *Vaya*, how she longed to set his erection free. To lick and nibble every pulsing inch of his huge erection...

"Not until you earn it, baby girl." As usual, the man seemed to read her damn mind. She was tempted to chuck him a prissy pout in return, but instinct stopped her short. She was glad she listened. She couldn't be wasting time on a pout with Shay's hands in her hair, yanking her to her feet and then angling her for the searing assault of his savage kiss. Only after he twisted her head in six different angles, ensuring his tongue branded every corner of her mouth, did he release her so harshly, it felt like finality. But she knew better, a perception that injected new fear to her blood—which, God help her, slammed like a shot of sexual heroin.

She waited, helpless and panting—and praying he'd shoot her up again.

He stared at her, his cuts and abrasions turning him into

a foreboding sight, the human version of a storm deciding whether to lay waste to a village. As the village who'd just begged fate for this, Zoe couldn't decide whether she was the universe's biggest idiot or most lucky submissive.

He didn't make her wait long for the answer. Scooping her hand into his, he yanked her along the window, back to the place he'd been occupying when she came in. He whirled her, making her face the black glass. A shiver rippled to her toes when he pressed behind her, flattening one huge hand against her belly while wrapping the other around the base of her neck.

"Take off your clothes," he dictated into her ear. "But keep facing the glass." Both of his hands dug into her flesh, emphasizing how firmly he meant the demand...as if the corrugation to his voice didn't communicate it already.

Her sexual high had officially gotten another kick.

Her hands shook as she shed her sweater and then worked the fastenings of her jeans. "*Mierda*," she spat after trying to free the button a third time. She could've launched an inner tirade, questioning all her nervous virgin behavior, but why? She already knew why everything about this felt like the first time with Shay—the terrifying first time. His defenses were compromised. The guard on his composure? Nearly nonexistent. He needed this...the untamed run of his darker, harder Dom. And though it scared the crap out of her, she was pretty sure she needed it too. The fullness of their connection...

Her romantic pep talk was ripped short. Literally. Just as she succeeded in pushing the jeans down, a loud tear came from the bathroom. Another, and then another.

Que pasó? Was he decimating the damn *towels*?

She didn't receive her answer for that until she was finished stripping and stood before the glass, listening to her rickety breaths against the whir of the air-conditioning, for what felt like a small eternity. The minutes were the longest of her life. Focusing on the *schrick*s Shay made did nothing to slow her heartbeat...or lessen the strange onslaught of self-consciousness about her full nudity.

Or *was* it strange? Lounging naked in her own bedroom, with nobody around to watch except the Gene Kelly and Ginger Rogers prints on her wall, was insanely different than standing in wait for the man who clearly intended on dominating every inch of her body...who finally reentered, two long white lengths trailing from his hand.

She dug her teeth into her lower lip. Her womb clenched. Her pussy seeped.

Caramba. He'd really ripped up the towels.

With the window doubling as a mirror, she watched him walk from the bathroom and drape his new creations on the bed—a pair of white linen ropes, formed of narrow strips he'd torn and then knotted together. Shay, still in his loose T-shirt and jeans with the open fly, looked every inch like Satan's single-minded henchman. As he turned and draped her in a hard, evaluating stare, Zoe guessed his solitary purpose wasn't catching up on the TV he'd missed this week. She couldn't discern anything about his thoughts from the brutal angles of his face. That didn't stop her lungs from shoving out her breaths in staccato bursts or her throat from rivaling the Mojave for negative humidity numbers.

He let her squirm in the light that spilled from the bathroom before reaching around the doorway and cutting the illumination with a strangely ominous *click*.

They were plunged into neon-tinted shadows again.

One word emanated from the depths of Shay's chest.

"Perfect."

He scooped up the ropes on his way back over to her. By the time he stood directly behind her, he'd stretched the lengths between his hands, winding his wrists to pull them taut. Zoe shivered anew, though she couldn't determine whether it was from watching his masculine move or the power of his presence, so close and heated and huge behind her.

He stepped even closer, lifting the ropes so he could slither them down over her face, into the valley of her neck, and then down over her breasts, brushing her nipples with both his thumbs, causing them to tingle with a thousand more electrons of awareness. "Ohhhh," she moaned. "*Vaya. Sí. Me vuelves loca. Quiero más...más...*"

He met her request, rolling her sensitive tips between his thumbs and the towel. A combination of sadistic and soft that had her writhing and whining for him.

"Your tits are so beautiful. They love to stand at attention for me."

She could only nod in response. His words mixed with his touch flooded her body, pooling in a thick, warm cream that lined every tissue in her throbbing sex. She needed him inside her about five minutes ago—though she knew, with dreading surety, the wait for his cock had only just begun. The man hadn't just destroyed a pair of hundred-dollar towels so he could give her a little sensual tease.

Sure enough, Shay left her breasts behind to slide the ropes lower, though he pulled them apart and let them drop after swiping her mons a single time...making sure both the lengths teased for moments at her pussy as they did.

"Oh!" she cried out. "*Bastardo!*"

She'd barely unleased the word than Shay pulled on

her hair, jerking her head back and plunging his tongue in, punishing her with violent sweeps of his tongue. If that weren't enough to turn her knees to flan, he finished the assault by raking his teeth along her bottom lip, stripping her mouth of any control it might've had on its own.

"The bastard says hold still." He ordered it before releasing her with another sharp jerk.

"The bastard" was also quite resourceful. Though Zoe's whole body trembled and swayed with lust, she noticed that Shay had torn holes into alternating corners of the towels, forming surprising fits for her wrists. He tucked the edges of the towels through the holes to fully encase her in bonds that were better than padded cuffs. Nevertheless, he rechecked the fit on both arms, confirming her skin had room for circulation. The brusque expertise in all his movements sent her suspicions rising about his ultimate purpose. He affirmed it by looking up, behind the scrim hiding the tops of the room blinds, to the rod that held them in place.

Ohhhh, shit.

Without speaking, he took the free end of one rope and then looped it up and over the rod. Zoe's arm rose too. She watched her muscles flex, an involuntary reaction against this very new form of bondage for her. With Bryce, she'd always been strapped down to a piece of equipment, shackled into weak positions. When Shay finished tying off both ends of the linen lines, she gazed up...and saw a bird in flight. Even her tethers were beautiful, their white lengths painted to rainbows by the shifting lights of the fantasyland below.

Shay circled around, fitting himself between her body and the glass. His eyes were dark and unreadable, his jaw still bracketed in tension, though now the essence of that strain seemed changed. In every inch of his stance and long breath from his lungs, Zoe felt him soaking up the potency of their new positions as deeply as she. Cotton and denim next to shivers and nudity. Freedom next to bondage. Power over vulnerability. Dark dominance...utter submission.

Zoe's eyes slid shut. "*Vaya*," she whispered. Just the situation itself jolted her veins with a fresh speedball of fear. She was quivering and didn't care. The high of his power was worth the price of her lucidity.

Shay brought his hands up to the sides of her neck by way of her hips, her waist, and her breasts. "Where are we at, baby girl?" His growl was a protective caress, modulated for her ears only. "Green light? Yellow light? Red light?"

"Completely green," she rasped, "but only if you touch me again like that."

He yanked her head close and bit into her lips again. "That's *not* how things work with me, little bottom topper—and you know it."

"Y-Yes, Sir." The syllables spilled out as he tunneled his hands back into her hair, streaming his fingers out to the ends, pulling hard every inch of the way. As he did, he pressed closer, his chest absorbing the rave-club pounds of her heart, his legs cushioning every new shudder that claimed her. With every motion or sound she gave him, he returned the energy with another bite or recession of pain, seeming to know just when she did and didn't need it.

It was as magical as dancing.

Though the metaphor fit, Shay left no doubt about who dictated every step they made. Zoe was more than happy with that. She sagged, letting the pressure of the ropes and the strength of his body support every inch of her...and letting her senses fall further over the side of coherency.

"My good girl," he said, continuing the Caligula advance of his fingers, clawing them down her back and over both swells of her ass. When he scraped them back up, she hissed from the pain but swallowed back a shriek. "You take it so well, dancer. Every bite I give...every blow I deal."

She rolled her head up, breathing him in. Smelled like Ghid had managed to help him clean up, though the unfamiliar soap didn't totally drown the perfect pine spice of his normal scent. "Because I belong to you," she professed. "I take it because *you're* the one giving it."

A husky groan tore from his throat as he pulled back enough to meet her stare with the potent gold power of his. "That's damn good to hear, because I want to fill this room with the smacks I give your sweet ass."

He soaked up the wide pop of her eyes with a look of dark, feral satisfaction before circling his body behind hers again. He stayed close, sweeping her hair to one side so his lips trailed along her nape, sending even more shivers through her body from the contact.

"Look up, baby girl," he finally ordered into her ear, meeting her eyes through their reflection in the window. "Watch yourself. Gaze at how beautiful you are when you give yourself to my hands...transformed into your freedom."

His words were like classic poetry. Zoe trembled and sighed again, swept in the splendor of them.

Right before he shattered them with his first spank.

"*Ayyyy!*"

She'd expected a brief swat. Maybe even some warm-up taps...though those did come after he rained fire through her entire backside with that initial blow. Okay, she was officially awake now. And after settling her heart rate into something do-able, she actually relaxed a little, settling herself into the pattern of the little raps he sprinkled across both her cheeks and the tops of her thighs...

Thwack.

"*Mierda! Cabrón!*" The smack hurt worse than before. And the brutally hard blow after that too. Only able to react to that with a choke, Zoe slammed her eyes shut and sagged her head.

"The correct response is 'Thank you, Sir,'" Shay directed. "And you'll raise your head to submit it to me."

She snapped her head up, teeth bared and glare ablaze, but taking in his face, its perfection enhanced by all the nicks, dissolved her resistance into a new puddle. He was so achingly gorgeous all the time, but never more than when he was given permission to let his Dominant run completely free. In every intense spark of his gaze and every proud angle of his posture, she witnessed what she gave to him right now...and what she had to trust he'd give her in return.

Swallowing back her anger, she instead stated with meaningful softness, "Thank you, Sir."

He returned a nod of assertive approval—right before dealing another strict slap to her buttocks.

Ow, ow, owwwww.

"Thank you, Sir."

Another, twice as hard. At least it felt like it.

"Th-Thank you, Sir."

Three in a row this time. She couldn't hold back her scream or the jerk of her hips, trying to get away from him, but he held on with a grip like steel. One rigid arm circled her waist while he spanked again—*smack, smack, smack*—sending even more ribbons of fire across her tender globes.

"Ahhhhh!"

She had some choice nouns in her alternate vernacular that were set to be added whether he liked it or not, but they fled her mind as he abruptly switched up the intent of his touch. Instead of pain, he took the fire he'd just wielded, spreading it into trails of tingling warmth. Back and forth he stroked, the swaths of his care becoming the most enticing massage she'd ever received—

Especially when he tucked his fingers inward.

Yes. Yes. Yes.

The word resounded through her senses as he glided over the soaked folds that begged for him the most.

New rivers flowed up through her body as he openly bit at her shoulder. The stab extended all the way to her sex, clenching toward his fingers. Needing more of him to fill her up.

"What do you say, baby girl?"

"Ohhh...*Dios*...thank you, Sir."

He pulled his fingers back out. Smacked her again with hard purpose. "And now?"

"Th-Thank you, Sir." It tumbled from her on a gasp as he drove his fingers back to her intimate core—this time, twisting one up inside her. Two. She gasped and shifted. Her body was more than ready, clenching on him as he drove up with fierce thrusts. She began to grind deeper, reveling in his invasion, until he suddenly left, returning to his rain of sharp fire over her backside.

"Again, baby girl."

"Thank you, Sir."

The rhythm continued, a heated tease followed by an

assault of hard pain, until Zoe could barely tell the difference anymore. Shay yanked her back and forth between such extremes of sensation that her mind shut down, turning her into a being only capable of one purpose—to feel.

Through it all, she never disobeyed him. As commanded, she watched every moment through her languid lashes. The effort became easier. She no longer recognized the woman in the glass, anyway. She'd become a shameless slave, a naked offering to a dark god who catapulted her body between pleasure and pain like his private plaything.

Her eyes widened a little at the most recent crack he gave her ass. The ring from it seemed to bounce off the glass, ringing in her ears. Nevertheless, she forced the words to her mouth again. "Th-Thank you—"

"No," Shay interjected. In the glass, she watched him run his hand down her spine before swirling it across the hot spheres at the bottom. He tightened his other arm around her waist. "No more words, tiny dancer. Damn, I'm flying...and I know you are too."

He dropped his head around to find her lips with his. Melded with her in a long kiss, caressing her tongue like they'd never tasted each other before. And *mierda*, was he delicious. The tang of his beer, the salt of his sweat, and the musk of his desire... It was ambrosia to her, and she sent a little mewl up her throat to beg him for more. In Shay's chest, a responding thunder rolled, though it never reached completion. He tore back from her with a tormented snarl across his lips.

"Christ." His breathing was labored. "I thought the domination would be enough, but I can't get enough of you." He suckled at her chin, her neck, her shoulder blades with hungry abandon. "I want to fuck you, baby girl, and not just with my fingers."

Zoe felt her head rolling back and forth, as eager a nod as she could manage in the middle of this perfect, needy haze. "*Sí...Sí...echemos un polvo salvaje...por favor...*"

Being able to let it all out like that just sent her mind on a wilder ride. She was lost in his embrace, her body a horny mess, the fire across her ass now blending into the tissues of her labia and making her pulse even more for the fullness of his cock. She made the message clear by undulating her whole body, straining against her tethers, forcing him to see the erect points of her nipples and the gleaming folds between her thighs.

"Damn," Shay grated. "You had me at *sí*, tiny dancer."

She tossed a little grin back up at him. "*Sí.*"

His gaze seemed to darken—she couldn't tell between the shadows of the room and the haze of her arousal—before he reached into his jeans pocket and slid out a glistening new condom packet. "I'm glad Ghid stuck this into the jeans he brought for me."

"Yaaayyy, Ghid."

"And I'm going to be *really* glad to watch you use that beautiful mouth again."

"Mmmm. Yes, Sir."

She bit her lips and eyed the colorful foil, wondering how the man had discerned all the deepest ways to fuck with her brain. Just looking at the thing, encased in his long, strong fingers, sent a gallon of fresh arousal to the tissues between her legs. It matched the speed of every neuron in her brain. What did he have planned for her? How would he control her this time? Would he untie the ropes and send her back to her knees...let her finally get him out of those jeans in the best way possible? Or would he order her to open the packet with her teeth while he watched with those molten, magical eyes?

He didn't make her wait long to find out.

"Lick." He nodded when she flashed a questioning stare. "You heard me, baby girl. Lick the package as if it's the surface of my cock. Every inch. Every ridge. While I watch...and let imagination work its magic..."

His voice fell away into a raw diamond roughness, setting off a matching cascade through Zoe's blood as she extended her tongue in willing obedience. As Shay turned the packet in front of her mouth to let her get both sides, she closed her eyes and joined him in his fantasy, dreaming that she licked his true flesh, serving him in one of the most special ways she could. In her vision, he teased her with his length, feeding her an inch only to draw it back, and then giving her a little more with his next press in...

She moaned hard.

So did Shay.

Imagination really could work magic. The air in the room hovered on sexual tension, swirling like dawn about to break, impatient in its last minutes of darkness. Zoe smelled her sex on Shay's fingers and leaned forward a little to lick that from him too. When he hissed, pulling away the packet in order to slide his digits farther into her mouth, the cloud across her senses thickened with more delicious heat. Existing solely for his pleasure, the only object completing his passion... It was a dream she didn't even know she had. Now, this astonishment of a man granted it to her in the very same moment.

He was the Dom of all her fantasies...and more. The warrior of her fairy tales. The miracle she'd abandoned hope of ever finding.

"Zoe...fuck...you're so perfect."

And the guy who knew how to hit every arousal button in her body with his illicit words.

She accepted a third finger from him with a blissful sigh, opening herself for the incessant rhythm he established, in and out with a force that built in direct proportion to the energy turning her whole body into a pulsing isotope of carnal need. She swayed on the ropes from the heady spell of it, her womb tightening, her pussy shivering. She almost wondered if she'd orgasm before he ever entered her.

Until he did enter her.

The violent thrust was a complete surprise. Time had been weirdly morphed. She didn't remember him freeing himself or even sliding the condom on, but there was no doubt about the mass of flesh filling her now. His invasion hurt at first, a fact that was likely never going to change, but after Zoe pulled in a breath and welcomed him into her walls, the pain became the best kind of ache her body had ever known.

He pulled his fingers from her lips in order to seize her left hip. His other hand already dug into the right side, forming a double strut that gave him complete command of her body. He sure as hell used it, pulling her back in forceful jolts as he lunged up. His lusting growl matched the harsh coil of his thigh muscles, making her realize he'd somehow shucked his pants too.

She dragged her eyes open to gaze at their reflection now. Shay's arms bulged out of his T-shirt as he controlled her, bent and flexed anew with every slam of their bodies. His legs were ropes of solid muscle, bent to accommodate their height difference but balanced by her weight as their passion escalated, fast and frantic and feral, into an animal-style fuck.

In every flex of his tendons and drive of his body, one truth blared for Zoe, brighter than the dawn that was about to crest for them both.

He needed this. Needed her.

Making her wish the sunrise would never come.

Her body, the traitorous bitch, had a thoroughly different desire. Every time Shay drove into her, he took another shred of her restraint against the sweet, sharp pressure in her body... the rays of her sun just beyond the silhouettes of the night. His flesh was everywhere, buried so deep inside her that the sack at his base tapped an enticing rhythm against some of her most sensitive tissues. She sobbed against the encroachment. Wasn't heaven supposed to last forever? And couldn't heaven be just as beautiful in the darkness as the light?

Shay increased his tempo. Grunted harder as his cock swelled bigger.

"Oh, Zoe. Sweet baby girl," he growled. "Here it comes. Here it comes."

No. No.

Yes. Yes.

The sun burst over them both, brilliant and blinding as the hugest star in the sky. Certainly that was what he'd transformed her into, a consideration that made Zoe smile as her limbs transformed to light, her mind became a cosmos, and her heart flew into a sky that glowed forever, bright and blue and warm...so wonderful and warm...

No. No.

She heard the words fall from her lips out loud as Shay slipped her wrists free from their bonds and caught her limp body against his. "Ssshhh." It was a murmur and order in one, vibrating from his mouth into her forehead as he scooped her up and carried her to the bed.

She protested again as he placed her beneath the sheets. "It's c-c-cold," she managed, beginning to shiver.

"I know," he said, climbing in next to her. "Come."

Like he had to bother with that one. Zoe fitted herself to the crook of his arm in seconds, sighing in bliss as he raised his hand, so big and warm, to stroke the length of her back.

"Air-conditioning," she mumbled, suddenly swept by exhaustion. "Damn force of nature."

Shay's answer came with the first smile she'd heard in his voice since he returned. "Force of nature? I think that's you, my little hostage...not the air ducts."

★ ★ ★ ★ ★

"*Mierda.*"

She whispered the word before even looking for the clock.

They'd both fallen asleep fast and obviously slept like a pair of corpses, because sunlight bathed the room now. Judging by the heatwaves pulsing on the outside of the glass, it had to be close to the middle of the day.

Laughter from the living room caught her attention. It sounded like Ryder—and Dan Colton, the CIA agent. Music, sweeping and dramatic, was a backing soundtrack, interrupted by a bunch of video-game explosions. Well, *there* was an interesting friendship in the making.

She snuggled a little closer to Shay, breathing in the perfect smell of him. The cotton of his T-shirt. The natural pine of his skin. The lingering spice from their sex. As she rubbed her foot along the inside of his calf, the scent was stirred a little—and instantly awakened all the juices in her body that mattered the most. A smile bloomed on her lips. She'd never really gotten to wrap her mouth around him last night. Maybe now was the ideal opportunity...

"Hey." Shay's sleepy mutter tilted her gaze up. "Good morning—errr, afternoon?"

Zoe laughed. "I guess we were tired."

He hooked an arm behind his head, angling his gaze a little better at her. "How long have you been awake?"

"Just a couple of minutes." She curled an impish grin. "Don't worry. I kept busy."

That made his gaze narrow before he drawled, "Doing what?"

"Hmmm. Well, smelling you, for one thing."

"What?" He glared like she'd just admitted to being the mastermind behind Rickrolling. "Smelling me? Why?"

"*Ay.*" She threw back a mock scowl. "Because I couldn't before now, all right?"

"I stink."

"Not as bad as Ryder's cat." She rolled her eyes. "He thought I was pining for you. He got really worried, so he lent Fluffy to me."

"Did he really name his cat Fluffy?"

"He rescued it. And he was drunk."

During the explanation, Shay took a tentative whiff at his armpit. And grimaced. "Shit. That does it. No more smelling until I'm out of the shower."

Before Zoe could object, he lurched out of the bed and headed for the bathroom. While the shower started, she got up and lowered the blinds on one side of the room. She wasn't able to do anything with the other side, since she couldn't reach high enough to release the linen ropes from last night. In a way, she was glad for that. Gazing at the ropes made her long for the night again already.

She walked over and wrapped a hand around the soft white length, pulling the rope taut while gliding her fingers down until she got to the aperture her wrist had fit through. Simply connecting to the rope like this beaded her nipples, sent demanding pulses to her pussy, and made her excruciatingly aware of her harsh sighs on the air.

She needed Shay again.

Screw waiting on him to finish the shower.

CHAPTER NINETEEN

Shay clenched himself back from bellowing the F-word for the fifth time in as many minutes but succeeded in peeling the last bandage away from his torso without a sound. When he freed the worn gauze, he tossed the bloody mess of it over the shower glass, his muscles protesting the action.

Okay, so giving in to the temptation of screwing Zoe wasn't the best idea for facilitation of his physical recovery. But damn, the wonders it had performed for his soul.

If it had been real.

Half his mind still expected to wake up on the gurney back at the lab, having dreamt every incredible second after Ghid drove him free from Area 51. But his ears confirmed the *thunk* as the wadded bandage touched down in the trash can across the bathroom, and his lips felt real as he gave himself a mental high-five for the swoosh. He hadn't been as lucky with his other attempts. Several bloodied squares littered the floor around the receptacle, a gruesome graveyard in memory of his nightmare.

His nightmare.

If it were only that easy...

Being in Spec Ops ensured he'd seen enough mind-benders over the years to logically pick apart what was going on in the gray matter. Thinking of trauma as a dream made it easier to handle in the short run. They even encouraged the tactic, at least for a limited time, until a guy had the ability to "adequately process" the ordeal. The thing was, Shay had always laughed at all that crap. Adequate processing? *Pffft*. Separation from missions, and any horrors they'd involved, was as easy for him as turning off a shitty TV show. Out of sight, out of mind.

Out of sight? Fat fucking chance now, when the simple act of washing his balls made him look at half a dozen incision sites inflicted by those science shits. *Out of mind?* Not when he'd spent days staring at white prison walls and wondering how an act of boyhood innocence had turned him into a freak, sliced and diced like experimental sushi.

He rammed the soap back into the holder. Then let his hand trail down his chest and stomach, stopping to run a finger over the thick black threads they'd used to sew him back together. Some of the incisions were newer than others and stung when he fingered them. The older ones were still sensitive but painless, the skin light pink in its freshly healed state.

He wrenched his hand away. And wondered if this was how Frankenstein felt after the lightning storm passed.

A movement in his peripheral snapped his head up. *Shit.* This was the moment the dream would end.

No. Worse.

Zoe stood there, doing her best to rein in the shock dropping her mouth and the horror darkening her eyes.

He actually wished for the fucking gurney again. Even that was better than witnessing the revulsion on her face. And the sadness. And the goddamn pity. This was why he'd kept his shirt on last night and why he'd waited to shed his jeans until she was swept away by too much lust to notice the gouges on his thighs.

It was why he spun from her now, driving a fist against the stall wall. "You want to respect the closed door and go out the way you came?"

"Shay—"

"I said *get out,* Zoe. This time I mean it!"

"And if I don't? You'll do what?"

He froze, gut churning. He was furious with her but enraged at himself. Her insolence was unacceptable, but so was his shame. She was right. How could he discipline her if he couldn't even look at her? But he was stuck in this mental space, unable to get the fuck over it. He'd finally met a woman he burned to be a hero for—and the first who'd never see him that way.

"Go. Away. And take the fucking pity with you."

There was no backtalk to that. Not a sound from her side of the glass at all. Had the stubborn little thing actually listened to him? Ten more seconds of silence passed before he let out his breath in relief and then grabbed the soap again—

Just as Zoe opened the shower door and stepped in with him.

"Zoe! Fuck!"

"Shut up."

His brows shot up before he could stop them. "What the— *no.* Goddamnit, this isn't—"

"Shut. Up."

She shoved on his sternum. The push wasn't hard, but astonishment added a wallop he didn't anticipate, knocking him against the wall. An incensed growl rushed out of his chest, but the string of profanity waiting on his verbal tarmac never took off—officially grounded by the sweet, wet kiss she pulled him into.

Shit. It was weird yet fucking exciting to be the pursued for once, to feel *her* needing *him* with the passion he'd always instigated.

For just a few seconds, he let himself revel in the switch.

Through the next few, he braced himself for the return of her repulsion.

It would come. Any second now. As she stepped back and got her close-up view of his mutilated flesh...

Slowly, Zoe drew her lips away. Carefully, she pushed back by a step. In agony, Shay waited for her gaze to drop—and her disgust to begin.

She might as well have shoved him back another time.

Her eyes did drop. But so did her head. As Shay watched, his lungs hoarding his breath and shock clamping the rest of him, Zoe closed her lips over the first set of his stitches. He gaped at her for several stunned seconds before the indignation and fury crashed in, pulling one of his hands up in preparation to shove her free. He'd take her revulsion over her pity; her honesty over her obligation.

But then she moved her mouth to the second wound.

And never once lifted her lips off his skin.

Her tongue flicked out, trailing fire to his flesh in open oral adoration...

Matched exactly by the twin blue flames of her eyes as she looked back up to him.

"Christ," he rasped. "Zoe."

She pressed him to the wall again. He moved willingly this time, letting his hand continue to her, now trailing his thumb along the exquisite line of her cheekbone. She pulled her mouth off his torso for a second to turn and kiss his palm before grabbing his fingers and lowering his hand. After gently worshipping the third set of his stiches, she spoke a supplication into the hollow of his navel.

"You're so beautiful. *All* of you."

An incredulous laugh tumbled from him. He couldn't help it. "*I'm* so—"

"Ssshhh."

She rasped that across the tip of his cock.

Her ministrations down his torso already had him half-erect. With the perfect wisp of her kiss, his penis surged to full attention. He stared back down just in time to watch her lowering completely to her knees, already going for his ball sack with her fingers.

"Fuck!"

His precome rose, hot and thick. His beautiful little toy was ready, cleaning the drops from his head before the shower could, her tongue soft and perfect against his head. A groan tumbled from him as she continued on, wrapping her mouth completely around his tip, teasing mercilessly at his throbbing crest. At the same time, she cupped his balls with fearless pressure, somehow knowing he liked being on the receiving end of intensity too.

"Damn." He choked it out, now petrified to look away, certain that a break in concentration would take him back to the white-walled prison and the gurney. "This has to be a dream."

Zoe gently shook her head at him before taking more of his length into her mouth—and now her throat too. When his hoarse groan resounded through the bathroom, she deepened her pressure and mewled around him in subbie satisfaction. He still wasn't convinced this could be reality, but he made a vow—he'd stow the doubts and simply enjoy every new journey into the honeyed heaven of her mouth. If he tumbled back into the nightmare, he would do so with a grin on his face.

It was paradise. *She* was paradise. With every embrace of her tongue, squeeze of her mouth, and kiss at the back of her throat, she took his dick to realms of pleasure it had never felt before. The cascading water and the rising steam turned the shower into their own tropical grotto, complete with the passion all the tourist guides promised but never delivered. A postcard he'd cherish in the scrapbook of his mind forever...

Which meant he needed to get in the picture with her.

The effort wasn't hard. His inner caveman had already been roused by the efforts of trying to keep her out of here, a mission of insanity if he'd ever known one. He let the Neanderthal stomp free while lifting his hands to her hair and tunneling them deep. The strands were wet and thick between his fingers, perfect for aiding his control. Zoe's high sigh of response told him she had a fondness for primeval man too. A veil of serenity seemed to fall over her face, all her sass relinquished to the joy of letting him rule the cave for a while. And Christ, did the look work for her. She was breathtaking, his enticing one-night trinket transformed into one of the best gifts fate had ever given him.

And coming down her throat was going to be his big red bow to finally pull free.

But something happened on the way to unwrapping the present. As Shay began fucking her mouth in earnest, sliding himself in from crown to base in long, commanding stabs, Zoe's answering moans, harsh with desire, hitched at instincts even deeper than his caveman.

He didn't want to come without her.

He needed to watch the big red bow open for her too.

Needed to see every second of her climax race across her exquisite face, knowing he'd made it happen...letting his tiny dancer spin in the enormity of her submission.

The commitment sealed itself in his spirit, lending his muscles the fortitude to push her free. When Zoe glared up at him, he simply jerked his head, directing her to the tiled ledge inlaid into the shower. "Plant your sweet ass here, baby girl." He weighted his growl with enough gravel to let her know that denying the order shouldn't be a fleeting thought in her head.

He pivoted a little as she settled onto the seat. Sweet fuck, she robbed his breath, with the shower light playing over her drenched skin and her hair trailing like exotic black snakes against her erect olive breasts. His dick swelled again simply from gazing at her, and he made no effort to hide that from her wide indigo stare.

"Spread your legs."

She obeyed without a word, exposing the dark-pink fruit of her pussy. His lungs held on to his breath again, likely jealous of the treat laid before his eyes. Fucking stunning. She was his own slice of sinful fruit from the bacchanal gods, kissed by nectar, fascinating as a flower—waiting to be stabbed open and decimated.

Which meant the dagger had to be perfectly prepared.

He raised a hand. And began stroking himself.

Zoe's breath audibly hitched. She gazed without blinking, mesmerized by the sluice of the water and his fingers over the length of his dick. Her gaze heated, and she ran her tongue eagerly over her lips.

"No," Shay ordered. "You only watch now."

"Yes, Sir."

He rubbed again, dragging hard at his crown, grunting

from the mix of agony and ecstasy. "Like what you're seeing, baby girl?"

She pulled in a labored breath. "Very much, Sir."

"You want it to fuck you?"

An adorable little hum spilled out. "*Dios*. Oh *yes*, Sir."

"I don't have another condom."

She turned her head up to directly meet his gaze. "It's all right. I'm tested during my yearly." A funny wince creased her features. "And there hasn't been anyone to worry about for that year anyway."

"A year." He released a wry laugh. "Longer than that for me."

Her gaze widened. "What?"

"Afghanistan for a year, and then Cameron Stock and his gang for six months. Take a guess which one killed the sex drive the most."

She tipped her head to the side as if to agree, though she gave a wry smile while stating, "It's a major upset to the cosmic balance to think of *anything* killing your sex drive, *amigo*."

Shay chuckled. "Oh, dancer, you have no idea...especially with you looking like the juiciest fruit in the jungle like that."

He expected a giggle from that. To his surprise, her stare went mushy instead. *Really* mushy. The thick tears turned her irises mysterious as midnight once again.

Shay dropped between her knees and grabbed her waist, yanking her close and kissing her hard. "Hey...what is it?"

She shook her head, one of those dismissive girl things that normally drove him ballistic, until she whispered words that slammed his chest like thunder and his spirit like lightning. "Every word that comes out of your mouth... It's like you've excavated my mind and pulled out the things I crave to hear."

She lifted a wobbly smile. "The things...I *need* to hear."

He frowned. "What do you mean?"

She tried to shrug that one off. Shay forced her gaze back to his with a thumb beneath her chin. She flipped his move on him, dipping her head to tenderly kiss the pad of his thumb. "I'd lost hope of being special to someone. Of being...good enough."

"Christ." He silenced whatever the hell else she had to say by sealing his mouth over hers again. After releasing her from the kiss, he didn't let her go from his grip—or his stare. "You're not *good*, tiny dancer. You're fucking perfect."

More mush. A lot more. Shay didn't care. Maybe he did have the power of reading her soul, but maybe that was because his already knew it...recognized it as the universe's answer to his own. But how much of that soul was still his own? How much of him was *him*, and how much the beast that had been roaming through his blood for twenty years? How much of himself would be left once he found out? And how free would he be to express it? The government was surely hunting for him now. Cameron, missing after the raid, was probably seeking out his ass too—and more than that, if he'd started connecting the dots and figuring shit out.

A lot of questions. A lot of answers he didn't have. He only had the fulfillment to one unknown, and that was the certainty of here and now. The deliverance that began with the very next kiss he lowered to her, plunging into her with all the desire in his body, the spiraling need in his blood. He could be perfect for her too—at least in assuaging the sexual fever between them.

He groaned as Zoe met him for the quest, surging her breasts into his chest, and roping her arms around his neck and her hands in his hair. As their kiss ended, she added a sweet vibration in her throat, erupting off her lips into a decadent whimper. "Ohhhh, Sergeant Bommer..."

Her plea turned his shaft into a goddamn missile, ready to be fired. "You rang, ma'am?" he teased in a sultry drawl.

"No ringing," she panted. "Just need. Need. *Need.*"

"Need what, baby girl?"

"Fuck me, Shay. Please. Now."

By now, he'd guided the tip of his sex to the waiting tunnel of hers—and could even feel the lips of her pussy, eager and hungry, struggling to draw him in. But he held his position, gazing down at her upturned face, and softly told her, "No."

Zoe's lips pursed. "Huh?"

Even as she snapped it, he nudged his cock another inch into her. Her confusion was pretty damn cute.

"I said no," he repeated—while stuffing into her by another inch. "No fucking, Zoe." He rolled his hips now, letting her feel every last sensation of his bare skin against hers. "Entering. Merging. Uniting." He smiled a little, exulting in the effect of each word on her lips, her eyes, her cheeks, her chin, even the gorgeous sweep of her neck, moving with her heavy swallow.

"And feeling."

Her whisper fanned his lips. He answered her with a soft smile.

"Yeah. And feeling."

"And how does it feel?"

His lips dropped as his jaw clenched. "Like perfection."

Like home.

He kept the addendum to himself. He had no right to fill her head with fantasies like that. If things weren't complicated enough before the little come-to-Jesus gig with Ghid last night, they sure as hell were now.

For now, this was what he could give her. Not just his body but his passion. Not just his kisses but his adoration. Not just a fuck but a union.

Everything except the seed that pummeled at his balls now, ready for its rocketing release. Still, he held back. Her skin was so slick and wet and tight around his, as if her body were made to welcome him. He tried rocking a little slower, focusing on the pleasure that gleamed all over her flawless body. For a few seconds here and a few seconds there, it worked. He was able to forget about the pressure that built like a bullet train, preparing to shoot from the station as soon as he punched the green light.

By now, Zoe rolled her hips in time with his, meeting every thrust with a mewling grind of her own. "Shay," she cried out, plowing her nails across his shoulders and locking her legs around his waist. "Oh, Shay...*mas duro...sí!*"

He was pretty damn sure what that meant, and it made him grimace. "Baby girl, if I don't pull out now—"

"I know," she countered. "I know, and I don't care."

Fuck.

He scraped both her hands off his shoulders. Used his grip on them to force her attention. "You *have* to care. We're not sixteen. We're not *married.*"

She flung him a look he'd never seen on her face before. One brow arched along with a sexier-than-shit wiggle of her head. "So if I find you in a month and tell you I'm knocked-up, you'll do...what?"

He actually came to a full stop. The woman was either the smartest bird he'd ever met or the biggest brat. Or maybe both.

Probably both.

"Throw a fucking party. Then make sure I never let you

out of my sight."

Her expression changed by one more element. The luscious little grin that spread across her lips, sparking the most breathtaking blend of blue and purple he'd ever seen in her eyes. "Then what are you waiting for?"

He grabbed her by the neck, kissing her harder than ever. He'd always avoided talk of babies, even when they happened to other people. In his life, "family" wasn't a word that brought fond memories of themed birthday parties and vacations at the lake. The species could propagate without his help. But now, thinking of Zoe with a little basketball belly, growing with *his* child...

He plunged his tongue even deeper into her mouth. Claiming her had never felt more important.

"Are you sure?" he murmured when they finally dragged apart.

The woman had the gumption to roll her eyes. "You going to keep yakking at me, Sergeant, or are you going to do something better with that steel between my legs?"

Goddamn. Her naughty mouth made his shaft feel like real steel. As he lunged up into her, reveling in her stunned gasp and arched neck, he snarled, "Like make you ride it, baby girl? Like this?"

She cried out as he drove into her even deeper. "*Sí*, my Sir. Just...like— Ohhhh!"

Forget the pretty adjectives. It was time to fuck his gorgeous little subbie. To drive her high and hard into the stratosphere of her pleasure until her walls converged on his cock and milked his seed deep into her body.

Like so many other things in this unexpected explosion of their relationship, it was a bungee jump of faith. A wild belief in what could be. Another careen into crazy.

In all the most perfect ways.

★ ★ ★ ★ ★

Where the hell had forty-eight hours gone?

For the first time since he was a kid on summer break, time had been pressed into a strange mix of both the meaningless and monumental. The little things just didn't seem to matter anymore, while the big stuff, like spending as much time as possible with his brother and Zoe, were now Shay's hugest priorities.

Because in every minute of those precious hours, he never forgot the price he paid for them.

Conveniently, the monsters had left the tags on the merchandise. Every row of stiches was a fresh reminder that this escape wasn't going to last forever. That the boys in the land of the thick black thread were hunting for him even now.

He'd only go back to that hell in a body bag.

Put the morbidity away, shithead. Enjoy the moment, remember? The sun is shining. The sky is blue. Your subbie is smiling, and you should be too.

Dr. Seuss had to take a back burner too. Shay looked up to endure his brother's sarcastic stare. He wasn't sure if the reason for the eyeballing was good or bad, so he waited for Tait to wrap his call to Kaua'i and walk back over to the pool cabana that Dan and Oz had secured for their use during the afternoon.

A victorious shriek from the plunge pool grabbed his attention. Ryder and Zoe were Ellie and Brynn's opponents in a water volleyball game, and it looked like Zoe was ruling the action. Shay smiled at the joy on his subbie's face. Though Dan and Ghid had decreed it was best for Zoe's friends to stay here since their homes were likely still being watched, the edict had valuable residual benefits. Seeing her rested and content provided a glimpse into a future he was determined to fight for. To live for.

Zoe spiked the ball over the net for another team point. Ryder whooped and high-fived her. As Zoe jumped to meet the move, sunshine and water gleamed across her body, clad in a pink bikini he loved and hated for all the same reasons. The thing was only held on her body by little string ties...

Time to adjust the towel in his lap.

As he slid the cover higher, he mandated himself to focus on something else. It was a damn good thing the Vdara had all these pools. Another that they were the only crowd at this one. The first time some douche ogled Zoe with the same intent that burned his mind right now, the guy would probably be without a dick.

Sprawled on the cabana's second lounger, Dan glanced at him and chuffed. "Fuck, man. Put us all out of your misery and make her throw on a T-shirt."

"Sure," he sneered. "And that'll make a difference...how?"

Colton frowned. Shay would've laughed if his imagination weren't on fire with the answer to that. Getting to the bikini top would be just as much a no-brainer for him if Zoe wore a T-shirt. As soon as he had her pretty tits free of the little pink triangles, he'd enjoy hardening her nipples right through the shirt's fabric—with his tongue. Wouldn't be long before he pulled the strings off the bottom of the suit, too. Then he'd slip inside her, taking her in a long, luxurious fuck that would give her at least three orgasms before he started pounding harder, and—

"Well, Kell got home from training," his brother announced, "and took a break from screwing our subbie in the rain in order to relay his asshat hello to everyone."

"Awww." Dan smirked. Tait had updated the agent about his unique relationship status back on the island—ensuring that Dan ribbed him about it whenever the chance arose. "Is somebody dunking his head in a big ol' barrel of oh-poor-me?"

"Bite me," Tait drawled.

"No, thank you," Dan quipped. "But maybe your brother'll be up for the task." He whacked a hand to his thigh. "Oh, damn. Wait. The only person he's 'up for' these days is currently leading the spike count in the volleyball game."

Shay snorted. "And boy, do I have a celebration trophy for her."

Dan snickered. "Make sure she kisses it after she holds it up."

"She always does."

"Then you gonna show it off to T?"

Tait glared while dropping into a chair and then adjusting the discomfort of his junk. "You done with your fun yet, Teabaggin' Tex?"

"Gah." Shay threw the orange peel from his drink, hitting the center of T's chest. "Dude, I can't believe you reached for that one."

Tait laughed and tossed the fruit back. "I've had to step up my game. I think the SHRCs are going to petition for shit-slinging as an Olympic event."

Dan's brows hunkered. "For the winter or summer games?"

"Probably winter." T took a sip of his own drink. His had a pineapple instead of an orange. "They could stick it in during lulls in the curling matches."

Shay rolled his eyes. "Isn't curling one giant lull?"

"You have a problem with curling?" The charge came from the cabana's newest guest, a scowling Ghid. As usual, the man wore a dark T-shirt to completely shield his back, joined by black nylon shorts and a pair of flip-flops. "You know what kind of skills are required for that sport?"

While Ghid grabbed a bottle of water from the mini fridge, Shay kicked his chortling brother in the shin. *Hell.* T of all people should be sympathizing with Ghid's tension, misplaced this time to a rant about big stones, little brooms, and a lot of ice. Personally, Shay shared Tait's point of view—a real sport usually involved protective gear and blood—but if Ghid wanted to bluster again about the guy he caught counting cards last night, he'd support it.

Mom had missed her normal check-in call last night. Then again this morning.

"Yo, Ghid." Maybe a redirect was the best plan here. "It's nearly ninety out here. That black shirt has to feel like a wool blanket. If you keep to the back of the tent, just shuck it and nobody will be the wiser."

Ghid sat in the chair next to Tait. The wicker creaked, not used to supporting over two hundred pounds of solid muscle. "Kid, half my blood once roamed across Africa. What makes you think this isn't my idea of heaven?"

Tait threw over a scowl. "Could've fooled the rest of us."

Shay didn't hide the kick he dealt the dork this time. "Can you just zip it the hell up now?"

"Sorry." T took a sheepish drag of his drink before raising a sincere stare at Ghid. "She'll call soon, dude. I know it."

The guy grunted and shrugged. "Meh. I'm just being

a paranoid pussy. She's got a lot to deal with right now, with everyone but Oliver, Nika, and Damian now at the compound."

Shay straightened. "Those are the three guys we couldn't bust out of A-fifty-one with us?" Ghid held his gaze and nodded tightly. The guy's eyes were touched with teal today because of his stress, but Shay also observed a warmer shade of understanding. He knew what it was like to feel almost a brother to a guy because your screams hit the same roofs.

Shay nodded in return, giving Ghid his thanks even as he joined the guy in a silent promise to those three men. *We'll go back for you. We swear.*

"Right." Tait submitted the assertion with empathy drawn on his face for Ghid. "I feel you, G. I want to talk to her again too." He exhaled. "Fuck. I can't wait to *see* her again." He tossed his stare at Shay. "You think she'll recognize me? I mean, I'm taller now. And cuter..."

Shay joined Ghid and Dan in a round of disgusted groans. After that, silence took over the cabana. It seemed T's humor had instigated deep thoughts for all four of them.

After a couple of minutes, Ghid cocked his head. Shay could almost predict the question he'd pose but waited for the discomfort of it anyway.

"You have any ideas about the beasties lurking in your CBC test, kid?"

The man hadn't let down his expectation. *Shit.*

Shay started his response with a shrug. "I've never turned a weird color, howled at the moon, or grown to abnormal proportions."

Tait chuckled. "Except for that thing between your legs."

Shay's pulse froze for a second. He pinned his brother with a stare. "You mean yours isn't—"

"What?"

"The same...uhhh..."

"You mean am I hung like a goddamn race horse? Apparently not. But I heard all about *you* from Sylvia Cooper. In excruciating, inch-by-inch detail." Tait set down his drink, shaking with laughter. "Christ wept, brother. Are you blushing?"

"Damn. I think he is," Dan drawled.

Ghid folded his arms and glowered. "Well, fuck. I get the backside of a Teenage Mutant Ninja Turtle, and he gets to be Babar the Elephant?"

Shay whipped a glare of his own to Colton, who fully enjoyed the shared snicker with Tait. "Guess you're happy now with *Teabaggin' Tex.*"

Though Ghid looked tempted to jump on that dig, he kept his regard fixed on Shay. "So that narrows things down to a list of critters on the...errrm...well-endowed side. Stop looking soggy as a Jane Austen novel, kid; I know you've been curious."

Shay pushed out a rebellious snort. So what if the guy was right? So what if *curious* only chipped the tip of the mental chaos he'd been dealing with in all this? So what if he felt like he'd been in a turbulent ocean already, only to be whammed by a goddamn tsunami? And so what if the only anchor he kept swimming to was a five-foot-three beauty he'd only met a week ago? Wilder shit had been known to happen to people, right?

People.

Yeah. And wasn't that the bitch of things?

He couldn't validate even being a *person* anymore...even if he'd never felt more ecstatically, uniquely, a man.

A cell phone started ringing. The look on Ghid's face conveyed that the call wasn't just a prayer answered for Shay.

After Ghid frantically pulled the device from his pocket, his lips quirked in his version of jubilation. "It's her."

"Thank fuck," Tait said.

"No shit." As Ghid rose and walked away, he added over his shoulder, "You can blab at her once I'm done, T."

"*Mahalo.*" Tait swiveled back toward Shay with a chuckle tempting his lips. He shook his head as he gave into the mirth. "Wow."

Shay inclined his head. "Wow what?"

"What do you mean, wow what? In the last seventy-two hours, I've learned my little bro pulled off arguably the slickest secret mission since Neptune's Spear and brought our mom back to us in the process. Not only that, but you're now some kind of badass super-hybrid something, *and* you found a woman who digs the hell out of you—who lives in Las Vegas, Nevada. I sure as hell know where Kell and I are taking our dream girl on our next vacation."

Shay couldn't help indulging his own laugh. "What happened to my sibling who always made things as dark as a Brontë novel?"

Tait flaunted a lopsided grin. "He moved to Kaua'i. Swims in the ocean before breakfast. And has the love of his life to come home to every day."

He studied the guy for a long moment, hardly believing his brother was the same man. A year ago, the only thing that got Tait out of bed was a bottle of Grey Goose and a semiclean glass. A soft smile replaced his chuckle. "It's really that simple, isn't it?"

Tait gestured toward the pool with one hand. "Sometimes you just have to believe it's the best day of your life, brother."

Like a bizarre magic spell, T's words seemed to set

everything into slow motion. The bad B movie kind, like rocks in Jell-O—which was exactly what Ghid looked like as he fell to his knees on the deck. The phone popped out of his hand and plunked into the pool between Zoe and Ryder, who joined Brynn and Ellie in gaping at him with confused horror in their eyes.

"What the hell?" Dan bounded to his feet.

Shay rose with him. "Not. Good."

He might as well have said *holy shit.*

Zoe. She had to get out of the water. He had to have her back here, next to him. Now. *Now.*

But the second her name started to buzz off his lips, his phone rang. Also listing a northern Nevada number.

Shay jammed the line open as fast as he could. "Mom? What the hell's going on? Ghid just collapsed like a deck of cards, and—"

"Sergeant Shay Bommer. My, my, my. Hello there."

It wasn't Mom. The voice was low. Calm. Cultured. Male.

Sometimes you just have to believe it's the best day of your life...

Until it became the worst.

"Where the hell's my mother, Homer?"

CHAPTER TWENTY

Despite the heat of the day, Zoe shivered as if she'd been dunked in a vat of ice.

She'd been trembling since the moment Ghid's proud stance had given way to a collapse of defeat. If that hadn't turned the day into a giant blast of surreal, Shay's snarl worked out the finale for the job.

Homer Adler. Like the captain of the *Titanic*, he was all too happy to guide a ship of dreams, right up until the iceberg. Then he'd abandoned it but found time to leave a "parting gift" for Shay—an adder in a shiny box called Mom.

Before even hearing his sickening professor voice, Zoe hated the man.

Where the hell had he come from? Why was he calling? And how did he know both Ghid's and Shay's numbers?

Caramba. If the answer was a snake, she would've been bitten and killed by now.

After one look at Shay's face, she wondered if she was going to wish for that anyway.

There was only one person on earth with both Ghid's and Shay's numbers stored in their phone. She knew that because she'd personally programmed Shay's number into the device.

Right before saying her goodbyes to Melody Bommer.

Shay paced to the cabana's table, his steps erratic. Half a dozen drinks and a plate of nachos occupied the space until he cleared them in one sweep. After slamming down the phone in their place, he stabbed the speaker button and leaned over the device, hands planted like he'd reach in and grab Adler through the phone if he could.

"I asked you a question, maggot. Start talking, or I'll track you to within an inch of your puckered little asshole and then implant it with enough bullets, you'll shit lead for the rest of your sorry days."

"Really? Hmmm. You and what army?" The man sounded like Shay was a boy again and he'd simply asked if Shay wanted his ice cream in a cone or a cup. "The big green machine who's officially listed you AWOL after you slipped away from the facility at A-51? Or the CIA spooks who have joined in on the manhunt, since Mr. Colton is on that same outlaw list with you?"

"Surprise, surprise," Colton whispered.

"You think they locked you out just because you had bad breath or something?" Ry retorted, also beneath his breath.

"He doesn't have bad breath," Brynn snapped. Colton's light smack on her ass ended any extension of that debate.

Besides that, Adler was just getting started. "Hmmm," the man repeated. "Perhaps you're enlisting the Las Vegas Police Department, who are getting ready to break the news that three young dancers from the Sunset four-oh-three drama were recaptured by one of their hijackers three nights ago, along with their handsome model friend, and are believed alive...for now."

This bastard was starting to piss Zoe off. "Nice try, *cabrón.*" She closed the towel around her waist with a harsh jab. "You're too late. We've all called our families already. They know we're safe, happy, and protected."

"Do they, Miss Chestain?" His voice, a combination of

Agent Smith from *The Matrix* and Hannibal Lecter, sent a hundred more ice cubes down her spine—with spikes in them. "I *am* speaking with Miss Chestain, yes? How pleasant it is to hear your voice. It's as lovely as your face. Your friend at the police department, Captain Donner, was generous in sharing so many...interesting...images of you in his urgent concern for your safe recovery."

The ice blended into her stomach. The spikes too. "C-Captain D-Donner," she stammered. "*Bryce* Donner?"

Adler hummed again, a creepy confirmation. Shay's posture curled into a tension she'd never seen before.

"As I said, the man's been very helpful in our efforts. He's still very fond of you."

"But he's not a captain."

"He is now."

Forget the ice. Zoe's skin crawled with cockroaches of disgust. "You're vile."

Ghid, who'd managed to stumble back to the cabana with Ry's and El's help, shoved back up with his stampeding rhino face on. "No more happy tea party, asshole, until you put Mel on."

Adler's huff distorted the line for a moment. "Now, Gabriel," he chided. "That's not the way it works and you know it."

Shay rotated the phone so the speaker was closest to him. "His name's Ghid. Call him Gabriel again, and you won't have an anus to speak of. Secondly, that's exactly the way it's going to work, Adler."

The man's chuckle made her think of fava beans, Chianti, and having the stomach flu. "Oh my, little Shay, how magnificently you have grown up. Having to watch you from afar was never as interesting as this."

Zoe's heart clenched to watch Shay take in that confession. She'd had a weirdo fan of the show try to stalk her for a few months who was eventually thwarted when she started dating Bryce. It was a nightmare that ended after a few weeks—nothing compared to what Shay now had to comprehend. The clench of his fist and the tension in his back confirmed that harrowing fact.

"Glad to know it was so fucking fascinating for you," he finally snarled at the phone. "Can we move on now?"

"Oh, fascinating doesn't even scratch the surface, boy. I have to know... Which part did you feel the most, do you think? Was it Hercules or Scout? Or maybe it changed as you got older..." He interrupted himself with a soft grunt. "Good Lord, I'm digressing."

"No shit." Shay didn't relax an inch of his rigidity, though he visibly battled to stay focused on the conversation now. "My mother, you dickwad. Put her on the phone, or you don't get one more tight hair of cooperation from me."

The bastard released a heavy sigh. Zoe tucked her arms to her sides to avoid throwing the phone—or anything else—out of furious frustration.

During the same interim, Tait stared over at his brother. "Hercules and Scout? The horse and the family dog. That's poetic, in a fucked-up kind of way."

"Shut up," Shay growled.

"Shay?"

Ghid joined Shay and Tait in lunging over the phone. "Mel?" His voice wavered. "God... Mellie, are you okay? If he's touched a hair on your head, I swear I'll—"

"I'm fine. We're all fine. Shay...are you there?"

"Right here, Mom. And Tait too."

A determined growl vibrated over the line. It was so impressive, Zoe forgot her trepidation for a moment. One musing, crossed off the list. Shay got the talent straight from Mama Bommer, not the family dog.

"Listen to me, Shay. I'm still your mother. If you give in to this douche, I'll rain hell on you like you've never— Ahhhh! Noooo!"

"Adler!" Ghid bellowed it as Melody's shrieks exploded through the line. The sound ripped horrified tears out of Zoe, while her empty stomach churned on its own bile. Brynn and El hugged her from either side, their faces bearing the same grief.

As Melody's screams diminished into sobs, an incoming image flashed on the phone's screen.

A newly severed human finger. Slender. Female.

Ghid's back heaved and dropped in time with his tormented breathing. His arms curled up and back, his hands like paws of quaking fury. Zoe didn't doubt he'd choke the life from the first creature that crossed his path. No sound spilled from him except those lurching breaths. Shay's and Tait's faces were grim, conveying the stark understanding of soldiers who'd experienced this kind of brutality before—though it had never been their mother.

Nobody said a word except Ryder, who often had obnoxiously accurate ways of expressing things. "I've met gobs of testicle sweat with more class than that."

Adler added his smug chuckle on top of Melody's steady weeping. "Oh, aren't you a clever bunch? That's such a sweet sentiment, but I'm not in the mood for sweetness today."

"You don't say," Tait snarled.

Shay straightened. His arms coiled at his sides at similar angles to Ghid's, fierce and tense, only his hands were slack, as if he prepared to render his damage by grabbing a rifle instead of ripping someone to shreds. "He's in the mood for business," he intoned. "And about to tell us that if we're not, Mom has nine more where that came from." He stared at the phone as if tempted to spit on it. "Am I warm, asshole?"

"You forgot the part about letting my men arm wrestle for who gets to use her cunt first, but sure...that's warm enough."

Ghid still didn't say a word. Instead, as they all watched, he departed the cabana on steps that threatened to crack the deck with their intensity. He didn't stop his incensed prowl until he got to one of the palms that bordered the pool—and rammed the top of his head into the thing's trunk. With a roar, he shoved. And shoved. And shoved. The palm gave way, Ghid's force hauling it out by its roots. It crashed into the pool, soaking the deck, though Zoe was certain the surface of Ghid's face was wetter.

More sobs erupted up her own throat in empathy for his pain. As little as a week ago, his act would've had her urging the hotel to skip the call to security and dial the local mental hospital. Now she understood every drop of his grief. It was exactly how she'd feel if Shay were in captivity under Adler's filthy thumb.

"You've made your point, Adler," Shay finally stated. "Now let's talk logistics and terms."

Colton angled in, making sure his glare was acknowledged. "Damn it, I-Man. No!"

Zoe shoved away the ice cubes. Barely. As for the iceberg that waited behind them? Adler made sure nobody forgot it today, didn't he?

"Shut up, Dan." But Shay locked his gaze with Tait's as he issued it. "This is my decision. And I decide it's going down."

"Wh-What's going down?" Zoe stammered. She reached and grabbed Tait's elbow. "What the hell is he talking about?" Then shifted her hold back to Shay. "What the hell are you—?"

"It'll be okay, dancer." He pressed his fingers over hers. "Everybody gets what they want. Mom will finally have her compound in the hills, and she'll be safe."

The iceberg flowed on top of her chest before she could rasp her reply. Before she could bear to know what Shay would render as his answer.

"And what does that *bastardo* want?"

"Me."

★ ★ ★ ★ ★

There was such a thing as life moving fast. Then there was the speed of light. Then there was the acceleration taking place as she watched, blinking and speechless, from the corner of Roklan Reed's palace-sized living room in the city's luxurious Southern Highlands neighborhood.

Rok, arguably the world's most recognized male model in the world for the last two years, wasn't just Ryder's mentor. He'd become a good friend to Ry—probably with benefits from time to time—which was a damn good thing, since they'd all shot out of the Vdara as soon as Shay hung up with Adler, and Ryder called Rok beseeching this huge favor.

That was all after the conversation that had Zoe losing her lunch on top of the tree Ghid had uprooted. The little chat in which Shay had agreed to turn himself over to Adler in exchange for his mother—tomorrow at dawn.

During the two and a half hours after that—spent mostly inside Ghid's van in a convenience store parking lot—Zoe had refused to look at Shay, let alone acknowledge his assurances about how everything was going to be "copacetic." Apparently, he and Tait had used their bond of brotherly connection to mind-meld back at the hotel and there was already some kind of plan in the works. The moment Rok had pinged back at Ry with a green light on them all invading his home, they were on their way. During the trip, Colton had kept showing both thumbs up, assuring Shay and Tait that all parties involved in their plan were on board for the challenge.

She'd succumbed to the royal eyebrow spike with that one. What the hell did "all the involved parties" mean when they were being hunted by every military, police, and special intelligence officer within a fifty-mile radius? Did they plan on recruiting mercenaries from the strip clubs and bars at the other end of town? The way they'd chattered on about "the team" and "the op" made her seriously ponder the idea, tempting her to vomit all over again. Did Shay actually think his ragtag little crew would stand with him the second anything went sideways with this plan?

And things *would* go sideways.

They always did when she loved the person at stake.

Mom had returned from Greece with tuberculosis. Ava moved to LA for a dream job and ended up working for a lunatic—and then was nearly killed by another.

And damn it, now it would be Shay.

Whom she loved just as much.

And maybe, in certain parts of her heart and soul, a little more.

She gazed at him crossing the room, joining Tait in the

foyer to greet the newest arrival at the house: Sergeant Garrett Hawkins. She recognized Garrett at once from the photos of Ethan's team that were now part of the décor in Ava's Hermosa Beach, California, bungalow. He was a muscular hunk with thick, dark-blond hair that spiked naturally at the top and a proud jawline that spoke to his Iowa farm-boy origins.

"Well, *alooooha*, asshat!" Garrett threw the warm greeting to Tait, who volleyed a mock sneer in return. Zoe figured he was allowed. The men had been on the same Special Forces team for years, until Tait's transfer to a new assignment in Hawaii back in September.

"That's my line, you pussy." Tait took Garrett's mission pack from him and tossed it along the wall next to a pair of nearly identical dark-green bags. "How have you been, man? How are Sage and Racer?"

"Good...and great." Garrett pulled out his phone to proudly show off an image. "As you can tell, he really loved his first birthday cake—though I think Sage is already worried. Seven out of the ten kids at the party were girls."

"Let me guess," Tait drawled. "*Star Wars* theme?"

"You think Uncle Zekie would have it any other way?"

A man the size of a small mountain strolled in behind Garrett. He yanked the sunglasses off his formidable face, making Zoe shiver more than the first time she laid eyes on Ghid. Like Garrett, his hair was also thick. Unlike Hawkins, his near-black waves tumbled to kiss the collar of a shirt in a blinding lime-green jungle print and scuffed khaki pants, a look that likely served him well if he needed to masquerade on an op as a slumming-it sheikh. Or a tree. *Mierda*. Ava was right. Zeke Hayes's pictures were awful stand-ins for the man's real-life command of a presence.

"What kind of mayhem are you blaming on me while I'm not around, Hawk-Man?" He barked it while hooking his elbow around Tait's and Shay's necks and then yanking them into a pair of gruff holds, apparently his version of "hugging it out." Or in. Zoe wasn't certain she wanted to truly find out.

"Nothing requiring bail, Psycho Zsycho."

"Holy fuck." Zeke took in Rok's place, with its gold-plated Greek columns, moss-green walls, French Rococo furniture, and swagged satin drapes, and promptly choked. "This place looks like Liberace had a wet dream."

"Thank you." Roklan emerged from the dining room, looking like one of the Hemsworths but preening like June Cleaver. "Some of the pieces actually came from his estate."

"You don't say." Zeke looked as interested in that as the sidewalk he'd just walked on. "So are those Rhett's and Rebel's packs? Are they already here?"

"They're setting up in the dining room." Zoe offered it before thinking twice. She needed to help the poor guy. He looked as comfortable as a punker at the opera. She just wasn't sure if she had the heart to tell him the dining room was just as gold, gaudy, and swirly. Maybe she'd let him be surprised.

Though it looked like him staring at her accomplished the job first. "Holy fuck," Zeke blurted.

"Huh?" Tait questioned. "Z, what're you—"

"I thought she was Ava." He blinked and flashed a dopey grin that turned the cliff of his face into pulse-grabbing charisma. "Sheez," he muttered, stepping toward Zoe. "Sorry for gawking, but it's like harmonic convergence. You could be twins with somebody I know—who also happens to be a cousin to my fiancée."

Zoe relished the chance to slide his smartass words back

at him. "You don't say."

"Seriously. You've got me believing in doppelgangers now."

"Is that a good or bad thing?"

He shrugged, still a goofball in the skin of a hulk. "I think it depends on whose side you're on."

Shay appeared at her side. Correction—loomed at her side. "Zoe, this is Zeke Hayes, bull-in-a-china-shop extraordinaire. Zeke, meet Zoe Chestain. She's my china."

Zoe dug her teeth into the inside of her lip. *Mierda*. If the man thought he'd turn her nerves—and her pulse and her pussy—into fifteen kinds of gooey with proclamations like that, he was totally right.

She forced her attention back to Zeke, who'd gone semi-apoplectic when hearing her last name. "It's awesome to finally meet you. Sorry it couldn't be under more pleasant circumstances. I've been trying to get Rayna to bring you down here to see the show for months."

Zeke grimaced. "Yeah, I know. Our absence is my fault. The bad guys of the world don't take a lot of breaks. The team's been everywhere from Manila to Mumbai lately."

Shay clapped him on the shoulder. "Yet here you all are, spending your leave doing this one off the books. I can't thank you guys enough."

"From what I hear, nobody's done *off the books* better than you the last six months, dude. Now we get to be a part of the fun too. Hell, *we* all might be thanking *you* when the fireworks are done." He cracked his neck with cocky swagger. "I'm going to get a world-class boner off this, aren't I? Might as well order Rayna's ass on the next flight in from Sea-Tac right now."

"Great plan. Maybe we can talk her and Ava into the *I-dos*

right now."

That interjection was issued by the next guy through the door, who received a double set of head-to-toe assessments— and subsequent approvals—from Rok and Ryder. Zoe sprinted to him in three seconds, nearly bowling him over with the enthusiasm of her hug.

"Ethan!"

"Hey there, *hermana*." The guy warmed her with his smooth laugh, letting enough of his rogue's grin linger to fill her eyes with grateful tears. His face darkened with concern. "You okay? I-Man promised me you were safe and would stay that way..."

"I am," she rushed out. "I...am. It's just so good to see family."

Her tears dampened the shoulder of his black T-shirt as he drew her into another embrace and murmured, "I know. And it's going to be okay." He tightened his hug. "Ava's on her way too."

So much for attempting to keep her composure. Joyful sobs crashed over her like a hurricane surge, making her sag a little more against him. Ethan's encouraging hum brought even more of the emotions to the surface, and *Dios*, did it feel wonderful to let them free.

"Archer." Shay didn't hide a note of his accusation. "What the hell did you—?"

"*Ay*," she shouted. "*Callate*, silly! They're good tears, okay?"

All the guys, including Ethan, were silent for a long moment. When they all burst into chuckles, Shay was the only one to abstain.

"Welcome to the world of being smitten by a Chestain,"

Ethan finally drawled.

"Down with your bass on that, brother." Zeke pumped a solidarity fist. "At this point, I still have one burning question for the I-Man."

Shay scowled. "Do I even want to encourage you?"

"How the hell did you snag a gem like her—in the middle of working undercover for Cameron fucking Stock?"

Zoe was thankful for the chance to join their laughter, despite how Shay reclaimed her from Ethan's arms and tried to move in for a little peck on the lips. *Not happening, amigo.* He might have just cranked up the moisture readings in all the right places in her body, but she was still incensed as hell at him. The thought of him walking into Adler's lair, even with some well-trained, badass Special Operations backup, still terrified her soul in corners she never knew it possessed.

"That's an interesting story," she said to Zeke. "I can tell you, but then you'll be questioning how many shots of *loco* I got in first."

To her surprise, Zeke and Ethan shook in harder laughs. "Ohhh, little Zoe," Zeke explained, "this team has downed so much *loco* already, it's a wonder they don't call us the wild boys."

"Maybe they should."

The comment cracked the air like a whip—wielded by a Dom who knew exactly what he was doing with it. Before she even looked toward the newest arrival in the doorway, Zoe knew who it was. The six-foot-six man—a dark, skull-haircutted cross between a Samoan god and a Special Forces recruitment ad—could be none other than Captain John Franzen. Ava had gushed plenty about Ethan's CO. The man's presence could be felt before he entered a room and long after

341

he departed, not only eliciting the obvious respect of the men already standing here but pulling Rhett and Rebel back out of the dining room to greet him.

"Look what the transport dragged in." The Creole-accented gibe came from the self-described "explosives man—in more ways than one" for the team. To the rest of the guys, he was known as Moonstormer, a call sign derived from a 1700s pirate legend about one of his ancestors. It had taken Zoe five minutes to decide it completely fit. With his jet-black hair and fully-tattooed arms, the only thing Rebel was missing was a real brigantine. Or a Harley.

"Yo, Moon." Franzen swapped a fist bump with his man. "You and Double-O finding a crap-ton of trouble to get into?"

Double-O was the call sign for the man who emerged from behind Rebel. That fit too. Rhett Lange was a stealth-quiet, brilliant-minded, completely hot ginger with biceps that stretched his dark-blue polo to capacity. The shirt matched his eyes to breathtaking perfection, not that the man seemed to care. Rhett focused on his work with such force, it frightened her. Fortunately, his expertise was comm, tech, and intel, which meant his laser beam was mostly directed at the three computer screens in the other room.

"Hawk just declared he and Zsycho haven't needed bail dough yet," Rhett issued. "So I suppose Moonstormer and I will pick up the slack somehow."

Garrett lobbed a glower. "Who're you calling slacker?"

Rhett eyed a hangnail. "If the shoe fits, man..."

Zeke cracked his neck again. "Hey, uhhh, Double-O?"

"Hmmm?"

"I really dig that new Powerpuff Girls screen saver on your phone."

"*Pfffft*. Like *you* hacked my phone."

"Like *you* unlocked it on the plane so I could earn that Chuzzle trophy for you."

Garrett and Zeke high-fived while Rhett dug his phone from his pocket.

"Fucker!" Rhett jabbed and swiped at the screen.

Rebel, clearly unable to hold back anymore, surrendered to a soft snicker. "That was righteously cool, Z, but you know payback's a bitch with Double-O."

Zoe dared to move into the fray. If she didn't do something, Rok's chichi décor was going to need therapy from the abuse it suffered beneath a bunch of Spec Ops studs in the mood to be puppies. "How about some fajitas?" After all the guys eyed her, instantly conveying one message—*fuck, I hope she's not kidding*—she broke a bigger smile. "Roklan was kind enough to take a grocery list from me and then called one of those cool delivery services, telling them he was having a party as a cover. I'm making beans and salad as well, and there's chocolate cake for dessert. I can make veggie, chicken, pork, or—"

"Beef!" The round of alpha male enthusiasm made her giggle. It didn't hurt for drowning out the prayer resounding through her spirit either.

Please, any saint or espíritu *listening, don't let the first meal I fix him also be his last.*

★ ★ ★ ★ ★

Later, with the clock fast approaching midnight, everyone was stuffed full—and still hard at work. Though the activity through the night had included everything from gun cleaning to mission-pack prep to letters for families "just in case,"

343

everyone on the team now gathered at the dining room table, concentrating on the schematics flashing across the three large computer monitors.

They'd been able to borrow the screens from the eight Rok had in the house. And the model called this his "winter place"? Zoe's imagination soared about his summer digs, with the Central Park views and private lap pool, in one of Manhattan's most exclusive high rises. Not that she didn't love it here. Cooking in this kitchen was like driving a culinary Cadillac.

After cleaning up, she reentered the dining room as Franzen directed Rhett to restart the digital mock-up of their logistics plan for the morning. The images, showing grainy shots of the little mining camp Melody had converted for the compound, had clearly been pulled off the internet. There had been no time to gather anything fancier. Even with that shared understanding, the team shared a groan. They were used to working with much more sophisticated intel, making this scenario something that probably felt like walking on tacks after strolling on grass. She was moved and amazed that, though the conditions weren't optimal, they were all alert and on fire about getting this done—all for two guys who weren't even on their real team.

"Okay, let's run the plan again," Franzen prompted. "I want to be sure we're not missing a goddamn thing."

"Great idea," Tait murmured.

As Rhett reset the simulation program, Franz turned a probing gaze to Tait. "Speaking of great ideas... T-Bomb, we need to talk."

All of Tait's features expanded except for his mouth, which flattened. "Ohhhh no, we don't."

"Tait, my boy..."

"Don't you 'my boy' me, damn it. Don't you dare do this to me."

"You want to hear me out? We have enough guys for the op, okay? If you weren't—"

"I don't report to you anymore! Even if I did, in case you haven't noticed, we're operating just a few thousand miles below the radar." He rose so violently, his chair toppled behind him. "No matter how you slice it, you can't command me to sit this one out."

Franz scooped up the chair and shoved it back under the table before following Tait's stomping path down the length of the room. "Damn it, Bommer. What do you think your mother is going to tell me if this op trips into the mud like a blind duck, loses its head, and then ends up being *foie gras* on Homer Adler's fucking cracker? You think that woman is going to let me keep my balls after learning I led her sons, neither of whom she's seen in twenty years, into an off-book rescue mission for her ass—that killed them both?" The man's jaw grinded like he crunched on nails. "You want to know what kind of a padded room that'll land her in for the rest of her life?"

That seemed to penetrate Tait's gray matter—for two seconds. He shook his head, hands on hips, before glaring at Franz again. "She understands the pain of giving yourself for a cause that's right. She'd... She'd understand."

Franzen folded his arms and braced his massive legs. "Good thing you're not on trial, Bommer. You would've just gotten the electric chair."

"Are you done?"

"Ohhh, I'm just getting started." One of his eyebrows hitched up. "You think I've taken out the heavy artillery yet?"

Tait blinked slowly. When he was done, incensed fire blazed in both his eyes. "You wouldn't dare."

"You know me better than that." Franz widened his stance, settling into the confrontation with confidence. "So let's talk Hokulani."

Tait wheeled away. "Let's not."

"Okay, Dick Tugnuts, you want to spin it like that? You want me to remind you that the only reason I let you *or* Kell keep sniffing around that girl was because I saw how happy you two make her? You also want me to remind you that she's just as much a *kaikuahine* to me as my biological sisters, and if you cause her a single splinter of pain, I'll hunt your ass down, even if you're on the other side, and chop your dick into bite-size chunks for hell's Crock-Pot?"

Tait growled. "She'll still have Kellan."

"'She'll still have Kellan.' That's the best you can do, assmunch?"

"He's good to her. He's good *with* her."

"Oh, shut up. You have no damn idea what you mean to her, do you?" When Tait answered with nothing but fuming silence, a surly sound prowled out of Franzen. "You know what two sides of a triangle is?" He narrowed his eyes. "Broken, T. That's what. So hey, go ahead. You need to feel like you stuck with your brother until the bitter end because he made the big sacrifice for Mom and you didn't? So are you going to ride with him off the cliff, just to prove you can?"

Rocks of anxiety weighed Zoe's gut all night. With Franzen's rant, that pit turned into a whole quarry. Logistically, she understood his tactic on Tait. Emotionally and spiritually, the man might as well have put her on a stretching rack and started cranking the handle.

"Stop," she pleaded in a rasp.

Franzen didn't hear her. "Which one are you going to be, T? Thelma or Louise?"

"Stop it. Please."

Shay got up, his chair grating the floor with a vicious sound. "Christ, Franz. He gets it. We all do. Now—"

"Guess it doesn't matter, right? Because Lani won't care about getting your remains back. Shit, this won't affect her at all. She'll just move right along, like you did after Luna—"

"Franz!" Shay bellowed. "For fuck's sake!"

"Stop." Zoe screamed it at nearly the same time. Or thought she did. The sound wasn't like anything she'd ever heard herself make before. It was desperate. Grieving. Pathetic. A world bursting in her heart, needing him—*loving him*—and no time to express it.

No more time before he left and risked it all with that madman.

How could they have no more time? They'd made an art form out of turning minutes into eternities...yet now they were filled with this dread. This pain. This hurt she'd never asked for.

On sobs she couldn't hold in any longer, she pushed past them all, out of the room. Past the living room, she walked out onto the Italian stone patio, overlooking Rok's Fantasy Island of a pool area. Five different rock waterfalls cascaded into a curving pool, with the middle waterfall serving as a "curtain" to a swim-up bar connected directly to the wine cave.

She could use half the cave's inventory.

She settled for stumbling across an arching stone bridge, onto a round island that extended into the far end of the pool. It was the perfect retreat, dark and solitary, especially because the majority of the island was a padded bed with a lot of pillows that screamed *go ahead, bawl on me*. Their only downfall was their colors. Gold, tangerine, red. She blinked hard, wishing for Samantha Stevens's powers to simply change everything into graveyard grays, browns, and black. *Sí*. Shitloads of black.

Forget it. She was almost too blind to care anymore, anyway. Letting the tears blast her senses as hard and fast as they wanted, she fell onto the mattress and instantly hauled three of the pillows close, wrapping her trembling body around them.

She tried to laugh it off. She tried to tell herself she looked as lame as a fifteen-year-old counting the hours until her boyfriend left for camp. But that washed as long as it took for her to look back through the glass at the living room and view everyone's rifles lined up against the couch, clean and shiny and ready for action.

This wasn't lame. Or adolescent. It was the reality of realizing that she'd fallen in love with the wholeness of a woman's mind, heart, and soul and now faced the grown-up pain of accepting the more-than-decent chance she'd lose it.

In less than ten hours.

She grabbed another pillow and stuffed it against her face, hating the ache that weighed on her chest and the effort of pulling in every breath.

Nothing changed when long, strong fingers pried that pillow away. Then the one below that. And all the others too, until her arms were empty...but only for a moment. After he tossed the pillows aside, Shay replaced their weight with his. He was everywhere, beautiful and huge and warm and solid, pulling her even closer, tangling their legs into each other. It was impossible not to breathe him in, his forest spice blending with the wildflowers on the desert wind, enticing her even closer...but Zoe froze. Locked down. How could she give any more when he was about to take it all away?

There was only one answer.

"I can't." Her rasp was a desperate sough into his chest. "I can't, Shay... I can't, I can't... Oh *Dios*, I can't..."

"But you already have." His declaration was even softer than hers, given as he tracked her tears with his lips before ending at hers and taking her in a kiss that felt like a prayer. "And I already have too, my beautiful, tiny dancer."

Her heart skidded to a stop. She jerked her face up to meet his gaze, glowing with molten shadows that confirmed so much without having to say the words. Oh *Dios*, if he said the actual words, she'd shatter like one of Rok's Limoges vases. It meant enough—the whole damn world—simply to see it in his eyes. "Shay..."

"Ssshhh." He kissed more fervently at the moisture on her face. "Baby girl, listen to me. Franz...he feels like crap. He didn't mean to freak you out."

"You don't say." It was working as the go-to sarcasm for the evening.

"The guy has substance for his weird willies, okay?"

"What do you mean?"

"After Luna died, they activated Tait back to the unit prematurely. He fucked up the coordinates on a kill shot—bad. One of *our* guys almost bought the farm for it."

"*Ay Dios mio*," she uttered.

"No shit," he commiserated. "The whole thing happened on Franz's watch, so needless to say, he's a little freaked about Tait tagging on an op that's going to involve a lot of fluidity— and stress." His jaw firmed and his eyes warmed. "But I've been talking to my brother a lot over the last two days, Zoe. I heard all about the training he endured for this new Sharks program. The *H* in their acronym, SHRC, is for *hostile*—and they mean it. He's gotten smarter and tougher in his training for the team, so he's ready, in every way, to end this shit with Adler. And so am I."

Zoe let her hands flatten against his chest. She could feel his heart thudding through his T-shirt, and she wished she could save every miraculous beat into the pads of her fingers. It made her response even harder to get out. "But at what cost? To perhaps both of you?"

Shay breathed slowly in. Then out. He dipped his head in order to fully meet her gaze again. *Oh, hell.* His eyes were brilliant with the solid gold of his inner Dom now. Sure enough, his next words were a quiet but definite command.

"Listen to me well, baby girl. I'm not going to die. Neither is Tait. Is that understood?"

"Yes, Sir," she whispered.

"Then look at me again, so I know."

Zoe slipped her hands up to frame the sides of his face. They were set in such determination, her thumbs and forefingers formed ninety-degree angles. "You take my breath away, Shay Bommer."

A slow grin, full of a devil's mirth and a satyr's sensuality, curled the edges of his lips. "Well, not yet, tiny dancer."

She let him lean in, settling his mouth over hers in a tender yet carnal exploration, filled with teasing stabs of his tongue that soon had her sighing into him, wordlessly begging for more. She raised her hands and pushed them into his thick hair, savoring the honeysuckle on the wind that sifted through the strands along with her fingers.

Shay groaned as she pushed her hips up against his, parting her legs at the same time. He roamed his hands over her breasts, pulling at her nipples through her bra, as they opened their mouths and mated tongues in unbridled passion.

"I need you." She finally dragged her mouth away long enough to plead it. "Being with me...merging with me..."

"Yeah." He filled it in, again taking the pressure of the words away from her. "Yeah, baby girl." After fitting his mouth even harder over hers, he reared up on his knees, trailing a hand over the simple bathing suit cover-up in which she'd left the Vdara. "Let me see you, dancer. All of you."

By the time she was fully nude, he was too. Zoe lowered back down, making sure there were pillows behind her head so she could simply gawk at him in a long moment of greedy delight. His shoulders were as broad as a linebacker's and sculpted with equal care, sloping flawlessly down into his biceps and triceps. His pecs, the part of him her fingers always craved to explore the most, were a matched set of gleaming, oh-my-God perfection. Two more rippled rows defined his abdomen, but they were no decent preparation for the molded steel of his thighs—and the shaft that extended, massive and equally muscled, from their juncture.

Her breath snagged, and she was certain he'd heard it. She was also certain she saw the edgy tic fire away in his jaw.

"Shay?" she prodded.

He smiled a little, but the look seemed forced. "Yeah, baby girl?"

She sat up, deliberately taking him by the balls with one hand and his dark-purple crown with the other. As she moved her hands toward each other, exploring every ridge and vein in his glorious cock as she did, she told him, "I don't give a shit if you got shafted by a gamma ray, or gnawed by a spider, or probed by an alien to make you this way. I'm just damn glad you *are*."

Looking like the cat who'd just devoured the canary, Shay impaled her with a heated stare and pushed her back into the bed. This time, his knees shunted hers apart—landing the pulsing head of his sex at the needy wet lips of hers.

"Probed by an alien?" He hunkered his brows while giving her lips a couple of fierce bites. "I should *probe* you brutally for that, earth female."

"Oh, yes." She smiled and kissed him back. "You definitely should."

As Shay lunged his length all the way into her pulsing core, Zoe cried out in a perfect mix of pain and pleasure. Her heart tumbled end over end. She let her head fall back, giving in to the heaven of letting this man fill her, fuck her...love her.

She was fifteen again. Alive only for the moment again. Desperately seizing every second that passed, working with Shay to stretch it into an eternity for the ages, filed under the heading of *Magic*.

They'd make it count—because they had to. Because they always did.

Because they always would.

Please God...because they always would.

CHAPTER TWENTY-ONE

"Be safe."

"Or die trying."

Shay allowed himself a thin smile as Hawk and Zsycho uttered the final words before the team went radio silent. He wove the gritted comfort of them into his muscles, using the strength to maintain his stance in the middle of what seemed an abandoned mining camp. Fast glances, using only his periphery, confirmed the intel that Double-O was able to knit up about this place. Four buildings from the mid-1800s. One freshly built structure, which Ghid confirmed as Mom's sterile lab and a quarantine room if they ever needed it. There also seemed to be a newly seeded athletic field and a picnic pavilion under construction. Ghid had told them about all that too. Many of the guys hadn't been outside in years. The chance to work in the sunshine—or even the rain and the snow—was paradise to them.

Shay cued up a vision of his own heaven, girding his mind and soul with it in this eerie moment filled only with his breath and the wind. Her indigo eyes, thick with passion. Her exotic lips, parted on her climax. Her open arms and burnished nudity, given so fully and beautifully to him.

He'd know that heaven again. Soon. He swore it with every fiber of his being.

I'm not going to die, dancer. Neither is Tait. Understood?

Her answering smile spread across his mind like a

rainbow, helping him brace against the November wind that gashed down again from the mountains. It was a double scythe on this plain, gusting from the ranges on both sides and then converging into a blade straight down the camp's main road to cut through every layer of his head-to-toe white Gore-Tex.

White. *Shit.* While he understood Homer's mandate, he fucking hated it. The white made it impossible for him to blend with any of the landscape around here. On the other hand, it made him look like goddamn Storm Shadow—*not* his favorite GI Joe on the planet, if that was what they even considered the guy. He'd take Duke Hauser any day. Duke would refuse to go into an op in white *anything*, except his BVDs.

Sorry, Duke...but I'm doing this for a cause higher than you or me.

The wind whipped up again. Shay would've raised a middle finger to the mountains in retaliation, but he was damn grateful for those cliffs right now. They'd made it possible for the team to bribe a Grand Canyon sky tour pilot into changing up his course by a few miles and then letting them gang-bang it out in a jump that had Hawk and Zeke instantly begging for a do-over once they'd all gathered their chutes. Hours of crossed fingers had followed the jump, everyone hoping that Homer and his band of merry men didn't have radar sophisticated enough to notice their "creative" in-fil to the area. Since everything went smoothly when Shay met Homer's driver-cum-henchman at the front entrance of the Bellagio, climbing into the town car just as the crowd *ooo*'ed and *ahhh*'ed at the first morning performance of the hotel's famous fountains, the group paused for a small but short celebration over the radio. First hurdle cleared.

By that point, Franz had led the team over miles of harsh

terrain, still with a few left to go before they could rest in their ready positions for this exact moment.

The meeting they'd been preparing for.

Shay swallowed in an attempt to rewet his throat. Briefly wiggled the tips of his fingers, though he had no gun or knife to reach for. Homer's instructions were specific. He came alone in the town car. He wore the damn ninja outfit and nothing else.

He only thanked fucking fate that the driver goon was an amateur. Though the ape had been thorough about the frisking shit back at the Bellagio, he never thought to scrape Shay's ears for comm pieces. Didn't really matter since Double-O had insisted on supergluing a backup piece straight onto his scalp, then securing it by winding his hair around the base. That process had been as comfortable as a root canal.

"I've got eyes on I-Man." The voice, down to a whisper, was Ethan. "Repeat, eyes on I-Man but nobody else."

"Check," Zeke responded. "Nothing from our bird's nest, eith—wait. Cocksucker at two o'clock."

"Check," Hawk growled. "I've got him too, Zsycho."

Shay appreciated the confirmations, but they weren't necessary. From the second Homer stepped out onto the packed dirt avenue, thinning hair blowing against his craggy cheeks and haphazard beard, Shay's gut constricted as if a fully armed hostile had emerged. Homer wasn't dressed in a traditional *payraan tumbaan*, though. Beneath his thick bulletproof vest was a black turtleneck that topped khaki pants and rugged terrain boots. He seemed a harmless cross between Gilligan's Professor and Jeremiah Johnson. But Shay would be damned or dead if he believed that for a second.

As Homer got closer, Shay noticed more movements

from the doorways of the old wood buildings. The new arrivals were a lot more what he was used to—younger men dressed in camos or black battle gear, armed and tense as hell. But closer scrutiny showed him newer details...much more revealing information. One of the men had Ghid's missing rhino horn—sprouting from the center of his forehead. Another had bear claws in place of hands. And they all glared at him like the one guy who'd been taking a leak when the IED hit their truck.

"Shay." Homer rushed through his last few steps before giving a hug like a doting grandfather coming to visit. The bastard smelled like one too. Old mints, bad hair gel, halitosis that gave new meaning to the term coffee breath... The list went on, but fortunately the man let him go. "Welcome back. As you can see, your brothers are happy to see you."

Shay didn't bother to point out the obvious, that the statement couldn't be farther from the truth. These men felt no kinship with him, despite the fact that his side of the return-to-papa terms had been the granting of their freedom, including the deliverance of Oliver, Nika, and Damian from the Area 51 facility. But Shay didn't blame them for being suspicious of the dream. He would be too.

"Let's get on with it." He didn't bother inflecting the words one way or the other. "One way" would've encompassed his rage, "the other" his revulsion. Homer didn't give a flying crap about either. "Where's Mom?"

The words seemed to hit Homer like an insult. "Why are you being so nasty?"

Shay curled his hands into dual fists. "I didn't know nice was part of your terms, asshole. Awww, damn." He knocked one fist against his thigh in oh-shucks emphasis. "Guess you missed out on asking for that one. And forgive me for not floating you a freebie. When a guy knows he's returning to the life of a goddamn lab rat, the happy dance gets scooted to the bottom of the priorities list."

Homer expelled a long sigh, again pulling the Grandpa Joe card. "It troubles me to hear you say that."

"Fuck. So sorry. Oh, wait. *Troubling Homer*. That one's on the bottom of the list too."

The man pushed back the graying mop of his hair before grabbing Shay by both elbows. "Don't you understand this, Shay? Don't you see? You're the one, my boy—my perfect example that the serum can work without any hideous side effects. And it was because you used it *as a boy*. I'm certain of it!" His features turned gruel gray as anger fulminated across them. "I was certain of it all those years ago, Shay—but your mother wouldn't listen. Even though the evidence clearly pointed to it, she refused to use children as test subjects."

Shay glowered. "No shit. Imagine that."

He might as well have farted for the effect it had on Homer's royal roll. "We're going to figure it out now, Shay— together." He lifted a hand to Shay's face. "You're the key. You're... You're amazing."

Shay twisted his head away. "I'm just me, damn it. And I just want to stay me, as *one* piece, not chopped up into tissue samples for petri dishes."

The man rushed at him again. "That's not your complete truth, boy, and you know it." He seized the front of Shay's vest in order to jerk him closer. "You've been wondering too, Shay. You can't stare me straight in the face and tell me you don't want to find out the truth about that magic pumping in your veins."

The snakes of revulsion and rage coiled tighter together

in Shay's gut—because the fucker was right. Questions about all of this were now the subconscious demons that jolted him awake at night, the empty rooms his soul roamed in its quest toward defining who the hell he was anymore.

He'd fallen in love. And he was pretty damn certain Zoe felt the same. But had she fallen in love with him...or merely the beasts who roamed in his blood?

He needed to know...

"But not like this." The conclusion ripped from him in a snarl as he pushed back again from Homer. "Don't *you* see, Homer? We can't do it like this!"

For one moment, just one, it seemed as if the man heard him—and understood. That was before Homer shook his head with a resigned slowness and murmured, "There *is* no other way, my boy. You'll see that we'll find the answers fast. And then the fun part will begin, and won't you like that?"

The guy's stinky grandfather bit took on a fucking creepy vibe now. Shay almost gave himself a mental cock punch to avoid the question that tumbled from him in response. "The... fun part?"

"Making your babies, of course." Homer spread his arms, offering a full smile with it. "Your concubines will be hand-selected, of course. They'll be tested for fertility and genetic perfection, and—"

"No."

Homer stopped, his shock blatant. "Pardon me?"

Shay *didn't* stop. He wasn't sure he could, despite how Homer motioned forward several of his soldiers, implying the order to train their rifles at him. His mind careened, condemning himself for not foreseeing this would be Homer's ultimate scheme, while refusing to accept it as the plan he'd even pretend to concede to.

With impeccable timing, Franzen's bark filled the comm piece in his ear. "Good, I-Man. This is fucking good! Trip Adler up and draw out those guys from the porches. Keep it up, man."

Not the best metaphor for the moment, but Shay sucked up courage from the boost. "No," he declared again, meeting Homer's glare with tight lips, drawn-back shoulders, and the hint of fight-or-flight in his stance. Homer, clearly terrified he'd opt for the latter, waved more guys off the porches and into the street. He was so consumed with corralling Shay, he left only two guards on patrol at the back of the street—who showed where their loyalties really lay by greeting Ghid with robust hugs before allowing him to swoop Mom into his arms, off to safety.

"Mama B is secure," Ghid's voice, gritty from the effort of holding back emotion, rasped over the comm. "Repeat, I have Mama B and she's safe."

Franz jumped on right after that. "Proceed to *go* positions. Proceed to *go* positions!" After a few frantic seconds, he came back on. "We need one minute, I-Man. Just one."

A minute? Slam dunk. As long as he had Homer's undivided attention, it was a perfect time to tell the prick exactly what he thought about this idea of the "fun stuff."

"I'm not your superbeast sperm bank, Homer. I agreed to be the lab rat, and you need to be okay with that. You can have my blood, my hair, my tissues—make daisy chains out of my fingernails and fertilizer out of my spit for all I care—but I'm not fathering children for your personal Dr. Demento show. Don't think I won't lop the fucker off first, either."

Homer's spine straightened like a pissed cobra getting ready to strike. "Is this your way of telling me you want to go the messy way and not the civilized way?"

Shay jutted his lower lip and nodded. "Probably."

Homer rolled his eyes before extending his arm as if pitching Shay a baseball.

No ball—at least not the stitched-seam kind. But who was he to make that assumption? For all he knew, one of the soldiers now coming at him had those goddamn black stiches hanging from his scrotum by now. These men didn't want to be doing this shit any more than he did. As the dozen of them advanced, he confirmed his theory by directly confronting their gazes. Their rifles were raised and their feet were moving, but he was damn certain they made the charade happen only because they mentally overlaid Homer's face atop his.

He couldn't wait to see their reaction to the surprise Franzen was about to bring on.

"Gentlemen, that's far enough."

Speak of the devil, in all his awesome glory.

"You can throw the safeties on those weapons now and lay them at your feet before backing up this way," Franz instructed. As Shay accepted his own rifle, brought over by his brother, he noticed a few of Homer's guys visibly expel their breaths after putting down the guns.

"My, my, my. Visitors. What a surprise." Homer cupped his hands in front of his chest pope-style, giving off a wing nut air that wasn't entirely out of character but still suspicious. Really suspicious. Shay eyed the guy harder. The reaction didn't feel right. He'd expected anything from a slow seethe to a full you-took-my-toy-and-its-box tantrum—but not serenity. Not now. The man had just lost the magic key to his fucking kingdom.

"Somebody frisk Doc Asshole," he muttered. "Now."

As Ethan performed that duty, the pontiff-perfect smirk spread wider across Homer's lips. "All right, so I have a confession to make. I'm not *that* surprised. And what a shame." He glanced over to Franzen. "I love surprises. Don't you?"

Franzen's lips twisted. Shay imagined he was contemplating the perfect way to tell the guy to shut the fuck up.

He never got that chance.

The earth shook as the compound's new lab was ripped apart by an orange and red explosion.

As he hit the deck along with Tait, Shay thought he heard his mother's horrified scream. Or maybe it was the ringing in his ears. Or the shock in his senses. He couldn't confirm it, because the bomb blast was followed by a firestorm he hadn't experienced since his team last tangled with a band of pissed-off insurgents across a poppy field in the Helmand Province. He jerked his head up, half expecting to see the opposition advancing through the flowers with his head on a pike as their ultimate goal.

No flowers. No pikes. A sight much worse.

In less than a minute, the street was overrun by a small army of fighting men who looked like shiny movie extras, some running, some tumbling out of fast-moving jeeps. Every single one of them was outfitted in spanking-new mountain camos and classy black battle boots. On their heads were high-end battle helmets with GPS and heat-sensing capabilities that could see through walls.

"Start paddling, kids. We're deep in the shit." Franz greeted them with it as they scrambled on elbows and knees to join him, Zeke, and Dan behind a rusty horse trough.

Dan grunted. "Our buddy Homer's been busy with his

tongue on *somebody's* balls."

"Not-so-wild guess?" Tait returned. "Or am I just entertaining a wild fantasy that it's Cameron Stock, finally within striking distance?"

Sure enough, riding shotgun in the lead jeep, was Cameron Stock.

Shay joined his brother in a dark grimace. To borrow from Homer's knowing sarcasm, *my, my, my*. To borrow from himself, *we should've fucking known.*

He'd barely stabbed himself with the remorse before his attention was swerved. A second jeep sped up next to Cameron's, making it clear that the man in that passenger's seat was leader in equal standing with Stock. The guy, reeking of military might, was lanky, grizzled, and scowling hard beneath a black beret he wore in the Army Spec Ops style.

The moment the guy got out of the vehicle, Franz swore in what sounded like Polynesian profanity. Tait's eyebrows kicked high, but Shay only fired back, "Who the hell is that?"

"General Kirk Newport."

His jaw hit the dust.

"Whoa." Zeke snarled. "*The* Kirk Newport? Like, the boss of our boss of our boss?"

Franzen's burnished skin paled by at least three shades. "Yeah. That one."

"But what's he—"

"Damn." Shay laid his hand over his rifle and then dropped his head to his wrists. "During the hijacking, he was the military representative who got on the line to try to talk Stock down—whatever that meant."

Franz arched one incredulous brow. "I'll bet that's interesting in hindsight."

362

"They talked smack to each other for a few minutes before Newport disappeared, a la your friendly car salesman *going to see what he could do*. It wasn't long before he got back on the line, magically granting us clearance for the landing at Groom Lake."

"Mother*fuckers*." Zeke's growl was strengthened by the new volley of bullets that whizzed over their heads. "The three of them have been in on this all along!"

Dan shook his head, appearing like he needed to borrow a few ashamed ice picks from Shay. "I should've thought things out by more steps. Should've predicted this."

"Using what fucking intel?" Tait rendered a chastising whack up the side of the agent's head. "You were flying blind, Dan. We all were. Still are."

Dan ignored him. "We played right into their hands," he muttered. "They didn't just know that we'd plan something. They were counting on it. Probably saw us jump from that damn plane. Listened to our radio chatter too. Damn it!"

Shay longed to join their rants, but there was no time. He wasn't just the cause of this mess; he was the one who had to set it straight. Somehow...

Newport, still in his jeep, yelled into his head comm. The charge was like water to ants, making half the guerillas surge toward the old Mercantile where Ethan and Garrett were now cornered. The decrepit store was located on the same side of the street as the clinic, where the remains of Mom's lab seemed to burn higher than ever. Shay wondered why the flames didn't die down, seeming to whip higher and higher at the sky—

Because they were.

The wind had gusted embers from the blast across the narrow alley and onto to the roof of the Mercantile—where they caught like a match on tinder.

"Holy shit," he gritted.

"No kidding." Zeke put the pieces together just as he did.

"Not good," Franz growled. "Those boys need out of there faster than bodybuilders at a romance writers' convention."

Shay was already halfway done scoping out the opposite side of the street. "That pile of boulders, between the saloon and the assayers... I can make it there, given proper cover. It'll also break up the elephant, make this thing easier to chew."

"And then what?" Franz demanded.

Shay cocked both brows. "You won't have given half of them lead enemas by then?"

Franz conceded the compliment with a cocky head dip. "Fine, but half of a thousand cockroaches is still a lot of cockroaches. You're the one they're here for, I-Man. They'll reform and reswarm."

Shay unhooked a grenade from the guy's belt. "That's what this is for."

"You're going to need more than one." Zeke pulled a pineapple off his own belt and handed it over. "Just don't blow up your nuts with it, okay? Apparently they're hot commodities these days."

There were so many choices of how to tell the guy to go fuck himself. Shay had trouble picking one out.

The hesitation cost him the pleasure. The words, along with his breath, were strangled in his throat by a fist of pure panic, sporting fingers of disbelieving dread.

So this was what it felt like to hear his own mother scream. Then to watch her tear back down the street, arms outstretched and face contorted with horror. Pretty much sucked as bad as he'd expected.

"Stop!" Mom shrieked. "For the love of God, stop it! There are still innocent people in there! *My* innocent people!"

Next to him, a tight groan burst from Tait's chest. Shay's spirit cracked for his brother. The guy finally laid eyes on the woman for the first time in twenty years but was locked down from doing a damn thing about it. Especially now.

Ghid's appearance lent no more clarity to things. Though his delay was explained by the painful contortion on his face and the hand gripping his crotch, it didn't clean up the confusion now on board with Shay's amazement. What was Mom talking about? Even if she'd been watching this shit go down, why was she coming back in the middle of a gun battle for three experienced men like Ethan, Garrett, and Dan? But she was so frazzed-out, she'd broken away from Ghid by going for his balls.

Innocent people. My innocent people.

"Holy crap."

He spat it as the horror hit home. As if it needed any more fuel, Mom stomped in front of the soldiers, shoving their gun barrels toward the ground as she went. "And you call *my* patients the monsters? Three of my nurses are still in there, you cocksuckers. Did anyone ask about that before setting off bombs? Did anyone care?"

Her announcement clearly knocked the hired hoodlums on their figurative asses. They pelted each other with panicked stares, clueless as noobs tossed into a hypothetical crisis on the first day of training. Their hesitation was both a blessing and a curse. While this was the ideal distraction Shay needed to implement his plan, Mom's nurses couldn't afford another moment of delay. *Hell*. There was a good chance it was too late already.

"Thumbs out of asses, kids." While the words were pure Dan Colton, it still stunned Shay that the agent was the first to spring to action—not just figuratively. As the agent popped to his haunches, he nodded fast at Shay. "You handle the field trip across the street, I-Man. I've got the nurses covered. The extra commotion will help Hawk and Runway get out too. Zsycho and Dragon, you both ready with the lead enemas?"

"Fuck, yeah." Zeke propped his rifle against the trough and growled with gusto.

"Shit." Franz emulated the move. "I hate it when our best option still sucks bones."

With that send-off, Shay jumped into action at the same second as Dan.

His sprint was a blur of adrenaline, exhilaration, and fear. Past the blood pounding in his ears, he heard a soldier yell toward him in Spanish. A bunch more joined in, soon growing into a mob. As he cleared the last three steps before the boulders, bullets sent up dirt clouds around his feet.

Bingo.

"Come to papa, sweet little sheep." He muttered it while shucking the ninja jacket, reveling in the new freedom from his thinner, darker raglan shirt and the Kevlar vest beneath. The words lent him the focus to ease his breathing and reassess the logistics of all this chaos.

A laugh tempted his lips, and he gave in for a second. *Shit.* In what other job on earth did "chaos" and "logistics" exist in the same action plan? The realization was either cause for celebration or compunction—or ambivalence between both, depending on the moment.

Like this one.

He crouched on the balls of his feet, grenade in hand,

opening his senses for the right moment to lob the thing. Maybe a fast glance over the top of the rock would help. The boulders were stacked on a small rise of earth, which would give him the chance to study the area for about two seconds. Didn't seem like much, but as he'd learned so many times over the last week, moments could be turned into eternities.

Mmmhmm. Just ask a dancer trying to look sexy during a major show finale at a dance rave pace.

"Dancer." The whisper escaped him as the memory flared through him, a solid brick of emotional C-4. He promised her he'd live—and he would, damn it.

Even if everything had taken yet another terrible turn for the worse.

On the bright side, he watched Hawk and Runway break free from the Mercantile, ash flying off their shoulders but nothing else notably damaged or burned. Zeke was still in position behind the trough but waved them beyond his location to a group of old barrels, where they joined a trio of guys who'd originally been Homer's minions. Shay was certain their defection wasn't a stunner to anyone.

That was the good stuff.

The horror show didn't start until he did a double-take on Z's position—the spot he'd occupied five minutes ago with Franzen and Tait. But where the hell were they now?

"Fuck."

Shay almost added a crapload of choice names to call the duo, synonyms for everything from first-degree idiots to gigged-up morons, as he caught sight of them behind a dilapidated wagon—engaging easily thirty of the guerillas in a disgustingly uneven firefight.

"What the—"

He cut himself off, finally spotting the treasure they were all shooting to kill for. Mom, bound by her wrists and ankles, was draped over one of the jeep's hoods. Her eyes were so wide, Shay swore he could see their whites from here. Ghid, who'd clearly fought to keep the scumsuckers from recapturing her, was splayed in a beaten-to-shit heap next to one of the jeep's tires.

Shay barely kept his stomach from punching its way up his throat. While it was a damn righteous sight to watch his badass brother and that half-Samoan warrior giving as well as they got when outnumbered fifteen to one, it was torture to keep his ass planted where it was. But Stock and Newport's ploy was more obvious than a stripper spreading her legs. If Shay raced to join Tait and Franz, he'd play right into their fucking plan. Every visceral, vile reaction he endured right now was like dancing on their puppet strings, but the dick wipes weren't getting the whole puppet show.

All he could do was pray for the right chance at lobbing these grenades—and about a hundred miracles after that.

"Help! Oh God, help me!"

The scream didn't sound like anything close to a miracle.

Shay lifted his stare back over the rock and frantically scanned for the source of the cry. It was female but hoarse... and raw with desperation...

There. On the old boardwalk in front of the burning buildings. A woman emerged in soot-covered medical scrubs, every inch of her skin just as black from smoke. Her mouth was a stark grimace against the charcoal of her face, opened on imploring sobs as she dragged an unconscious body behind her.

A man.

"Christ." Shay sagged against the boulder. "Dan!"

At a fast snap from Newport, a medic appeared. The guy started a vitals check on Dan. Shay gripped both sides of his head to keep his sights steady—or maybe his spinning mind roped down—while the fucking exam stretched on. And on. *And on.*

When the medic finally lifted his head, Shay couldn't decipher anything from the man's movement. It wasn't fast enough to be urgent but not slow enough for complete somberness. He only knew one thing for certain. Dan was still much too still.

"Alive," the medic pronounced. "But barely. And the burns on his left side..." The guy shook his head. "They need immediate attention."

"He saved...my life." The soot-covered woman wept as she stammered it. "Viv and Megan...they were already gone...the smoke and the heat...and I knew I'd be next. Then he appeared, almost like he walked through the flames..." She dropped her head into her hands. "Oh, God! Don't let him die!"

Shay swallowed hard. It was the same fucking prayer in his heart too.

After the nurse revealed the news about her coworkers, Mom's throat ripped open on a long, grieving wail. She torched the sound into a furious scream. "We could keep him from dying if we still had a medical building, you monsters. And Homer, you're the leader of the goddamn pack. You signed this deal with the devil twenty years ago, and what's it brought you except blood on your hands? How many more will it take? The life of this agent now? Or the man after him? Or after that?"

Newport stalked forward. "*Enough.*" He paused next to the jeep, pulling off his aviators to lower a calm smile at Mom.

369

"Dr. Bommer, we're all sympathetic to your grief and aware of how you feel. But you know as well as Dr. Adler or anyone here that doing the right thing is not always doing the easiest thing." He stroked her forehead and gave her an encouraging nod. "You know who else knows it? Both of your amazing sons."

He kicked the last of that into a prominent shout. Shay grinded his knuckles into the boulder, as well as both sides of his jaw, to hold back from telling the ass fuck what he could do with his twisted take on the motivation banner. He just hoped Tait had the melodrama curtains closed today and would know to keep his own mouth shut.

"Take a dick deep in your backside, Newport!"

Damn it. The curtains were wide open.

The slur was all it took for Newport to order more men toward the cause of opening fire on T and Franzen. Though Ethan and Zeke ran and joined them, it was soon clear his four friends were destined to repeat the fucking Alamo. Shay grimaced to see Franzen take a bullet to his thigh, while Ethan was grazed in the shoulder. And still, the four men fought on—until it was clear they were about to run out of bullets and options.

Abruptly, Newport held up a hand.

Immediately, the firing stopped.

"Well, then, gentlemen." Though the general called it out, his voice held the condescending cool of teatime at the fucking Ritz. "I think we all agree now. Game time is over."

At Newport's nod, Cameron waved another throng of soldiers forward. The assholes stormed the little wagon like delirious Banshees. With two injured members and little ammo left, his friends had two choices: surrender or death. Reluctantly, they agreed to the former. Their rifles gone, their bodies bloodied, and their spirits exhausted, they didn't resist when the guerillas zip-tied their wrists and then ordered them to kneel in front of Stock and Newport.

All of them except Tait.

Shay looked on, his heart snapping, as a soldier rammed the middle of T's back with the butt of his rifle, forcing him to bow at the feet of the man who'd been responsible for Luna's death—and damn near Lani's too. But as Tait scrambled to his knees, he didn't miss the chance to spit hard on Cameron's boots. He followed it by jerking his face up at Stock too. From Shay's position, he could only witness the violence of the movement itself, but if T's face matched the action, Satan was thanking fuck he'd sent Stock as his proxy.

Unless the two were the same piss-sucking creature.

A supposition supported in disgusting detail by Stock's next move.

Motioning a soldier forward to keep Tait's head locked back, the bastard pulled out his pistol and jammed it to the middle of Tait's forehead.

At the same moment, Newport did the same thing to Mom—with a creative twist. His pistol went straight into her mouth.

"Choices."

Newport bellowed it, succinctly and purposefully, into air made harsher by the crackles and whooshes of the fire still eating through the lab and Mercantile.

"Easy ones, or right ones."

Shay laid his arm along the top of the boulder and then caged his face with his hand. He glared through his fingers at the blazes on the other side of the street. The flames consuming the lab were fluid and brilliant, their heat defined by dark-cobalt hues, the smoke twirling up with effortless grace....

A dancer.

As the Mercantile surrendered, it punched out thick black billows that were scented by cedar and pine, forcing its way up...

A fighter.

But higher in the sky, the colors blended.

Merged.

Mated.

For just a few moments, they painted the sky in one of those moments a person simply knew...and he knew.

Stare at this. Remember this. No photo will ever capture it right. Only your heart will remember it perfectly.

He let his hand slip down his face, dragging his tears with it.

He pushed away from the boulder, dropped his rifle, and raised his arms.

"You've made your fucking point, Newport. And now you have what you came here for, so do the right thing yourself and let them all go—Dan first. He needs a heli-vac. With paramedics."

"Fuck," Tait grated.

"Fuck." Now that Newport's pistol was gone from her mouth, Mom echoed it. Hers came with a big difference. The sheen of her tears.

"It'll be okay."

Shay repeated it after they untied Mom and let him hug them both one last time.

"You're a fucking liar, Little B." Mom's accusation was broken up between the tears she soaked into his neck.

"What she said." Tait's voice was just as ragged.

"Shut up, asshat." Shay gripped the back of his brother's head and held on tight. Tighter. He had no idea what the three caballeros of crazy had in store for him or if they'd ever let him see T and Mom again, so he clung to this moment like another precious curl of smoke in the sky—and once more said the words that had become his desperate prayer. "It'll be okay."

CHAPTER TWENTY-TWO

"You all think everything's going to be okay, *sí*? Well, I'm afraid I've got some tough news."

Zoe folded her arms and let her words sink into the thirty UNLV dance majors lined up against three sides of the studio classroom. But who the hell was she kidding? If anyone was listening at all, they only reacted with rolled eyes and impatiently tapping feet.

"I'm not trying to be your *puta*, okay? But if half of you turn in performances for your final that look anything like today..."

Nobody noticed she'd trailed off. Several kids yanked out their phones and started checking texts.

"*Mierda.*" The mutter was more surrender than anger. How could she blame them? Five minutes before the start of spring break, and she decided to drive the stake in about their lazy jazz hands and sloppy footwork? Damn. She'd be secretly calling herself a *puta* too.

But did they want to end up showcasing their "skills" at some club on the North Strip with bouncers and a two-drink minimum? They had to think about their futures. God knew, she hadn't. Not really. She'd been a fool, believing she had all the bases covered, all the plans handled.

Then she'd met Shay Bommer during an ordinary flight delay...that had been anything but ordinary.

Moral of the story? Life was a sadistic pitcher. It liked

switching up the throws. And if you weren't ready, you got hit in the head.

It felt important to pass along the knowledge, even vital. It was why she'd decided to take a leave of absence from the show and accept this guest teaching gig at the university for a year. It was challenging work but much easier than having to feign desire and passion during the show every night. After only a couple of performances, she'd realized the stupidity of that move. Only one face kept blazing in her mind—not the one she needed with four thousand people watching. His eyes seeking hers with dark-gold need. His jaw clenched in those two perfect right angles, leading to the intersection of gorgeous and dominant in his chin. His thick chestnut hair tumbling over his forehead as he pressed it to hers, laughing softly as she whispered how crazy they were...how perfect they were.

She took a deep breath and swallowed her eightieth pang of heartache for the day.

Just as someone burped.

The clock saved her from coming up with a reprimanding glower. As the minute hand officially ticked into the end of class, the kids cheered and raced for the door.

"If you're smart, you'll practice over the break!" she yelled. "And remember, beer looks like crap in spandex!"

Her parting shot seemed to get her back into a few good graces, not that it would tamp her irritation with most of them. It wasn't personal. She was frustrated with everyone these days, even Ry and Ava. Ryder, now wearing Rok's promise ring, couldn't stop talking about the trials of handling having to "open up the New York place" for their relocation to the Big Apple for the next six months. And Ava, now Mrs. Ethan Archer and a full-time stylist for the CW's Vancouver-based shows, was just as bad with the décor magazines. After her and Ethan's Bali honeymoon, he'd brought her home to her wedding present: a five-bedroom, three-bathroom "starter" place on the Columbia River.

That was right. The whole world was in rebirth, redecorating, and now, in the case of her students, rejoicing in a week off from responsibility. There were wildflowers on the hills and more convertibles on the freeway with their tops down. Everyone wanted to hit the Refresh key and wake up.

Except her.

I'm not going to die, dancer.

He'd kept his word, hadn't he?

He wasn't dead.

But heaven forgive her...she wished he was. At least then she'd know he didn't wake up every morning with only hours of pain in front of him. She'd fall asleep knowing he wasn't strapped to some bed, pleading for sleep as his only deliverance. She wouldn't wake up screaming from nightmares of him wandering endless halls alone, rows of those black threads holding his body together, wondering which part of him would serve as the next experimental meat for Adler, Stock, and Newport—who somehow, in the eyes of the military, was still untouchable in the whole "honor and character" department.

On the other side of the bullshit river, Shay had been officially discharged from the green machine as AWOL. Her fury about that fact only made her more determined about holding on to him with every piece of her heart and grasp of her soul. Every morning before she left for the university, she wrote journal entries to him. At night, she looked to the stars and whispered to him, wondering if his night sky was the same as hers. She restocked her pantry every week with his favorites.

The pretzels, Oreos, and apple chips—the soft kind, not crunchy—waited there for him. She did too...pleading with fate for the moment he'd come bounding through the door, sweaty from the gym, scarfing on the stuff like a puppy and kissing the back of her neck in thanks. She read everything she could get her hands on about loving a man in the Special Forces. Sometimes she pretended he was just away on deployment, out to run recon on bad guys and rescue kids before they stepped on landmines—until the memories returned, glaring and taunting, of what she'd seen in the hallway at Area 51.

Then it all returned. Including the helplessness.

Especially the helplessness.

Nothing was good enough to bring him back. Despite the AWOL status, perhaps because of it, Franzen had helped her get files reactivated at both the CIA and FBI. Their new agents didn't come close to Dan Colton, but it would be a long damn time before Dan donned his spook suit again. After months of burn treatment and therapy, the man was still unwilling to see anyone except Franz and even then for only ten minutes at a time. Despite that, Dan had turned in a detailed report about everything that had happened to Shay from the moment he signed on with Stock's gang. Like all the first sets of his notes, the report went "missing," conveniently deleted by CIA computer users who remained faceless, nameless...ghosts.

Just like the ghost into which Shay Raziel Bommer was turning, as she watched without a damn thing to do about it.

No. *No.*

She couldn't give up. She *wouldn't* give up.

"*Ay,*" she muttered while extending the handle on her rolling file bag. "Enough of the moping, damn it."

The edict would have to apply for at least the next few

hours. Brynn and El had a dark week for the show, so they'd invited themselves—along with Ryder and his drapery sample book—over for a dinner designed to get her head out of all things Shay Bommer. Despite the thirty excuses she'd tried for getting out of the plans, her friends held her feet to the fire. There *would* be pizza and salad tonight. And wine. And drapery samples.

When she arrived home, a couple of hours remained before the trio's scheduled arrival time, but a dark-blue Ford sedan already occupied her driveway. Alarms went off in her senses, remnant angst from the night half the government agents in the country had descended on her house, but when she saw the G-tags on the car, her curiosity piqued.

As soon as she parked her Prius, a man got out of the Ford. Bad suit. Classy haircut. Square shoulders. Proud chin. She'd met him once before, in his office at the FBI building downtown, and her impression was the same. Cary Grant had been reincarnated in the form of Caspar Menken, the agent for Shay's case.

Only what was he doing here, visiting her at home?

No. *Mierda*. No.

She approached the agent on legs that suddenly turned to icicles. When Caspar bypassed the pleasantries and went straight to "We need to talk," the icicles shattered and gave way to complete paralysis.

"Spare the damn sugar, Menken."

"Just Caspar, okay? And what the hell does that mean?"

She gripped the handle of her file bag tighter. "Don't give me platitudes, poetry, or pretty. If he's dead, just tell me—and then forgive me if I don't invite you in."

Caspar's stare, a Caribbean blue that was almost too

pretty on a guy who evoked Cary Grant, softened a little. He'd always been able to see the pain beneath her anger, and she was usually thankful, except misery had beaten the gratitude to her gut today. "Zoe..."

"What?"

"You need to invite me in."

Her heart burst at the same time it caved. She couldn't make it through the door fast enough or wait the agonizing three seconds it took Caspar to step inside too.

As soon as they got through the door, Fluffy ran to greet them. Over the months, the cat had simply become more Zoe's than Ryder's, especially with Ry leaving in three weeks to play house in New York with Rok. Nevertheless, kittah-girl instantly wrapped herself around Caspar's leg, having been well-trained that men were the ones with all the best presents.

Zoe hoped she *and* Fluffy would be receiving great gifts tonight. To kick-start the good karma, she broke out the expensive cat food as dinner for the feline.

She motioned for Caspar to come along to the kitchen so she could dish out Fluffy's pseudo filet mignon. As she prepped the food, Caspar once more didn't waste a moment to start speaking again.

"First, I owe you an apology."

Zoe let her eyebrows dip. "Why? You didn't come here to tell me Shay's dead. We're already off to a good start."

Caspar loosened his tie and readjusted himself on the chair he'd pulled out next to the dining table. "I...haven't been completely honest with you."

She let the empty can and the spoon clatter to the floor. Fluffy jumped four vertical feet and then bolted for the bedroom. "*Mierda.* He *is* dead. You just didn't want me to make a scene—"

"For fuck's sake, Zoe. He isn't dead."

She huffed and retrieved the mess off the floor. "Fine. Then what? *Dios*, Caspar. Spit it out."

He curled his hand into a determined fist and tapped it on the table. "I've been tracking General Kirk Newport for about two years."

She almost let the can drop again. "What?"

The agent nodded. "It was the reason I got assigned to Shay's file when Captain Franzen came in, demanding we open one. We already knew about Newport's connection to Cameron Stock. The two rammed their dirty peanut butter and chocolate together after meeting at some Hollywood grip-and-grin. Stock, of course, saw the immediate bennies of an evil partnership, especially when learning that Newport's status could get him back into Melody Bommer's panties."

Zoe grimaced. "Disgusting *cabrón*."

Caspar nodded more emphatically. "We knew all this in theory, but gaining enough evidence to put them both down was close to impossible. On the books, everything they both did was completely legit."

"Which was why you didn't looked too stunned when Franz and I relayed our version of the mess to you."

A trace of a smile crossed Caspar's screen-idol mouth. "The day you two came in was one of the biggest mother lodes of intel I'd landed in a long time. I was so over the moon, I damn near kissed your toes."

Zoe allowed herself to laugh a little. "Franz would've demanded worship for his own little piggies."

"Why do you think I held myself back?"

She approached the table after filling a pair of water

glasses. "I'll forgive you for the subterfuge if you tell me this has led us somewhere productive."

"It has."

She was glad she'd gotten the water. It helped combat a pulse that kicked into aerobic mode and palms that were now humid microclimates. "So why do you look like depression on a stick again?"

The agent took a couple of thorough breaths before flipping open his smart pad. "It's a good thing you don't like sugar, because this shit doesn't have a grain on it." If his words didn't underscore the severity of his message, the new lines at the corners of his mouth and eyes were damn effective. "You ready?"

She flattened her palms to the table's surface, emulated his breaths, and nodded. "*Sí.*"

Caspar swiped to a new page. "First, Adler may be a scientific genius, but he's an operational moron—and that's good news for us. After Shay gave himself up at the mining camp, it was pretty simple for us to track him back to his old haunts in the DC warehouse district."

Zoe raised a hand, stopping him. "Wait. What? You've known where he took Shay and didn't tell me?"

"So you could do what with the information?" the agent calmly countered. "*We* could barely do anything with it. Knowing where they were through exterior intel gathering was one thing. Getting inside the damn place was another."

She didn't want to let him off the hook. Not yet. This was like being the last one picked for high school PE because she was the smallest. "So when did all that happen?" she sneered.

"Three days ago."

She blinked. "Oh."

"Yeah. *Oh.*"

"And...?"

Within a second, she saw they'd come to the hardest part of the conversation for Caspar. He studied the condensation on his water glass for a long moment. "I know you love him," he finally murmured. "And that's why I'm going to give this shit to you straight."

"I appreciate that," Zoe returned. "I...think."

The man planted both his elbows on the table. "You know how you thought it would be bad for him?"

Damn.

"*Sí,*" she whispered.

"Well...it's been bad."

"*Mierda.*"

"As you know, Shay negotiated some things into his surrender to Adler. One of those things was the release of all the other Big Idea subjects into his mother's care forever...so Shay's been *it* in terms of test subjects for the man."

"*Ay Dios mio.*" She locked her own fist to her mouth, but the sorrow welled and spilled anyway. "That *higueputa* doesn't deserve to be pissed on by a rabid gutter rat."

"I can't do any better than that, so I won't try." Caspar waited a second before reaching to grab one of her hands. "But Zoe, we also have firsthand accounts that he's been heavily sedated through most of it. I know that's not much help, but stop and take a breath. At least he's been out of it. They've kept him in a nearly vegetative state a great deal of the time. I don't think Adler wanted to risk another escape attempt, despite the presence of Stock's guards on a round-the-clock basis."

"It does help, Caspar. Thank you." She wasn't lying. The knowledge that Shay wasn't cognitive of his torture made the news a little easier to bear. A *very* little.

"Wait." Caspar winced. "I'm afraid the roller coaster's just starting."

"Of course." She drenched it in grim sarcasm.

"Giving him the sedation for so long has been like keeping a drug addict on a constant fix. They're not sure what it's done... to his short-term memory."

Zoe yanked her hand back. The entire center of her chest felt rammed by an I-beam. She was so stunned, even her tear ducts refused to function. "H-How short term?"

"Like I said, they're not sure. And we won't be sure, either...until we get him out of there." He waited through the moment it took Zoe to wrench her head up. Then spike him with a don't-bullshit-me stare. "Yeah. We're going in as soon as we can get the mission together, including the undercover operatives for it."

Zoe nodded. Correction, swung her head like a spastic bobble head. "Oh. Okay. Good. Good."

But she glanced away, biting her lips. *Who's really the bullshitter of the night, girlfriend?* Did she truly believe this was "good"? What would she do if they broke Shay out again but he had no recollection of who she was or what they'd shared? "Short-term memory" sounded like a damn accurate description of a few shared days of passion before he went back under Adler's knife...

Caspar's grip, now wrapped around both her hands, yanked her back to the roller coaster. The agent gave as good as he promised. This was a premium ticket ride, for sure.

"Zoe. I'm telling you all this...because we want you on the op too."

One upgrade to the super*premium ride, please.*

"Me?" Her echo sounded as foggy as she felt. "Wh-What? How? Why?"

She reconsidered her thought that Caspar was at his most stressed a minute ago. As the agent closed the cover on his smart pad and then folded his white-knuckled hands on the table, Zoe could've sworn she saw red start to bleed up his neck. "The conditions of Shay's surrender... How much did Tait really tell you about them?"

The fog in her brain thickened. Or maybe it couldn't escape past the tribe of heathens pounding a strange refrain through her heart. She shook her head, unable to understand the feeling. She should be jumping up and hugging Caspar. He was offering her the chance to be there when they rescued Shay. Hell, she'd hold open the car door if that's what they needed.

Even if he doesn't recognize you? Or remember what he shared with you?

"Why would Tait leave anything out?" she finally challenged. "I don't under—"

"What did he tell you, Zoe?" The question was gentle, but Caspar's face was raw demand.

"Everything, I guess. I wasn't exactly in the best emotional state when we talked, you know."

"Good. So you know about Adler's plans for the breeding."

The air left the room. Which then tilted and swam behind the field of fuzz that conquered her vision. "The... The..."

She swallowed, battling to focus on the act to ground her senses again. No use.

Breeding.

Had she heard the word wrong? *Right.* Because this anguish was exactly what her imagination would have thrown together as the bomb she wanted Caspar to drop. Because she was so keen to remember the weeks that followed Tait's visit, telling her about the ambush at the mining camp and all its horrible fallout. Two of Melody's nurses, dead from the explosion. John Franzen with a bullet in his leg and Ethan with a rough graze on the shoulder. Dan Colton in an intensive care burn unit.

And Shay...gone.

She'd waited, counting the days, praying her body had already started to grow a part of him. But like clockwork, on the twenty-eighth day of her cycle, her period had started. It had been the day before Thanksgiving.

It had been a really shitty Thanksgiving.

Ry had forced her out of the house for the day-after sales, helping her redecorate the bathroom she'd obliterated in her grief.

"Okay." Caspar laced his fingers as he gritted his teeth. "So Tait didn't tell you everything."

She gulped again. "Guess not." Caspar's answering silence was a gift—not easily given. She could feel the urgency in his energy, sensing they were scrambling the mission fast, but he allowed her a long minute to push through her tumult of shock and pain. "So Adler plans on using him as a stud horse? That's the deal?"

"You have a pretty good grasp of words."

"I also have a good grasp of not being okay with this."

Caspar meshed his fingers tighter. "But you might have to be, Zoe. At least for one day."

"*Caramba. En tus sueños. Beso mi culo!*"

"Do you want to get Shay out of that place or not?"

She pushed up from the table, unable to sit still with rage roiling like this. While refilling her water, she rebutted, "Why me? You planning on sneaking *me* in as his fuck buddy? If that's the case—"

"She's already been selected." The red inched farther up Caspar's neck. Zoe would've called out the shit and enjoyed embarrassing the crap out of him if it weren't for the more pressing matter at hand—the concept of Shay with his cock inside anyone but her.

"Of course she has." She took a long drink of water. That was supposed to help in the whole composure recovery thing, right? "And let me guess. She's as tall as an Amazon with legs to her neck, breasts like a pin-up, and big, brown Bambi eyes. Wait. Her name *is* Bambi."

"Her name is Buffy."

She snapped her fingers. "Damn. So close."

"And yeah, she's blond. And actually, a pretty nice girl...for a high-end hooker."

Screw the water. Zoe jerked the fridge open and reached for the Chardonnay. "This just gets better and better. So what's my role in this whole op, Agent Menken? Do I get to hold the bimbo's purse and makeup kit while she mounts the man I love?"

She watched Caspar debate his answer to that. He even glanced to the front door, obviously considering the choice of accepting her version of *no fucking way* and leaving. At this point, Zoe verged on agreeing with that decision. *Undercover operatives.* She'd be there in the pretense of someone else, having to conceal her feelings. She wasn't certain she'd be capable of success.

In the end, Caspar stayed put and continued on. "They won't let the woman be alone in the room with him. They want an impartial observer to accompany Buffy, to ensure that full consummation happens."

That did it for Caspar's blush. As the red rose to his forehead, Zoe repeated, "Full consummation? You mean... they want somebody to report back that Shay..."

"Performed his duty. In...a matter of speaking."

Zoe downed the whole glass of wine. Then poured another. "And you want me to be this...watcher...person? Why?"

Caspar reopened his smart pad. Zoe suspected the motions were just for something to do, but how could she fault him? This was one hell of a strange conversation. "When the breeding takes place, they have to pull Shay off of many of his sedatives. We're not sure how he's going to respond to the change. He'll be close to fully alert for the first time in months. If he gets agitated, he may resist our efforts at extracting him, and we won't have a lot of time to pull this thing off. We need him to be as calm and cooperative as possible."

"So you think I can somehow calm his beast?"

"If it comes to that, yes."

"Even if he doesn't remember me?"

"He'll know the idea of you, Zoe. Though your face and name may not be familiar, he'll recognize your scent, your voice, your touch. Tait informs me that he's never seen his brother more connected to a woman. Though I've never had the pleasure of seeing you and Shay together, I'm inclined to believe that." The ends of the man's lips kicked up again. "You love him. I saw it, felt it, knew it from the moment you walked into my office. If Shay returns even half of what you feel for him, then you *are* the best 'operative' for this gig."

While the assertion warmed her with joy, it was still a lot to take in. Zoe paced to the patio slider and opened it. Twilight was already beginning, bringing with it the colors in the sky that matched Shay's gaze the most. How many times had she stood here in the last four months right at this time, to raise a hand and reach for the breathtaking mix of amber and gold and copper?

But it was impossible to touch the sky. Bringing Shay back had always been an equal impossibility...until now.

All she had to do was watch him "breed" with another woman.

"Okay, Caspar."

She heard the agent turn in his seat. "Okay? You... You mean you'll do it?"

"*Sí.* But only on one condition."

"What's that?"

"If Buffy comes out of this with an accidental black eye, you all look the other way."

★ ★ ★ ★ ★

Buffy was going to get her black eye sooner rather than later.

As the woman giggled again at one of Homer Adler's lame jokes, Zoe gripped her clipboard tighter and readjusted her glasses with another girl growl. Oh yes, the woman was an Amazon—to the point that she wondered if Adler, Stock, and Newport had really found her in the middle of the Brazilian rain forest.

At least they were finally walking down the dingy gray hall in the warehouse now, making their way to Shay's room. It had taken almost three hours to get here. After four security checkpoints, they'd taken an hour for lunch and then another hour for her and Buffy to fill out so much paperwork, she wondered if she was actually helping draft a Congressional bill.

If that was the case, then she'd just done so as Helena Troy—a cover name even two hours of pleading to Caspar hadn't changed. The agent assured her that nobody in Adler's offices would blink at the name after they looked at her disguise, a point Zoe had to agree with now. After a prosthetic nose, inch-thick glasses, and an outfit they literally bought for five bucks in a Salvation Army rejects bin, she looked like a cross between Emily Litella and the scarier side of Joan Crawford.

Just the look she wanted for seeing the man of her soul after four months.

Finally, Homer called the medical team to confirm Shay was "ready to shoot." He and Buffy had enjoyed a really good guffaw at that one. Zoe survived the moment by imagining her fist in the bimbo's left eye socket.

Just a few more steps, girlfriend.

She focused on the joyful certainty of it. Timing it to her steps helped as well. Her heart certainly wasn't going to cooperate with the effort. If it were capable of bursting out of her chest, it would've done so—then torn down the hall, escaped up the stairs they planned on using for Shay's escape, and run around the block five times.

Buffy let out an especially loud titter. "Oh, my God!" she cried at Homer. The final word lasted at least ten seconds, making Zoe wonder if the Buff-ster was secretly a mutant too. On the strength of that bray, she guessed a touch of donkey mixed with a bit of goat.

Wishful thinking.

"So what *did* the monkey say?" Buffy grabbed Homer's arm like the fate of nations rested on the joke's punchline.

"How about, 'My name is Buffy. Please punch me in *both* eyes, Miss Helena Troy'?"

Caspar's answering snicker resounded through her head. It took a moment to identify the sound, since they'd had to embed her comm piece into one of her teeth like a filling. She told Caspar it made him sound like God. Right now, it was more like God eating a cracker.

"Breathe," came the agent's quiet reinforcement. "You're doing well."

"Which means I *can* hit her in both eyes?"

"Zoe." God was back to his no-bullshit self.

"If she does conceive Shay's kid, somebody better hope the angels pick from the right box when it comes to locking in the brains."

"You need to chill, goddamnit. Focus on the plan. You know if we get the right opportunity, this will all go down before Buffy ever does."

"*That's* encouraging. Thanks."

Caspar didn't answer. She wasn't sure she'd hear him over the thunder of her heart anyway. They'd arrived. If Homer's all-stop didn't inform her of that fact, the retinal scan next to the door certainly did. Buffy bounced a little on her bright-pink strappy sandals, which perfectly matched her skimpy mini dress. Fleetingly, Zoe wondered if she'd just come off a shift with some businessman at the Bellagio. And wrestled back her hundredth desire to punch the woman.

Buffy didn't help her cause by leaning over and whispering in a just-us-girls tone, "Isn't this exciting? We're making scientific history!"

Zoe forced a smile past her careening senses and churning stomach. Thank God she hadn't eaten much for lunch.

Homer swung the door in.

Don't lose it. Don't lose it. Don't lose it.

She commanded her feet to move. And her eyes to lift. And her hands to stay where they were, instead of going for the throats of the two men who already waited in the room for them with proud grins on their faces—next to the bed containing the nearly naked, completely unconscious form of the man she loved.

Oh, God. Oh, God. Oh, God.

Caspar had tried to prepare her, but all he'd rattled off were the facts. The next-to-catatonic stillness. The shallow breaths. The skin that nearly matched his sheets for color. Well, his *sheet*. There was only one, draped across the middle of his body, though the cover accomplished very little at actually hiding the body part there. Even the cotton candy in Buffy's brain didn't miss it. Her stunned sigh was obvious in the room's tense air.

Tense? That only began to describe this chamber. Zoe peered around, certain she couldn't be the only one aware of it. The aura of despair. The stench of hopelessness. The palpability of brokenness.

She thought back to Tait's vow at the Vdara, to put a dagger into Cameron Stock's neck. She'd wondered how the man could talk of the act with such glee in his eyes...but wasn't so confused anymore. A blade in her hand, driven into Adler's carotid, suddenly became a very nice fantasy.

The bastard guided Buffy across the room. "Miss Buffy Walsh, I'd like you to meet the men who've made this research possible—Mr. Cameron Stock and General Kirk Newport. Gentlemen, I am pleased to present Miss Walsh, who has enthusiastically accepted our offer to be the program's first surrogate."

Buffy curtsied and giggled. "Well, what's not to accept

about fifty thousand dollars?"

Stock took Buffy's hand and leaned over it. "A pleasure, Miss Walsh."

Newport only nodded like the corrupt asshole he was. "You're doing your country a great service, my dear. A great service."

"Oh. Gosh." Buffy brushed down the front of her dress. "Ask not all the stuff your country does for you but how you can give back...right?"

"Sure." Stock smiled indulgently. "That's...uh...just fine, Buffy. Just fine."

"Miss Troy?"

Homer's prompting was sharp, as if it weren't the first time he'd issued it.

"Huh?" she stammered.

"Zoe." Caspar's voice was a boom in her head. "Snap out of it!"

"I'm...I'm sorry," she spluttered. "I was...uhhh...assessing the...uhhh..."

Dear God, what *was* Shay? Not their damn "test subject." Rats in labs were treated better than this. The bed was nothing but a wide plastic mattress on a dark oak frame, and he was tethered to it by chains connected to metal shackles, his arms raised over his head and his legs stretched out toward the corners. He sure as hell wasn't their patient, either. The fresh stitches and incision points proved that, as well as the pallor of his skin and the pronounced loss of his muscle tone. She couldn't bear wondering about the last time he'd seen the sun or been allowed to even take a walk up the hall...

If she called him their stud horse, that came a little closer, though thoroughbreds weren't shot up with so many sedatives that their arms rivaled a junkie's for needle tracks. Circus animal seemed too kind as well.

Today, he'd become nothing more than their whore.

And she swore that every breath she took and move she made in this room would be with one purpose in mind.

To free him from their filthy clutches.

"Yes, yes," the general declared, seeming relieved that "Ms. Troy" returned the atmosphere to a businesslike tone. "Excellent thinking, Ms. Troy. Feel free to check everything out and...mmm...carry on, as they say. The men will be keeping the leather warm in the waiting room."

Zoe forced a cordial nod to the man. Hypocritical *cabrón*. He liked the idea of reaping the financial benefits from selling Shay's sperm but not the mess required for it. It was frightening to contemplate the man and his ego ever leading men into real battle.

Stock followed in Newport's steps, leaving Homer behind with Zoe and Buffy, as well as the nurse who monitored Shay's vitals in masked silence. Zoe eyed him expectantly, but Buffy sidled up to him with a seductive sashay, pulling suggestively at both his elbows. "Homie," she said in a whine to rival a four-year-old, "can't you stay?"

Zoe pretended to scribble data on her clipboard. Between fighting the need to throw herself around Shay this second and the craving to knock Buffy out before she got anywhere near the bed, keeping her composure was a big enough win on its own. She didn't need to go for the bonus round with "Homie's" continued presence.

"I'm flattered, darling," Homer crooned, "I truly am, but it's not a good idea."

Thank God.

"But why?"

Maybe that client Buffikins had left behind had been into daddy-daughter play.

"I'm not Shay's favorite person in the building. It's probably best for everyone concerned if I wait with the other men. Besides, I think Newport brought a bottle of his good brandy."

"Mmmm. I love brandy." She pouted at him. "Save some for me?"

"Uh-uh-uh." He gave her nose a chiding tap. "None for you...Mommy."

Her dagger. The man's neck. It swirled into a better dream by the minute.

As soon as the door clicked shut behind him, Buffy turned and beamed a bright grin at Zoe. "So...whaddup, H?" She wiggled her shoulders rap-girl style, but the last thing Zoe wanted was some lame white girl humor. More awkwardly now, Buffy murmured, "You're supposed to give me the all-systems-go, right? I mean, Homie told me that they're going to make him a little more...lively." She glanced toward Shay. "I mean, the chains are fine. I can be a kink bunny as much as the next girl. But I'm not into necrophilia, you know?"

"Sure." She pushed it out by sheer force of will. With her remaining strength, she pushed down the ocean of nausea in her stomach.

Dios. She really wasn't any smarter than Buffy, was she? Just like the moment she'd first entered the room, she thought she was ready for this moment. Had drilled over the op plan a thousand times with Caspar, thinking that would anesthetize her to everything when it really went down—but like her students at the university, she'd gone through the motions as a lame simulation of the truth.

And now, with timing that sucked ass, Shay let out a long and painful moan.

"Hmmm." Buffy's eyes sparkled like she smelled fresh cookies. "Now *that* sounds promising."

"Sure." She was getting pretty good at this lying-through-her-teeth shit. Swallowing back another surge of bile, she followed Buffy to the bed.

Shay jerked weakly at his wrist chains, grimacing when they didn't give. He rolled his head from side to side on the pillow. As sweat broke out on his neck, Zoe had to clench the back of a chair to keep from grabbing a washcloth off his tray and soothing him. Homer had been specific in his instructions to "Helena." After the men departed the room, Buffy was the only person in the room who touched Shay.

It was a good thing that Buffy at least knew her way around a man.

Or maybe not such a good thing.

Part of Zoe's heart exhaled with relief when the woman automatically reached for the washcloth. The other part railed with the wrath of Hera at watching Buffy stroke Shay with it, slowly and carefully, murmuring words of comfort to him as she did.

Both sides froze into silence when he dipped his head toward her hand, his lips parting on a wordless entreaty for more.

"That's it," Buffy whispered. "That's good. You're okay, tiger."

Zoe whirled, pretending to write on her notepad again. Her scream of anguish began in the pit of her gut, roared its way up her throat, and was barely kept in by her clenching teeth. Nobody in the room heard it.

But Caspar, embedded in her filling, sure did. "Zoe," he barked over the comm, "you need to keep it together, girl."

"We'll handle it." The new voice on the comm delivered a double punch. First, it was another female, albeit with a rasp coming in somewhere between Courtney Love and Kirstie Alley. Second, and most weirdly, Zoe heard her words in stereo. "Won't we, darlings?"

Zoe breathed to school her features while she slammed her gaze over to the masked nurse in the corner. One of the eyes above that mask, glistening with dark amber wickedness, winked at her.

Tait.

For once, she was grateful as hell for the man's intrepid side.

"Everything's just fine." Buffy said it, thinking the "nurse" had spoken to her. She rewet the washcloth and started wiping down Shay's chest. "We're going to take this in easy steps, baby."

"Slower is better, I'd say." Tait flashed a stare that was filled with apology but told her he had the bigger picture in mind.

Even though Zoe didn't know how much bigger she could stand it.

Before Buffy even tugged the sheet away, she knew what the woman would find. Shay's erection was a mouthwatering sight even at half-strength. As the woman hummed her approval and began to circle the firm bulb at the head of his cock, she screamed at Tait with her eyes. *How far do we let this go?*

It wasn't a fair question. She already knew the answer

anyway. They couldn't unshackle Shay and expect him to stumble anywhere now, let alone walk.

"On the other hand, I don't know if our boy is on board with that thinking," Buffy commented. "Whoa, tiger. You really want to roar, don't you?"

"Mmmm. Fuck...yeah."

Dios. No.

As the words tumbled out of Shay's mouth, Zoe's heart really did beg her for a bungee jump out of her chest. She couldn't do this anymore. No matter what kind of platitudes her mind threw at her, that he had no idea what he was saying— that he barely knew where he was let alone to whom he spoke— they were meaningless against the pain of watching him struggle anew against his bonds, battling to reach for Buffy...as his sex lurched higher beneath her fingers.

"That's it," the woman murmured, letting her hand slide over his whole stalk. "You're doing great. God, you're magnificent."

"Mang—mal—magificant," Shay babbled back. "No. Not me. You. Bew-ba-ful. You."

Zoe glared at Tait. *I can't do this.*

"Hmmm," he murmured, seeming to direct every word at Buffy. "Just a few more minutes, I think."

Buffy shot back a questioning stare. "Are you sure? I mean, look at him."

"No." Shay's voice was clearer this time. The lunges of his head against the pillow were sharper and stronger. His eyes started to twitch. "Just wanna look at you—"

"That's it." Zoe slammed the clipboard into the chair.

"Zoe."

She already had her gaze locked with Tait's. His eyes

detonated with elated astonishment—the same stuff coursing through every inch of her soul.

"Zoe." It erupted from Shay in damn near a shout this time. "Don't...go. Need...you. Zoe. *Zoe.*"

Buffy stretched out beside him, continuing to work her hand over him. "Sure, baby. Call me Zoe, if that's what you want. I'm going to take such good care of you and your cock..."

The words were just as soothing as everything else the woman had said, but Shay reacted like she'd just told him she was a succubus. "No. Not right. This... This isn't right."

"Of course it is, baby. It's so good. So right."

"Wh-Where's Zoe?"

Zoe pinged her stare around the whole room. Tait joined her, clearly on board with the same task. There was a good chance, despite her presence there as Helena, that Newport, Stock, and Homer were also observing the party from the next room. But where would such a camera be?

Once Tait stood close enough to her, he relayed, "Yo, Cary Grant." It was their pet name for Caspar. "I-Man's rising from the fog a lot faster than I expected. Little B and I are hunting for the room cam now."

"Little B?" Zoe queried. "But..."

"You're the new Little B now," he explained. "Come on, it's just a matter of time—if we can get all our asses out of here in one complete piece."

"Save the wedding invitations for later," Caspar yelled, "and find the damn camera."

"Check. Hey, Double-O, you still with us?"

"Wouldn't miss this fun for the world," Rhett answered.

"You still want to try your hand at jamming these doors?" Tait charged.

"Is Scarlett Johansson the key to world peace?"

"God help me," Caspar mumbled.

"Every lock in that building should be tighter than a virgin in five...four...three..."

Rhett's countdown was drowned by the sound of cracking wood. Zoe joined Tait in whipping their sights back around in time to see Shay break both his wrist shackles free from the top of the bed. Coming along for the ride was the mounting plate for the restraints—and the monitoring camera embedded into it. Both were ruined.

"Uhhh...found the cam," Tait announced. "And disabled it too."

"Where the hell is Zoe?" Shay roared.

Buffy, who had to be either the bravest or most clueless woman she'd ever met, continued her seduction with a sultry game face. "Sssshhh, baby. It's going to be okay, I promise." Estimation option number three—maybe she really was that desperate for fifty thousand dollars. Undoubtedly, her payout depended on producing a healthy baby. But was it worth getting swung at with a splintered headboard and a couple of heavy chains?

"Zoe. Goddamnit, I need Zoe!"

"Okay, tiger. I'm Zoe, okay? Now let me show you what else I can be..."

Zoe smacked a hand atop the woman's thigh just as Buffy untied her string panties, preparing to straddle Shay's erection. "Oh, honey. Quit while you're ahead. And alive."

Buffy flashed her the pert cheerleader grin again. "Oh, it's okay, doll. Thanks for your concern, but I'm used to some rough stuff."

"Oh, it's not him you have to worry about, *doll*." She

flickered her own version of the bimbo smirk while stabbing her fingernails into Buffy's skin. "I'll break it down into simpler terms. You will not fuck my man tonight. You will not fuck him in the light. You will not fuck him on the bed. You will not fuck him on a sled. You will not—"

"She gets the point," Tait interceded. From his rolling medical cart, he yanked out parts of a rifle and began screwing them together.

"Yeah. I get the point." Buffy held up her hands and backed off the bed. After grabbing her shoes, she bolted from the room.

"On a *sled*?" Tait sneered.

"I'm under stress," she snapped.

"If you don't get the hell out of there in five minutes, you'll also be under siege," Caspar barked.

"Roger that," Rhett confirmed. "We've got a couple of hawks on the roof now, T-Bomb, and so far, those bozos think the threat has originated from there. Hostiles are racing for the higher ground like sheep to the cliffs. We've already confirmed Adler's flight from the building too. Someone in that place unjammed my door jam."

"What about Newport and Stock?" Tait asked.

"No sign of them," Rhett conveyed.

"Good. That's really fucking good."

"There's no time for cowboy games, T. We'll be able to keep up the ruse on the roof for only a few more minutes. You need to get I-Man up and moving now."

Tait looked over his brother while using an attachment on his utility knife to jimmy the locks free on all the shackles. "Oh, you don't have to worry about the 'up' part."

"I do *not* want to hear about it," Rhett retorted.

"Me neither," Caspar growled. "Zoe, can you still hear me?"

"Yeah." It was the first thing she said since getting her hands on Shay again, and it was a natural wobble of emotion. "Yeah," she repeated, as much to the man beneath her touch as the agent in her tooth. "I'm here. I'm here."

"This is coming down to you, girl." Caspar sounded like God once more. "You're clearly the only one he'll listen to. Talk to him. You can do this."

She nodded, struggling to keep her tears at bay. Right now, she felt like she could scale Everest if asked—except that holding Shay in her arms again felt like arriving at the summit already.

"Shay," she whispered. Then a little more forcefully, "Shay. Baby. You need to wake up, okay?"

His face flopped against her chest. "Zoe. Please. I... I need Zoe."

"I'm here, my love. Right here. Open your eyes." She kissed his forehead. "Good. You did it once. Try it again."

"Zoe." He kept his gaze open, but it was a bleary, straw-colored mess as he grabbed her sweater. "Can you get her for me? I miss her so much."

"*Mierda.*" Her voice splintered. She fought the total breakdown by sucking in another tight breath. "Oh, God. I *am* Zoe. Don't you know me?"

"She says that a lot. *Mierda*. She's so fucking cute when she spits it out. Then sometimes, she bites her lip after it, and I just want to kiss her..."

It was good inspiration. In desperation, Zoe went with it, grabbing his face and kissing him hard. When she finished, she kept her head bent over him, running soft fingers down the side of his beautiful face and letting him feel the rain of her tears. "Look at me, Shay. Look at me and know me...please. I'm here, and I love you so much."

He let out a weary sough. "I love her so much. I didn't tell her, and now I'm afraid she'll never know."

"Oh, Shay." She cried harder. Prayed that the love in every drop of her tears would baptize his memory and bring him back to her. "I know. I *do* know."

"Zoe. I need Zoe."

"She's right here. I'm right here. Open your eyes. See me."

"Zoe."

"I'm here. Your baby girl. Your tiny dancer. The heart you've taken hostage...forever."

As she rasped the words against his lips, she felt his breath hitch. Then his whole body seized. Hers did the same, raw dread jolting through her.

What the hell was happening to him? Was it a bad reaction to coming off the drugs? Was he going to try throwing her away like he did Buffy?

If that was the case, she was too late to stop him. He shifted his hand to her arm and wrapped a grip around her like a steel claw.

But he didn't hurl her away.

He jerked her closer.

Zoe stared down, nervously scanning his face again.

Her heart didn't stop again. But it sure as hell skipped a lot of beats.

His lips started inching into the grin that could stop traffic. The corners of his mouth and eyes crinkled. And his eyes...held all the hues of the desert sky. Only this time, they weren't the shades of the sunset.

They were the colors of the dawn.

"Zoe. My tiny dancer."

It wasn't his question any longer. Or his plea.

It was his certainty.

"Shay. My beautiful Sir."

It was her certainty too.

"Are you really here?" After her hard kiss of confirmation, a heavy breath left him. "I can't believe it."

The building shuddered. Zoe grabbed the back of his neck, compelling him to look at her. "We need to get out of here. Now. Are you strong enough to walk?"

"For you? To the moon."

She smiled. "Okay, overachiever, how about just up to the roof?"

They left the building as the waning day turned the desert sky into a thousand radiant colors—but to them, the sunset had just become a sunrise. A new beginning of forever, heated by the perfection of their crazy, fated love.

CHAPTER TWENTY-THREE

One layover, a few adventures, and a lot of love later...

Zoe Margarita Madonna Chestain
and
Sergeant Major Shay Bommer

request your presence at their wedding vows...
and a second celebration, too

Saturday, October 1, 3:00 pm
Spring Mountain Ranch
Blue Diamond, Nevada

Barbecue, Bar, Riding, and Roping
immediately following the boring stuff

In lieu of gifts, please make donations to
The Melody Bommer Institute for Progressive Gene Research
But if you insist—registries can be found at Babies Plus,
Infant-A-Go-Go, and Babies In Arms

RSVP to Zoe's cell: 702-555-7429
Please leave a message. She'll return the call...
when she's not tied up.

EXCERPT FROM *MASKED*
BOOK SEVEN IN THE HONOR BOUND SERIES

Dear God.

It bore repeating. Probably out loud. If she could only figure out where the hell all her air had gone.

He was beautiful. Almost unreal. She'd only had this sensation a few times in her whole life, like the moment she'd gazed at her first Michelangelo statue in Rome or gasped at a Cirque performer who supported three others in his palm. His lean but rock-hard build emphasized every captivating striation of his muscles: the hard ropes of his neck, the shoulders and arms that rivaled the ridges of Red Rock, the abdomen that was another mountain range all its own as well. He moved closer to her with grace that reminded her of an eagle's flight, deadly force honed for efficiency and grace.

Was he even real?

She yearned to reach out and learn that answer for herself.

She'd never been more afraid to move in her life.

She cleared her throat. Tried to straighten her stance but wondered if she should lower her head instead. Or bow. Or curtsy? Or shake his hand? Hell. She was the girl who'd read every research book on dungeon etiquette, right? But now she really did feel like the girl at the prom with toilet paper attached to her heel.

"Hi," she finally managed. "I...I mean hello. Hello, Sir. I...I mean..."

If she really had something to say after that, it would've disappeared as soon as he lifted her hand between both of his. Shivers. Everywhere. Her blood. Her skin. And yes, even in the deepest parts of her most intimate tunnel. His skin was so firm and warm, his grip a steady command, his eyes still impossible to read. That fact alone brought even more of the illicit tremors...

He stepped closer, peering at her harder, as if trying to figure her out more fully. "Ssshhh. Breathe, red."

Red. Though she liked playing up the unique color of her hair, she always cringed when someone used the too-typical nickname. But on his lips, it was transformed into something new. Magical.

"Breathe. Right. Okay...right. God. I am so sorry. You must think I'm so—" She injected a weak laugh. "I'm normally better at the whole conversation thing, I promise."

Why was she blowing this so badly? And why did he make it worse with his disarming grin and his tightening hold? And the intensity of his nearness. And the potency of his scent. How could the combination of Scotch and dust suddenly smell so incredible?

"Why are you sorry? I'm the one who intruded."

"Oh, yeah. 'Intruded.'" She blew a pseudo-raspberry. "Because there was so much going on here in my corner to intrude on."

"There would've been."

His mutter edged close to an animal's timbre, making her shiver. Tess had heard enough radio spy chatter over the years to know the small disk on his neck was a voice distorter of some sort—but instead of raising her wariness, it only added to his allure. A lot.

Too much.

The conflict hastened her reckless heartbeat, especially as he repeated, "Oh, yeah. You were going to have a waiting line tonight, I can guarantee it. Then I would've had to bounce a few skulls together."

"Why?" She knew how stupid it sounded. The possessive snarl beneath his words spoke enough meaning for anyone to figure out—except, perhaps, her. The protective thing was usually her gig, a default when one was looking out for sisters who were "the pretty one" and "the smartass." Grasping the concept that anyone wanted to look after her in the same way...

Weird. Very weird.

But nice.

Really nice.

Still, she braced herself for his teasing chuckle. Maybe some sarcastic quip at what a "silly subbie" she was for not comprehending his intent.

Once more, the man turned her expectations sideways. No. Fully upside down. Her senses careened as he released a hand, lifting it to her jaw, yanking up her face to the focus of his fathomless gaze. "Why?" he repeated. "Because I'm pretty well set on having you all to myself tonight, rose." His fingers pressed in. "Unless you aren't interested in what you see?"

She laughed. She couldn't help herself. "You're kidding, right?"

"At the risk of being trite, do I look like I'm kidding?"

"At the risk of being obnoxious, do I look like a nun? Because that's the only situation where I can imagine you being turned down, Sir Sexy."

Air pushed past his smirk. His thick stubble disguised the exact edges of his lips, but the flash of his teeth briefly showed her they were curved and lush...and maybe a little wicked.

Wicked. Right behind daunting on what she'd come here looking for.

"I ought to stamp your ass with my palm for that cheek, little rose. But I don't even know your name yet."

She couldn't help grinning. If "cheek" earned her comments like that, she was tempted to change her name to Cheeky.

"Odette." She supplied the name she'd used with Master Max when turning in her application. If Sir Sexy had asked about her before coming over here—and something told her he had—then it was best to be consistent. "And you are...?"

"Interested." His lips tugged up again. "And intrigued. And fully cleared by Max, if you'd like to ask him about me. He and I have been friends for a while."

She looked toward the bar, where Max was waiting with a reassuring nod. It reinforced the security she already felt with Sexy—but also the apprehension, delicious and decadent, that inched its way into more of the sensitive skin between her thighs.

Hell.

She was really stepping down the rabbit hole this time, wasn't she?

With a Dom she couldn't stop staring at.

Who hadn't stopped staring at her either.

Who turned her bloodstream to mush because of it.

"You're good," she finally blurted. "I-I mean, it's good. I like it...that you're interested."

"And intrigued," he prompted.

"Same difference," she volleyed. "Right?"

"Not necessarily."

She swallowed. How had he pressed at least six inches closer without her noticing? "Your semantics are certainly curious."

His kiss, soft yet sure, was the last response she expected—yet the perfect pin in her careful composure. Pin? Try a full arrow, piercing to her very core...a wound that felt so damn good. She moaned and then inhaled, ordering her brain to locate its This End Up sign. This was the craziest opener to a date she'd ever had—if this could even be qualified as a "date."

Damn good point. What the hell was this? Maybe they needed to talk about that. Set some parameters. Lay down ground rules for next steps, and—

Thoughts that flew from her mind the moment Sexy kissed her again. Longer. Deeper. Pushing her mouth open this time, coaxing her tongue against his, all but dictating her to kiss him in return—like she'd resist a single moment of this heat and fire and pleasure. He turned her into a firework. And like the song said, she was ready to let her colors burst.

Don't stop. This is so good. You feel so good...

But he did, all too soon, dragging away despite how she grabbed his shoulders to stay upright. His muscles felt even better than they looked, solid boulders beneath her fingers. Wow.

"Odette?" he murmured.

"Hmmm?" she managed.

"You still with me?"

She blinked, struggling through a dreamy fog. "If I said no, would you kiss me again?"

His laugh was a gentle rumble. "No." He compounded

her dismay by stepping out of her reach, steadying her with his hands instead of his body. "I want more than just your mouth, little rose."

She gave him a half-drunk smile. "Like what?"

She barely comprehended his hand lifting to her face. But oh, how she felt it when he grazed his fingers along her cheek, against her temple, into her hair. "Like what's in here."

She scowled. "Not the answer I was going for."

He tightened his grip on her scalp. "But this is where it begins." For a moment, he dipped a heated gaze down the length of her body. "As much as I long to discover all of this...it doesn't happen until I learn more of this." Then he was back to focusing on her face, as if committing her features to memory. Tess swayed toward him, a flower straining for the sun, needing more exposure. More...

"Then learn me."

He sucked in a deep breath, almost as if her words had become his air. As he released it, he snarled. "Damn it."

"What?" Her gaze snapped wide. "What's wrong? Did I mess up?"

He chuckled. Oh, yes. Chuckled. What the hell? Being with him felt like riding a rubber band. Dark mask but gleaming eyes. Hot kisses and then chaste clinches. Snarls and then chuckles.

"That wasn't messing up, red. Not one damn bit. You're just so new. So new. And open, and willing, and..."

"And what?" Her whisper didn't surprise her. She was amazed it had volume at all, considering how deeply his words tore at her. He sounded like he was in pain.

Yep. Rubber band. Wasn't the Mr. Interested and Intrigued just a minute ago? Hadn't he kissed her like it?

"And...well...I'm not new," he finally answered her. "And I don't know how to do this in your kind of way. And my kind of way is..."

He trailed into such a thick, dark growl, Tess wondered if she'd sprung a crimson cloak on her shoulders to match the forest in her imagination, looming around the path she had to take to "Grandma's house." Only, she wanted the big bad wolf to devour her—in any way he could imagine. But how to prove it to him?

The answer blared at her like a shaft of light in that forest.

And was as easy as tugging the ribbon that secured her own mask.

She let the covering fall all the way to the floor. Then tilted her bare face up at Sir Sexy, letting him see the surrender in her gaze.

"Your kind of way is what I came here to find," she confessed. "So show it to me...please?"

This story continues in **Masked: *Honor Bound Book Seven!***

ALSO BY ANGEL PAYNE

The Misadventures Series:
Misadventures with a Super Hero

Honor Bound:
Saved
Cuffed
Seduced
Wild
Wet
Hot
Masked
Mastered (Coming Soon)
Conquered (Coming Soon)
Ruled (Coming Soon)

Secrets of Stone Series:
No Prince Charming
No More Masquerade
No Perfect Princess
No Magic Moment
No Lucky Number
No Simple Sacrifice
No Broken Bond
No White Knight

**For a full list of Angel's other titles,
visit her at www.angelpayne.com**

ABOUT ANGEL PAYNE

USA Today bestselling romance author Angel Payne loves to focus on high-heat romance starring memorable alpha men and the women who love them. She has numerous book series to her credit, including the Suited for Sin series, the Cimarron Saga, the Temptation Court series, the Secrets of Stone series, the Lords of Sin historicals, and the popular Honor Bound series, as well as several standalone titles.

Angel is a native Southern Californian, leading to her love of being in the outdoors, where she often reads and writes. She still lives in Southern California with her soul-mate husband and beautiful daughter, to whom she is a proud cosplay/culture con mom. Her passions also include whisky tasting, shoe shopping, and travel.

Visit her here:
www.angelpayne.com